SCORPION

STRIKE

SCORPION STRIKE

JOHN J. NANCE

CROWN PUBLISHERS, INC., NEW YORK

Published by Crown Publishers, Inc., 201 East 50th Street, New York, New York
10022. Member of the Crown Publishing Group.

CROWN is a trademark of Crown Publishers, Inc.

Manufactured in the United States of America

Library of Congress Cataloging-in-Publication Data
Nance, John J.
    Scorpion strike / John J. Nance.
    1. Persian Gulf War, 1991—Fiction.   I. Title.
    PS3564.A546S28   1992
    813'.54—dc20   91-40638
                                                  CIP

ISBN 0-517-58565-0

10 9 8 7 6 5 4 3 2 1

First Edition

This work is dedicated with heartfelt respect and friendship to my compatriots, the men and women of the 97th Military Airlift Squadron and the 446th Military Airlift Wing at McChord AFB, Washington—my military "home" for the past sixteen years.

It is also dedicated to my fellow Reservists and Guardsmen from all branches of the service who, like me, instantly put civilian lives and careers on hold in the fall of 1990 to serve in Operations Desert Shield and Desert Storm.

And finally, it is dedicated to the active duty members of the U.S. Military who accepted and integrated their Reserve and Guardsmen brethren into a unified team of unprecedented effectiveness which, in one stroke, proved the brilliance of what someone years ago dubbed the "Total Force Concept."

JOHN J. NANCE
Tacoma, Washington
December, 1991

A C K N O W L E D G M E N T S

Flying for ten months on active duty for the Military Airlift Command (MAC) was the seminal event that inspired this high-intensity thriller. More precisely, it was the *people* of MAC that did it.

The key Air Force characters in this book are fictional, of course, but I know them like brothers and sisters. They embody the good traits and the intellect, the humor and the strengths, the weaknesses and the humanity of the men and women I've served with since 1971 in MAC. Desert Storm/Desert Shield brought home how fortunate I've been to know such people over two decades and through two wars.

After the storm—after we reservists returned to civilian life and this writer returned to his word processor—I leaned heavily on friends, family, and associates to help me elbow aside my other books in progress to bring this work into being.

As publicly as possible, then, I want to thank:

■ The impressive number of people on three continents who talked to me in person and by phone regarding a long list of technical questions aimed at producing a novel of authenticity and technical accuracy without compromising national security;

■ All the people who took time to read and comment on the manuscript, including those at MAC Headquarters and the Pentagon who helped complete a thorough security review on a tight schedule;

■ Captain Dennis Isaacs of the 97th at McChord, who fought a similar pitch problem and brought his C-141 home safely to tell us the story;

■ My editor at Crown, James O'Shea Wade, who first legitimized the idea that became *Scorpion Strike;*

■ My wife, Bunny, and my executive assistant, Patricia Davenport, for their extensive and professional in-house editing and guidance;

■ My literary agents, George and Olga Wieser;

■ And the short-lived but best-of-show aviating firm of Nance, Fernalld, Valkenaar, Barnes and Dellinger. The road to Rotterdam will never be the same, guys!

JOHN J. NANCE
Lt. Colonel, USAFR

SCORPION

STRIKE

P R O L O  G U E

The last few drops of water left the goatskin reluctantly, trickling onto the man's tongue and disappearing, doing nothing to relieve the thirst that was rapidly becoming a chasm of fear threatening to engulf him. With the other goatskin lost, there was no more water. He had miscalculated—again.

The man braced himself as he stood on shaky legs, leaning slightly toward the west—or what he hoped was the west—as the howling might of the wind blasted horizontal columns of sand and grit at him with a guttural moan that seemed to echo from the depths of hell. The sandstorm had overtaken him hours ago, or was it days ago? It seemed interminable.

As the wall of swirling, sickly yellow clouds had tumbled toward him the previous late afternoon and swallowed the setting sun, he had felt a sudden, naïve flash of Arab pride, expecting to be tested in the tradition of his desert heritage, and found worthy despite his earlier mistakes.

That conceit had lasted all of ten minutes—the time it took to realize he was in deep trouble.

The storm had enveloped him then, his mouth suddenly filling with sand and grit, as he tripped for the first of many times, sprawling facedown on the hard, gravel-strewn desert floor. He had struggled to his feet, gasping for breath, the ancient rationale of the linen cloth that swathed his head and face—the *howli*—all too obvious. He had fashioned the howli when he abandoned the car, leaving only a slit for his eyes, and feeling somewhat silly with clear air and temperatures only in the upper sixties Fahrenheit. Now he desperately needed its protection. His breathing came hard, the heavy air drawing in particles of dust and sand so tiny that even the cloth couldn't filter them out completely. He could taste the desert, even if he couldn't see it—an alkali taste of bitter grit.

It was pitch dark now and past midnight, the relentless, shrieking sandstorm more ominous than before. The man sat down suddenly to think, pulling his knees up instinctively, his head down, his back turned to the onslaught of the wind, eyes closed tightly beneath the white linen. His feet were numb and his back ached, but there was soft sand beneath his buttocks, a relief from the small rocks and hardpan surface that alternated with sand and gravel in the Al Hajarah, the northern reaches of the Arabian Desert.

His mind racing, weakened by fear, he struggled to examine his situation in the abstract, willing himself to use the practiced discipline of his scientific mind: define the elements of the problem, probe for a hypothesis, test the hypothesis . . .

When the sun came again, the temperatures would top thirty-eight Celsius, or one hundred degrees Fahrenheit to the Americans occupying one-third of his country. He could last a week without food, but how long without water? If he was truly off course, he could wander for days without finding the tiny Saudi outpost he had so carefully targeted on his map of the southern Iraqi desert.

He had abandoned his car hours ago in order to stay undetected.

A car could be seen kicking up dust plumes for miles. A solitary nomad would be all but invisible.

The man tried to peer at his hands, which were shaking, but the cloth of the howli got in the way. He was hardly a nomad, of course, and he knew it. The desert in the mild temperatures of springtime had not scared him as it would an experienced man. One hundred kilometers or so on foot—some sixty miles—had seemed easy. He had never figured on a sandstorm, or on losing his only compass and his spare water bag in a terrifying fall down the side of a wadi—a dry streambed.

He knew he must focus his mind, and when he did so, the proposition seemed simple, although the words echoing in his head were Oxfordian English instead of his native Arabic, and that disturbed him, as if his survival depended on thinking in Arabic.

Either I'm within twenty degrees of my original course, he concluded, *or I'm doomed.*

He tugged at a corner of the howli, opening a slit for his left eye as he held his digital watch inches away and pressed the button activating a tiny light. The irony made him chuckle through the gnawing fear: a tiny vestige of western technology obediently serving a western-educated Arab now in real danger of dying because he'd never learned to be an Arab.

It read 1:43 A.M.

He got to his feet just as suddenly and positioned the wind on his right sleeve as a physical compass, resuming the same steady pace as before, a renewed confidence pushing him on. There was no legitimate cause for panic. He could not possibly be off course more than twenty degrees, and there was an east-west pipeline south of the border he couldn't miss.

The monotonous impacts of his footfalls in the blackness, accompanied by the numbing shriek of the wind, was a form of sensory deprivation, blocking out all other inputs, leaving his conscious mind free to wander, painting vivid mental images before him. The bedroom of his house in the southern suburbs of Baghdad loomed before him, with Saliah, his wife, and their two sons and one daughter huddled together there. The pain of missing them was just below the surface, but he suppressed it.

There had been no electricity for weeks in Baghdad, and less water, and he had been able to visit them just once since the American attack began. His initial terror at reports that the capital was under siege had given way rapidly to a sort of confidence. Whatever horrors the Americans had planned for Hussein, wiping out the Iraqi population was not among them. By the time he had disobeyed orders and struggled over shattered concrete and clogged highways from Ar Rutbah to be with them for a while, Saliah and the children had settled down to a routine of basic existence. He was proud of them. He knew they could survive.

But now there was a terrible lie out there somewhere in the night that Saliah would eventually confront, and there was nothing he could do to prevent it. Your husband of eighteen years, she would be told, was found burned to a cinder beside the road from Ar Rutbah to Baghdad. Must have been American bombs, they would say. He probably died instantly.

The man stumbled suddenly, righted himself, checked his direction, and trudged on.

Day came in the form of a yellowish glow, stronger to his left, and still his feet obediently plopped one in front of the other, sometimes treading over a dune of shifting sand that slid and slithered under his weight, sometimes crashing onto a desert floor as hard as concrete. Thirst was an enemy struggling to consume him. The hours trudged by with depressing monotony as the light brightened and faded to darkness once again.

By 9:00 P.M. the storm had calmed. The clouds suddenly cleared overhead and stars popped out above him, changing his mood to brief elation. He pulled open his howli and scanned the sky, finding the Big Dipper, Orion, and the North Star, and fixing the compass rose around him in his mind.

Look at the horizon, you idiot! he roared at himself. *There should be lights, fires, or something ahead.* He was surely on Saudi soil by now.

But pitch darkness was all that beckoned, and the wind was rising once again.

By 2:00 A.M. the storm was in full force again, and it was obvious to the man that he was lost in every way.

I will meet death walking at full speed, he decided. His pace accelerated to almost a trot as he plunged with renewed purpose into the throat of the sand-laden winds.

He could tell that he was dangerously dehydrated now, his emotions floating on the calm seas of a detached mental state, his conscious thoughts occupied with speed and course as if those were the only reality. He counted his steps diligently, keeping his pace steady and rapid, moving at almost exactly 1.5 meters per second at the moment his weary body crashed headlong into the metal side of a parked truck.

The Saudi sergeant sat bolt upright, cobwebs clearing from his head instantly, aware that something had disturbed the steady moan of the wind and the intermittent clanking of the rusted metal door to the broken-down masonry outpost. His two companions, a lieutenant and a private, still slept. They were from the city. He was a Bedouin who preferred a tent to a cold stone floor.

He heard nothing more, but that noise had not come from his dream. The sergeant got to his feet and slipped on his sandals, picked up his American M-16 rifle, and padded outside cautiously, taking the sandblast full in his face before stumbling across the collapsed body of a man on the other side of the truck.

* * *

Shakir Abbas regained consciousness in a chair, the foul breath of a Saudi soldier assaulting his face, his explanation disbelieved. He heard the Arabic word for *spy* before being handcuffed and driven into Badanah, where he was given a small cup of water and thrown in a filthy cell that reeked of human waste.

It seemed endless hours before a higher-ranking Saudi appeared, only slightly more interested in his explanation. This one, too, disappeared, and his frustration grew enormous as he felt the time crawl by, knowing what had to be happening nearly three hundred miles to the north. *That* schedule would not wait, and neither could he.

When at last yet another Saudi officer came down the hall, Abbas summoned his strength, stuck his face through the bars, and, with as much rage as he could muster, yelled at the man.

"You idiot! I have information vital to the Kingdom of Saudi Arabia about Saddam Hussein! If you don't take me to military intelligence immediately, your life will soon be worth nothing!"

The Saudi gave him the sort of impassive look one gives to a screaming hyena in a zoo.

"At least tell them I'm here!" He tried again.

The Saudi moved closer, his eyes impassive.

"Tell whom?" He asked in Arabic.

The man felt his shirt. The pen was still there, and perhaps he still had paper.

Yes, there it was. He pulled it out and knelt down suddenly, using his knee as a writing board, his hand hastily sketching the design of a particular molecule along with its chemical description.

"Please come quickly," he wrote in English. "I have important information."

He signed it, stood, and pushed the scrap of paper at the Saudi, who had remained impassive but somehow clinically interested in the prisoner's odd behavior. The Saudi took it, looked at it, and raised a bushy eyebrow in question.

"The Americans will understand this," Abbas said in Arabic. "Please, give it to them quickly and tell them where I am." He realized his voice was little more than a pleading whine that echoed slightly against the unyielding stone walls. The expression of the Saudi reflected those rock walls as he turned away, and Abbas watched with sinking heart as the Saudi folded the paper and made a movement as though tossing it into a distant corner as he left.

Abbas slept then, the sleep of one who can do no more. How long the confusing dreams and nightmares played, he wasn't sure—the guards at the outpost had taken his wristwatch. It was dark outside, however, when the sounds of a helicopter vibrated through the building, followed by the clank of a heavy steel door and hurried footsteps echoing through the stone corridors. He was too weak to leap to his feet, but his eyes opened in time to see the guard swing his cell door wide, admitting an American army officer and a civilian.

"Are you . . ." The officer looked down at a piece of paper. "Dr. Shakir Abbas?" He looked up again, his steel blue eyes locking onto Abbas's.

"Yes. Yes, I am." He got to his feet, hopeful.

"Did you draw this, Doctor?"

The American officer held out the scrap of paper with the molecular notation, but as soon as Abbas nodded, the officer yanked it away.

"Yes!" Abbas confirmed. "I wrote that. I knew someone would—"

"Reproduce it for us. Now." The officer, a lieutenant colonel, was holding out a notebook and pen, and Abbas understood instantly. He knelt down as before and quickly reproduced the same biochemical molecule with its full chemical description, a notation only someone schooled in the most sophisticated forms of biochemistry would understand.

The man in civilian clothes took the notebook and studied it carefully for no more than half a minute before looking up with a thin smile.

"Dr. Abbas?" His hand was outstretched in a halfhearted handshake, and Abbas took it gratefully in both of his.

"Please come with us."

Keflavik Air Base, Iceland
Wednesday, March 6, 1991—3:30 P.M. (1530 GMT)

Jan Bae of the International Red Cross returned the small, conservative wave of the captain of the Balair DC-10 as the pilot closed his cockpit window. The portable stairs had already been moved back from the essentially empty passenger plane, and the American Air Force ground crewmen were moving into position for engine start. Bae smoothed his thinning blond hair with his right hand and glanced at the leaden skies overhead, and then at his watch. Thirty minutes early. That was typical of charter operations. He wished they could have talked Swissair into using one of their 747s directly from Geneva, but the Swiss were so zealous about guarding their neutrality that involving the nation's flag carrier was impossible. Even with the sudden, mystifying change of heart of the American government, the Swiss perceived a postwar International Red Cross humanitarian rescue mission to Baghdad as somehow potentially partisan. So they had offered their charter subsidiary's aircraft instead—Balair—at a substantial price, of course, and then only if they departed from some country other than Switzerland.

The delegation had chosen to meet in Iceland for reasons that were known only to the Americans. From here, the flight to Baghdad would take just under eight hours.

Bae turned and walked briskly toward the terminal, enjoying the cool air of what had turned out to be a balmy day with temperatures in the forties. At home in Oslo a snowstorm was in progress. There he would need a heavy coat.

He reached the entrance to the old wooden breezeway and walked to the main military terminal waiting area, long habit forcing him automatically to the large glass windows, where the quiet approach of another man completely escaped his notice.

A familiar voice suddenly reached his ear.

"You couldn't slow them down, then?" the man asked quietly.

Bae turned suddenly and recognized Colonel Richard Kerr of the American Defense Intelligence Agency, who had set up the charter and flown in with the DC-10 crew the night before. Bae smiled at the big pilot, whom he knew from his days in Washington as a wicked chess partner and an intimidating golfer. At well over six feet, Kerr towered over him; he was like a grown-up kid who still loved to play with airplanes, but he had a first-class mind. Just the sort to be an effective air attaché—if he'd ever accept such a position.

"No, Richard, I tried, but the captain wanted to leave as soon as possible, and you never gave me a sufficient reason to protest."

"I couldn't. It wasn't anything sneaky, though."

"Of course it wasn't." Bae tried hard to look like a disapproving schoolmaster faced with a ridiculous lie. The effort was not in vain. Colonel Kerr was suddenly very uncomfortable and searching for a response.

Bae, with practiced timing, beat him to it, raising a hand as if to dismiss the need for a defense, a sly smile on his face. "Well, you will, no doubt, report this flight's early departure to some command post around here with that portable radio you're hiding in your right hand"—Bae noted with satisfaction the look of mild alarm that now flashed across Kerr's face—"and I suppose they'll simply have to adjust their thoroughly innocent plans." Bae turned further toward the Air Force colonel, looking him in the eye. Kerr was always great fun to toy with. "You wouldn't want to tell me what's going on, would you?"

Kerr tried to look hurt. "Nothing at all, Jan. Except normal operational caution for a dangerous mission to a criminal country. Air traffic control clearances and diplomatic clearances are hard enough to coordinate without changing the times."

Bae fixed his gaze on the taxiing DC-10 and smiled. "Nothing going on, eh? What's the phrase your big general used at that briefing last month? 'Bovine scatology'? I do know it when I hear it."

Sandy 101—Classified Coalition Air Base in the Arabian Desert (southeast of Bi'r Fardan, Kingdom of Saudi Arabia) Wednesday, March 6, 1991—6:35 P.M. (1535 GMT)

The food smelled surprisingly good, probably because he hadn't taken time out all day to eat. At sundown, Major Jerry Ronson had chased him out of the ALCE, the tiny portable airlift command post, asking one of his sergeants to escort the visiting colonel to the brightly lit mess tent, with instructions to get him to eat.

Colonel Will Westerman, commander of a Special Operations–Low Level (SOLL) squadron at Charleston Air Force Base in South Carolina, moved past the steam tables with detached curiosity, collecting an assortment of hot food in the various scalloped sections of the gleaming stainless steel tray. Westerman retraced his steps back through the connecting tent corridor then, drawing a cup of coffee before sitting down at the closest table. The mess tent was indeed a tent, but it was also the latest version of military field equipment, with Velcro flaps and air conditioning and bright lighting—yet it still felt like the ones he remembered from Vietnam.

Westerman looked around and chuckled. If Colonel Potter and Hot Lips Houlihan had walked by at that moment, he wouldn't have been surprised. It looked like the set of "M*A*S*H."

Poor Ronson, he thought. Westerman knew him well enough to perceive that the months away from home had been rough on the man. Ronson had been uprooted in mid-August from Charleston Air Force Base along with three sergeants and one lieutenant and sent to man a tiny twelve-by-fourteen-foot folding metal box full of radios in the middle of the Arabian Desert for an indefinite period of time. The collapsible ALCE box, which was to serve as a forward Military Airlift Command Post, had been airlifted in by a C-5 and plunked down on August 14 at what was then a sleepy Saudi air base. Now it was a busy U.S. Army maintenance and staging center, with a contingent of British fighter pilots thrown in to irritate the Saudis even more. For seven months Ronson had coordinated Military Airlift Command—MAC—flights to a base which officially didn't exist.

Poor guy! I've been here less than two days and already hate it, and he's been here seven months so far. Lord!

Westerman realized he was toying with his chicken fried steak. He wasn't hungry after all, and his mind was elsewhere, searching for problems in the hastily assembled mission he was in charge of launching within hours. It was a strange and worrisome secret operation that had landed in his lap out of nowhere two days ago, just as it looked like the war was over and everyone could begin breathing a sigh of relief.

Suddenly he was embroiled in a whirlwind of activity and fatigue. One minute he had been sitting quietly in his office at Charleston, the next he was on a four-engine jetliner from the presidential fleet in Washington, headed east while glued to a scrambled satellite phone, trying to assemble his people and the equipment they were going to need. The use of the VC-137—a Boeing 707-type jetliner from the 89th Wing at Andrews Air

Force Base, occasionally used as Air Force Two by the Vice-President—had been a real shock. But it was a measure of the importance of the assignment.

This one came directly from the White House.

The first problem had been finding his aircrews, since they were scattered between the States and the Persian Gulf, flying airlift missions for MAC in the venerable C-141B cargo jet. That had been quite a challenge.

Westerman focused on a forkful of potatoes au gratin he had been balancing for the past few seconds. Pure calories, but then he had always been able to eat as much as he wanted and never gain an ounce. For someone who loved food, it was a blessing, and this wasn't bad at all—especially for an Army field kitchen. The potatoes disappeared in his mouth as Major Ronson's voice crackled from the hand-held portable radio he had borrowed from the ALCE. There was alarm in Ronson's voice.

Westerman swallowed quickly and brought the walkie-talkie to his mouth in a practiced, singular motion.

"Go ahead."

"Colonel, you may want to get back here. The inbound mission's just checked in on our ALCE frequency, and he's got a problem. He wants to talk to you."

"What kind of problem?"

There was a moment's hesitation before Ronson responded. "Sir, he's got a major flight-control problem."

Westerman covered the hundred yards through the tent city to the ALCE in seconds. The prefabricated metal door had barely closed behind him with a solid *thunk* when the familiar voice of the aircraft commander of the inbound C-141 filled the small metal box office.

"Sailor Zulu, how copy? MAC five-zero-two-four-zero, calling for Ramrod." The voice was obviously strained. Something *was* significantly wrong, Westerman thought, but the pilot was at least controlled enough to use the proper code name for his mission commander.

"This is Ramrod, two-forty." Westerman scooped the microphone from the hand of a sergeant, his eyes focused out the rectangular window of the ALCE box into the desert twilight. "What's up?"

"Sir, something's bad wrong in the elevator system, and we can't figure out what's going on. We got a nose-up runaway pitch trim going through thirty thousand on climb out from Riyadh, so we disconnected the trim at eight degrees nose up, but now we can't get either electric or electro-hydraulic trim to reset, and the straight hydraulic trim lever won't work. We've tried turning off hydraulic systems—every combination we can think of—but we can't get the trim back, and the pitch control keeps slamming us up and down. It's all or nothing. We pull slightly and it goes full nose up. We push on the yoke just a little, and it goes full nose down. There's no in between! We've been leapfrogging through the sky for the last twenty minutes, and I wouldn't be surprised if we've bent the tail."

Will let his mind race through the C-141B's trim system, a combination of hydraulic and electrical motors that moved the huge horizontal T-tail up or down to keep the pitch control balanced. If the trim weren't frozen in an extreme nose-up position, Collinwood could fly easily without the trim motors. With eight degrees nose up and something else wrong with the elevator—the pitch control—it was a life-threatening emergency without question.

"Have you done a controllability check?"

"Yes sir. Pitch control is marginal, but we're learning how to fly it, and I think we can land it—since I've got bank control with my ailerons. At one point back there we had the yoke full forward and we couldn't get the nose down! I had to go into a forty-five-degree bank to keep from stalling!"

Westerman could picture Jim Collinwood's serious face in the cockpit of the Starlifter. He was a young captain, but one of the Special Operations–Low Level squadron's best pilots. In the dead of night over the Atlantic, Westerman had located Collinwood and his crew in the MAC "stage" at Torrejon Air Base near Madrid, and had picked them up when the Andrews AFB–based VC-137 stopped there for fuel. The crew had been as excited as children at Christmas to be whisked away suddenly by a jet normally assigned to the White House—a plush flying boardroom with a stocked galley and thick carpets. Will had briefed them thoroughly on the secret mission before they reached the Saudi capital of Riyadh, where he dropped them off while he went on to Sandy 101 to set up the rest of the mission. Jim Collinwood and his crew were to get thoroughly rested, then oversee the outfitting and loading of the C-141 chosen for the mission before flying it into Sandy for what was supposed to be the beginning of a very long night. But they had apparently drawn the wrong C-141B.

"How far out are you, Jim?" Westerman asked.

"Forty miles, at twelve thousand feet and descending." There was a long pause. "We don't know what else might be ready to come apart. I think we're all in agreement up here that we'd better get this bird on the ground."

"Stand by, two-forty." Westerman turned to Jerry Ronson. "Get Lighthouse on the satellite line. Fill them in on what you're hearing, tell them to patch through to the MAC command post at Scott, and check the weather for Riyadh and Dhahran." He raised the microphone again.

"Two-forty—Ramrod. How's your fuel?"

"We've got . . . wait a second . . . fourteen thousand pounds. Not really enough for Dhahran, sir, if that's what you're thinking, and Riyadh's supposed to get another sandstorm in the next hour. I know they've all got better maintenance and stuff, but I think you're the only reasonable base in range, and we've got some things aboard you, uh, need."

Westerman knew he was right, even as Ronson confirmed the marginal weather in Riyadh, three hundred miles to the north-west. Most of the people and vehicles he had assembled for this operation were already in position at Sandy 101, out there in the dark, waiting to be loaded aboard a serviceable airlifter. But Collinwood's C-141 was bringing in some key equipment as well—not to mention Collinwood and his crew, who were supposed to fly it. They had specialized SOLL training that the average C-141 crew never received.

Murphy's Law wins again, Westerman thought. *I was afraid this was going too smoothly.*

Westerman turned to Major Ronson again. "How good's your maintenance, Jerry? Can they fix it here?"

"Probably not. We've got three mechanics and their toolboxes, and I have to scrounge maintenance stands from the Saudis. That's it."

"Okay. Tell Lighthouse that Colonel Westerman wants them to start looking for another C-141 to divert in here. Now. We won't be able to use two-forty. Use the scrambled line."

Westerman raised the UHF microphone to his mouth again. "Two-forty, Ramrod."

"Yes sir." No hesitation in the reply.

"I have no disagreement with your plan, Jim. Just try to stabilize her on a long, flat, straight-in approach and change your pitch as little as possible. Don't worry about your approach speed. You've got ten thousand feet of runway and a hard-packed desert beyond that for at least a hundred miles."

"Roger." There was a hesitation. "Sir, you mean do a no-flap?"

"If you decide that's best."

"No, it seems to fly better at lower speeds, and we've already got the flaps to approach position and the gear down."

"It's your call, Jim. Just get it stabilized and don't plan to flare. We'll have the emergency equipment standing by." Will turned to the sergeant. "Make sure of that, will you? The emergency equipment, I mean—tower notified and all?"

The man nodded smartly, his eyes reflecting intense concern.

Sandy 101 belonged to the Saudi Air Force, and the Saudis who ran the control tower did not respond well to Americans telling them what to do. The sergeant, however, was an expert at massaging them diplomatically. He moved immediately to an ordinary phone at a small desk in the rear of the ALCE.

Will Westerman peered into the night, his mind running through his memory of the C-141B pitch-control systems as he suppressed the gnawing worry that the entire mission was now threatened. Collinwood, he knew, would know the systems with even greater precision, but Collinwood was also under tremendous pressure at the moment, though he was apparently handling it well. Will had approved Collinwood's upgrade to Pilot Flight Examiner just last year, even though he had only eighteen hundred flying hours and had been promoted to the rank of captain just six months earlier. The SOLL missions could be dangerous. They involved flying big four-engine jet transports at treetop level to drop troops and equipment on clandestine missions behind enemy lines, and for the average C-141 crew, that was an unnatural act among nonconsenting adults. Strategic airlift crews operating what amounted to huge, unarmed targets in the sky, had a distinct aversion to flying low and trolling for ground fire.

But this young man had asked for the assignment, and from the first had shown an unusual ability to coordinate his people and sufficient maturity to listen to them. Even Will had learned things by watching him instruct and give check-rides.

Will picked up the microphone and fingered the transmit button, intending to remind Collinwood as aircraft commander to make the landing himself from the left seat as MAC regulations required. But he stopped himself. He had picked good people. He ought to trust them. Collinwood knew the rules.

Another radio transmission cut through his thoughts. "Ramrod—two-forty. Just to let you know, we're lining up now on a thirty-mile final."

"Roger, two-forty," Westerman replied, recognizing the voice of First Lieutenant Jeff Rice, son of a longtime friend, Brigadier General Walt Rice. Ever since young Rice had joined the squadron, Will hadn't been able to shake a feeling of special responsibility for the young officer's welfare, especially after choosing Collinwood's crew for the first really risky SOLL mission since Operation Just Cause in Panama. Will had fought the temptation to call Walt Rice to let him know his boy was going in harm's way; that would have been inappropriate and embarrassing to both father and son.

"Colonel?" Jerry Ronson had pulled his chair into the forward left corner of the ALCE, next to the desklike counter that ran for a full fourteen feet across and beneath the main rectangular twelve-foot window that took up one complete wall. With the glowing dials of UHF and VHF radios on his left, and the rack-mounted stack of computers and high-frequency and satellite communications to his right, the man looked overwhelmed—as if cornered and trapped by the sophisticated electronics.

Will glanced at him, then back outside, preoccupied with finding the inbound 141 in the field glasses he was holding.

"Sir, Lighthouse says Scott wants to know if they've turned off hydraulic systems one and two, one at a time?" Lighthouse was the call sign for CENTCOM, the central command post for the Coalition in Riyadh. Scott Air Force Base was MAC headquarters in Illinois.

Will relayed the question to Collinwood.

"I thought we did, but let me try it again," was the response, then, "whoops! Geez . . . *Damn!*" The transmitter switched off, leaving a void.

The three men in the ALCE froze, waiting for agonizing seconds before Collinwood keyed his transmitter again.

"Ramrod, tell whoever's asking that we turned off number one and nearly lost her a second ago. But then we turned off number two and she jerked violently the other way. I think both elevator packs are bad, but I'm afraid to try the emergency pack alone. Remember, we've still got a ridiculously high nose-up trim."

Will punched the mike button immediately. "That's enough experimenting, two-forty! I'll tell them you tried."

"Roger. Thanks. That was scary."

Will put down the binoculars suddenly and turned to Major Ronson.

"Jerry, hand me that tower radio. I'm going to take your van and go watch him from the taxiway."

Will drove quickly to a position abeam the three-thousand-foot mark on the runway and parked. The sound of Lieutenant Rice's voice talking to the tower split the silence with clipped professional tones as the airplane drew closer. If the copilot was working the radio, the aircraft commander was flying the airplane, which confirmed his faith in Collinwood.

Two-forty's landing lights were on now, and very visible not so far in the distance, their brightness almost painful. Two lights extended out from below the wings with four more taxi lights in the wheel wells, and they were amazingly effective against the black velvet background of the night sky. The constellation of lights seemed to just hang there a few miles to the northwest as the 165-foot-long, 180-thousand-pound jet transport approached the airfield. Will noted with satisfaction that their descent angle was shallower than a normal approach. Collinwood would be thinking the same thing: Set up a steady descent and just hold the controls in the same position until the wheels touch the concrete. Do *not* flare! If the yoke was moved slightly and the elevator decided to reverse position too close to the ground while they were flying near stall speed, there might be no time and no altitude to recover.

That triggered the shadow of another thought—a disturbing nudge of something forgotten—which flickered unidentified across the periphery of Will Westerman's mind, irritating him slightly by vanishing as fast as it had come. There was . . . what? What had he been thinking? Something about the hydraulic checks they had run.

The C-141 was less than two miles out now, the sound of the

powerful Pratt and Whitney turbojet engines rising in Will's ears, its landing lights now bathing the runway threshold.

They had turned off the hydraulic power units to the elevator one at a time, yet—there was something logical that they were all missing. *What?*

They were over the perimeter road now, less than 150 feet above the ground. Collinwood had boosted his engine power slightly to keep his speed up. Will could hear the pitch of the engine whine increase.

The splash of white illumination on the desert sands from the advancing transport's lights finally crawled up to the threshold and shone on the two large numbers that designated the runway heading: 15.

Did he wait long enough each time he turned off a hydraulic pack? Could he have reacted too fast? Dammit! That's probably it!

Westerman's mind raced back and forth over the problem, remembering Collinwood's words, and his right hand reached for the radio to recommend a go-around. In a sudden flash of insight it seemed very simple: Collinwood could regain complete control by simply turning off one switch.

Wait! Westerman willed himself to stop. *What if I'm wrong? They could lose the airplane while trying to go around.*

His hand gripped the portable radio with indecision as the C-141's descent flattened slightly around one hundred feet above the threshold. Collinwood had changed back-pressure for some reason, or something had happened—the C-141 was too high for the cushion of air known as ground effect to be altering their pitch attitude.

As soon as it had pitched up, the nose of the C-141 began pitching back down in the direction of the proper pitch angle— back down toward the previous attitude.

Good! Good! Too late to change things now. He'll have to ride it in. I should have figured this out before.

But something *was* wrong.

The pitch-down had not stopped. As the airplane passed over the end of the runway, the nose of the Starlifter continued a slow push-over and the rate of descent increased perceptibly as the cargo jet began to dive at the surface.

They were fifty feet in the air and coming down dangerously fast now. Will felt the words "Pull up!" form in his mouth, but the radio cut him short as one of the pilots unconsciously triggered a microphone switch, his disgusted, amazed words running like an Arctic chill down Will's back.

"The stick's dead! I've got it full back!"

The words hung there as the nose of the Starlifter dove through the last fifty feet with a suicidal vengeance and impacted nose-wheel first, the fuselage bending upward instantly as the main gear slammed into the concrete and the gear struts exploded up through the top of the landing gear pods. The wingtips of the Starlifter slapped the ground before springing back up, flinging the right outboard engine completely off the wing.

The jet was skidding down the centerline now, nearing a point abeam Will's position on the taxiway, the severed number-four engine bouncing and bounding right off to the side and right at Will's van, the sounds of its various impacts with the ground bone-jarring.

Will's hand clawed unsuccessfully for the ignition key. The disintegrating TF-33 turbojet engine, dragging what remained of its pylon, almost filled his windscreen now with malevolent energy. Time had dilated, and he could see with fatal clarity that it was going to tumble head-on into the lightweight, Japanese-made van he was occupying and obliterate it. The prospect of being crushed was not a fear, it was a fact.

His hand flailed for the key, his eyes watching the final split seconds as the engine filled the windscreen and dug into the sand one final time before disappearing from view.

The sound of something huge passed overhead as the mechanical apparition leapfrogged cleanly over the top of the van, leaving Will unscathed, small parts raining down on the roof as the body of the huge engine thudded harmlessly into the desert behind him.

Thoroughly adrenalized, Will simply accepted the fact that he was alive. There was no time to analyze the point. That was that.

His hand finally gripped the keys. He started the engine and jammed the automatic transmission in drive, accelerating to the right, following the wrenching progress of the broken C-141, which was now sliding sideways, parts separating in all directions as it went, the left wing taking the brunt of the impact as the disintegrating wingtip slid along the tarmac, the truncated fuselage now aimed forty-five degrees to the right of the runway, showers of sparks marking the friction between tortured aluminum skin and runway surface, the wings flexing and drooping. Two-forty had touched down at over 130 miles per hour, but it was now down to sixty knots or so, the wreckage beginning to grind to a halt, the orange flicker of fire suddenly mushrooming to a huge blaze as the remains of the left wing ignited.

The sounds! He had been unaware of how much horrific noise the crash landing was causing until it stopped. Suddenly, there was quiet, flame, and a towering column of dust now mixed with smoke. The wreckage was four thousand feet distant, and Will accelerated toward it, barking orders into the ALCE hand-held radio as he saw the red beacons of the fire trucks converging on the scene as well.

"We're going to need ambulances. There are five crew members on the plane. Five!"

In the macabre combination of flashing red lights and the hot orange glow of a fire somewhere close by, Jeff Rice, the copilot, realized he was alive. As with Westerman, it was a matter-of-fact realization. There was no pain, but his chest felt strange as he pulled open the seatbelt clasp and tried to find the lever to push the seat back.

There *was* no lever, and only then did he realize the seat wasn't on the tracks. It was somewhere near the middle of the center console and twisted.

Jeff looked over at Jim Collinwood, whose eyes were open, his headset gone. He looked back at where Robbie Jamison, one of the engineers, had been sitting, and saw twisted metal, darkness, and flickering lights through a huge gash in the floor where the rear cockpit seats had been. There had been horrendous noise after the hellacious impact with the runway.

Jim was moving his hand and trying to speak. The plane was tilted somewhat, but Jeff managed to crawl toward him, noticing for the first time that his head was canted at an odd angle and resting against the shattered glass of the pilot's sliding window.

A sudden burst of heat and orange light from the left propelled him to action. They'd burn alive if he didn't get them out of there. Jim couldn't move. Robbie, the other engineer, and their loadmaster were simply gone. It was up to him to get the aircraft commander out.

Pushing and hauling at the seatbelt, Jeff finally felt it give, hearing a guttural cry of pain as he half-pulled, half-lifted Jim Collinwood past the shattered right side of the pilot's seat and across the back of the navigator's table. The angle of his head was immaterial. There was fire.

Other hands and voices, some speaking a language he assumed was Saudi, began intruding, coming for some strange reason through the gap in the floor, trying to grab Jim away from him. He heard himself yell that he was okay—he had the aircraft commander—but the voices and hands overwhelmed him anyway, someone ordering him in English to lie down on a stretcher. He didn't need a stretcher. He needed to help the others, and he was in the process of heading back into the aircraft when his legs became rubber and his head became an echo chamber.

* * *

Will Westerman arrived at the wreckage at the same time as the first fire truck. As the firefighters began spraying foam on the burning wing, trying to keep the raging fire from spreading, he ran to the front of the aircraft, where a huge breach had opened the fuselage like a tin can from the bottom of the crew entrance door to the bottom of the structure. The interior of the flight deck was mostly intact—except for the rear cockpit bulkhead seats, which were just—*gone*. Will could see a lone figure moving inside the cockpit. It was Jeff Rice, hauling out what looked like the body of the aircraft commander. Will joined two firemen in lifting the aircraft commander clear of the shattered flight deck, which was a maze of sharp, twisted metal. Time was critical. The heat from the raging fire behind them threatened to explode any remaining fuel in the wings.

They laid Collinwood on a stretcher just outside the fuselage, conscious but in great pain. Will felt sick inside as he knelt down momentarily to reassure him. What kept playing in his mind as two medics rushed him off to an ambulance was the distance to the nearest U.S.-staffed field hospital.

Over three hundred miles.

The sounds of shouting behind him heralded a new intensity to the flames, probably from number-one fuel tank.

Will caught the sleeve of one of the Air Force paramedics as they lifted the now-unconscious form of the copilot onto another stretcher.

"I'm telling my command post to get a rescue bird on the way in here now to air evac these people, okay? You do have a doctor here, don't you?"

"Yes sir—but only one."

"You have a hospital set up?"

"No sir. Only a field clinic."

"Get him to it as quick as possible. Then have someone report back to me at the ALCE. Understood?"

"Yes sir." The man turned with his partner and disappeared

back to the ambulance as Will issued a stream of orders to the hand-held radio.

There were three more of his people unaccounted for, and he assumed the worst, a cold knot of guilt sitting in his stomach. Why hadn't he seen the simplicity of the hydraulic problem before? Only one of the elevator hydraulic units could have been causing the problem, but if you turned it off and back on too quickly, the other unit would reposition the elevator and make you think you were still in trouble. Why hadn't he told them to go around?

Will clambered through the gap where the crew entrance door had been, working his way into the tilted cargo compartment, the garish light of the fire making odd shadows inside through the small windows. He was startled to see another man standing near the wadded-up metal that had been the cockpit bulkhead, apparently oblivious to the fire. He was just standing there, looking down at something as Will approached, and that was aggravating. The rescuer should be moving, looking for survivors. There was precious little time.

A powerful flashlight beam suddenly cut through the interior gloom as someone else began climbing in behind them, and in the shaft of light he realized the man he had assumed was a rescuer was wearing a flight suit with their squadron patch sewn on one sleeve, which made no sense at first.

Senior Master Sergeant Bill Backus looked up then and met the eyes of his commander, before glancing down again at the twisted body of Staff Sergeant Sarah Andrews, the loadmaster, who had been entwined in the wreckage of the forward bulkhead. Backus's eyes were filled with tears. He looked at Westerman again and pointed weakly into the shattered hull. "Robbie's back there a ways. He didn't make it either. Sarah and he were on the flight deck on the rear seat. They must've . . . must've . . ."

He couldn't finish, and sat down heavily on the upturned bulk of the sidewall seats with his face in his hands. Will stood there a split second in confusion, trying to focus, the twisted wreckage, the smell of burning fuel and metal, and the flashing emergency lights all screaming for an emotional catharsis. He wanted to bury his face as well. These were his people.

But they might have only seconds left. As if from a long distance away, he could hear the voice of the other firefighter who had climbed in the cabin after him, yelling, "GET OUT GET OUT GET OUT!"

Will hauled Backus to his feet suddenly and passed him to the firefighter, who helped him out the door with Will on his heels. The heat had risen to blast-furnace proportions, and they all ran hard toward the line of fire trucks and cars.

Will reached the van and stood there a second, closing his eyes and rubbing his head, realizing he had no time for the luxury of grief. As a child, he had confronted the same dilemma with his father's alcoholic rages: in order to function, he had had to suppress the fright and the pain and the grief. He had learned very well how to put his feelings on hold. And he was still in command of a mission of critical importance, now with no airplane and no crew, but still in charge. As usual, he would have to grieve later.

The fire flared hotter yet, the entire upper wing involved, small splashes of molten metal dropping onto the tarmac, and the firefighters ordered everyone back. The bodies of the other two crew members were still inside, but the flames had now spread to the rear fuselage. There was no way anyone was going to risk going in.

Will left Backus in the care of another officer and climbed into the ALCE van, lifting his hand-held radio to his face and taking a deep breath, struggling to produce an even voice as the sound of a muffled explosion heralded the loss of number-two fuel tank behind him.

"This is Ramrod," he began. "I . . . we've got a lot of work to do to save this mission. I'm on the way back."

**In flight aboard MAC 60141 abeam Riyadh, Saudi Arabia, at flight
level 350
Wednesday, March 6, 1991—7:05 P.M. (1605 GMT)**

Colonel Doug Harris, commander of the 97th Military Airlift
Squadron at McChord Air Force Base near Tacoma, Washington,
sat in the right-hand copilot's seat of a C-141B and shook his
head in disgust, his lap covered with classified code tables. Lighthouse had ordered them out of the blue to change destinations
and divert to a particular set of coordinates over the middle of
the desert, which was an unusual request, to say the least. Harris
had been instantly suspicious that someone down there didn't
have a clear idea of what he was doing, but now, after Lighthouse
had twice failed to reply with the proper authentication code from
a very simple code table, Harris was incensed. Lighthouse, after
all, was the code name for alliance headquarters in Riyadh, and
they'd just fought and won a war. They couldn't be *that* incom-
petent!

Harris keyed the interphone, speaking only to the other crew
members in the airplane, all of them activated reservists and
members of his squadron. ''I don't believe this!''

He glanced at Pete Tilden, the aircraft commander in the left seat. Tilden had gotten nowhere trying to get an explanation for the diversion order. Controlling agencies tended to run all over captains. Full colonels were not treated as lightly.

Now it was his turn.

Doug keyed his microphone again. "Lighthouse, MAC Alpha two-five-five again. Authentication incorrect. We're proceeding to the original destination. Your divert request is disapproved."

They were close enough to Riyadh to be using UHF radio, but since anyone including Saddam Hussein could listen in, it was hardly a secure channel. Asking for authentication of a message to divert a mission was not only reasonable, it was technically required.

A disgusted voice came back from below.

"Okay, two-five-five, let's cut out the cute nonsense, okay? You've had your fun, and no, we're not too fast with the authentication tables. But you were directed to divert to the coordinates I gave you—and I mean right now! It's a matter of great urgency."

"Who's talking?" Harris could feel his blood pressure rising.

"Say again, two-five-five."

"I say again, exactly who is talking, and I want name and rank."

There was a sneer in the reply. "This is *Major* Walker at Lighthouse."

Doug glanced at his partner in the left seat and winked as he pushed the transmit button. "And this, Major Walker, is Colonel Harris, as in O-6, as in full colonel, asking who in hell you think you're issuing orders to when you can't even authenticate? For all I know, you're a clever Iraqi with a stolen radio hogging the channel."

Silence from below, and Doug could imagine the wide-eyed scramble in the command post as one stunned major realized his gaffe, and some superior grabbed for the microphone to smooth it over.

Predictably, a different voice filled their headsets almost immediately. "Uh, two-five-five, sorry about the confusion. We now have the appropriate book and are prepared to authenticate again, sir."

This time the codes matched exactly, and the aircraft commander punched the latitude and longitude coordinates into the FSAS, a small computer on the center console that the crews called the "heads-down display." Another three keystrokes and the Starlifter began a gentle bank to the right and headed southeast as Doug keyed the radio again.

"Okay, Lighthouse, now what do we do when we get there? You realize a major sandstorm's moving over this area? We were barely going to have enough time to load up at Dhahran and get off again before it hits there."

"Yes sir, we understand." The new voice was different, and a great deal more cautious. "We need you for an air evac."

"But all you've given us are latitude and longitude coordinates. How do we know we've got enough fuel? Do we have legal alternates? Has someone checked the weather at whatever destination this is?"

"Sir, do you have at least twenty-six thousand pounds of fuel left?"

Doug keyed the interphone to the flight engineer. They had thirty-two thousand. "That's affirmative."

"Okay, two-fifty-five, then I confirm that you're completely legal to do what we're asking. Twenty-six thousand is the minimum fuel required for this divert with legal alternates. You've got visual weather conditions at your destination, and that will continue until at least an hour after your projected arrival. I checked personally. Also, Dhahran remains good as an alternate. When you get to the holding fix, enter holding, and come up on blue frequency for Sailor Zulu. If no contact within five minutes, call us on the appropriate HF frequency. If still no contact, after twenty-five minutes total hold time, depart and recover at Dhahran."

Doug shook his head again and punched the interphone button again. "The damn war is over, guys. This is weird."

Tilden was nodding, obviously relieved to have a full colonel's horsepower driving the questions a mere captain couldn't get them to answer.

Doug turned partway around in his seat, looking back at one of the flight engineers on the jump seat. "One of their emergency air evacs last fall turned out to be a sprained wrist and a broken arm going back to Germany. Someone down there probably has a stomachache or a hangnail this time."

"More likely a case of terminal acne," the engineer added.

Doug keyed the radio again.

"Lighthouse, two-five-five. You say we're an air evac . . . Are there any med crews down there waiting for us?"

"Uh, no sir."

"Then there's no way we can do a legal air evac. Why don't you scramble a C-130 from Dhahran? They've got real air-evac crews and medical technicians standing by."

The four-engine turboprop 130 transports were a slower and smaller Lockheed-built cousin of the C-141, but they could do the job just as well for short distances.

"Uh, we need you, sir. That's all I can say."

"You're aware we have cargo for Dhahran?"

"Yes sir."

"And that doesn't matter?"

"No sir. This is a true emergency." There was a long pause before the transmitter clicked on again. "Sir, we've got some severely injured people in critical condition down there. You may be their only chance. They need your help."

Doug looked at the aircraft commander and shrugged. "They just said the magic words."

In a particular room in the middle of a nondescript building in downtown Riyadh, Saudi Arabia, known as Lighthouse, an agitated Lieutenant Colonel Jensen replaced the microphone and sighed. After eight months he was mentally and emotionally exhausted, and ready to go home. No one was supposed to know yet that there had been a major accident with a MAC aircraft at the classified staging base known as Sandy 101, and he couldn't tell two-five-five anything about the destination.

And he certainly couldn't tell him that the real reason for snatching him out of the sky had nothing to do with evacuating the crash survivors.

He didn't blame the angry colonel in two-five-five for being upset. He was going to be even angrier when he discovered he'd been lied to, and that the real air evac would be handled by a C-130 now getting ready to leave Dhahran on the coast—just as the colonel had suggested. Screwing around with a full bull colonel could be hazardous to the health of your career.

Jensen glanced over at Major Walker, who had been watching anxiously a few feet away. He'd have to have a few words with Walker about authentication codes, as well as about the distinct advantages to one's career of taking the time to check the rank of those you intend to intimidate.

Sandy 101
Wednesday, March 6, 1991—7:10 P.M. (1610 GMT)

Will had made the decision on the brief dash back to the ALCE. As he saw it, there was no other way. Sending in one of his highly trained SOLL aircrews was one thing, but diverting a C-141 crew on a routine mission and forcing them into a combat situation while he directed things from the rear was entirely another. He couldn't stay behind. He would fly this one himself.

Will Westerman blew into the ALCE unit with the sound of ticking clocks in his head. They had less than two hours to launch.

"Any word?"

"Yes sir." Major Jerry Ronson was holding the satellite phone as Will crossed the floor in a heartbeat. "They've diverted a 141 headed from Jiddah to Dhahran. The crew spent the night in Jiddah, so they're fresh if you need to use them. The mission is MAC Alpha seven-two-five-five, tail number six-oh-one-four-one. They had some trouble getting them to accept the divert, but they're on their way."

"Trouble?"

"Lighthouse blew the authentication codes twice."

"Wonderful example. How about the air evac?"

There was a hesitation and Will read frustration in Ronson's eyes.

"He's supposed to launch from Dhahran in forty-five minutes. That'll put him in here in two hours, which is when you're scheduled out, and about the same time the storm front is supposed to roll over us."

"Jesus."

"I begged for an earlier departure. By the way, two-fifty-five's crew think *they're* the air evac."

"I wish they were," Will replied. "I also wish this were a MAC base with other crew members we could press into service, not to mention a backup airplane. We should have planned this mission to launch from Riyadh, dammit!"

Ronson watched Will Westerman and said nothing, which was always the cautious response to rhetorical statements by senior officers.

I wish the hell this mission was in Riyadh too! Ronson thought to himself, being careful to keep a poker face. From his point of view, the whole operation was an unwelcome intrusion into what had become a routine, if painful, exile. Before Will Westerman had breezed into town thirty hours ago, Ronson had been able to keep a low profile in what, for a MAC troop, was a backwater of the war. All he and the two sergeants had to do was take care of two or three MAC flights that dropped in each day to unload cargo, refuel, and leave. The rest of the time he could spend writing letters, sleeping, or just feeling generally miserable at being away from home and family.

But now, with the special mission and the crash, the whole goddamned Air Force would be swarming all over the place for weeks, and he'd be in a fishbowl.

Ronson raised an index finger to snag Westerman's attention.

"Sir, one more item. We've received word that the Balair DC-10 was airborne at four-five, the last hour. He's twenty-two minutes ahead of schedule."

Will just stared at Ronson for a second as the other members of the ALCE crew—a chief master sergeant and a technical sergeant—wondered what DC-10 they were talking about. Only Major Ronson had been briefed fully.

Will Westerman slapped the desk gently with his hand, looking back over his shoulder. "Chief Taylor? Sergeant . . . what was your name again? Richards? Sorry. You fellows come here a second."

They assembled silently next to Jerry Ronson.

"Here's what we've got to do. I'm out of time, and I'm the interloper on this base. You guys have been here awhile—you know the ropes. Now, I've got two pilots hurt, two crewmen dead, and a fifth in severe emotional distress even if he's not hurt. The A/C may have a broken neck—I'm not sure about the copilot. We've got to get them to a properly equipped hospital, and I need all your creative energies to get that done, sandstorms or no sandstorms. For my part, I've got to concentrate fully on launching this mission on time." They all nodded solemnly.

"Item one: We've got to bulldoze that wreckage off the runway within fifteen minutes. Try not to crumple it, but get it off, and if you can unload the one pallet of material—provided it didn't burn—do it. Chief Taylor, can you manage that?"

The chief master sergeant looked startled. "Uh, two problems, sir. One, MAC and Air Force regulations say we can't move the wreckage, and in fact we may do far more damage to the fuselage if we push or pull her off without lifting her with a crane onto dollies and all the other procedures you're supposed to—''

"We have no time for that, Chief. It's on my head if I'm second-guessed wrong, but at this point, even if it was a perfectly serviceable airplane, I wouldn't care if we tore it up. We *have* to clear that runway."

"Yes sir."

"We can discuss the legalities at my court-martial. What's the second problem?"

"The Saudi colonel who commands this base, sir, will want to follow regulations and shut everything down. He has already. The airfield is technically closed. You may need to talk to him."

Will looked the chief in the eye for a moment. "Set it up, and brief me on where the tripwires are before he gets here."

"Sir, you mean I should summon *him* over *here*? To a Saudi commander, that would be considered a deep insult, I—''

"Invite him, beg him, bribe him, or trick him. I'm not kidding, I don't have time to go to *him*. Do we have bulldozers?"

"The Army guys do, sir."

"Call them. Get them out there right now. Don't wait for permission."

"Colonel al Rashir will go berserk, sir!"

"Let him. Second item: I need the K-loaders and forklifts standing by, manned, gassed, and running the second two-fifty-five parks. I need someone to meet the crew and escort them here—*all* of them. I don't want anyone left out there to argue and slow us down. As soon as they're away from the airplane, unload it and dump the pallets anywhere you can. Take their personal bags and put them in one of the pickups and bring them here. I'll need one of their pilots and all of their enlisted to fly with me. I'll kick that colonel loose, whoever he is."

Ronson looked startled. "Sir, *you're* flying the mission?"

"No choice, Jerry. Now, upload the mission vehicles just as quickly as you get her emptied, and put the planned fuel load on board. Start fueling her the second the crew is clear."

"In other words," Taylor volunteered, "we steal the airplane."

"In so many words." Will felt himself smile slightly. "Item three, call the British squadron and ask them to please launch a Jaguar or something out there to meet two-fifty-five at the holding point and escort her in. It's stupid, but even though the war's over, we still can't talk about this base in the clear. We can't just call up two-fifty-five and tell him where we are. We can't even turn on the navigation aids until he's within twenty miles, and I guess we'll have to violate the rules and give him the Tacan frequency on the air.

"Item four, I need the Special Forces commander in here in forty-five minutes for a pre-boarding conference to coordinate things. Okay, that's it for now. It's nineteen-fifteen local. We have to have this mission off the ground by twenty-one-hundred local. Let's get moving!"

They all scattered as Will headed for the door, then turned back to Jerry Ronson, motioning him over to where only he could hear.

"Jerry, make sure—make absolutely sure—that Lighthouse is launching the tanker and the surrogate thirty minutes ahead of planned schedule. They can orbit and wait for us if we're slow. Make sure they've told the AWACS crew as well, and see if there's any way they can screw up Balair's clearance through Greek airspace and slow him down."

"Yes sir."

"I'm going over to that Army medical tent. I think I know where it is." He raised the hand-held radio into view and waved it slightly. "I've got the radio."

Jerry Ronson shook his head as Westerman pushed out the door. There was no way, *no way,* they were going to make it in time.

Colonel Tariq al Rashir felt a rush of power as the lights of his base flashed by, his driver under instructions to floorboard the expensive black Mercedes to get over to the side the Americans were being allowed to use. Unconsciously he pulled at his mustache and patted his uniform to make sure everything was in place. He almost wished he had a scimitar—he was certainly going to kick some American ass for presuming to order American bulldozers to push American wreckage off his Saudi runway without his permission. Perhaps he should use that exact phrase— "kick some ass." He knew Americans paid more attention to you when you spoke profanely in a loud voice. Americans in general seemed so obnoxiously direct. They were incapable of understanding the use of civilized nuance and careful hints. Especially these Air Force people.

Rashir fingered the button for the electric window and felt the cool desert night air rush past his ear with a soothing roar. How well he knew the Americans! He admired them and he hated them as a people at the same time, and saw no contradiction in that. They had taught him to fly at an American Air Force training base in the sixties, and treated him like some backward country cousin. Tariq al Rashir, the oldest son of a first cousin to the crown prince of the House of Saud, had learned much profanity that year, as well as the offensive American habit of simply telling you to your face that you were wrong.

Colonel Rashir's driver purposefully skidded the car to a halt outside the small expandable box they called an ALCE, so as to throw up a cloud of dust and dirt in front of the window. Rashir waited for his door to be opened before charging toward the entrance of the ALCE with the meanest expression he could manage.

Chief Taylor and Major Ronson were already on their feet as Colonel Rashir burst in, Taylor holding out a satellite phone receiver.

"It's for you, Colonel Rashir."

* * *

Will Westerman pushed past the loose flap of the medical tent and walked a few steps into the night, feeling very depressed and ill. He glanced up. Stars were everywhere, and even the Milky Way was starkly visible above the tent city the allied forces had constructed almost overnight eight months ago. He wished he could take some pleasure from the celestial canopy. The desert could be beautiful in its stark simplicity, and the phrase "smell the roses" echoed again in his head. Janice had tossed—no, lobbed—that phrase at him a dozen times in the past few years, whenever work won out over her desires to do "something fun."

"You're too damn serious, Westerman," she was fond of saying. "I don't marry overly serious sticks-in-the-mud. You want me? Lighten up." For ten years they had shared a house and sparred about marriage, yet neither would ask the other. Neither would commit to the other.

What a crazy damn time to be thinking about Janice!

Will looked down at his watch, which read 11·35 A.M. She'd be at work now—at a hospital, which was where these kids needed to be.

He hadn't taken time to change the time zones on his watch since leaving Charleston, which was eight hours earlier than Saudi. Local time would then be 7:35 P.M., or 1935. One hour and twenty-five minutes left.

Ronson had warned him by radio that Colonel Rashir was headed his way, a somewhat kinder and gentler host now than he'd been ten minutes before. He would have to find out what Chief Taylor had done to defuse the man. It was well known that chief master sergeants ran the Air Force. At least they thought so, and few officers were brave enough to argue the point with them.

Got to focus. Got to think.

Will spun around suddenly to look to the west, straining to see whether the storm front, bearing a ten-thousand-foot-high wall of dust and sand, was visible. It wasn't. Not yet.

The C-130 simply had to get in. How could he leave, otherwise? How could he fly away with the only other aircraft large enough to do an air evacuation of Rice and Collinwood? He couldn't even drop them off in Riyadh without canceling the mission that he'd worked so hard to piece together. The Balair DC-10 was already airborne, and its steady, ominous progress now governed all his decisions.

Maybe he should call Lighthouse and abort the mission. Maybe that should be the backstop option in case the air-evac C-130 couldn't land. Weren't the lives of his two pilots more important than some nameless, faceless Arabs who had let themselves be led by a butcher?

The thought of the Iraqi scientist who had started all this made him sick. Suddenly the little bastard becomes morally conscious and wants the allies to set it right for him, while two GIs die and two more fight for their lives. At least in Jeff Rice's case. The report of the beleaguered doctor trying to save the copilot had not been hopeful.

General Rice would have to be called. Will was dreading that. How do you tell a man his only son may be dying ten thousand miles from home without ripping his heart out? There was no time right now, and no way the man could do anything from back in Washington that wasn't already being done. The 130 was just getting airborne from Dhahran, according to Jerry Ronson.

"Dammit to hell!" Will kicked a Styrofoam cup on the ground as hard as he could, watching it bounce off the rubberized canvas of an adjacent tent—a useless, futile gesture of frustration. The copilot's yoke had injured young Rice internally when his seat broke away in the crash and hit the front panel. But all his noble efforts to pull his aircraft commander from the wreckage were done under the anesthesia of shock, and he had made things infinitely worse for himself, doing massive internal damage with shattered ribs. His internal bleeding now was critical, and the doctor—Will couldn't remember his name—had already performed emergency surgery. Rice was stabilized for the moment, but he needed a sophisticated hospital—fast.

Jim Collinwood wasn't much better. The poor guy's neck was broken without question, but somehow, thank God, the struggle to get him out hadn't seemed to damage his spinal cord. So far, there was no paralysis. He, too, needed the type of care you don't get in the middle of the Arabian desert.

When the Saudi commander had been gone from the ALCE for a full two minutes, Jerry Ronson turned to Chief Master Sergeant Taylor and offered him a high five, which the chief met.

"Brilliant, Chief. Absolutely brilliant. How'd you know you could ignore the chain of command, risk a diplomatic incident, and call a Saudi general without getting us court-martialed? When I heard who you were asking for on that phone, I seriously considered shooting you."

Taylor let himself look smug for a few seconds. "You know I'm a ham radio operator, right?"

"Right."

"And you remember I spent a week working at CENTCOM in December?"

"Yeah?"

"There was this one high-ranking Saudi officer there who's also a ham operator and has been for years. Turns out we've exchanged QSL cards before. He treated me like a friend, and I happened to overhear him chewing up one of his base commanders for not cooperating with a Coalition commander at King Fahd. I figured he might want to offer a few words of guidance to Colonel Rashir before Rashir unloaded on us."

Ronson paused, a puzzled look on his face. "You're not talking about General *Akhmed*? Rashir's commander?" he asked at last.

"None other."

*   *   *

The sound of footsteps approaching rapidly over the hard-packed sand reached Will Westerman's ears before the image of the Saudi colonel loomed out of the darkness. Will waited until Tariq al Rashir was within a few feet before turning and trying to manage a smile as he extended his hand.

Rashir spoke first.

"Colonel West . . ."

"Westerman."

"Of course. Westerman. I am Colonel Tariq al Rashir of the Royal Saudi Air Force, the base commander here."

Will pumped his hand warmly, remembering his briefings on Saudi customs: stand close, look them in the eye, shake hands firmly.

"Colonel Rashir, I appreciate more than I can tell you your kindness in coming over here tonight to speak with me and help us out. I'm sorry I was not able to pay a formal visit to you before. I only arrived yesterday."

Rashir's face changed from puzzlement to a smile. Perhaps the American major back at the command unit had not had time to tell this senior officer of the embarrassment he had caused Rashir. "It is my pleasure, Colonel. My commander in Riyadh has asked me to personally help you in every way."

"We lost two of my crew members in the crash. Two others— the pilots—are in critical condition, with internal injuries and a broken neck. Very serious. We have a C-130 coming in from Dhahran to evacuate them, and I'm sweating out which gets here first—the sandstorm or the 130."

The Saudi brightened slightly. "You may not be aware that we have a very fine hospital at Al 'Ubaylah with excellent Saudi doctors. It is only one hundred eighty kilometers or so by road. We could begin at once."

"Thanks, but I think it will be faster by air evac."

Rashir hesitated, studying the American. "I assure you, Colonel," he said more slowly, "our hospitals are quite well equipped."

"I . . . have no doubt of that, sir, but these injuries . . . I mean . . . by road . . ."

"We could use a helicopter, then. I will use my radio and get a helicopter for them."

Will raised his hand, palm up. "I . . . appreciate that very much, Colonel, but I think, if you'll permit the 130 to land and take off again, that we'll just stick with the original plan. We also have another C-141 inbound, and I'll be flying that one out in about an hour on a special mission."

"What is this mission?"

"I, ah . . ." Will saw the tripwire too late. "I really can't discuss it, sir. I'm acting under instructions from Riyadh."

"Can I help with this mission?" Rashir asked, his face clouding up.

"Other than letting us get the airplane back out whether the sandstorm has hit or not, no sir."

"I am commander here, Colonel. I have a secret clearance. My country is your host and a member of the coalition that has achieved such a glorious victory over Hussein. Do you not think I should know about a mission that operates from my base?"

Why the hell did I say anything? Damn, damn, damn, damn!

"I'm very sorry, Colonel, but in the rush of things, CENT-COM apparently failed to specifically authorize me to discuss it with you—or with anyone. I could call them . . ."

Colonel Rashir's face progressed through several shades of red and purple as he studied Will's eyes. His hospitality had been rejected, his authority trivialized, and his dignity offended.

"I am instructed to cooperate, Colonel. You shall have that cooperation, even if you think our hospitals and our security reliability are below your standards." Making no attempt at a farewell handshake, he nodded his head curtly in dismissal, obviously furious, then began to turn away.

"Colonel Rashir, I did *not* mean . . ."

Rashir pivoted around and moved back toward Will, standing uncomfortably close, his eyes aflame and narrowed, his hands behind his back, watching with obvious pleasure as the American groped for a way to mollify him.

"It is interesting," he said at last, "that you are posted to Saudi Arabia, Colonel. Wester-man . . . Wester-man." He turned the name over on his tongue as if tasting it. "That is a *Jewish* name, is it not?"

A sudden flash of old and primal anger welled up from somewhere inside, fighting unsuccessfully to get out, as Will feigned a smile and said simply, "No, Colonel, I'm from Texas. Westerman is an *American* name."

Rashir snorted, turned sharply, and left.

The message from Ronson crackled from the hand-held just before Will pulled open the door of the ALCE, brushing by the U.S. Army Delta Force officer who had been waiting impatiently for ten minutes and had every intention of letting the Air Force colonel know it. Two-fifty-five had just reached their holding fix and called in, and the British fighter that was going to rendezvous with them in the holding pattern and literally guide them back to the top-secret location had just lifted off. Will could hear the roar of the Jaguar's afterburners in the distance.

Ronson tipped his head in the direction of the Army major dressed in combat fatigues, who cleared his throat a bit too loudly and introduced himself as James Moyer, Army Special Forces. "I was told to be here ten minutes ago, sir. And I was."

Will gave him a neutral stare and waited until Moyer became uncomfortable with the silence.

"Ah . . ." Moyer said at last, "we're ready to go as soon as we have an aircraft. I'm told you're flying us in *personally*?" There was the slightest hint of amazement in his voice.

"That's right. Any objections?" This man is an ass, Will concluded.

"Why, no sir, I was just concerned, Colonel, in light of the crash, I mean, that we aren't straining too hard to get the mission off."

"Meaning?" Will's look was hard and cold, and he hoped the major got the point.

"Meaning that I'm told your two injured pilots were specially trained for this sort of mission. Forgive the question, but do you have the same training, sir?"

"I'm the commander of their unit, Major. Of course I'm trained for it. I'm the one that teaches many of the courses."

"No offense meant, sir. It's just that you fellows are used to dropping paratroopers, and this time, since we'll actually be landing that pig in the desert . . ." Moyer stopped, aware of Will's growing anger.

" 'Pig,' Major? You referring to the C-141B?"

"Uh, sorry, sir. I'm used to landing my men in helicopters or, at the worst, C-130s, and *jumping* out of 141s. I don't know who the harebrained idiot is who decided to use a four-engine jet for this, but I think it's nuts . . . sir."

Will glowered at him and struggled to control his temper.

"Major, you are speaking with the so-called harebrained idiot who made that decision."

Moyer's eyes widened and he looked slightly stricken as Will continued.

"Since you question the decision, I'll tell you the rationale."

"That's . . . that's okay, sir, I apologize for second-guessing—"

"Shut up and listen, Major. We couldn't carry all the vehicles you need in a C-130, especially the one you'd have to use to haul out the, uh, target, if it can't be destroyed on site. We'd have to use two C-130s. Point two: we're not allowed to fly in and land from the south now, by presidential order. We have to sneak in from the west, and there's no way to do that with a C-130. They aren't fast enough. Neither are your Pave Low helicopters.''

''Yes sir.''

''You may not have been around long enough to know it, Major, but this is almost exactly the sort of mission that we were poised to run to get the hostages out of Tehran in 1980 after the fiasco with the C-130 and the helicopter at Desert One.''

''Yes sir.''

''And that would have worked if Carter hadn't been too wimpy to order a second try.''

''Yes sir. Colonel Westerman, I'm *sorry*. That was a stupid comment I made.''

Will nodded. ''You're damn right it was.''

''I . . . I do want to make sure, though, that you know that this could get nasty while you're waiting for us, Colonel. We could even drag a firefight back with us.''

Will looked around at Major Ronson, who was pretending to look elsewhere. He looked down at his feet then, and rocked back and forth for a second with his hands behind his back before letting his head and eyes snap up to lock on Moyer.

''Where have you seen action, Moyer?''

''Sir?''

''Were you in Panama?''

''Why, no, I missed that one.''

''Were you in the ground campaign last month?''

''We were standing by, but my particular unit is a Special Forces—''

Will cut him off.

''I flew sixty-three combat missions over North Vietnam,'' he said very quietly, ''and punched out once near a place called Pleiku, then came back a year later in command of a C-141 to the very same field and almost lost my copilot to ground fire while carrying out three hundred and thirty South Vietnam Army soldiers sitting on my cargo deck with cargo straps tying them down and bullets whistling through the machine. I was in the lead ship into Grenada, and in one of the few C-141s to collect bullet holes in Panama. In other words, Major, I really don't think I'm going to come apart on you if the lead starts flying. Your job, however, is to prevent that lead from being fired in the first place. Correct?''

''Yes . . . of course. Provided our intelligence and the assistance of our guide is all it's cracked up to be.''

The designated ''blue'' frequency came to life suddenly behind them, the voice of the British Jaguar pilot boosted over an inordinately effective speaker.

''Good evening, MAC two-five-five. Ascot forty-four with you, closing at range twenty nautical, climbing to angels three-five-zero. How are you chaps hearing me?''

''Loud and clear, Ascot. How do you want to do this?''

''You stay steady in the hold, I'll join you as wingman, then take over as lead and bring you in to a final and break off.''

The two pilots continued exchanging necessary information on the 141's speed and rate of descent as Sergeant Richards came in the door and Ronson began relaying wind and runway length and surface temperature to MAC 255.

Will turned his attention back to the Delta Force commander. ''Where were we, Moyer?''

''I was making a fool of myself, Colonel. I apologize again.''

Will's eyes bored into Moyer's, verifying his contrition.

''Okay,'' Will said at last. ''Get the personnel carriers and your men in position on the ramp where we're going to park him, and be ready to help them unload. You'll probably have less than ten minutes to get everything on board once the airplane's empty.''

Sergeant Richards moved toward the two of them, a look of grave concern on his face. ''Colonel . . . sir, could I see you a minute?'' Will gave him a just-a-moment crook of the finger and turned back to Moyer.

''It's twenty-hundred hours local, Major Moyer, and we need

to be off early if possible. We need to be taxiing by twenty-forty.''

"Yes sir.'' Moyer gave a snappy salute and left the ALCE. Will heard, rather than saw, the Humvee race away toward the far end of the tent city. For security reasons, the Delta Force unit had turned down the regular tent city and pitched their own camp after arriving twenty-four hours ago. According to the Department of Defense, no such force existed, and the less contact with other troops, the better.

Will turned to the sergeant who had just come from the medical tent with news that Lieutenant Rice had slipped into a coma. The beleaguered doctor estimated a maximum two hours before an operation was absolutely necessary to save his life. That left little choice about phoning Washington, where it was noon.

Walt Rice was in, and as Will had expected, the news hit him hard—all the harder for being unable to affect the outcome. The 130 was on the way, the hospital at Dhahran was waiting, and the sandstorm was approaching. Only Lieutenant Rice could provide the missing glue to keep the rescue together—by staying alive. Will gave the general the direct line to the ALCE, and pledged Major Ronson's support in passing the latest information back to his office at the Pentagon.

Doug Harris read through the Engine Shutdown Checklist and the Before Leaving Aircraft Checklist as he tracked the sudden frenzy of movement outside the parked C-141. They had seen the dark hulk of a wrecked Starlifter on the side of the runway as they landed. It had loomed large and eerie in their lights— all the more so because no one had warned them that there was anything that close to the runway, let alone another 141.

There were vehicles everywhere, far more than seemed necessary for a mere emergency air evac. Doug was beginning to get an idea what was happening. There had been an accident, all right, and no one wanted to let it get out to the rest of the world. They really *were* to be an emergency air evac.

Doug raised a quizzical eyebrow at the aircraft commander and pushed his seat back, shedding the headset as he clambered out of the copilot's position. The scanner had materialized up the three feet of ladder from the cargo compartment to the flight deck at the same moment.

"What's going on out there?" Harris asked. "That's one hell of a reception committee."

"Sir, there's a chief out there wants us all to come in to the ALCE immediately. He says that crash we saw occurred just an hour ago."

"Okay." Doug turned around toward the aircraft commander who was signing the 781 maintenance log. "You hear that?"

"Yes sir."

"I suggest we go in and leave the engineering department to get her fueled."

"Uh . . ." The scanner looked stricken. "They want us *all* in there, Colonel."

Harris cocked his head and smiled a now-seriously-folks smile. "Why?"

The scanner shrugged his shoulders. "I'm not a chief, Colonel, I'm just an Indian. They want us in."

"Yeah, because they're going to steal our airplane, I'll bet anything!"

As they pulled away in a van with Chief Taylor at the wheel, the sight of several men throwing their crew bags into the back of a flatbed seemed to answer the question. As they rounded the right side of their aircraft, the sight of three tracked fighting vehicles and a small platoon of armed soldiers wearing berets answered the other: they had not been yanked out of the sky for an air evac. Doug Harris was ready to take someone apart by the time they arrived at the ALCE, and the aircraft commander simply hung back and waited for the explosion as Harris yanked open the door of the olive drab foldable, transportable ALCE box and charged inside.

"Who the hell is in charge of this place?" He stepped into the enclosure as the six-foot-two frame of Will Westerman moved from the far end to confront him. Both men stared at each other in stark silence for what seemed to Ronson and Taylor like an entire minute. Harris's hands had been on his hips. They now slithered to his side, an involuntary gesture Westerman was mirroring, shocked smiles slowly crossing both faces as Will extended his hand.

"This I don't believe! My God, Doug, what on earth are you doing *here*?"

Sandy 101 ALCE
Wednesday, March 6, 1991—8:10 P.M. (1710 GMT)

Doug Harris gripped Will Westerman's right hand and gestured toward the door with his left. "This is what happens, Westerman, when you snag something out of the sky without looking. You get me!"

"Geez... Doug, we gotta talk, fast. What an awful time for a reunion! I'm in the middle of the mother of all crises."

"That phrase is getting overused, you know."

Will turned to Ronson. "Hold the fort for a moment, Jerry, while I brief..." He glanced back around at Doug, checking the silver eagles on the shoulders of his flight suit and feigning amazement: "My Lord in heaven, they'll promote anybody..." Then back at Ronson: "... while I brief *Colonel* Harris here."

"Yes sir."

Will turned back to Doug. "Or should I call you Colonel *Captain* Harris?"

"Yeah, well, I'm a 747 captain now, but 'Colonel' will do nicely," Doug replied, noting the puzzled look on Major Ronson's face.

Will saw Ronson's confusion as well, and gestured at Doug. "Jerry, this turncoat got off active duty fifteen years ago and joined the airlines while I stayed on to keep Charleston safe for democracy. He's a United Airlines pilot now, moonlighting as an Air Force colonel."

Doug shook Ronson's proffered hand before following Will out the door of the ALCE. The two colonels walked a few yards away into the stark blackness of the desert night at the edge of the tent city.

"Doug . . . Lord, it's been too long. Let me tell you quickly. I'm in charge of a very vital, very secret mission, but we lost the mission bird on landing a while ago . . ." His words tumbled out quickly, the ticking of the clock in his head becoming compelling.

"I know, I saw it on rollout. Quite a surprise."

"Yeah . . . well, we couldn't say anything about it on the radio."

"I gathered. What on earth happened?"

"I'll . . . have to fill you in later. Right now I've got to take your airplane, and . . ."

"That's okay. I guessed that much."

"*And* I've got to shanghai some of your crew."

"They're not mine. I'm just hitching a ride. I mean, they *are* mine in that I'm their leader, but not their A/C. Did you follow that?"

"Not a word."

"I'm their squadron commander, but not the A/C, you see. We'll need to involve the young captain back there, Pete Tilden."

"*You're* a squadron commander? I haven't gotten over the shock of your being a full colonel! Doug, the resident rebel? God's gift to United flight attendants?" Will was chuckling as Doug wagged his finger at him.

"Okay, pompous-ass-with-the-eagles-on-active-duty. I'm commander of the 97th Squadron at McChord, a goddamn *active-duty* squadron, I'll have you know."

"Me, too."

"Like *hell* you're commanding the 97th."

"No, I mean at Charleston. I'm commanding a SOLL squadron."

"I knew you were at Charleston."

"Yeah, Harris, but you never write."

"Nor do you."

The two old friends fell silent for a second, a decade of no communication a yawning gulf between them, but both of them startled at how quickly the old familiar rhythms of friendship—the give-and-take barbs and humor—had returned, cutting through the pretensions and posturing of rank and position in a microsecond. It was like falling into a time warp, as if they were back in school growing up together again and *pretending* to be in the middle of a desert facing a mountain of challenges. Which was reality and which was make-believe? The disorientation lasted all of a few seconds, but it opened an anthology of memories.

"Okay," Will said at last, "back to business."

"*Bidness*. We're from Texas, remember?"

"Yeah. Come on, man, this is dead serious." Will looked pained. "I've got less than thirty minutes to get in the seat. They're refueling your airplane now and loading it. Your bags have been pulled off and should be by the ALCE back there. I need some of the crew to go with me. Is the A/C, Captain... what was it?"

"Tilden."

"Tilden. Is he AR-qualified? Aerial refueling, I mean?"

"Hey, I know what AR means. I am a qualified 141 jockey, okay?"

Will's right hand went over his eyes in mock embarrassment. "I'm so sorry. I *forgot*."

"Who else do you need?"

"He can serve as copilot. I need the full complement. Two engineers and a loadmaster. We've got a contingent of Delta

Force Special Forces types we're taking up north. That's top secret.''

"North?"

Will nodded.

"The war's over, Will."

"Not for us."

"You're going to fly whatever this mission is *yourself?*"

"No choice. My two SOLL pilots are in critical condition."

Will quickly shared his deep worries over Rice and Collinwood, and the inbound C-130 trying to beat the sandstorm to the base.

Doug nodded. "That sandstorm was beneath us. It can't be more than an hour away. You could see it even in the moonlight."

Will looked at his watch again; it was 8:14. A small twinge of panic roiled his stomach, and his mind focused on that, almost shutting out Doug's next statement. "What?"

"I said *I'm* going. Leave Tilden here. He's not AR qualified, and I am. Noncurrent, but qualified."

Will smiled and shook his head. "No . . . nothing doing, Harris. We're both too old for this sort of thing, but I have no choice, and all I need is a copilot."

"Yeah, bucko, but—"

"*Bucko?*"

"Yeah," he was chuckling, "would you prefer 'meathead'?"

"*Bucko?* No one uses 'bucko' anymore."

"*Look,* Will, cut the crap." Will was doing his best to look incredulous. "You need a copilot ornery enough to take the airplane away from you if you start screwing things up. We're both full bulls now and inherently intimidating. These young troops may have had aircrew coordination training, but in most cases they'll sit on their hands and watch respectfully while we fly them into the side of a mountain. I don't know what this mission is, but it sounds demanding, and you need my help. That's that."

Will was still shaking his head. "*Bucko?*"

"What do you say?"

Will sighed. "Doug, you're a civilian. You've got a life."

"I'm active duty at the moment, and this *is* my life." Will turned away slightly to think, and Doug repositioned himself in his field of view.

"Think, Will. You'll intimidate the hell out of that young captain. I've been running roughshod over him since we left Torrejon yesterday, without trying." He suppressed a laugh as he gestured back toward the ALCE, remembering an incident at the visiting officers' quarters. "Hell, he . . . he even came to my VOQ room when we were alerted and tried to carry my bags to the crew bus, for crying out loud."

Will raised the palm of his hand to stop the onslaught of arguments, and Doug ignored him.

"Hey, guy, whatever it is we're supposed to do, it's in a good old 141 and we own the skies over Iraq, if that's where we're going. And . . . *and* . . . it'll be the old Westerman-Harris team on deck again. What do you say?"

"Okay."

"Okay?"

"Okay, dammit. I don't have time to argue."

Doug nodded. "Okay." They both fell silent, until Doug broke the moment.

"So where are we going?"

"Come on." Will gestured and wheeled, with Doug following, as they returned to Tilden and his crew. Tilden would stay behind to ramrod the C-130 evacuation of Rice and Collinwood, but his crew would go with Harris and Westerman. Directions were given, bags moved, and the enlisted crew members dispatched back to the aircraft at high speed.

"One more thing." Will had already briefed Ronson in the ALCE box. They were back outside.

"Yeah?"

"There's someone you'd better meet. He'll be going with us, but you may have to restrain me from booting the bastard out of the plane on the return leg. He's the cause of this whole thing in more ways than one." Will, who stood six-foot-two with long, powerful legs, put on a burst of speed as he headed into the tent city, leaving the five-foot-eight Doug Harris scrambling to keep up.

"Doug, what time are you showing?"

Doug fumbled for the light button on his digital watch as he half-trotted to stay up with Will. "Twenty past the hour. *Which* hour I'm not sure."

"I am. We gotta be in the airplane, ready for engine start, in fifteen minutes."

Dr. Shakir Abbas sat on the side of the U.S government–issue cot in the small, portable accordion-fold building, and listened to the sounds of airplanes coming and going—sirens, cars, engines, and other unexplained noises in the night. He had no idea when the Delta Force commander would come for him. He had spent hours briefing them on the layout of the lab, and who would do what once they reached it. In effect, he would be in the lead—with a gun at his back.

Once again he looked at his watch, reading a local time of 8:20 P.M. He had never expected to see the watch again, assuming the Saudi guards who took it when he came over the border had no intention of returning it. It was a Seiko he'd bought in London in 1988, a gold digital calculator watch with memory capacity for fifty addresses or numbers, and it had become part of his memory—a vital part. In fact, he had trusted it too much.

In the cell at Badanah he had sat in a panic, trying hard to remember all the information he had stored in the fifty tiny electronic pigeonholes of the watch's silicon chip. The watch, he figured, was long gone. But the numbers he desperately needed were in his head—somewhere. It was amazing how many he could recall when he really tried, but two of the most vital numbers had eluded him. For hours he had tried, almost seeing them—almost able to read them in his mind's eye. But each time he had attempted to mentally sharpen the focus, the numbers had evaporated like a heat mirage in the noonday desert.

And then the Americans had come like a breeze of cool air, and the Saudi officer who had appeared to have tossed his note aside—but hadn't, Allah be praised—suddenly handed back his watch! How poor was his opinion of human nature to have assumed otherwise.

Little victories, little defeats. He had oscillated from confidence and purpose to the depths of despair and back a dozen times in the past few hours while waiting, waiting, waiting. Time was slipping away, and if these bright-eyed, confident, sturdy westerners he had always admired didn't—what was the phrase?—"get their act together" very rapidly, the canisters would be moved, and the consequences would shake the planet.

He had never for a moment thought Saddam could be a Hitler. He thought he understood Saddam. Butcher, bully, master manipulator, and demagogue—but not a madman like Hitler. While studying one weekend in the library at Oxford, during his baccalaureate years, when he had been absorbing everything western, he had run across the newly discovered plans of the Third Reich for the British people. The incredible brutality of the postwar blueprint was beyond the comprehension of a sane mind: all British men would be exterminated; all British females would be enslaved, many for the casual sexual use of German males; all male children would be slaughtered; and all British institutions and museums would be not only dismantled but eradicated, as if there never had been a Britain. Shakir had been shaken to the depths of his being that such a monster existed. Surely Saddam could never approximate such evil.

And yet, with Shakir's self-indulgent help, that was exactly what he had decided to do. The Israelis thought they were the focus of Saddam's rage. They had no idea it was mankind itself that stood in his crosshairs, and mankind came in many forms and cultures.

The image of his children and Saliah, his wife, came again, and his composure slipped. *How I miss them! How I miss her!*

She was so beautiful, even after all these years of marriage and children. So many Iraqi wives stopped trying after a while, but not Saliah. She began the day and ended the day trying to look beautiful and desirable to him—and she succeeded. *How I want her!*

Strange, Shakir thought. What a curious response to separation. His smile broadened as the thoughts and memories of her became more sensual. How lucky he was. Their hunger for each other had grown, not diminished, especially with the lonely months of separation. When Saddam had ordered him to the desert in 1989 to stay and work at Saad-18, one of the bunkerlike underground desert labs he had helped build, only occasional visits home had been permitted. It had been an agony for the family, and a special agony for Saliah and Shakir. Iraq was anything but a traditional Muslim country when it came to females. There were women provided to serve the masculine needs of Saddam's loyal workers in the desert; Shakir had never been interested in them. Only in Saliah. He lived for the trips home.

And now what had he done? Slammed the door on his life.

So it all comes down to this in the end. The worth of what I'm about to do is nothing compared to what I may lose for myself.

Once again, a crushing sadness and feeling of shame fell over him like a shroud, the energy draining away, the purpose that had driven him the past few days seeming trivial. He was an enemy of the state now, whether they knew it or not. Saliah and the children could become targets at any time. If they ran an autopsy on that charred corpse he had left at the side of the road . . .

Logic told him there was no way such sophisticated forensic detective work would be done in a bombed-out country fighting a civil war. But the mere shadow of a possibility that Saliah might some night open their door and find a two-footed animal from Saddam's secret police waiting there paralyzed him with fear. How would such horrors begin? With a knock? Or do they just burst in, guns firing?

With his mind in Baghdad, the sudden opening of the door echoed the nightmare, and Shakir jumped from the cot in confusion at the noise, searching for a place to run before realizing where he was.

Will, who had stepped in first, was startled to see the Iraqi scramble toward the flimsy wall, his eyes dilated with fear.

"Abbas? What the hell's the matter with *you*?"

Doug switched on the light, as Shakir slowly regained his composure.

"You startled me. I'm sorry."

"Colonel Harris, meet *Doctor* Abbas, otherwise known as Doctor Death." Will's words were tinged with acid, and as Doug began to extend his hand, Will quietly tugged his arm back. "Don't shake this individual's hand, Doug, until you hear what he and his little Saddamites have been doing up there in Iraq for the past few years. Tell him what this is all about, Abbas."

Will sat heavily on an opposite cot and added, "And make it quick. We take off in a few minutes."

Doug sat too, slowly, feeling somewhat awkward in the heat of the hatred Will obviously felt for the man. "What's your field, Doctor?"

Abbas sat down on the opposite cot and looked Doug in the eye.

"I am a microbiologist and biochemist," he began. "The Iraq government paid for my education in London and in the United States. My Ph.D. is from Johns Hopkins. I have worked as a researcher in what we call the Iraq Research Institute since 1972, long before Saddam. I . . . this . . . Colonel, this gets to be a long story, so I'll just say that I have become a traitor to my country and come to Saudi Arabia and to the allied forces for help because one of the terrible things I helped invent—something that was never supposed to be used for anything but a threat—is about to be used by Saddam, and we have to stop him."

Abbas let that sink in. Doug turned and searched Will's face before continuing. "What the hell is it we're doing?"

"You do not know, then, Colonel?" Abbas asked softly.

"I just got here," Doug began. "There was a crash . . ."

Will raised his hand slightly. "Abbas, we had a last-minute change of flight crew, but the assault team you've met and instructed will be the same. Colonel Harris here will be my co-pilot."

Will turned to Doug. "Okay, here's the deal. We're flying the assault team in quite close to where his underground lab is located. We don't drop them in by parachute—we actually land. A combat support team did a high-altitude, high-open drop in there yesterday from a C-130. They're on the ground now and talking to the AWACS, and everything's secured. Early in the morning, we land, the commandos take Abbas here and go to the bunker, Abbas destroys these bugs he's invented, they take anyone they find down there prisoner and blow up the place, then they scramble back to the airplane and we get the hell out of there and go south in time for breakfast."

Doug looked at Abbas, then at Will, then at Abbas, and back at Will, and laughed. "That's all?"

"That's enough for one night."

"Is he . . ." Doug turned to Abbas. "Are you trustworthy, Doctor? Why are you doing this?"

Will stood up and snorted. "Because after all this time he's had a conscience attack! Interesting timing, isn't it? His pip-squeak criminal country loses, and suddenly he needs our help. Come on. Let's get going."

Abbas got up slowly and reached for Doug's sleeve. "Colonel, my family and my life are still in Iraq. When this mission is complete, I've still got to get them out. I'm putting myself and my family in great danger. This is no trick."

Will whirled on him, the frustrations of the past hour boiling over and spilling out at the only target in sight.

"Abbas, I don't think you know what you're asking, and what the cost has already been. I don't think you have any idea of the destruction and pain this mission has already caused. I've got two flight crew members dead, a man and a woman—true professionals—and I've got a pilot with a broken neck and a copilot bleeding internally so badly he may not make it. All because of your germ-warfare experiments and the fact you came running to us to clean up your mess." Will stood with his hands on his hips, glowering at Abbas.

"I am sorry, Colonel. I needed your help . . . to prevent many more from dying."

"From a virus you created!" Will snorted.

Abbas nodded. He could feel Westerman's frustration. It didn't make it any easier, but he understood. In many, many ways, he now shared the loathing of what he had done—the realities to which he had blinded himself for so long.

Major Ronson leaned out the open door of the ALCE, genuine concern showing, and shook Will's hand. "Good luck, sir. You'd better get moving. The winds are picking up, and the gust front is only about five miles away."

"Thanks for all the support, Jerry. You say she's fueled?"

"Seventy thousand pounds, sir. They just finished. I checked weather for Jiddah, by the way. It's clear for a bingo alternate. That'll put you on the refueling track with at least thirty thousand pounds. The C-130's going to make it in just before you launch. The patients are already in the ambulance, and the doc said to tell you there's no change. The copilot's hanging in there."

Will gave Taylor and Richards a small wave through the open door and swung into the right seat of the Humvee, which rushed them to the aircraft.

Senior Master Sergeant Bill Backus was waiting for him, an anxious look on his craggy face. "Sir, I'm going with you."

Will studied Backus in silence, the flight engineer's six-foot frame bent toward the window of the Humvee as his arm balanced against the roof. He had a slight paunch and jowls that made him look older than his forty-eight years, but his eyes were lined and sad, like those of a basset hound, and the effect in the subdued light was that of a supplicant enormously afraid his request would be denied.

"I need you *here,* Bill," Will said. The image of Backus standing in the middle of the burning fuselage of the crashed C-141 was indelible in his mind. He should be in a hospital, not flying the mission.

Yet he was unhurt, and well trained.

Will tried again. "I think you should stay with Jim and Jeff. The 130 called in before I left the ALCE. He'll be here in ten minutes."

"The medical people can do that, sir. I didn't get a scratch in the crash, I'm SOLL-trained, and you've fully briefed me on this mission already as we were flying to Riyadh, remember? The other two engineers are neither SOLL-trained nor up to speed on what this is all about, sir." He jerked a thumb in the direction of the lighted cockpit.

"Bill . . ."

"Please, sir. What if something goes wrong? I'm trained to shoot and escape and evade. You've got two engineers up there who aren't. And you and I've flown together before."

Will sighed and looked at his feet as Doug hustled past and disappeared up the crew entry ladder.

"Sir, I *want* to do this. *Please!*"

Will looked up at him, trying to read his eyes. "You're sure you're okay?"

"Yes sir!"

Will nodded. "It's against my better judgment, assuming I

have any, and it's probably against regulations, but all right. Hurry. Get up there and find out who wants to stay. You have your—''

''Already arranged, Colonel. The other guy's ready to leave, and I'm going to borrow his headset and manuals.'' Backus fairly leaped at the ladder as Will followed him onto the flight deck and dropped into the left seat, hurriedly connecting his seatbelts, headset, interphone cord, and oxygen mask. In the right-hand copilot's seat, Doug was already working rapidly, his abbreviated checklist open on his knee, the present position punched into both INSs—inertial navigation systems.

''Okay, pilot,'' Doug began, ''the INSs are aligned, the engineers already put in present position, and we're down to state five on both INS one and two. Ready on the APU, engineer?''

The auxiliary power unit—the APU—a small jet engine in the left wheel well, provided electrical power and pressurized air for engine start.

''Ready.'' It was Backus's voice. He had already taken over. One of the other two flight engineers was disappearing down the ladder with his briefcase.

''Who's left in the engineering department?'' Will asked.

The incongruity of a sudden cascade of feminine blond hair and a hint of perfume over the center console completely confused Will's senses for a second. Staff Sergeant Sandra Murray leaned over to shake his hand as Will fumbled to remove his headset.

''That's Sandra,'' Doug announced over the interphone, as if the name told the story. ''One of my people.''

Will's eyes met hers and lingered for a second. Her mouth was exceptionally wide, he noticed, turned up in a permanent smile on both sides of a rectangular face set with a pug nose, her eyes china blue, round, and huge. Will shook her hand briefly and disengaged, trying unsuccessfully to push her pleasing image from his conscious thoughts, her shoulder-length blond hair still catching at his peripheral vision. It was amazing, he mused, what a well-proportioned female like Sandra could do to a standard Air Force flight suit.

"She'll start off as scanner," Doug was saying, using the job description that applied to whichever flight engineer was not sitting at the panel that leg. The scanner stood outside during engine start and retrieved the chocks and landing-gear safety pins before climbing on board.

"And our loadmaster is Phil Casey." Doug's thumb arced toward the rear of the airplane.

"Yo," said another voice on the interphone. "Glad to fly with you, Colonel. The vehicles are all in place and tied down and our passengers are all aboard, the Form F weight and balance is done, and I've already been briefed about the waiver for the overgross cargo load, and the cargo doors are closed and latched. By the way, sir, the Army major down here says to tell you he's ready too."

"Thanks, Load," Will said.

Sandra Murray had already left the flight deck and plugged into the outside interphone cord. "Scanner's on, walkaround complete, APU's clear, sir."

The thought crossed Will's mind that he was either going blind or she had been hiding when Tilden's crew arrived at the ALCE. Not that it mattered, but how could he have failed to notice an attractive female engineer? Will looked around the cockpit once again, watching for a few moments as everyone went about the pre-start duties with practiced competence. The previous hours had been filled with confusion and frustration, horror and surprise. He had no idea whether he'd made the right decisions—there had been so many. But the irony of it all was that starting the mission itself seemed to be the easiest part. It was as if he could relax now, and get to work.

"Before Starting Engines Checklist," Will announced on interphone, and the comfortably familiar litany of checklist items began, taking them through engine start until all four were running, the chocks were removed, and the crew entrance door was closed.

"We take off visual, climb visual, then pick up our instrument clearance from Riyadh, is that the plan?" Doug asked.

"Exactly. We pop up. Riyadh radar doesn't need to know where we came from."

The scanner reported, "Check complete," and Will shoved the throttles up and manipulated the nosewheel steering wheel, guiding the 141 down the taxiway at an alarming rate to the end of runway 33. The landing lights of the arriving rescue C 130 were already visible on short final, and as they finished the lineup check and Doug obtained clearance for takeoff, the 130 touched down, slowed rapidly, using the massive reverse thrust of its paddlewheel propeller blades, and turned off the runway toward the line of vehicles and one ambulance waiting for them—a column of flashing red lights. If all went as planned, Collinwood and Rice—and the bodies of the other two crew members that had been recovered from the wreckage—would be on board within five minutes. By doing an engine-running onload, the C-130 could be back in the air within ten minutes of landing.

"It's gonna be a photo finish, pilot." The voice was Doug's. The winds were already picking up, the wall of dust and sand now obscuring the westernmost lights near the perimeter of the base as they advanced power to 1.92 engine pressure ratio on all four engines and the big jet began to accelerate through fifty knots, then eighty, and past rotate speed, 134 knots.

"Go." At the required call from the copilot, Will eased the yoke back, letting the ship accelerate as it lifted off the main gear with a series of thuds. He glanced at the vertical velocity and confirmed they were climbing before calling for gear-up.

And just as suddenly they weren't climbing.

"Wind shear!" Doug's voice was steady but strained. The radar altimeter was showing fifty feet now, but the needle was beginning to unwind with the end of the runway coming under the nose and the gear in the wells, up and locked. The headwind they had nosed into had suddenly become a tailwind with the onrush of the gust front, robbing them almost instantly of nearly thirty knots of wind across the wings.

Will was only marginally aware of Doug's left hand gathering the four throttles and pushing them all the way forward. His voice rang clearly in Will's headset, even calmer now.

"I've been here before, Will. Pull it back till we get the shaker. She'll fly."

He pulled against all instincts, the airspeed now hovering around 110, the engines screaming, and the radar altimeter finally stopping its decline at thirty feet and beginning a slow reversal into a climb. Thank God for a flat desert beyond the threshold.

"Back farther, a little more . . . *There!*"

The stick shaker, a small eccentric motor at the base of both yokes, began vibrating both control columns, indicating they were nearing a stall with just a little margin left.

"Okay, let off a hair of back-pressure until it stops, then nibble it in again." Will could feel the pressure from Doug's hands following him on the control yoke as the shaker stopped, then started, then stopped again.

The radar altimeter was at fifty feet once more, and just as suddenly leaping through 150 as they pulled the throttles back to normal takeoff power.

Will waited for the speed to shoot through minimum flap retract by ten knots before calling "Flaps up"—and letting his breath out.

"Copilot, better let them—"

A radio transmission from the right seat cut him off. "Sandy tower, MAC Alpha two-eight-four. Has the C-130 taken the runway yet?"

A Saudi voice struggling with the international language of aviation, English, replied hesitantly, "You are asking, sir, about . . . who . . ."

Doug forced himself to slow down. "Has the C-130 that just landed called for takeoff clearance yet?"

"Negative, sir."

An American voice cut into the channel just as quickly. "Air Evac fourteen-twelve here, MAC. You calling?"

"Roger. Bad wind shear on takeoff. We probably lost thirty knots, headwind shearing to tailwind. Are you guys ready to roll?"

"Visibility's going to hell, but we're closing the doors now. We'll carry extra speed on liftoff. Thanks for the warning."

The buzz of the C-141's engines at climb power and the electronic hum of radio circuits and the interphone formed the background as Will climbed them through five thousand feet. Their ears were on the tower frequency behind them, their imaginations geared to following the C-130 out to the runway.

At last: "Air Evac fourteen-twelve's ready for takeoff."

"Roger, fourteen-twelve, the airfield is closed. Permission denied."

Will punched the transmit button. "Fourteen-twelve, this is MAC Alpha two-eight-four. Disregard the tower. I'm personally clearing you for takeoff on the authority of the base commander, Colonel . . . ah . . . Rashir. Tariq al Rashir. He has already approved your departure despite weather. Get that tub off the ground."

"Hey, MAC, you can't play tower up there." The accent was deep southern.

The Saudi voice in the tower cut in again. "Air Evac fourteen-twelve, you are not cleared for takeoff. The airfield is closed."

Will looked at Doug. "Copilot, take the aircraft. We're cleared to flight level two-five-zero until we can contact Riyadh control."

Doug nodded and Will diverted his gaze somewhere on the other side of the instrument panel as he concentrated on moving a mountain.

"Air Evac fourteen-twelve, who's the A/C?"

"Major Daniels speaking, MAC."

"Major, Colonel Westerman here. I'm giving you a direct order to take off as long as you can do it safely. You are to disregard the control tower. You have my word that it has already been arranged, and Colonel Rashir has already approved takeoff regardless of weather.''

"I don't know, Colonel. I don't think you can do that. I—''

The Saudi voice came on again, somewhere between anger and hysteria at the subjugation of his frequency and authority.

"You are no cleared to take off! Acknowledge! Not cleared, MAC and Air Evac! You are not having authority to talk this way on my channel!''

"Air Evac, Westerman. Can you take off safely with the winds and visibility the way they are?''

"Yes sir. It's bad, but it's safe. I can even see the far end of the runway.''

"Then for God's sake, man, do it now! It's my authority and my ass on the line—as long as it's safe.''

"Okay, Colonel, this one's for you. Sandy Tower, Air Evac is rolling.''

"NO NO NO NO NO, Air Evac! You do not have—'' The Saudi voice had reached a higher pitch before being interrupted. Another voice came on then without warning, the tones low and precise—accented but understandable, calm and icy. It was Colonel Rashir.

"Air Evac one-four-one-two *is* cleared for takeoff.''

There was silence for more than a minute before the 130 pilot reported, ''Airborne,'' and the crew of MAC Alpha 284 breathed a collective sigh of relief.

God willing, Will thought, Rice has a chance.

He looked at Doug then, who seemed remarkably unaffected by the wind shear and the cliffhanger C-130 departure.

"You insisted on coming, Harris.''

"Just like old times. You're just as pushy as you used to be.'' Doug was grinning behind the boom microphone. ''And besides, that sort of wind shear is old hat.''

"You've gone through *that* before?''

"Not in a 141, but in a Boeing 727 simulator in our Denver

training center. We practice it in the commercial world. Textbook example of wind shear on takeoff. Like that Pan Am crash in New Orleans in 1982. We now know that they could've flown out of it if they'd known how to do what we just did.''

''Next you're going to tell me it's a piece of cake, Harris!''

Doug grinned. ''It's a piece of cake, Harris.''

And Backus chimed in from the engineer's seat.

''I think I've changed my mind, Colonel Westerman, sir. I don't want to go after all.''

''Great,'' Will replied. ''I've drawn a crew of comedians.''

With cruise altitude reached, Doug let himself relax for a few minutes. He turned the panel lights down and leaned forward in the copilot's seat, his chin almost resting on the glare shield. A sparkling canopy of stars spread before the Starlifter like a secret feast prepared only for aviators and astronauts. There was such a peaceful grandeur about it, especially with most of the cockpit noise all but eliminated by the state-of-the-art David Clark headsets MAC had finally purchased for its aircrews. Doug could almost imagine some moving orchestral piece playing in magnificent accompaniment to the symphony of stellar images outside. He wished he had a Walkman along. Many of the C-141 and C-5 aircrews had fought the boredom of endless hours of Desert Shield flying by putting a soundtrack with their transoceanic flights—sticking a pair of stereo headphones under their headsets. Digital stereo and position reports at 39,000 feet. What was the line Bill Tilden had used? Roxette with Roma Control, Connick with Cairo, and Madonna with Madrid.

Doug toggled the interphone switch on the control yoke.

''I think this is where I came in.''

''Say again, copilot?'' The voice of the flight engineer came back in response.

''How old are you, Sergeant Backus?''

''Forty-eight, sir.''

"You're old enough to remember this. When your folks took you to the movies when you were a little kid, did they just charge right in as soon as they got there, regardless of whether the movie had started?"

"No sir. My dad had a thing about getting there before it started."

"You're lucky. My folks would walk in whenever, let the damn movie end and begin again, and then my dad would stand up and say, 'Okay, this is where we came in, people. Let's go.' "

"I've heard the phrase, sir."

"Anyway, this is where *I* came in, about three hours ago"—he looked over at Will, who was riffling through paperwork in the left seat—"before I was rudely yanked from the sky by some banjo-pickin' active-duty clown from Charleston."

Will looked over and grinned. "Watch your language, weekend warrior."

"That's 'active-duty weekend warrior' to you, bub."

"Uh, copilot, are you saying Colonel W. plays banjo?"

Will raised his hand in protest, but it was too late.

"Better than Grandpa Jones, engineer. He and I had a professional folk music group back in the sixties in Dallas. I played twelve-string guitar, sang, kept the books, and got the gigs and the groupies, while he tortured a banjo and screeched."

Will was shaking his head in disgust as the engineer's voice came back with a tinge of wonder. "Really? Our colonel?"

"You bet. We were called the Mavericks."

"What do you mean, 'screeched,' Harris?" Will asked. "*You're* the goddamn tenor! I'm a baritone. And we never had groupies."

"I'm impressed, sirs," Backus said.

"A long, long time ago," Will said.

"In a galaxy far, far away," Doug added.

"Engineer, this is the pilot. Would you monitor Victor Two, please? That's Riyadh Control. I need to fill Colonel Harris in on the flight, and for security reasons we can't do it on interphone, so we'll have our headsets off.''

''Roger, sir. I've got it.'' Backus reached up and adjusted the switch for the number-two VHF radio while the two pilots shed their headsets and leaned over the center console.

''Doug, there are some details I haven't told you.''

''I figured.''

''First, you know we're headed to the refueling track over the Red Sea, and you saw the location of that.''

''Yeah. I'm familiar with the track.''

''Okay, we'll meet a KC-10 tanker on the refueling track, but he won't be alone. There will be a C-141 with him. When he left his base, the 141 was to move in on his wing with his transponder off. The KC-10 had some preplanned 'trouble' about that point: his transponder got stuck in the indent position, so while the 141 quietly flies along with him, the KC-10 is showing up as an overly large target on any radar that might be looking at him. They'll both be up there on the track, waiting for us. Now, while the other 141 stays off to the side, we'll refuel. When we part company with the KC-10, however, we go north- west toward El Dab'a on the north coast of Egypt in tight for- mation with the other C 141. As we depart the refueling track, the other 141 will take our transponder squawk and our call sign and we'll turn our transponder off and just pretend we're not there. Meanwhile, as far as Cairo or anyone else knows, a single MAC flight—us—goes on to Europe.''

''I don't understand. Why the subterfuge? Aren't we going to Iraq?''

Will coughed a few times. Trying to make yourself heard in a 141 in flight meant almost yelling, with a very dry throat as a result.

''When they ginned this mission up several days ago, they realized they needed the tracked fighting vehicles we're carrying to take the assault force in, but the 130s that would normally do a combat insertion like this can't carry that many in one run, *and* bring back an eight-man combat support team plus POWs, and they can't fly as fast as we can.''

"Which is how a 141 unit got involved," Doug finished.

"Exactly."

"These damn things are strategic assets, Will. We shouldn't be using them like C-130s.''

"I know, but my squadron is, in effect, tactical. Low and fast, sneaky-pete drops—all that. You know the SOLL mission.''

"Yeah, I'm familiar with it."

"Okay. By order of, well, I guess the President, we can't just fly in and land and blow up something in central Iraq at the moment. I'm not privy to—''

"What? I didn't hear that last."

"I say, I don't get the top-secret briefings on *why* the policy is the way it is; all they do is tell me the policy, which is that we can't just fly north and land openly. We have to sneak in and out. We can't officially be doing what we're doing, and this entire thing is top secret.''

"But why?"

"Hell, man, I'm not a diplomat, but the whole reason—I'm guessing now—the whole reason for the President stopping Schwarzkopf short of Baghdad was to prove we weren't out to conquer Iraq. So if we're not out to conquer Iraq and we've liberated Kuwait, we have no business messing around in Iraq north of the ceasefire lines. At least that's why we can't just fly north across the border with God and everybody watching.''

"So is this trip really necessary?"

Will motioned Doug a bit closer, speaking directly into his ear, his voice urgent and worried. "Doug, remember those bugs Abbas mentioned back there? He came across the border the other day with news that Saddam's about to unleash a biological holocaust. He's telling our people that his lab has been ordered to make ready for use a batch of the scariest biological agent any of our people have ever heard of. I really didn't understand most of what they told me, but I *do* understand its potential, and

Doug, it scares the hell out of me! Abbas says it will not reach maturity, whatever that means, before day after tomorrow. But they could ship it as early as tomorrow.''

"What kind of bugs? A virus?"

"That's what's so frightening, Doug. Most biological agents have to infect by contact. Some can be spread temporarily by air, but they're fragile. This mother of all viruses''—Doug pulled back and winced—''okay, okay, it's overused, but hear me out.'' He leaned back again. "This bug is the first our side has seen that can be spread by water. It doesn't die easily, and when dry, it stays dormant like anthrax.''

"Good Lord, Will. It's a human virus?"

"From what I understand, yes. An awful way to die. Abbas claims he nearly revolted when they tested it on some captured Kuwaitis in their lab last month. He said it was gruesome. When Baghdad passed the word to ship it out, he says he reached his breaking point and came south.''

"Pretty brave of the man, don't you think?"

"After inventing it? No, I don't think he's brave. I think he's a little rat trying to save his skin. But we need him.''

"How . . .'' Doug cleared his throat as well and began again. "How do we . . . I mean, why are we flying a two-ship to Europe?"

"We're not. Cairo Control is not supposed to know it's a two-ship. To them, it's just MAC Alpha 284. We're tucked in below with our transponder off and our lights off. We go like that to El Dab'a.''

"They'll see us on radar. They'll see the skin paint.''

"No, they won't. This was my idea, Doug, and it's basically the same thing the Israelis did to bomb the Iraqi nuclear facilities several years back. I tried it a few years ago one day over Canada with a sister ship. We were bored, the controller was bored, and I got to wondering, if two big airplanes like this were flying close together and only one had his transponder on, what would radar see?"

"Only one?"

"Right. Our air defense radars and those the Soviets use can do better, but with the radars the Egyptians and everyone else but the Israelis are using, they can't see us when we're tucked up there in a modified close trail."

"Geez. I never thought of that. What happens at El Dab'a? We dive and run on the water?"

"Come on, Doug. We'd never get a 141 in under radar. No, this is where it gets interesting—and challenging. There's a DC-10 headed to Baghdad from Switzerland. The Red Cross chartered it with our help. He doesn't know it, but he's going to carry us over Beirut, over Syria, and into Iraq. We break off and land several hundred miles out of Baghdad under the wildest burst of radar interference the Coalition has mounted since the war started."

Doug straightened up and looked at Will admiringly. "You thought all this up?"

"Part of it."

"In two days?"

"I've been busy."

"I'll take back my statements. You're good enough to be a reservist. In fact, you think like an airline crew scheduler."

"Is that a compliment?"

"Depends on your point of view. One question."

"What?"

"I . . . no regrets I came along, okay? But what happens if, uh, they spot us going in?"

"Gross navigational error and we're *real* sorry."

"How about if they force us to land in, say, Syria or Jordan, or goddamn Beirut?"

"We don't do that."

They stared at each other for a second in silence. The 141 had no defensive systems. Defying a fighter who wanted you to land was suicide.

"And if we get jumped in Iraq?"

"That's different. We're in touch with the AWACS every second once we get across the Syrian border. We have fighter CAP nearby and rescue choppers with blades turning just over the Saudi border, and even on the ground we'll have the combat support team to guard us."

"We landing at an airport?"

"No."

"The *desert*?"

"No. A road. It's wide enough, and a combat support team was dropped in twenty-four hours ago to secure it and mark it with lights—of a sort."

"What do you mean, 'of a sort'?"

"There's . . ." Will began, ". . . there's one other thing."

"What? These surprises are killing me."

"You ever used night-vision goggles?"

Doug pulled back and looked incredulous, a tell-me-you're-joking sort of smile creeping across his face. "No-o-o!"

"Well, I've had a little instruction, but . . ."

"This is where you tell me we've got to land on a rural road in the middle of Iraq in the middle of the night wearing night-vision goggles, right?"

"Afraid so. That was the part I couldn't quite work out of the plan. The team down there will be marking the runway with fluorescent light sticks that only show up on the goggles."

Doug was nodding slowly, a thoroughly serious expression on his face.

"You've succeeded, Will."

"In doing what?"

"In scaring the hell out of me, too."

MAC Alpha 284, in flight over central Saudi Arabia
Wednesday, March 6, 1991—9:40 P.M. (1840 GMT)

Technical Sergeant Phil Casey, the loadmaster, leaned awkwardly against the folded crew entrance ladder and surveyed his airborne cargo compartment while sipping a cup of rancid, re-warmed coffee. The seventeen-ton M-3 Bradley fighting vehicle and the two M-113 armored personnel carriers—tracked, tanklike vehicles, the Bradley festooned with guns—barely fit in the interior of the Starlifter. The members of the strike force were sandwiched on each side of the huge machines in what he considered the least comfortable seats in aviation, the ubiquitous red canvas folding sidewall seats, now occupied by eighteen Army commandos, most of whom were sleeping in the universal GI position: any way they could. Casey thought about offering coffee to their commanding officer, Major Moyer, a ramrod-straight infantryman with a perpetually grim expression and a crewcut, but rejected the idea. *I don't really dislike the man* that *much,* he chuckled to himself. The coffee was terrible, even by MAC standards.

The aircraft commander, Colonel Westerman, had promised

to give him and Sandra a thorough briefing sometime in the next hour, and he was looking forward to that. Whatever they were getting ready to do, the Delta Force major had already told him he wanted the rear cargo doors open and the ramp down before the plane rolled to a stop. *Where* they were going to roll to a stop was still a mystery. The two pilots had gone off headset to discuss it. Iraq, he figured. Some airport up there in the dead of night, perhaps. The thought of bullets crashing into his airplane gave him a momentary chill, but that sort of thing didn't happen to MAC reserve crews in C-141s. Or so he hoped. Besides, the war was over and the Coalition had won.

The Iraqi sat only a few feet from the cockpit ladder on one of the sidewall seats, apparently consumed with his own thoughts. Phil had never met an Iraqi before. The man seemed gentle and well-spoken, thanking him for a cup of water in perfect English with a British accent. Interesting. As a struggling artist, he had found himself studying the man's face carefully, trying to memorize its subtleties. Perhaps he could sketch it, pen and ink, before he forgot. The features were angular, with prominent cheekbones and slightly sunken dark brown eyes, a slight underbite, and a powerful brow. The man had jet black hair combed loosely forward and close cropped on the side. The eyebrows were what made him memorable, though. Dark, bushy, wild eyebrows, as if he'd never trimmed them. He had no mustache, and Phil wondered if he'd look more Arab if he had one. His skin was not as olive in complexion as most Saudis he'd seen, but perhaps the fellow didn't spend as much time in the sun.

Phil closed his eyes and checked his memory of the face again. He specialized in portraiture, his part-time flying in the Air Force reserves keeping him from being a starving artist in the truest sense. With the public's interest in things Arab following the war, it might prove valuable if he could do a classic portrait of this fellow.

"How you doing, Load?"

Casey jumped as Colonel Harris touched his shoulder. He'd

been concentrating too hard. Harris had somehow come down the ladder undetected.

"Just fine, sir. Can I get you anything?"

The words had to be half-yelled over the tremendous noise of the air-conditioning ducts. Harris bent down next to his headset. "No. Just coming back to talk to our guest." He moved on past Casey, navigating carefully past the stack of crew bags to where the Iraqi was sitting and staring at the floor.

"Dr. Abbas?"

Shakir Abbas looked up to find Doug Harris leaning over him, trying to talk above the amazing din of the airplane.

"Yes?"

"It's too damn noisy down here. Why don't you come up to the flight deck so we can talk for a few minutes?"

Abbas nodded and followed Harris up the four-foot ladder through the offset entryway to the large cockpit compartment and paused at the top, noting the single sidewall seat tucked to the left of the doorway, the navigator's station directly forward of the entrance, and the three seats to the right along the aft bulkhead of the cockpit.

"This is very large," he said, his words lost in the background noise. Doug motioned him to one of the seats along the aft wall, behind the flight engineer's side-facing seat and panel, and sat beside him. The white noise of the slipstream was still ferocious, but conversation was not impossible.

"Doctor, this has been one of the wilder evenings of my life. I just got involved with this mission at the last minute, so there are some things I'd like to ask you."

"I heard Colonel Westerman say that there had been a change of crew."

Doug nodded, smiling. "I didn't have any idea Will was even *in* Saudi Arabia until two hours ago. I walk through a door, and here's my old friend!"

"You have known each other a long time, then?"

Doug laughed. "Just about forever. You ever have a friend

you grew up with, went to school with, chased girls with, worked with, and—in my case—even joined the Air Force with?''

"No, not exactly." Memories of his childhood flickered by, a childhood of few friends and many taunts—especially the two years after his father disappeared, when they had been forced to hide with cousins in the desert. Those had been the worst years of his life.

"Well, that was the case with Will and me. Although we've kind of lost touch over the years." Doug glanced forward for a second, remembering Will's sudden departure from McChord— what was it, seventeen years ago? The day after Doug's wedding, he had vanished.

Doug focused again on Shakir. "I'm sorry to get sidetracked."

Shakir had been gazing forward as well. He turned then and met Doug's gaze. "I heard one of your men say you were an airline pilot, but how are you also in the Air Force?"

Doug laughed at that. "Sometimes I wonder that myself! No, I was on active duty for five years before I joined what we call an associate reserve unit. That means I fly the same airplanes on the same missions that I did on active duty, but *I* tell *them* when I want to come out and fly. Unless a war breaks out and my whole unit gets called to active service, which is what happened last fall when your sumbitch president decided to invade Kuwait."

Shakir nodded, his eyes locked on Doug.

"So," Doug continued, "Will up there has always been on active duty. He was never with the airlines, but I've been flying airliners in the U.S. for fifteen years, and flying these 141s in between commercial flights. In fact, I had just been promoted to full colonel and was just getting ready to retire when all this broke out, and suddenly I'm commanding an active-duty heavy airlift squadron and shuttling to your part of the world. It's been a bit of a shock."

"Iraq has reserve military people, too, but they are used differently, I think."

"I'll be frank with you, Doctor. I don't think much of your country's military or its so-called leader, okay?"

"I understand, Colonel. I apologize for mentioning it," Shakir replied.

"That's all right. What I came back to ask you about, this . . . this . . . *bug,* for want of a better name, that you developed, is it that deadly?"

Abbas studied Doug's face and nodded solemnly. "More so than we ever thought possible, Colonel."

Doug began to speak, but Abbas raised his finger. "Please . . . let me tell you something . . . about how this happened. Would you permit me to do that?"

"Sure."

"Thank you. Colonel Westerman has been . . . too busy to hear me on this." He studied the floor for a few seconds and glanced forward with a concerned look before turning back toward Doug. "You do not need both pilots in the front seats to fly?"

"No. Don't worry. We've got nearly forty-five minutes to go before we join up with the tanker to air-refuel, and in the meantime, as long as we've got the autopilot on, one pilot up there is sufficient. You were going to tell me something."

Abbas nodded, shifting position slightly, folding his left leg on the seat to face Doug more squarely.

"You have no reason to believe me, but I never for a moment thought that any of the things I was working on would ever be used. They are all too terrible. Weapons that can kill your own army and citizens are exceedingly poor weapons. You have people in your country—the Soviets do in theirs—who spend their lives developing bigger and more terrible bombs. These scientists can live with this because they do not really believe such weapons will ever be used, because to do so would be insane. They build bombs like I built what you called 'bugs,' to scare the adversary into not attacking, or, in Saddam's case, to scare others into letting him have his way, whether with Kuwait or somebody else."

"But you created something terrible, didn't you?"

Shakir nodded again. "More awful than something that just explodes. This could contaminate—ruin—entire regions. If it gets into a water table, it could contaminate it perhaps for decades, killing all mammals, including man, who come in contact with it."

He studied Doug's face for a few seconds before continuing. "It was a complete accident. I was doing a series of genetic-engineering manipulations of a certain promising viral strain that was mildly infectious, bombarding it with ultraviolet radiation to cause mutations. We would always test the various mutations with mixed results, but when we exposed a rack of lab animals to this, they were all dead within two hours. The more we tested, the more incredibly lethal it turned out to be, *and* the more resilient! I found it could live in water. Not just an isotonic solution, but *any* water! And, partly because it is encapsulated in a common bacteria, it can survive heating to nearly boiling, it can be dried or frozen, go dormant for an indefinite period, and still regenerate and kill. More important, it is horribly infectious and kills very rapidly. The more I tested, the more excited I got, because, after all, I was trying to build a biological equivalent to your triad defense. I was trying to build a bio-chemical neutron bomb. And I succeeded beyond my wildest dreams." Shakir took a deep breath, the effort of talking over the background noise greater than he'd expected.

The flight engineer pulled his headset aside and leaned toward Doug. "Sir? Colonel W. wants to know when you're coming back up front."

Doug looked distracted. "What's up?"

"Nothing, sir, except he needs to visit the head, and he'd rather leave someone flying the airplane while he's gone. His words, not mine."

Doug laughed at that and motioned him away. "Tell him he'll just have to hold it till the next rest stop."

"Yes sir."

"You were saying, Doctor?"

"It was all pure research, you see. Not the real world. That's what I stupidly thought."

"So did Dr. Nobel when he developed dynamite."

Shakir nodded. "I tell Saddam's people in Baghdad—this thing can never be used. Threaten, yes, but never plan to use it. He has ordered us, you see, as of 1989, to go live at the laboratory until we give him the weapons he wants. Remember the Israeli raid on our nuclear facility? It made Saddam determined to build a terrible weapon the Israelis couldn't reach. Nuclear bombs require triggers and other telltale supplies. A biological bomb requires only a few dozen scientists working sixteen hours a day in a hole somewhere—people who were put through school by the state—people who have a comfortable life and families who are safe to live and grow only as long as they obey and keep researching. People like me."

Doug turned to the flight engineer again. "I guess he's suffered long enough. Tell the pilot I'll be up in two minutes."

"Roger." The engineer punched his interphone button as Shakir continued. "As soon as the BBC announced that the ground war was over and our army was destroyed, those of us in my facility rejoiced and got ready to burn the virus and the lab. Then the message comes. We are to package the virus in containers for shipment to the front. What front? I ask. I am told to shut up."

"You don't know where he's planning on . . ."

Shakir shrugged, hands out. "Perhaps the Kurds. He hates the Kurds as Hitler hated the Jews, maybe more. He hates the Jews, too, especially Israelis, but how can he reach them with this weapon? More than that, I think he plans to send it south."

"To Saudi?"

"And Kuwait, and perhaps even the United States and England if he can. Once we have lost control of this, who knows?"

"How powerful is it?"

"It is difficult in biological terms to speak of a virus as being powerful, but are you aware how deadly the botulism bacteria is to human life?''

"I've heard. A teaspoon could kill a thousand humans?''

"Yes, approximately. But this is potentially much worse, because it continues to multiply rapidly when it attacks a living host.''

"Can a cure be found?''

"Not in time. Not in time to prevent thousands—maybe tens of thousands—of deaths. Will quarantine work? Perhaps, but it is not like the HIV virus. It is very aggressive, very infectious, and because of the incredible speed with which it causes our own cells to produce lethal toxins, it's worse than the ancient black plague. There are no human antibodies in any population built up to oppose this, and it doesn't give the human immune system time to manufacture any. All of mankind stands completely vulnerable to a virus like this.''

Shakir Abbas leaned forward, his eyes boring into Doug's.

"Colonel, Saddam has tricked your President again. He has succeeded in getting everyone worried about nuclear weaponry and bomb-grade plutonium—chasing and bombing those facilities—while the real doomsday weapon is buried in the desert, in my lab.''

"Yours was the only biological lab?''

Shakir shook his head vigorously. "Oh no! There are many more. Whether anyone else has had a breakthrough, I can't say, but my lab was only one of many.''

Doug breathed heavily and sat back a bit. "The opportunity for terrorism with this stuff is mind-boggling.''

"Kaddafi wanted it. So did some of the PLO. Even Saddam wasn't crazy enough to consider their requests—but now I don't know.''

"If we do get you into your lab, can you destroy all the virus?''

He nodded slowly. "If it's all still there. I know exactly how, and in the lab I have the right equipment.''

Abbas looked down, his mind racing. *If it's not all there, how can I tell this man the possible consequences?* He looked up just as quickly and locked eyes with Doug once again.

"All the cultures *should* still be there," he said with feigned conviction, "and when they are destroyed, the virus is destroyed. There are no formulas for this, as there are for chemical weapons. Not even I know how to create this again. It was a random, unexpected mutation."

"But are you sure it's all still there in the lab?"

Abbas ignored the scream of apprehension echoing through the hallways of his mind. "I left instructions that none of the canisters could be shipped before March eighth, or the contents would be useless. This is not true, but they will have believed me."

"Why? Why would they believe someone who defected?"

"They do not know I defected—yet. I . . . forgive me, it was most unpleasant . . . I knew of a funeral in a nearby village. After I left, I went to where this man was buried and dug up his body, carefully closing the grave again. I drove halfway to Baghdad before putting him in the driver's seat and making the car go off into a wadi. I soaked it with gasoline and everything burned. Some of my papers were there. There is no time for autopsies, so they will think I am dead. I had to do it. There are many, many who will die if we do not stop this."

"Doctor, if this does slip through, how could they spread it?"

He shook his head slowly, sadly. "An aqueous solution sprayed into a cloud, and when it rains, it rains death."

Doug recoiled as if hit. "In a *cloud*? You're saying this can contaminate *clouds,* and *rain*?"

"You understand now. If it gets out of that lab, it will be easy to rain Iran out of existence, as well as anyplace else Saddam wants to infect."

Doug sat back, thoroughly stunned. Even an airplane flying through such a cloud at high altitude could suck in the virus through its pressurization ducts, compress the infected air, and pump it into the lungs of everyone aboard.

"How long, Doctor . . . how long could such a cloud remain, for want of a better word, contagious?"

"Perhaps long enough for the water vapor to circle the earth. I do not know how far it could travel. I pray no one ever has to find out."

Refueling Track Charlie, over the Red Sea northwest of Jiddah
Wednesday, March 6, 1991—10:20 P.M. (1920 GMT)

Exxon 92, a KC-10 tanker— the Air Force version of the Douglas DC-10—began its fourth turn in the racetrack-shaped holding pattern as the crew finally made radio contact with the approaching MAC Alpha 284. With the proper air-to-air channels relayed and set in on both flight decks, the respective aircrews watched as their navigation radios—Tacans—locked on the opposite aircraft, giving precise distance and direction to each other's position.

Heading north with the accompanying C-141 flying some fifty feet off his right wing, Exxon 92 began his turn at last—a left 180-degree course reversal back to the south.

In the cockpit of MAC Alpha 284, Sergeant Sandra Murray adjusted her headset and fastened the lap belt on the flimsy cockpit jump seat, an almost makeshift folding chair anchored just aft of the center instrument console, between the pilot's and copilot's seats.

"You guys hear me now?"

"Loud and clear." Doug took the opportunity to glance around at her again appreciatively. She didn't know it yet, but her squadron had already submitted a recommendation that Sandra Murray receive a commendation medal for singlehandedly finding and fixing an engine problem that had threatened to scuttle an important mission to Turkey early in the war. As her commander, Doug had signed the recommendation letter with enthusiasm.

"How far out are we?"

Will looked around briefly at Sandra and smiled. "About twenty-three miles now. You see that white light out there at ten o'clock?" He pointed to the left, where a twinkling light hung against the black velvet background of the night sky.

"Yeah."

"That's the tanker. He's in his turn now and level at twenty-five thousand feet, and we're at twenty-four thousand. We'll fly up behind him, get clearance to climb up under him, plug up, hang on through several turns, get our fuel, and go. I figure the transfer will take about fifteen minutes." Will looked back at Sandra again. "You know what a holding pattern looks like?"

Sandra nodded impassively as Doug reached for the interphone button. "Will, Sandra's a licensed private pilot, and she's sat at the panel through a hundred of these ARs."

Will glanced back apologetically. "I'm sorry, I assumed . . ."

"No problem, sir," she said quickly. "Actually, I'm not finished with my instrument rating, so any information is appreciated."

Exxon 92 rolled out at last, a distant constellation of position lights and rotating beacons—with no visual trace of the four-engine jet flying formation just off his right wing.

They finished the rendezvous checklist and Will keyed the transmitter. "MAC Alpha two-eight-four's moving into pre-contact position."

"Roger, MAC. Cleared to come up."

Will's hand tightened on the control yoke, his eyes glued to the tanker's belly as he eased the throttles forward and brought the 141 closer. Time was the critical variable. With the Balair DC-10 ahead of schedule, they had raced at a fuel-inefficient speed of nearly Mach .80—eighty percent of the speed of sound—all the way from level-off, but they still had less than twenty minutes to complete the refueling, and that was barely enough, even when everything worked perfectly.

It was getting warm in the cockpit by Will's estimation. "Engineer, this is the pilot. Would you cool us down a bit, please? I'm going to be working up a sweat here in a minute.''

"Roger, sir." Backus reached up and toggled the flight-deck temperature control toward the cool side as Will brought the Starlifter steadily up and forward toward the rotating red beacons and position lights of the KC-10, which loomed larger and larger in the upper windscreen.

"What do you think, copilot? Is that about right for the pre-contact spacing?''

Doug turned toward Will and feigned a startled expression. "You're asking me? I haven't done one of these for six months. I'm noncurrent.''

Will paused briefly, and Doug saw him grin. "So am I."

"What?" Doug looked to the left again, now in mock panic. *"Good grief,* Westerman, we're up here in the middle of the night, needing sixty thousand pounds of gas from the flying gas station ahead of us, and you tell me you don't know how to air-refuel anymore?''

"I didn't say I didn't know *how!* I just said I'm noncurrent. You're going to scare the crew, talking like that.''

"Really?" Doug paused, then hit the interphone button again. "Crew, this is the copilot. Are you scared?''

Sergeant Backus answered immediately. "Yes sir. The engineer's scared.''

Another microphone clicked on. "Loadmaster's scared.''

Sandra was reaching for her interphone button as well when Will cut her off.

"Okay, okay!" Will was shaking his head, his eyes still riveted on the tanker's belly. "My last plug was two months ago, everybody. Don't panic. I can still hang in there.''

"Now he tells me!" said Doug.

The deceptive stability of the huge Douglas jet suspended just above them seemed to deny the fact that they were merely matched in airspeed—a 600,000-pound, three-engine jumbo-jet tanker with a 250,000-pound, four-engine transport less than one hundred feet away, both traveling at over three hundred miles per hour.

When the pre-contact checklist was out of the way, the voice of the boom operator—the "boomer"—approved the final closure from the pre-contact position to actual connection. Will eased the throttles forward and gently nudged the yoke back a hair, the KC-10 swimming ever closer; the huge refueling boom—guided by two small fins "flown" by the boomer—was already extended and in the ready position, a small white light marking its end.

A muffled roar announced the engineer's opening of the UARRSI, the universal refueling receptacle on top of the aft cockpit area—a target marked with lights for the boomer to use in making the final adjustments as he flew the refueling boom into place and locked it.

The control yoke was now beginning to move in small jerks backward and forward, left and right, the throttles walking forward and backward slightly, constantly, as Will jockeyed the ungainly 141 into position, the bow wave of the massive KC-10 causing predictable turbulence across the horizontal T-tail of the Lockheed jet. The end of the boom finally disappeared over their heads, the position lights along the belly of the tanker guiding Will's slow advance beneath the tail of the tanker, and within seconds the sound of a muffled thump marked the final connection.

Suddenly the boomer's voice was coming more clearly through their headsets on the interphone circuit through a connection in the boom.

"Connected, sir. Ready fuel."

Backus called, "Ready," flipped the appropriate switches, and watched with satisfaction as the pressure gauges swung into proper position on his fuel panel. "Fuel pressure, fuel flow," Backus reported.

With a small movement of the boomer's hand, 5,500 pounds per minute of JP-4 jet fuel began rushing down the tube from the KC-10 to the 141 as the engineer routed it to the appropriate tanks. Will fought to stay inside a narrow zone beneath and behind the tanker within which they could stay safely connected. If he got to the edge of that envelope, the boomer would pull back his probe, stopping the fuel flow instantly, until the pilot could get the 141 back in position.

Doug, whose right hand had been resting lightly on the control yoke, looked away from the tanker for a second, glancing down quietly, unhappily confirming what his hand had been feeling. Will's movements of the control column and the yoke were becoming staccato and slightly excessive. *He's struggling*, Doug thought.

"Twenty thousand pounds onloaded so far." The voice of the boomer came over their headsets again, followed by the voice of the KC-10 pilot.

"Starting turn in thirty seconds."

The yoke was gyrating even more now, the throttles jockeying more rapidly as well, and the 141 was beginning to move around within the boom's vertical and lateral envelope more than it should on what was essentially a night of smooth, turbulence-free air. As the gyrations increased and Will struggled harder to control them, Doug felt his hand tighten around the yoke, just in case.

"Start turn."

The KC-10 pilots, flying their airplane on autopilot according to normal operations, had begun a gentle bank to the left for the 180-degree course reversal back to the north. The star field and the distant lights of Jiddah out to the left tilted now, and the moon began a weird and wobbly transit from the left across their field of vision. First up a bit, then down and to the side, banking a bit too much to the left, using an excessive roll rate back to the right and coming down too fast, back up with the yoke, jerk back left, a bit of rudder to the left to skid her around, Will struggled to stay within the envelope—to hang onto the boom—to maintain perfect formation with the KC-10.

But he was losing it, and Doug could see and feel what was happening.

For a second it looked as though he had settled down. The gyrations suddenly slowed as Will dampened his control inputs. But just as suddenly they drifted much too far to the left as Will overreacted, snatching the yoke back in the wrong direction. In a heartbeat the C-141's nose canted up, and the windscreen was suddenly filled with KC-10.

"*Break away!*" The boomer's words were spoken at the very instant he yanked the boom out and away, as Will shoved on the yoke, throwing everyone up against the straps as the 141 lurched downward. He let the airplane descend over a hundred feet before stabilizing—Doug's hand still guarding, but not taking over.

"Jesus!" Will pushed the transmit button. "Sorry, Exxon. I'll stay in pre-contact till you roll out."

"This is the boomer, sir. You got to the limits with that last correction. I barely got it out."

"Roger. I'm sorry."

"We'd rather not have you go back as a unicorn tonight," the boomer added. *Bad time for humor, fellow,* Doug thought to himself. The image of a C-141 flying to an emergency recovery base with the ripped-off refueling boom still stuck in the refueling receptacle was not amusing.

Beads of perspiration were all over Will's forehead now. There was little time for such mistakes, as he knew well.

"How much did we get?" Will asked the engineer.

"Only twenty thousand, sir. We need an extra forty thousand pounds." With every second's delay, the rendezvous time with the Balair DC-10 grew closer. Will took a deep breath again, and tried to concentrate.

Once again the two huge airplanes were streaking through the night sky less than fifty feet apart as Will inched toward the tanker, fighting hard to dampen his control inputs and average his corrections, trying to get his responses in sync. Once again the boom moved over the cockpit out of sight behind them and thunked into place in the UARRSI, the engineer calling fuel flow.

And once again the gyrations began.

I'm up and to the right a bit too much, bring her back to the left and down, not too much, back right, RIGHT, and down, just a little . . . little bit more . . . too far . . . DAMN!

Will was fighting harder and harder, with less and less success, to dampen the control inputs, sweat beading up on his brow and dripping into his eyes as the tanker seemed to wave and bob in the upper windscreen. Once again the KC-10 seemed to lurch to one side with a momentum that seemed guaranteed to take it beyond the limits . . .

"Breakaway!" The boomer's voice again, this time slightly calmer. The gyrations had told the tale. He had been anticipating another disconnect.

They stabilized in the pre-contact position again as Doug studied Will's face and toggled the interphone. "Hey, old buddy, how long since you've had any sleep?"

"I'm okay."

"I know you're okay, but how long?"

Will shot him a questioning glance. "Last night. Why?"

"Let me give it a try, Will. Fatigue is what's getting you. I'm more rested."

Will Westerman felt a flash of anger as he looked to the right, ready to snap at Doug. He was perfectly capable of doing this, thank you. A sarcastic retort rocketed through his mind, but he suppressed it.

"Let me give it one more try," Will began.

"Will . . ." Doug was watching his face carefully. "We're out of time."

Will Westerman glanced to the right in a quick turn of his head and read the look of concern on Doug Harris's face, realizing he was right. This wasn't a contest. They either got the gas, or the mission failed. *This is not a testosterone check, Westerman!* The voice in his head was his.

"Okay, Doug. Your airplane." Will felt Doug's hand wobble the yoke slightly to indicate he had the airplane.

"Nope, just gonna borrow it a few minutes," Doug said. "If I bend it, it's your fault." He was trying to smile at Will, who was trying to let go gracefully.

Once again they approached the tanker. Time was running out. Will was acutely aware that Balair would cross Tansa intersection north of El Dab'a on the Egyptian coast in just over two hours and twenty minutes, and that it would take their clandestine flight of two C-141s about two hours to get to the same point. Either they were there at the same moment or the mission would have to be quietly scrubbed, and all the effort would have to be repeated a day later—if it wasn't too late. In addition, the last update of the DC-10's time would have to come through the interphone connection in the refueling boom. Such information could *not* be transmitted in the clear on the radio. Even if they had enough fuel, they would still have to plug up one last time just to get that update.

Doug brought her in steadily, all the old instincts coming back. He had always been good in formation. In pilot training, Will had been the master of instrument flying, Doug the master of contact—or visual—flying, especially in formation and acrobatics. It had been a massive shock to the rest of the class when Doug, the pilot with the "golden hands," got a C-141 transport, and Will, the "hood master," took an F-4 Phantom, the contact pilot's dream-machine of that decade.

The boom moved over the top of them again, followed by the sound of a solid connection and the confirmation of fuel flow. Doug worked the throttles back and forth along with small movements of the yoke that he wished were smaller and more precise, but this time at least they were steady.

In the left seat, Will's mind was racing ahead, recognizing

the futility of maintaining the refueling track and accepting another turn to the south at the end of the northbound leg. That would lose more precious time. They were far enough to the south already. If they ignored the racetrack pattern and flew north for the remaining seven minutes it would take to transfer the fuel, they could still finish before crossing the major air routes between Egypt and Saudi. And it could only help Doug hang on.

"Exxon, MAC. Delay your turn. Let's stay straight until we're filled, even if we bust the area."

"Ah , , , okay, MAC."

"Thirty thousand." The boomer again, calling the onload increments. "MAC, Exxon 92 cockpit here on interphone. We have your target update from our satcom link, if you're ready to copy."

"Go ahead, Exxon."

"Okay, the estimate for Point Alpha is two-one-one-eight Zulu, and for Point Bravo it's two-one-four-four Zulu. Monitor frequency one-two-three-point-two for Playmate's position reports at that time. Off the west coast of Italy, Playmate was thirty minutes ahead of flight planned time at thirty-five thousand feet."

The reference to Greenwich Mean Time as "Zulu" was a standard for aviators.

"Roger. Thanks." Sandra had been waiting for the message. While Doug hung on to the boom and the last few thousand pounds of fuel coursed into the 141's fuel manifold, she consulted a small table Will had given her an hour earlier and traced the column of figures with her finger as Will looked back to his right and watched her. "Playmate" was the Balair DC-10. Will was relieved that the Balair captain was apparently maintaining the slower airspeed of Mach .78 as he had been instructed by his company. The message had been relayed by satellite connection to the KC-10 from U.S. intelligence sources monitoring the progress of the Balair flight through Roma Control in Italy. Balair was estimating the position known as Paleochora in Greek airspace over the island of Crete at 2118 GMT, and Tansa intersection at 2144 GMT. Tansa, a navigational fix that exists only on aviation charts, marks a point in midair halfway between Crete and the north coast of Egypt—the jurisdictional dividing line between Cairo Control and Atheni Control.

Sandra keyed her interphone. "Pilot, jump seat. I calculate that if we're finished here in five minutes, we'll just make the rendezvous at Tansa."

The boomer's voice cut in.

"That's a total of sixty, MAC."

The sound of the refueling boom withdrawing from the C-141's refueling port echoed through the cockpit as Sandra quietly reached to her left and positioned her microphone selector to the same radio carrying the young male voice of the KC-10's boomer.

She waited for his next call.

"Okay, MAC, we're clear."

Sandra keyed the transmitter then, her feminine voice suddenly filling the boomer's headset as she purred with exaggerated sensuality and feeling.

"Oh wow! Was it good for you, too, Exxon?"

Doug whirled around to his left and tried to shoot Sandra a stern look of disapproval, but his grin was ruining the effect.

"Sandra!"

She repositioned her radio switch and tried to look wide-eyed innocent. "Yes?"

"No telling how long the poor guy's been out here," Doug said. "That's cruel!"

Will bit his lip and said nothing.

Doug eased the aircraft down about fifty feet as the KC-10 pilots said farewell and began a climb, the aircraft's lights diminishing rapidly overhead.

Doug shifted his gaze to the other C-141 as Will pointed to their sister ship and keyed the interphone. "Bring us into a modified pre-contact position beneath our friend out there, co-pilot."

"Yes sir, Captain, sir. And I'll take the chicken," Doug replied, eyes straight ahead.

Will toggled the interphone button and held it for a few seconds before speaking, looking at Doug in confusion. *"What?"*

Doug chuckled. "I'll explain later. It's just something junior flight officers say to their captains in the civilian airline world."

"Are reservists always like this?" Will asked.

"Like what?" Doug replied, affecting as innocent a look as Sandra's.

The radio call to the other 141 on the secure radio channel was next on the agenda, Will reminded himself. He should have checked the radio already, but in the confusion of the departure from Sandy 101, he had forgotten. The special type of secure frequency-hopping radios was vital to the mission, especially now, he thought. The other C-141 now flying formation with them less than a hundred feet away had been specially configured for this mission and had special UHF radios. The other crew was supposed to be standing by and monitoring those frequencies already, waiting for MAC Alpha 284 to initiate the frequency-hopping procedures, which would let the two airplanes communicate in almost impenetrable privacy.

Will glanced to his left at the pilot's side panel then to find the special control head—and stopped cold.

Many C-141s already had the frequency-hopping secure radios installed.

This one didn't!

The pilot's left side panel was, in effect, bare, leaving them no way of communicating safely with the other C-141.

Will's heart sank. *Another mistake! I should have checked to make sure they were installed before we left!*

He glanced up at the dark bulk of the other 141 now ahead of them in the windscreen, acutely aware that both of them were wasting time by flying north at the sedate cruising speed of .74

Mach. The other flight crew was obviously waiting for instructions from Will *over their secure radios!* Without them, there was no secure way to coordinate the changeover of the transponder, the turn on course, the call to Cairo Control, the airspeed, or the plan for crossing Tansa some two hours ahead. Time was indeed running out. They would have to race toward El Dab'a now at red-line speed to have any hope of intercepting Playmate, but how could he tell the other aircrew all that without telling the world below as well?

Will suppressed the additional butterflies and tried to think through the options. The 141 ahead was probably monitoring what MAC crews called "button ten," a particular UHF frequency for air-to-air conversation. It wasn't secure and it wasn't private, but anyone hearing what he needed to say wouldn't be likely to figure out what they were doing unless they already knew.

He reached down to UHF radio number one and dialed in preset frequency 10, then moved his radio wafer switch to the UHF-1 position and hit the transmit button on the yoke.

Keep it cryptic! "Up button ten, friend?"

No response. The 141 was looming large in the windscreen now. He tried again, on UHF-2, with no response, then on the VHF radios tuned to frequencies they had used with the tanker.

Still nothing. No response.

They *had* to establish some sort of contact, and fast.

Doug glanced toward Will with a question on his face. "Are you talking to them?"

"I wish I could. They're monitoring their frequency-hopping radios, but we have a small problem: we don't have any in this aircraft. I just now realized it."

"Oh boy. The other airplane did? The one that crashed back there at our departure base?"

"Yeah," Will replied.

"Well, what now, Kemo Sabe?" Doug was maintaining position about fifty feet behind and below the 141, which was still heading north, waiting for instructions.

"Pull out to his left, Doug. Make it a safe distance, but make sure he sees us."

"Okay. We'd better turn our lights on."

Doug reached up and snapped on the leading-edge lights, position lights, and rotating beacon as he slid the airplane to the left and began to gain on the other Starlifter.

"Engineer, pilot. Do you have a large-tipped felt marker of some sort?"

The answer took a few seconds in coming. "No sir . . . I don't think so."

"I do, pilot."

"Who's that?" Will asked.

"The loadmaster. I've got one. Passing it up now."

"Good. Now I need two sheets of paper, around standard letter size. Blank and white. Anybody?"

"Okay, pilot, this is the engineer. I've got the back of some computer paper here."

Will swiveled around toward the engineer. "Okay, take that marker, and in as large a format as you can make it, with one number per sheet, write down a one and a zero."

The image of the other 141 was now coming into the two-o'clock position several hundred yards to the right.

Will turned to Sandra again. "Jump seat—Sandra—when the engineer has those ready, I'll need you in the copilot's window. We've got to get the other crew to come up button ten. Hold up one number at a time until you think the pilot over there's seen each one of them. Got it?"

"Uh, sir. Can I make a suggestion?" Sandra asked.

"Please do," Will shot back.

"We've got the Aldus light over there. Why don't we use Morse code? I don't think they're going to be able to make out these numbers in the window in the dark."

The engineer was nodding vigorously. "I concur, pilot."

Will shook his head as if to clear it. "The pilot's embarrassed," he began. "That's obviously the better solution. I completely forgot we had a signal lamp. Sandra, do you know Morse code?"

"Yes sir. I have a ham radio license."

Her seatbelt already off, Sandra knelt in the right-hand cockpit window and plugged in the high-powered signal lamp, holding it against the glass and aiming it carefully at the other 141 as she found the trigger and waited for them to pull abeam of the other airplane, which was now about two hundred feet to their right. She saw the outline of the pilot in the other cockpit, and saw him look left. Now! She triggered the light, flashing it off and on several times as the sound of an irritated voice crackled in everyone's headsets.

"Hey! Cut it out! MAC, you up button ten?"

Will moved his wafer switch back to UHF-1. "Roger. You see the light?"

"Have I been blinded, d'you mean? Hell, yes! Turn that off!"

"That's our man," Doug added.

Will thought through his phraseology for a few seconds and triggered the transmit button. "Okay, here's the deal. Wrong radios installed here, so button ten is our channel. Increase to point-eight-two-five Mach immediately, get clearance, blaze the trail, and head for Point Alpha as agreed. Copy?"

"Hold it, I'm writing." The radio fell silent for a full twenty seconds.

"Okay . . . roger. You sure about eight-two-five?"

"We're sure," Will replied. "It's lights-out here, and we're going to have an identity crisis in one minute. Yours will end at the same time."

"We . . . ah . . . wait a second." There was a pause lasting no more than ten seconds. Sandra could see the pilot looking to his right, obviously talking the meanings over with the other crew members.

"Roger, all received and understood. Identity in thirty seconds, mark."

Will let his hand drop from the transmit switch, worrying that he'd said too much or maybe too little. At least they understood over there that "identity" meant the point at which they would become MAC Alpha 284. He reached over and snapped off all the lights, and turned the transponder off at the twenty-second point, motioning to Doug with his thumb to drop back. "Take us back to the trail position as before."

"You got it, pilot."

The position lights, formation lights, and leading-edge lights of the other aircraft snapped on as the frequency for Cairo Control came alive at once with a voice from the other cockpit. "Cairo Control, MAC Alpha two-eight-four, flight level two-five-zero, estimating Wedj at one-nine-four-two Zulu, requesting flight level three-five-zero."

"He's accelerating." Doug's hand pushed the throttles up smartly to keep pace with the lead Starlifter as he suddenly leaped ahead. Mach .825 was the red-line speed, the fastest cruise permitted for a C-141. Doug turned to Sandra, who was already punching the waypoint that corresponded to Tansa into the inertial navigation display. Within seconds the distance remaining and time estimate would be displayed.

Will sat back, noting that Doug seemed to be settling in and enjoying the formation flying, although nothing more than a few lights marked the position of the other 141 just out front of the cockpit.

It always seemed so sedate and simple and even elegant, two airplanes perfectly matched in speed and direction, one of them appearing to float effortlessly in the windscreen of the other. But the realities were brutally different. Behind the lead Starlifter was a trail of disturbed air streaming over them and barely clearing their huge T-tail, 160 feet behind the cockpit. If Doug should get too high and run the horizontal stabilizer into that slipstream, the consequences could be anywhere from startling to disastrous.

The thought of two huge airlifters colliding in the night was an apocalyptic vision Will pushed out of his mind. Better to enjoy the almost poetic image of those lights hovering just above and ahead.

Doug caught Will's eye and inclined his head toward the sister ship. "Thank God he thought to turn off the anticollision beacon. I can't imagine that thing flashing in my face for the next two hours."

Will nodded as he toggled the interphone. "Now, for the next two hours, people, we play like we're invisible." He turned then to look at Sandra, and beyond her at the engineer, then back at Doug. "Copilot, scanner, engineer, loadmaster—all of you, this is the pilot. Thanks, team. That was excellent response and coordination to my lousy performance."

Doug looked at him and raised an eyebrow. "And you think we didn't know you were just testing our responses, huh? We know you did all that on purpose, just to see if we'd be assertive."

The green display screen of the FSAS flight computer flashed the figures Sandra had been waiting for. She scribbled down the time estimate, compared it, and triggered the interphone—a concerned frown crinkling her face.

"Pilot, this is the jump seat. Ah . . . I think we've got a problem. The DC-10's supposed to cross Tansa at twenty-one-forty-four Zulu. We're already at maximum speed, and the computer says we're not going to get there until twenty-one-forty-seven!"

Will and Doug both checked and rechecked the figures and the FSAS, but the estimate was accurate.

Sandra couldn't hear Will Westerman sigh, but she could see his chest fall, and read the weariness around his eyes.

It was Doug, however, who tried to sum it up. "Okay, this is the copilot. We have only two choices," he said. "Either we speed up—and we can't do that—or we alter course. To alter course, we've got to call the other flight crew, and we've already said too much on the air."

Will had been deep in thought and staring through his instrument panel. Now his right hand went up slowly. "No, there is a third option. We can wait. We've got two hours to Tansa, and within ninety minutes we'll be able to hear the DC-10's position report. Until we know when he's *really* going to cross Tansa, we're playing a roulette game of chronological dead reckoning."

"Yeah," Doug replied. "And if we reckon wrong, we're dead."

Cairo Air Traffic Control Center
Wednesday, March 6, 1991—11:35 P.M. (2135 GMT)

Farouk Hammedi reached over and switched off the circular polarization function on his radar display—a handy feature that kept pesky thunderstorm cells and other weather from clogging the scope. Ten minutes ago he had been sleepy. Now he was wide awake—and getting angry. Most American Air Force transport crews were reasonably polite and very careful to comply with their clearances. This one—MAC Alpha 284—was becoming a major irritation.

As I suspected! Not a weather cell anywhere on the scope.

Hammedi checked his transmitter control switches. He was broadcasting on 123.5 VHF, and simultaneously on 246.55 UHF. Ultra high frequency was supposed to be the common frequency for the U.S. military, but most Military Airlift Command pilots chose VHF. He had always wondered why.

"MAC Alpha two-eight-four, Cairo."

Nothing. *Damn them! Why don't they listen to the frequency?*

"MAC Alpha two-eight-four, MAC Alpha two-eight-four, Cairo, Cairo. Do you hear me?"

The distance between the MAC flight and his assigned course was increasing by the minute. He mentally projected the track forward, startled to see it would cross another midair navigational fix some fifty miles east of Tansa, known as Aioa, and, like Tansa, on the dividing line between Cairo Control and Atheni Control.

"MAC Alpha two-eight-four, do you hear Cairo?" He was half-yelling into his headset microphone now, and one of his fellow controllers in an adjacent position was looking at him with puzzlement.

Finally, a laconic American voice cut through his headset. "Roger, Cairo, MAC Alpha two-eight-four with you."

"Where are you going, two-eight-four? You are twenty-five miles now to the right of your assigned course."

There was a pause on the radio channel as Hammedi watched 284's blip flare once again in the same strange way it had done earlier.

"Ah . . . Cairo, two-eight-four. We told you, sir. We've had to deviate around thunderstorm buildups ahead of us."

Hammedi snorted to himself and keyed his transmitter again. "Two-eight-four, I show no weather tonight in your area. I repeat, no weather. Where is this weather you are trying to avoid, sir?"

"Cairo, two-eight-four, I'm sorry you can't see it on your radar, but we see it on ours, and I'm just not going to fly through it. If I have to use my authority to deviate in the interest of flight safety, then consider that's what I'm doing."

The answer made no sense. What "authority" was he talking about? Cairo Control had the authority in Cairo's airspace, and, at the moment, only Hammedi could grant or take away authority to fly through that airspace.

Hammedi keyed his transmitter again, deciding to be as diplomatic as possible. "Can you come back to course now, two-eight-four? When can you return to course?"

The pilot's casual, unconcerned attitude was becoming infuriating. *Is he unaware of the trouble I can make for him?* Hammedi realized he was grinding his teeth, threatening to dislodge a loose filling that had been bothering him. He willed himself to stop.

"Cairo, this is two-eight-four again. I think we'll need to stay on our present heading until, well, we'll probably need to cross Aioa intersection."

Hammedi sat back a second and thought hard. Something was very wrong about this. American Military Airlift Command flights just didn't disobey air traffic control directives.

He scanned his flight strips. Two-eight-four was at flight level 350. Behind him was a MAC Alpha 299, also at FL350. There was also a Saudi 747—Saudi flight 334—at FL330. Coming in from Greek airspace and headed for both Tansa and then Aioa was a DC-10, Balair 5040, but he was safely at FL370. There was a westbound 707 headed for Aioa at FL330, and . . . *there* . . . an Egyptair Boeing 737 out of Cairo was climbing north and due to cross Aioa at 2147 at FL350! That meant that MAC Alpha 284 was headed straight for the same position at the same time.

"MAC Alpha two-eight-four, you cannot cross Aioa at flight level three-five-zero. It is impossible, sir, due to conflicting traffic."

"Cairo, two-eight-four, you're breaking up. Say again?"

Hammedi repeated the message twice with the same response. He switched transmitters. Same response. He asked the following MAC flight to relay. Again, the same response. Hammedi slammed his pencil on the floor and keyed his transmitter again, speaking in Arabic.

"Egyptair one-twelve, descend immediately to flight level three-three-zero."

Someone on the Egyptair flight deck acknowledged, but in English, and for a second Hammedi felt himself off balance, as if he were losing part of the picture. His eyes swept the scope again. Egyptair should be descending to FL330, no other conflicts—that should do it. Now for the disobedient American. He was chomping at the bit to take care of that matter. Hammedi turned and caught the eye of his shift supervisor, motioning him over.

Scorpion-1 (formerly MAC Alpha 284), in flight
Wednesday, March 6, 1991—11:37 P.M. (2137 GMT)

"There he is!" Sandra's voice broke the interphone silence as the distant flash of strobe lights from the wingtips of the oncoming DC-10 caught her eye. The strobes were followed by the hint of a pulsating reddish light, probably a rotating anticollision light, barely visible against the background of stars to the northwest. The lights were exactly where they were supposed to be—at last.

Sandra was feeling fatigued, but since Bill Backus wanted to stay at the flight engineer's panel awhile longer, she had no intention of leaving the jump seat just before the real show began.

The previous two hours had been very tense as they dashed in formation behind the other C-141 toward El Dab'a on the Egyptian coast, hoping the Balair DC-10 would be slower than his original estimate. For the past twenty-five minutes she had strained to catch Balair's position reports, turning off the squelch control on one of the VHF radios and tuning it to the frequency used by Atheni Control, straining to pick the voice of the Balair pilot out of the background static. At one point she thought the words were there, just behind the hiss and roar, but she couldn't make them out. They were still too far apart.

The Westerman-Harris crew had no call sign now, but the Coalition would have their positions listed on various command-post display boards as Scorpion-1.

Before going "feet wet"—as the act of crossing over a coast-line and flying over a large body of water was called—she had recalculated their estimate for Tansa a dozen times, but the estimate had stubbornly remained 2147. That meant that if Balair crossed Paleochora any earlier than 2121, the rendezvous at Tansa would be impossible. The time-to-fly between there and Tansa at Mach .78 was only twenty-five minutes.

Nearly twenty minutes before, just as they approached El Dab'a, Sandra had managed to overhear Balair's position report to his company on one of the high-frequency radios. Through the background static that had been numbing her senses, the DC-10's pilot reported they had crossed Paleochora at 2115, and were southeast-bound toward Tansa, estimating the Tansa intersection at 2140, *seven minutes before Scorpion-1 could get there.*

It had been painfully obvious that northbound MAC Alpha 284, as the lead C-141, needed to make an immediate course change to the right to catch Balair farther to the east. But there was the same dilemma again: how to tell them without telling the world? After all, there were people with sophisticated radios in Egypt and certainly in neighboring Libya who would gleefully inform Baghdad of anything that might jeopardize American military operations.

In the lead airplane, MAC Alpha 284's crew had heard the same position report and already figured out what they had to do to be able to pass precisely under the Balair DC-10 as their courses crossed over the Mediterranean. As they soared over El Dab'a with Scorpion-1 behind them, Will reached for the rocker switch on the control yoke to order a course change, but before he could transmit, the lead 141 was banking to the right, rolling out on exactly the right heading, and reporting to Cairo the need to deviate around nonexistent thunderstorms.

"That," Will had said, "is performance in the 'above and beyond' category!"

For twenty-two minutes they had listened in silence to the sparring as Cairo became increasingly agitated, and MAC Alpha 284 became increasingly devious, and now it was all about to pay off. Balair 5040 was in perfect position, even if MAC Alpha 284 and his silent wingman weren't.

Will reestimated the distance remaining and keyed the interphone.

"Crew, this is the pilot. We're about to change partners. Loadmaster, have the passengers strapped in tight, yourself included. Engineer? The refueling port is closed and dark, correct?"

"Yes sir."

"Okay, all lights down here in the cockpit, and Load, I want it pitch dark back there in the cabin. I don't want anyone spotting a lighted window."

"No problem, pilot. Everyone down here's ready, and the lights are out."

"You ready to take it, Will? I'm beginning to see double." Doug's eyes remained on the tail of 284. The two pilots had traded off formation duties since leaving the Red Sea, but Doug had flown for the past forty minutes.

A small shake of the yoke marked the transfer of control as Will leaned forward, his chin over the edge of the glare shield, trying to calculate the right moment to bank away.

"Copilot," Will began, a shadow of a grin on his face, "you remember that cartoon with the two guys hanging by their thumbs in a dungeon, both with long beards, and one says to the other, 'Now here's my plan . . .'?"

"Sure do."

"Okay. Well, now here's my plan. We can't generate more than point four-five Mach closure rate on Playmate once we get behind him, since he's already doing point seven-eight and we can't exceed point eight-two-five. Right?"

"Right."

"So I'm going to try to time this to come out of the turn almost exactly under him. That means in the turn—which will be steep—I'll need all the help I can get watching where he is and where we are. Jump seat, could you get behind me here and monitor him as I start the—"

Doug's voice cut him off. "Traffic at three o'clock, pilot." His face turned to the copilot's side window.

The confusion in Will's mind was momentary but profound. The Balair was to the left. What traffic could be to the right?

"What altitude, copilot? Above or below?"

"*Our* altitude—and closing!" Doug's voice was intense.

Sandra yanked her seatbelt clasp open and moved quickly to the copilot's window behind Doug's seat as Will glanced in the same direction.

"Will—" Doug began.

Sandra's voice cut in. "The traffic's level with the horizon, and he *is* closing on us, pilot!"

"We'll have to warn two-eight-four if we need to climb or turn," Will barked, his eyes remaining glued to the underside of 284, just ahead. The Balair DC-10 was at their ten-o'clock position now, and less than ten miles away. The breakaway turn would have to be made momentarily. This would immensely complicate his timing, to say the least.

"He's closing fast, we're dark, and 284's beacon is off. He can't see us." Doug grabbed for the wafer switch on the copilot's interphone panel, turning it quickly to UHF-1, then grabbing the transmit button on the yoke.

"Two-eight-four, traffic closing three o'clock, collision course. Climb, climb, climb! Now!"

Another glance to the right brought the rotating beacons of whoever it was into Will's view at last, the sudden proximity taking his breath away. He felt adrenaline rush into his bloodstream. He had to do something instantly, but they were literally trapped by the looming hulk of the lead C-141—which began to rise in the windscreen, a small suggestion of a climb at first, then rising like a fighter, clearing the way for Will to maneuver clear.

"*Climb,* Will! NOW!" The voice was Doug's, and it came out as a strained shout as Doug's right hand joined Will's on the yoke, both of them pulling hard, Will banking to the right as the sudden flash of a lighted tail insignia and the roar of jet engines passed just below them.

On the flight deck of Egyptair 112, what sounded like the roar of jet engines passing just above them scared both pilots speechless. They had been assigned FL350. Could someone else have been at the same altitude? The captain changed the radio frequency to Atheni Control and reported level at FL350, his face ashen when he learned where they were supposed to have been: level at FL330.

Doug lunged at the windscreen, searching above for 284, who was out of sight above them now. If 284 somehow failed to see Balair, they could climb right into him. "Two-eight-four, go no higher than three-six." The prospect of avoiding one midair just to send a companion into another flashed through their minds as the voice of 284's aircraft commander cut through with a strained grunt. "Rog."

The lights of the Balair DC-10 were now just to the left and slightly above at FL370. He had to be closer than four miles. Will had planned to start the turn when the DC-10 was exactly four miles away, as measured on their weather radar. Now there was no time even to look at the scope, and the Douglas-built jumbo was passing almost directly through their course.

With 284 out of the way, Will banked hard to the right, running the bank angle to forty-five degrees and pulling it around, realizing he had started late. They needed to be exactly beneath the Balair when they rolled out, but they weren't going to make it. To Sandra's eyes, from her position on the jump seat, the DC-10 appeared to angle down in the windscreen, and then slowly, steadily, float back up and move ahead as they came around on the same heading, overshooting slightly to the left and too far behind to stay radar-masked.

Will reached over and selected a range of five miles on the weather radar, then moved his hand to the center console, raising the antenna tilt to its limit to "see" the target aircraft. The DC-10 suddenly appeared on the radar scope in front of them, just under a half-mile away.

Will said it first, the same thought setting off alarms in Doug's head. "If we're unmasked here for more than a minute, every radar in the eastern Mediterranean will see us!"

The throttles were nearly to the firewall now, and the flight engineer saw the vertical tapes shoot toward the top of the two engine RPM gauges as his foot toggled the floor-mounted interphone switch. "Overboost, all four. Bring 'em back to two-point-two-zero maximum, sir."

Doug complied as the lights of the DC-10 stayed stubbornly ahead. They were closing, but they were still exposed, the metal skin of the dark 141 reflecting radar bursts back in the direction of a dozen air traffic control and air defense radars at a slightly different time than the electronically enhanced return from the transponder on the Balair aircraft. Cairo, Cyprus, Greece, and perhaps even Israel could be getting a small, shadowy target behind Balair 5040. If it didn't go away within a couple of radar sweeps, someone was going to take it seriously.

"What's our worst-case scenario, Will? Fighter interception from Syria? I know the Iraqis wouldn't dare launch any."

The occupant of the left seat nodded, his eyes locked on the brightly lit airliner now only a few hundred yards in front of them and still somewhat above.

Will's voice was slower now, more metered, as he struggled to suppress the effects of the adrenaline he couldn't purge from his system.

"I'm, ah . . . not going to slow down until we're right under him. Be ready on the spoilers, copilot. I'll come screaming under and then put on the brakes, so to speak."

"Will, don't forget the pitch-up tendency. Make sure we have some vertical room, okay?" Doug cautioned. MAC crew members were supposed to address each other on the interphone only by their crew positions, not by first names. Reservists, who tended to maintain friendships over many years across the officer-enlisted lines, were the worst offenders in using one another's names—especially when things got tense.

"Understood," was the left-seat reply.

The bulk of the DC-10 seemed to be coming at them fast now, the closure rate around thirty knots. No more than thirty seconds had elapsed since they had rolled out on the same heading, but the closure rate was half a mile a minute. They had thirty seconds to go—more, if they tried to slow down from behind and match speeds gently.

Doug loosened his seatbelt and threw the shoulder harnesses off, placing his head as far forward over the glare shield as he could manage as the DC-10's tail slid backwards over them.

"Now!" Doug called. Will brought the throttles to idle and the spoiler handle rapidly down to the full flight position, raising the large panels on the wings that acted as speed brakes in flight. The C-141 suddenly shuddered and protested, the nose wanting to leap up, the aircraft fighting to climb as Will kept the altitude constant.

The huge jumbo appeared to slide backwards into position directly above them, then stop, exactly matched in speed, the lower rotating beacon barely visible in the topmost corner of the C-141's windscreen.

"Retract the spoilers now." Doug was trying to look straight up, at considerable expense to his neck muscles.

Will brought the spoiler lever up rapidly and increased power on all four engines back to cruise, the 141 suddenly returning to smooth flight, the DC-10 moving slightly ahead as Will began to ease them up and into what was essentially the refueling position—less than fifty feet down and back from the tail of the aircraft.

"Amazing," Doug said. "That crew hasn't the slightest idea we're back here."

"Which is why," Will continued, "we're going to have to watch him like a hawk. He could dive or climb with virtually no notice, and we're right below."

In the engineer's seat, Bill toggled a generator switch and scowled at the electrical panel. Another problem to report.

"Pilot, engineer."

"Go ahead."

"I'm going to disconnect number-one generator, sir. It was unstable and getting worse. Way out of limits."

Will turned to his right and surveyed his panel. "We still have the other three, right?"

"Absolutely."

Will gave his approval, and the interphone fell silent for a minute as Bill completed the disconnect and the two pilots took stock. Over four hundred miles ahead and still out of sight was the Middle Eastern coastline. The Balair DC-10 would fly over Beirut and then Damascus before proceeding into Iraq on a direct course for Baghdad, all the while oblivious of the presence of their silent partner below.

Every mile of the way, however, the DC-10 would be watched carefully by the radars of several different nations who would not take kindly to such a trick.

"Well, did we make it, pilot?" Doug was watching carefully for Will's reaction, which was slow in coming. As Sandra changed places with Bill Backus back at the flight engineer's station, Will looked over finally in Doug's direction, a weary smile creasing his face, his head shaking slowly. "I don't know. We were too far back there for over a minute. Cairo had to have seen us."

"And if they did?"

"Maybe they'll ignore it." Will gestured in the direction of Lebanon and Syria. "And maybe they won't."

One thing's certain, Will thought to himself. *I was too damn cocksure I could pull this off!*

* * *

Farouk Hammedi looked up as his supervisor returned. "We have informed Atheni, and they will violate MAC Alpha two-eight-four for entering off course."

Hammedi pointed to the radar display. "When this Balair flight passed the MAC flight, for about a minute, if I didn't know better, I'd say someone was following Balair. There was a return just behind him. Then it stopped. I recommend we tell military control."

The supervisor scratched the side of his face and considered that for a moment. He remembered the last time he had reported something odd to military control, and fighters had gone up to take a look. There was nothing wrong, they said, but a supervisor who couldn't read his radar. That had not been a pleasant experience.

"You saw nothing," he told Hammedi, "unless it reappears as a steady target."

Scorpion-1, in flight
Thursday, March 7, 1991—2:20 A.M. (2320 GMT)

Shakir Abbas sat bolt upright suddenly, his forehead slamming inadvertently into the portable oxygen bottle strapped to the ceiling of the crew rest pallet. The horrifying image of his wife being dragged from their home began to fade, but his heart was still pounding as his mind searched frantically for a way to save her. The image was confusing and wrong. Saliah was in her wedding dress and beautiful as always, but her face was contorted in fear, and she had tossed her veil aside in anger as she looked at him and mouthed the word, "Why?"

He rubbed his eyes and tried to find reality.

Thank God, it was only a dream! I must calm down.

The bruise from the emergency oxygen bottle asserted itself at last, and he felt the spot on his head, relieved he wasn't bleeding. He was still shaking slightly, or was it the airplane? It was hard to tell.

Shakir looked around again at the tiny space, grateful for the offer of a place to lie down, but amazed that anyone could ever get rested in such a pigeonhole. The pallet hung from the ceiling seven feet or so above the cargo floor, and extended back about five feet behind the cockpit bulkhead, just enough space for two single mattresses separated by a ceiling-high stack of canvas bags full of life vests and other emergency equipment.

It was too cramped to sit all the way up, so he let himself lie down once more, studying the battleship gray padding around the air-conditioning ducts and the maze of control wires running, he supposed, from the cockpit back to the control surfaces of the C-141.

The dry heat was incredible. Almost as bad as the desert. He was overheated and consumed with thirst. Despite the nightmare, it had been good to sleep for a while—especially with the little yellow earplugs the loadmaster had given him as a defense against the amazing noise levels.

Shakir closed his eyes and tried to capture his wife's image again, the gnawing worries washing over him in a wave of fear and despair. If the mission succeeded and they took him back to Saudi, how would he return to his family? Would the Coalition or the Saudis arrest him? Would they give him political asylum? They would have to let his family in, but how could he get them out of Iraq? What if Saddam was not overthrown? What if someone fingerprinted that burned corpse he had left in his place? What if, what if, what if!

Someone grabbed his right shoe and wiggled it, and he had to stop himself from sitting up too fast and hitting the oxygen bottle again. He peered down one side of his body and recognized the loadmaster standing at his feet on the cockpit ladder.

"We're getting ready to start down. They want you up."

"What?" The noise was masking the voice, but so were the earplugs. He worried one out of his ear and motioned to the man to try again, leaning around as far as he could.

"I said it's time to get up, sir. We're starting down."

* * *

Doug Harris pushed in the button on the high-frequency radio known as HF-1, shutting off the irritating cascade of static. Like all MAC C-141 drivers, he had been listening to the same damned HF radios all the years he had flown the airplane—twenty years in his case. He shook his head and looked out the right window, his body language complaining to no one in particular. *Here we are in an age of satellite communications, and we're still dependent on Korean War technology!*

Except for the night-vision devices, of course.

Doug looked at his partner in the left seat and triggered the interphone. "We've got the go-ahead signal. Hard to hear, but it came in from Croughton on one-one-two-one-five upper sideband."

Will nodded. Every fifteen minutes for the past two days, most of the USAF aeronautical radio stations had broadcast a series of codes, most of them background gibberish until now. "Wallflower sequence Alpha Charlie Zulu" had virtually no meaning other than to confirm to Colonel Will Westerman and crew that they were "go" to penetrate Iraqi airspace—which they would do now in less than two minutes.

The DC-10 banked gently to the left, making a small course correction, with Will following it smoothly. So far the ruse was working. The communications between the pilots of Balair 5040 and the Lebanese controllers, the Syrian controllers, and now the weak signal of the Iraqi flight control authorities had all proceeded as planned. No one was supposed to know that Scorpion-1 was back here, and so far no one did.

So far.

Doug glanced at Will, gauging the intensity of his concentration as he worked to stay in tight beneath the DC-10 that had filled their cockpit windscreen for the past two hours, the lower rotating beacon flashing monotonously. They had both taped folded maps to the windscreen to block out the beacon, but as Doug watched his companion, the reflected bursts of reddish light illuminated Will's face like some sort of bizarre disco strobe, highlighting lines and creases and sags in those familiar features that he hadn't noticed before.

It had only been seven hours since he had stumbled into the ALCE and found himself face to face with his former best friend. Or perhaps Will still occupied that category, despite the long years of mutual silence. How could two friends as close as they had been drift apart so completely? Doug realized he had been evading that question for nearly seventeen years.

The night sky was still visible beneath the Douglas jumbo, the moon almost at its zenith and nearly full, the softness of the moonlight cascading in through the copilot's window. The bright disk was starkly visible, hanging just forward of the dark mass of the DC-10's right horizontal stabilizer over their heads. Without a cloud cover ahead, the moonlight would make it a dangerous night for a commando-style raid and an assault landing in enemy territory. But the weather forecasters had been reporting a solid undercast at around five thousand feet—solid enough to hide them, yet high enough to permit a visual approach to a darkened desert highway.

"We're over the line, crew." The voice was Will's. Iraq was below them now.

At 2330 GMT—2:30 A.M. in Baghdad—an exhausted Iraqi military radar controller saw his screen bloom into useless lines and splotches of phosphorescent nonsense yet again. For days he had manned a temporary trailerful of radar screens and communication gear with eight other controllers and attempted to masquerade as an air traffic control facility. Their real mission was military radar intelligence, but the problem of how to watch the skies without drawing an American air strike had unnerved them all.

Most of his colleagues were dead now—all those who had been trained with him as radar operators. One by one the Americans had taken out the military radar sites, destroying Saddam's expensive network and blinding his commanders. This last one was supposed to be left alone—supposed to be considered civilian—but he was almost resigned to dying at any moment from an unexpected Coalition bomb dropped by an invisible stealth aircraft without warning.

The scope was now useless. The Americans had been doing this all night at regular intervals. When the first episode had come in early evening, everyone had gotten excited, and in the absence of telephone communications, a messenger had been dispatched to military headquarters. The Americans were up to something, they were sure!

But each time the terrible burst of radar interference had ended, he had searched the skies again and found nothing there. His commanders had originally suspected the radar interference was a cover for some new Coalition assault, but he knew otherwise. There had been no fighting, no reports of bombed cities, no Scud sites attacked—nothing. After fifteen such episodes, it was obvious to all of them that the radar bursts were American harassment aimed at Saddam, and not a cover for some military operation.

Several hundred miles to the west and invisible in the "noise" of the radar picture, the commander of Scorpion-1 was counting on exactly that conclusion.

At long last, the image of the DC-10 began to move up in the windscreen as Will eased the 141 into a descent, accelerating toward the red-line airspeed of Mach .825 once again. The descent profile had been carefully computed to keep the 141 positioned directly under the Balair flight as Scorpion-1 dove at the desert.

Will's hand had been resting on the spoiler lever. He armed it now and began pulling the lever back and down, everyone aboard feeling the spoiler panels extend into the airstream on the top and bottom of the wings, the aircraft beginning to shake and shudder as the spoilers acted as speed brakes, enabling the aircraft to descend at a far steeper angle without exceeding airspeed limits.

As Sandra struggled at the engineer's panel to keep up with the changing cabin pressurization, Doug frowned and craned his neck to look directly above them, verifying that the diminishing form of the DC-10 was still in the right place as his hand held on to the ungainly combination of his flight helmet and the night-vision goggles. They had already taped the sheets of colored gel over the instrument panel. Otherwise the flight instruments could overpower the goggles.

Eight thousand feet per minute, nose down now and screaming through thirty thousand feet, Will held the speed at red line, metering the extension of the spoilers to maintain the right combination of descent rate and speed, the throttles now fully retarded.

"Twenty-five thousand." The voice was Doug's. The hundreds column of the altimeter's vertical tape was almost an unreadable blur.

In the jump seat, Bill Backus reached to the middle of the center console and changed the electronic "page" on the FSAS flight computer screen, checking the latitude and longitude of the target highway once again. The computer projected a white line on the radar screen from their present position to the destination, and Will had switched it to the 150-mile range minutes before. They were less than fifty miles out now.

"Okay, jump seat, this is the pilot. You have the hand-held?"

Bill Backus raised the small portable FM transceiver into Will's view and nodded. Somewhere ahead and below, a member of the combat support team who had dropped in by parachute the night before should be waiting.

"Go ahead and call them," he ordered.

Backus nodded and pressed the transmit button with a short,

coded sequence of words. A steady voice came back instantly with the proper reply, and then a quick stream of information, which Backus relayed to Will:

"They're standing by, sir. The markers are set, no road traffic in sight, and both ends are covered."

"Thanks."

"Fifteen thousand," Doug reported.

Scorpion-1 slid into the undercast, which replaced the star field with dark gray for several thousand feet, then descended out of the bottom of the clouds at 4,500 feet. The steep descent rate continued through two thousand feet as they came up on the turn point, which was planned to be five miles north of the highway and fifteen miles northeast of the underground lab the strike team members were getting ready to visit.

Will leveled the 141 at five hundred feet above the ground and pulled in the spoilers, the engines now at idle, the airspeed still around three hundred knots and slowing rapidly.

"There's your turn, pilot." Doug called the fix and looked right into a vast blackness. A few lights were visible in the distance, but nothing to provide a reference or a differentiation between roadways, desert floor, or buildings. It was a "black hole" approach they would be attempting, and for every minute it took to find the highway and land, their risk of exposure rose.

"Get the helmet and goggles on, Doug. Come on." Will gestured impatiently at the ensemble in Doug's lap. Doug began pulling it on, flipping the NVG-6 binocular night-vision device in place, and looking in Backus's opinion like a fugitive from a grade-B science-fiction movie. Doug adjusted the controls as the enhanced images flared like daylight in front of his eyes, somewhat fuzzy whites against darker backgrounds, but every available photon of light utilized and amplified. They had practiced this briefly at altitude an hour back, but actually tracking the ground on these things was going to be an entirely different experience.

There was a road out there somewhere, running roughly east and west as they headed south. Even without the direct moonlight, even with an overcast, there was enough light to see it clearly with the goggles when they finally located it. That, at least, was the theory.

But the road wasn't there.

Doug toggled the interphone. "Nothing yet. How far are we supposed to be from it?"

"Three miles. You should see it now, even at five hundred feet."

"Nothing. I see some . . . lines . . . and what looks like maybe a building to the right, but no roads. This is a highway we're looking for, right? That's what it looked like on the maps."

"It's more of a rural highway, but paved," Will said. "We should be almost on top of it."

"You better put the bug-eyes on too, Will. I don't see anything out here that looks even remotely like a road."

"Your airplane." Will began fumbling with his helmet and the goggles as Doug acknowledged and automatically tightened his grip on the yoke, looking down to check airspeed and power. They were coming down through two hundred knots now, ready to extend the landing gear and flaps the second they spotted the road.

Doug let his thoughts race back over the possibilities. If they weren't in the right place, then either they had the wrong coordinates punched in, or the inertial navigation systems had drifted off.

Will's voice filled the crew's headsets again. "Turn back a hundred eighty degrees and head north. We've probably gone too far south."

Doug peered hard at the white images and tried to imagine what a road would look like. Instinct told him it was still ahead. "Maybe we should continue on a bit longer," he said.

The response from the left seat was abrupt.

"No. We've overflown it. Let's turn."

Doug hesitated. "How can you be sure? Let's give it a few more miles, just in case."

"Do you see anything out there in front of us?" Will asked, irritated.

"No, but—"

"Then turn the damn airplane!"

Doug bit his lip and toggled the interphone.

"Give me three more miles, pilot."

There was silence from the left seat for a second. Then, "Roger."

They were laying down one hell of a noise footprint, and even without running lights, any military units in the vicinity who heard the whine of the C-141's jet engines would instantly suspect something was up. Will knew they mustn't get within ten miles of the lab, but if they were mispositioned . . .

Will searched the fuzzy images before his eyes, praying for something resembling a road. There was nothing but flat white desert with clumps of bushes here and there. That was far enough.

Bracing for Doug's objection, Will made the decision to turn back north, and was surprised when Doug complied without a word, the 141 beginning the turn to the right, the nose passing through southwest at the moment Doug's voice cut through the rising tension.

"*There!* Right ahead, pilot. See that? It's a road."

Will squinted and saw the same thing.

Doug banked hard right then, aligning the 141 with the road, rolling wings level as Backus's voice came on the interphone.

"The ground team is hearing jet sounds to the east now, sir. That's got to be us!"

Bright points of light on each side of the road up ahead began to come into view, tiny fluorescent light sticks almost invisible in flight to the naked eye, but as bright as normal runway lights in the enhanced-light world of the NVG-6. The markers extended off into the distance, outlining the landing strip beautifully.

"Flaps approach, gear down, before-landing check." Doug gave the requisite command, his left hand pulling the flap lever to the approach position and then snapping the landing-gear lever to the down position as Will acknowledged, the sounds of the flap motors and the rush of the slipstream through the nose landing-gear door beneath their feet filling the cockpit. The throttles were back to idle now, the ground coming up fast.

"Flaps landing." Doug called the setting as he brought the flap handle the remaining distance to full extension. "Your airplane, pilot."

"Roger, flaps landing," Will repeated. "Keep flying, copilot, I'm monitoring." There was no reason to change control.

"Roger. In that case, I've got it." Doug's voice was steady and calm, in sharp contrast to the tension he was feeling. "Jump seat, start your callouts. What's my airspeed?"

"One hundred forty," Backus replied. With no night-vision devices to distort his eyesight, Backus had been assigned to keep his eyes glued to the airspeed and altitude gauges to back up the pilots. Will kept his eyes ahead, his hands following Doug's on the controls, checking the alignment, which was dead on.

"One hundred thirty-five, and your marker speed is one-thirty, sir. Three hundred feet above the surface, sink twelve hundred."

Doug nodded, but no one saw the gesture. They were too close now. The first set of light-stick markers slid past the cockpit.

"Jesus, Will. Are you sure this is wide enough for our main wheels?"

"It's forty feet wide. The wheels need twenty, and the shoulder is hard-packed sand."

"One hundred thirty-two knots, almost on marker, two hundred feet above, sink rate thirteen hundred feet. Sink one thousand now, you're one hundred feet above, sink eight hundred, on marker speed, sink eight hundred, fifty feet, thirty, twenty . . ."

Doug flared the aircraft slightly and let it settle hard and firm.

"Spoilers!" On Doug's call-out, Will grabbed the T-handle

lever that deployed the large panels on the wing known as spoilers and pulled it to the full down position as Doug pushed hard on the yoke to keep the tail from dragging, and brought the throttles to idle. They would not use reverse power to stop. Too much noise.

Doug worked hard to hold the airplane to the center of the two-lane concrete road, amazed the landing gear was still within its borders.

"Jeez, this is narrow! I don't know, pilot. Speed?"

"One hundred and five."

Doug pressed his toes into the top of the rudder pedals to apply the brakes hard, and they pitched forward in the seats as the Starlifter slowed.

"I'm killing one and four," Will said, his hand snapping off the engine fuel and ignition switches for the two outboard engines as they had rehearsed. "Doors armed, Load, cleared to open. Watch your step. And, copilot, you're eighty knots."

One hundred forty feet to the rear of the cockpit, the loadmaster, who had pre-positioned himself at the folding cargo-loading ramp, struggled against the deceleration to stand against the left side of the cabin and toggle the switch that opened the clamshell cargo doors. The pressure door had been retracted into the ceiling while they were on approach. Now, as the clamshells came into position, he began lowering the ramp. In the cockpit, Will took control to taxi, cranking the nosewheel around to the left, taking the nose gear off the roadway and onto the hard-packed ground alongside the road as he reversed course to park back on the road facing east. Four of the strike team members were standing by to put the two portable ramps in place as soon as they stopped, and almost immediately the engines of the armored personnel carriers and the Bradley fired up, the troops already in place inside—including Dr. Abbas, who was in the third vehicle.

There were no lights outside as Will brought the aircraft to a complete stop and set the parking brake, killing engines two and three. Within two minutes the first of the APCs raced by the cockpit toward its objective. The speed of the attack force's departure was amazing. It had gone like clockwork.

Will removed his helmet and the goggles as Doug was shedding his, both of them fumbling through the final checklist. The cockpit was pitch dark now, with the engines stopped and the battery switch off. The auxiliary power unit—the small jet engine in the left wheel well that normally provided power and pressurized pneumatic air on the ground—would be left off as well, since it could be heard for some distance.

Doug scanned the panel again, as much in his mind as visually. They had done the shutdown checks and turned everything off, but something was nagging him—something left undone—and he found himself feeling off balance.

The silence was overwhelming. The sounds of turbines and pumps winding down to complete stillness let the now-distant roar of the strike team's engines rumble through the cockpit momentarily. And then they, too, were gone. After more than six hours of nonstop noise, it was disorienting to find that the squeak of a seat cushion and the scraping of a metal log book on the darkened flight engineer's table were the loudest sounds in their ears.

The presence of someone new on the flight deck startled Will, an offered hand almost invisible in the gloom, until the owner turned on a dim red pencil flashlight and shone it on his face momentarily before turning the beam toward the floor.

"Welcome to Iraq, Colonel!"

The man pulled off his black watch cap, revealing a perfectly bald head, and Doug concluded he looked like Mr. Clean of household detergent fame.

"Sergeant Dale Johnson, combat support, sir. Glad you could join us."

Will felt himself relaxing. "Everything quiet and secure out there, Sergeant?"

Johnson grinned a toothy grin under a Gordon Liddy mustache.

The effect made him look older than he was, which by Doug's estimate fell in the range of the early thirties. His accent was definitely Oklahoma.

"A small truck rambled by from the direction of the target about an hour back, as we were setting up the markers. About a half-mile east of here there's a side road from the south that intersects this east-west road you've landed on. Whoever was driving didn't see a thing, and we didn't mess with him. Since then, we've shut down the road about four miles farther to the east by blowing a hellacious trench through it with plastic explosives. Any fool could drive around it, but the trench will slow them down, and two of my men are guarding that approach. Behind us about ten miles to the west, by the way, the road ends in a sand dune, so we shouldn't be bothered from that direction either."

Will nodded, his face dimly visible in the illumination of Sergeant Johnson's pencil light. There was a strained silence for a moment as the sergeant struggled to decide what the two pilots wanted to hear.

"Uh, I . . . can also tell you there's no activity from the target, and my guys took out the four guards a half hour ago very quietly. They're waiting near the bunker now for the attack team to arrive. I just talked to them by radio. The Delta guys should have no resistance outside."

Doug, who had swiveled around in the copilot's seat to face the center console with his arm resting on the glare shield, slapped the plastic surface and grinned.

"Speaking as a United Airlines pilot, I think I resent hauling around passengers I have to describe as 'a bunch of Delta guys.'"

Johnson didn't reply, and Will stepped in, arcing his left thumb in Doug's direction. "Colonel Harris, here, is a reserve pilot, Sarge. He flies for United and makes an obscene amount of money."

"When I'm not trolling for triple-A in enemy territory in a Goodyear blimp, that is," Doug added.

"Oh," was Johnson's puzzled response.

Will began maneuvering out of the pilot's seat, forcing Johnson to move back. Doug followed, swinging his leg over the jump seat.

"Is it safe to talk outside?" Will asked.

"Sure," Johnson replied.

The three men emerged into the desert night, the smell of cool air mixing with the familiar aroma of partly burned kerosene as a gentle breeze blew through the tailpipes of the jet engines.

Will zipped his leather flight jacket against the chill and tried to find a comfortable way to stuff his hands in the awkward horizontal pockets. The overcast was solid, with just a hint of moonlight glowing through the cloud layers. On the ground it was almost pitch dark, the facial expressions of Doug and the sergeant all but invisible. He could hear the loadmaster moving tie-down chains across the floor of the aircraft, the sound of flight boots crunching on the hard-packed desert floor as Doug shifted his weight, and the metallic pinging of hot engine parts cooling down—but he could see nothing, and indiscriminate use of flashlights seemed rather unwise.

"You came in yesterday?" Doug asked Johnson.

"Yes sir. A HA-HO—high-altitude, high-open—drop. They pushed four of our four-wheel motorcycles out of a C-130, and we stepped out of the other 130 at eighteen thousand about sixty miles from here, opened, and glided the rest of the way in, homing on the beacon in one of the Humvees. Worked perfectly, except the opening shock hurts like hell when you jump that high. You're goin' awfully fast, y'know."

"There's something here I don't understand," Doug said. "If you could use C-130s yesterday, why are we using a C-141 tonight?"

"Sir, all I know is what they told us, which is that U.S. aircraft can fly anywhere we want to over Iraq, but the UN won't let us land anything but rescue missions. A couple of C-130s descending and landing out here would be very visible, especially coming in from the south the way we did yesterday.''

"But 130s can fly in low.''

"Not that low, sir. You're thinking of the Pave Low helicopters. They can fly in at fifty feet at night. They've got the equipment.''

"So why not use them?''

"Not big enough to carry all the vehicles they needed for this strike.''

Doug nodded and looked off in the distance, a gesture unseen by Sergeant Johnson.

Doug turned back to him. "What'd you guys do during the day?''

"We camouflaged the motorcycles, dug ourselves a large hole, put netting over that, and just kept out of sight. We set up our little satellite communications antenna and hunkered down. We had a good view of the entrance to that bunker, though. We watched 'em all day long from about two miles away and waited for the AWACS to confirm you were coming and when.''

"A HA-HO jump, huh? I've never understood, Sergeant Johnson,'' Doug began, shaking his head in mock wonder, "why any sane person would jump out of a perfectly good airplane.''

" 'Cause we don't trust your landings, sir.'' Johnson chuckled. He'd heard the same barb and answered it the same way a hundred times with pilots, but it was still fun. Like friends from different schools poking each other over a football rivalry.

Johnson was suddenly tired of the small talk. "Colonel, I'll be monitoring my people and the Delta team. I'll call you on the hand-held the second they start back.''

"Okay, Sergeant. We'll be out here or in the cockpit. How long do you figure?'' Will cocked his head for the answer, which was a few seconds in coming.

"Could be forty minutes. More likely an hour and ten—unless things go wrong. You best be ready to crank up within five minutes of my calling you.''

"Understood." They had rehearsed that as well. Either Sandra or Bill Backus would remain at the engineer's panel, ready to turn on the battery switch, fire off the hydraulic accumulators to start the APU, and then start the engines as the team rolled on board. They'd close the doors as they taxied toward takeoff. It was all set—but something was still worrying Doug. Something not worth mentioning. Just a vague uneasiness. He pushed it aside, picked up two soft drinks from the loadmaster's stash in the galley, and followed Will out to the end of the left wing, which hung over the hard surface of the Iraqi western desert.

"Buy you a drink?"

"What've you got?" Will asked, fumbling with the proffered can in the dark and sitting down cross-legged by the edge of the road.

"It's a naïve little cola without much breeding . . ."

Will laughed through the last line, ". . . but you knew I'd be amused at its presumption. Good Lord, Doug, in pilot training you used that old line at least once a day."

"James Thurber never gets old."

"Yeah. Doug, look, I'm . . . ah . . . sorry about snapping at you back there. If you hadn't insisted we keep going south . . . well, I would have screwed it up, and you saved it."

"That's what your faithful copilot is for, Will. To kibitz, suggest, point to, niggle, and otherwise respectfully second-guess the esteemed aircraft commander."

"Who should have had the good graces to be more civil."

"Well . . . I didn't take any offense. We got here, didn't we?"

Will was silent for a second. "This is unreal, Doug. I'm tired, so maybe that's why, but does this all strike you as . . . weird?"

"What?"

"Sitting here, I mean, under the wing of a huge fifteen-million-dollar airplane by an Iraqi highway in the middle of the night, sipping a Diet Coke and listening to what I swear sounds like crickets, while that team of gung-ho commandos are off in the distance saving the world. You remember a certain evening at Tak Li in, what was it, '72?''

The memory came back to Doug in living color. As a newly minted aircraft commander he had flown a load of cargo to Will's F-4 base in Thailand for a twenty-four-hour crew rest. They hadn't seen each other in six months, and when Doug burst into Will's hootch, they decided on the spot to have a two-man party and catch up on each other's war stories. Lugging sandwiches and a case of San Miguel beer out to the flight line, they sat most of the night beneath the wing of Doug's C-141 getting generally smashed and taking bets on whether a passing cobra would be more likely to bite a transport pilot or a fighter jock.

"I spent that whole evening," Doug began, "tryin' to talk you into transferring to 141s at McChord."

"Yeah. And I did, didn't I?" Will countered.

"For a couple of years." They fell silent again, Will's sudden departure from McChord playing in both minds.

Doug turned to him finally. "What the hell happened, Will? Why did you leave McChord so suddenly? I mean, we get back from the honeymoon and you're in Charleston! Wendy never understood, and I know I didn't."

"How is she?" Will asked at last.

"Who?"

"Wendy. Your wife, remember?"

There was no answer, and Will searched the dark form next to him for a clue as to why. Finally Doug spoke. "You didn't know? You *don't* know?"

"I don't like games, Doug. Know what? Don't tell me you two aren't together anymore?"

"In . . . in a manner of speaking."

He hadn't written Will about it. He hadn't called. He had just assumed the news had made its way to Charleston. After all, they really hadn't been in touch for well over a decade.

Will heard a long sigh before Doug's voice broke the silence.

"She's dead, Will. Eight years now." There was a small gasp

in response. "I've remarried . . . have two little boys, ages two and five . . ."

"*What?* How . . . I mean, what . . . happened?"

"It was, ah, an accident, okay?"

"A car accident? What *kind* of accident?"

Images of her danced across Will's mind instantly, transporting him back, the night suddenly filled with the primal beauty of her honey blond hair blowing in a Puget Sound sea breeze, and the memory of her emerald green eyes flirting with him on the Seattle waterfront one very special evening that had turned into day. Memories of sensations and emotions he had thought were dead washed over him like a warm wave: the sensual peace of her silky body in his arms at sunrise, the contentment of waking up in a rented cottage on an Oregon beach with sounds of the sea in his ears and the scent of Wendy in the air, and the way she purred like a kitten at his touch. How could she be gone? He had lost her to Doug, and somehow that had been bearable. But . . . *dead*?

"Just . . . just an accident," Doug was saying slowly, unconvincingly.

Will's head spun with conflicting emotions of disbelief mixed with memories of long-suppressed desires— memories he assumed Doug Harris had never known about.

Doug turned toward him and took a long, somewhat labored breath. "It's . . . a pretty painful memory."

Will's response bubbled up from a reservoir of hurt he had sealed years before, forming into words that left Doug puzzled.

"Painful for me, too."

Southeast of Ar Rutbah, western central Iraq
Thursday, March 7, 1991—3:05 A.M. (0005 GMT)

A beefy hand reached out without warning and grabbed his shoulder, causing Shakir Abbas to look up much too rapidly. The nauseating pitching and bouncing of the armored personnel carrier's windowless interior had already tied his stomach in a knot. The sudden movement of his head was almost too much.

The master sergeant tapped his radio headset and pointed in the direction of the lead vehicle. "Doctor, the boss wants me to brief you on what's about to happen, okay?"

The sergeant was obviously pumped up with anticipation and adrenaline, his face covered with dark charcoallike makeup, his impatience showing. He loomed unreal and menacing in the gyrating darkness of the vehicle's windowless interior. The voice, however, was not unkind.

"I have already been briefed, Sergeant."

"Yes sir. But we need to do it again."

The major was in the first vehicle—the Bradley—and Shakir was in the second of the two M-113 APCs. According to the plan, they would come up behind the small blockhouse that protected the stairway down to the bunker complex. The Bradley—which was armed to the teeth with a stabilized 25-mm turret-mounted cannon and a couple of TOW antitank missiles—would be the first vehicle in to clear the way. The two lightly defended APCs would then follow, the strike team dashing from the rear ramps to establish a safe perimeter. At the radioed signal that all was ready, Shakir would be hustled out and rushed to the entrance, where the first squad would be waiting to descend the first flight of stairs. If they were pinned down by gunfire at any point, Shakir would be expected to describe the areas beyond in great detail, including side doors, escape routes, windows, and any other place someone with a gun could hide in waiting. As soon as each segment was "safe," his "keepers" would pull him along to the next staging point. Every member of the team had memorized the detailed makeshift blueprint Shakir had drawn. They all knew that the living quarters were on the third level down, the lab itself on the fourth, the virus in the lab's isolation chamber. The squad members carried a frightening array of killing machines, from standard assault M-16s to what resembled tiny Uzi machine pistols with silencers, as well as knives and several varieties of stun weapons—one of them a military version of the Taser. The group included demolition experts who would set the charges to pulverize the facility after Shakir had destroyed the batches of virus below.

They were an impressive and chilling bunch, these young men, Shakir thought. He was already scared to death of the situation, but knowing these men were trained to end his or any other life in a heartbeat made them something other than human, and all the more threatening. They smiled, they joked, they talked among themselves like any soldiers, but there was a keen edge about them that was unnerving.

Hours before, while in flight, Shakir had carefully approached the major who led them. "Many of the people in that laboratory," he had begun, "I have worked with for years. They will not fight you."

"If anyone down there so much as raises a gun," the major had replied, "he's dead. I'm not going to risk my men."

"Yes, but please remember, most of these people would have left the country too, if they could have. Please don't kill them automatically."

The man had looked at Shakir long and hard.

"Is that what you think of us?" he had asked at last.

"I just—"

"Doctor, we don't automatically *kill* anyone."

"Okay, Doctor. *Now.*" Two of the team members guided Shakir out through the small oval door in the back of the vehicle and into the cool night air, which felt wonderful. They were inside the familiar entrance all at once, without resistance, and down the flight of steps to the first corridor, the sound of steel doors being opened, again without resistance, clanging below. The next level was the same, and a cold apprehension began to creep unspoken into his gut. Could they have already moved everyone and abandoned the facility? The thought that the Pandora's box he had filled might already be open and empty was chilling.

Another loud clang and the sound of angry, shouting voices, all in English, followed by another urgent cordon of American hands pushing him into the living quarters where, to his relief, a half-dozen familiar Iraqi faces waited. They stood wide-eyed and frightened, but alive—their hands on their heads.

Sandar Almeany was in the middle, his eyes flaring even wider when he saw Shakir, his jaw dropping open as he searched for the words in Arabic. "Shakir! We thought you were dead! You were captured, then?"

With an Arabic-speaking American corporal standing to his right, Shakir was acutely aware of the consequences of any misunderstood phrase. He ran the words over in his mind in an instant, inspecting them for trouble before finding his voice, his hands gripping his assistant's shoulders.

"There is no time, my friend. I will explain later. All the prepared canisters are below, correct?"

Sandar's eyes shot from Shakir to one of the soldiers and back again several times.

"*Sandar!* This is important! Is it all there? They have not . . . no one has moved the canisters yet, have they?"

"I . . ." Sandar's head jerked toward the door, where more members of the research team were being marched in at gunpoint, their hands being quickly bound with plastic tie strips, their bodies rapidly searched for weapons.

Shakir gripped his shoulders and shook hard. "*Sandar, answer me! Is everything still here?*"

That same cold fear which had gripped him before for a split second grabbed him again as his research assistant's head began to nod, then changed direction, moving slowly from side to side in a universal negative.

"*Where? How many are gone? When?*"

His voice recovered at last, the Arabic words tumbled out rapidly. All but two canisters were there.

"*Where are they, Sandar?*"

"Ansallah . . ."

Shakir's response was instantaneous, interrupting Sandar.

"When did he leave?"

"An hour ago, but I'm not sure he had both canisters. A helicopter came the day before."

Shakir stepped back and almost shoved the man away. "You must go, you all must go with these soldiers without resistance."

Two canisters gone! Enough for a holocaust. But there were far more below to take care of. Shakir motioned to the soldiers with him and headed for the stairway and the lab. As they watched, he turned on the lights and inserted his hands in the isolation gloves, working the levers and turntables to assemble the twenty-one gleaming, glass-lined stainless-steel canisters while what could best be described as an electric kiln warmed rapidly.

One of the attack force moved over beside him, catching his attention. "Talk me through this, Doc. You can't kill all of that at one time, can you?"

Shakir looked up, appreciating the curiosity. "It will take two cycles of five minutes each. I don't have enough room in the kiln for all of these."

One by one he unscrewed each of them, lifting the glass container with its lethal contents out of each protective shell, inserting it in the transit rack, moving half the group into the kiln, and shutting the door. The temperature inside was already approaching one thousand degrees. He wanted one thousand degrees for five minutes for each load to be absolutely sure.

The soldier asked some more questions about the safeguards, the filling and emptying procedures, and how the German company that had built the bunker had gone about designing the lab. Shakir was almost enjoying the discussion when Major Moyer came in the room hurriedly.

"We need you upstairs for a minute, Doctor. Can you leave?"

Shakir looked around. The first batch had been at one thousand degrees Fahrenheit for almost five minutes. He turned back to Moyer.

"I should load the second and last batch in."

"After this. Come on. Now. There's a compartment up here we don't understand."

Shakir left with a warning to the two soldiers to touch nothing. As he cleared the room, the one who had been standing in the background quickly secured and bolted the door, while the one who had asked the questions pulled a tiny steel container from a belt pouch with practiced efficiency and moved expertly to the small safety hatch between the lab and the isolation chamber. He had been well trained, and the German-built equipment chamber was easy to figure out.

* * *

Shakir returned to the lab irritated and resumed his seat, moving the second batch into the kiln. What kind of disease affected the military mind to such a degree that someone obviously as intelligent as the major would pull him away for such a minor matter? An ordinary refrigerator was not a secure lab storage device, even with a lock on the front. Any idiot should have known that!

Major Moyer pushed into the lab again and approached Shakir, his M-16 still in one hand, his hand-held command radio in the other.

"How much longer, Doctor?"

"One more minute." On the excursion upstairs, Shakir had tried to bring up the subject that was burning for resolution, but Moyer had refused to listen. He would listen now.

"We have a problem," Shakir heard himself say.

Moyer's eyes were everywhere at once, taking in the isolation chamber, the long gloves through the wall, the stance of his two men on either side of the room watching Abbas, and finally back to Abbas himself.

"What?"

"I have destroyed all the virus that was here. But you see those canisters?" He pointed to the open collection of metal behind the thick glass. Moyer nodded.

"Two have already been taken out of here, and we must get them as well."

"Where are they?"

"I . . . just a minute." Shakir checked his watch. Five minutes had passed, but they were going to blow everything up anyway, so why not just let it cook? He abandoned the idea of turning off the kiln and withdrew his hands from the gloves, turning back to Major Moyer. "They left just an hour ago, just before we landed. I know the scientist that took them. He is a Ba'ath loyalist—the only one we had here. He will be headed straight for Baghdad. We can catch him if we start quickly. I would recognize the van."

Moyer was shaking his head. "Not in the plan, Doctor. We kill the bugs here, blow the lab, and get everyone out. Those are my orders. Going after that guy's another operation for another day."

Shakir was astounded. There was no choice. How *could* there be a choice? No one could rest until all of the cultures had been found and incinerated.

"Major, there may not be another day. There may not be another *opportunity!* Don't . . . don't you understand how deadly this thing is?"

"I'm sorry. I have my orders."

Shakir was on his feet then, pleading, but without effect. Stunned, he was led from the lab, with Moyer and three of his men clearing the area as they climbed. Only the demolition team remained inside now. Shakir was hustled out the entrance and back toward the second APC, but stopped suddenly, yanking the sleeve of the master sergeant he had ridden in with.

"You took all my people prisoner, didn't you?"

"Yes sir. They're in the second machine there."

"I have to speak with one of them."

The sergeant hesitated, then nodded. So far, Abbas had been no problem. He guided him to the rear of the APC and let him motion Sandar Almeany outside. As the sergeant watched carefully, the two men stood at the corner of the vehicle and began speaking urgently in Arabic. Shakir was grateful for the absence of the Arabic-speaking American corporal.

"What kind of vehicle was Ansallah driving? Do you know?"

"The Toyota van. The white one. The green one is still here."

"You're sure it was an hour ago?"

He nodded again.

"Was anyone with him?"

"One of the soldiers. They had new orders not to let any of us leave alone after your . . . your accident. What happened to you?"

"Later, Sandar."

Sandar caught Shakir's sleeve and stared at him, eye-to-eye. "Tell me now!"

Shakir nodded. "I could not let this happen, Sandar. I could not let them use it. I had to stop Saddam's plans the only way I knew how."

A sly smile crept across his colleague's face. "So you *did* go south. Ansallah said you had faked your death. He didn't trust you. He thought the virus would be ready sooner than you said it would."

"He knew I had . . . defected?"

"No. Ansallah didn't know. He suspected. He knew we didn't trust Saddam. He knew how determined you were to prevent the virus from being used."

Saliah's image came to him again. "Did he say these things to Baghdad?" Shakir must have looked panicked, and Sandar understood at once. "Calm down, my friend."

"But now that we've raided—"

"He never had time to tell anyone. That's why he left tonight. There were no phone lines, and no one to report to." Sandar thought for a second before continuing. The game had changed with Ansallah gone. "If he *does* get through, however . . . you had better get Saliah and the children out of the country."

A strong tug on his arm propelled him toward the other APC as Sandar was pulled back inside his.

"Time to go, Doctor."

Shakir complied easily as he spotted the rickety metal shed where they kept the cars, identifying at last in the gloom the green Toyota van.

The squad leader was quite pleased that Shakir had turned out to be trustworthy. With the major walking over for a last word with the sergeant before departing, Shakir let the others get in ahead of him. As the major and the sergeant compared notes on the return off to the side, the rear ramp was drawn up and latched and the oval entry door once again swung open, waiting for Shakir and the sergeant.

The major turned to Shakir and touched his arm. "All your people are fine, Doctor. No one resisted except the guards outside. Everyone else is safe. I thought you'd like to know that." Shakir thanked him, and watched him turn and trot toward his vehicle as the sergeant smiled and motioned him in the door.

"It is an old Arab custom," Shakir lied as convincingly as he could, "that after a dangerous but successful battle, the honor of entry into the tent must go to the fighter. I know it is silly to you, but please . . ."

He could see the professional soldier's mind enter a temporary feedback loop of indecision. Shakir wasn't trustworthy, but he had just proven himself trustworthy. He wasn't there to be a diplomat, yet CENTCOM, Schwarzkopf, and everyone under them had pounded in the need to respect Arab customs. In that split second, Shakir knew the likable American was going to make a major mistake that would give him the one chance he needed.

"Okay, Doctor. In accordance with custom, then." The sergeant swung his left leg into the oval doorway, holding his Uzi lightly in his right hand as he propelled his trunk through the entrance. Shakir deftly snatched the Uzi away with one hand while slamming the armored door with the other, the sergeant's momentum propelling him cleanly inside before he could react. The rear door closed with a clang, and Shakir turned one of the latches before dashing toward the shed as fast as he could run. About twenty yards on the other side of the shed, there was a small emergency exit from the bunker below—just a long steel ladder attached to the concrete walls of a vertical shaft covered by a steel door flat on the ground, but a place to hide nonetheless. If he could get to it in time, they wouldn't follow even if they could find it. The charges had already been set and the demolition crew had reported clear of the bunker, and they wouldn't expect him to do something suicidal like going back inside, even if they knew about the exit.

Angry voices were replaced by the clanging of metal as the

entire rear ramp of the third vehicle crashed open on the ground and the sergeant and several others came pouring out like angry hornets. Shakir was already rounding the shed, the objective somewhere just ahead. He heard the confusion as they yelled back and forth, trying to figure out which way he had run.

Shakir dove into the sand then, and crawled in the darkness the remaining distance, his hands feeling frantically ahead as shouts and footsteps behind him indicated that an energetic search was under way, with at least one soldier heading toward the shed. He felt a metal surface then, and his fingers flew over it, trying to find the handle. The running footsteps came closer, and he could hear the heavy breathing of someone just fifty feet or so away.

At last he touched the handle and grasped it, but it wouldn't budge. He had no leverage lying on the ground, but if he stood up, he'd be visible instantly to any flashlight beam. He pulled and hauled nevertheless, throwing sand in his eyes, but feeling no movement.

Engines were firing up behind him as strong headlights cut the air above, filtering through the shed and around the van as at least one of the machines came his way. More shouting now. His footprints had been seen going into the shed. They were assuming he would shoot at them, and that assumption was slowing the search.

A fingernail tore painfully as he hauled away at the handle. The hatch hadn't been opened in some time. Too much sand had drifted over it, or perhaps it had been latched somehow from below. He hadn't opened it in a year.

Heavy footsteps ran toward both sides of the shed now as they ordered him to come out with his hands up. He froze, then his head triangulated the sounds, and logic interpreted what was happening: they had assumed he was hiding in the van, some forty feet behind him.

Someone pulled open the van door, then cursed loudly.

At last! The hatch moved a tiny bit, a deafening screech from the metal hinges assaulting his ears. He froze, hoping they hadn't heard the noise through all their shouting, and knowing he couldn't move the hatch again without alerting them.

That was that. He could do no more. Defeated, Shakir relaxed, totally out of ideas. They would find him or they wouldn't, and if they did, he was confident they wouldn't shoot him lying facedown in the sand. If he stood up, they might. After all, when last seen, he was carrying the sergeant's gun.

More footfalls, this time coming in his direction from behind the shed. He recognized the sergeant's voice in the distance, and knew the man felt angry and betrayed. He felt guilty about tricking him. The sergeant had tried to be respectful of Arabic customs, but Shakir was sure the next Arab who tried to appeal to the man's diplomacy would be in for a rude shock.

There was an unexpected shout, and he recognized Major Moyer's voice. "Break it off, people! Forget it! We don't have time to chase the little sonofabitch."

One of the men nearest Shakir yelled back, "Sir, I think he ran over this way."

Major Moyer understood why Shakir had bolted. He couldn't sanction it, but he understood. He turned to the squad leader of the demolition crew. "You weld that main entry door shut?"

"Yes sir."

"How long to get back in?"

"Sir?" The man looked profoundly shocked, the thought of reentering a ticking bomb anything but pleasant.

"If someone tried to get back in, how long?"

"Too long, sir. He'd get blown up trying."

As he figured. "Let's go, everyone!"

"Should we shoot the tires on that van, sir?" another asked.

Moyer looked in the direction of the shed from which his last few men were returning, and shook his head. If the Iraqi couldn't get it started in time, he would go up when the bunker detonated, which would be one hell of an explosion. If he *could* get it started, he had a fighting chance.

Good luck, you Iraqi bastard.

"No. Leave it alone," Moyer answered.

The collective roar of powerful engines and the sound of squeaking tank treads rose to a crescendo and faded rapidly to the north, toward the airplane. Shakir knew the charges were set to go off sometime after the assault team was at a safe distance, but how long was *that*? There was only one safe assumption: he had no more than a few minutes to hot-wire the van and get away.

Shakir scrambled to his feet and ran for the vehicle, amazed to find the key in the ignition and gas in the tank. He turned the key, and the small engine sprang to life. Another amazement! He seldom talked to Allah, but he did so now, a quick prayer of thanks and a glance skyward. Shakir carefully placed the stolen Uzi on the floor, snapped on the headlights, and roared off toward the east. Ansallah had already branded him a traitor, and now the man had an hour and a half's lead time in getting to military headquarters in Baghdad. Those facts kept going around in his head.

There was probably no way he could catch Ansallah, but he had no choice.

There were still two canisters left.

Southeast of Ar Rutbah, western central Iraq
Thursday, March 7, 1991—4:00 A.M. (0100 GMT)

Sandra had seen it in the small beam of her flashlight as they shut down. The image of the spoiler handle in the extended position had registered in some recess of her mind, but it had taken nearly half an hour to ferment into a conscious jolt. Now, shaken at the sudden realization, she fumbled for the flashlight, splaying the beam on the center console, hoping she was wrong.

She wasn't. When they had shut down, the spoilers had been left extended with the number-three pumps on, big as life. As the power had died, the hydraulic pressure had drained away from the accumulators.

"Oh God!"

Without pressurized hydraulic accumulators, they couldn't start the APU. Without the APU, there was no way to start the engines.

The combat team would be back any minute, maybe with a running gun battle in pursuit, and here sat their getaway vehicle, unable to move.

Sandra took in a ragged, frightened breath and scrambled down the ladder, fighting panic and guilt, finding the pilots under the left wing.

"Sirs, we've got a big problem. We screwed up. The accumulators are flat, and we've got to start pumping now!"

Sandra explained rapidly what had happened, and Doug shook his head as they scrambled to their feet. "*We* didn't screw up, engineer, *I* screwed up," he said. "You read the checklist, but I'm the one who said the spoilers were closed and disarmed."

Will put a hand on Sandra's shoulder as they headed back toward the crew entry door. "Sandra, get the hand pump going while I round up Backus and Casey and some of Johnson's men back there to help us. If we all take turns, how long to get them recharged?"

"Twenty minutes, if we're lucky, sir."

Sandra raced to the vacant midsection of the cargo compartment, removed the side panels covering the hand pump, and began working away at the handle as the others assembled, each of them taking turns, the tiny pressure gauges staying nearly at zero at first, then slowly, painfully, beginning to register, each stroke of the handle becoming more and more difficult as they built toward the three thousand pounds per square inch needed in each accumulator. Sandra was taking her third turn at the handle when word came that the assault team was on its way back with fourteen prisoners and the rest of Johnson's men.

Sandra ran a quick time-and-distance estimate in her head as she put all her strength into the downstrokes of the handle.

Jesus! That leaves us ten minutes to finish this!

The living black-and-white fresco by flashlight resembled some classic surrealist film on industrial oppression, one of them at a time pumping madly with beads of perspiration and heavy breathing marking the urgency of the effort, the others leaning over in support, watching the gauges and waiting to take their turn at the pump each time the count reached twenty-five, the noise of the struggle echoing off the walls of the empty cargo compartment.

The sounds were replaced all too soon by the distant roar of engines as the Bradley and the M-113 APCs charged around the open rear of the aircraft and up the ramp, their powerful headlights cutting the gloom of the darkened cargo compartment as they clanked toward the front under Phil Casey's guidance, rumbling past Bill Backus as he took his latest turn at the pump handle while balancing on the left side rail, barely clear of the huge machines.

The gauges were up to 2,400 psi now, which *might* be enough—if both accumulators were fired at once. Will and Doug had already headed for the cockpit as the troops began piling out of the APCs. One of the combat support team's motorcycles was the last to rush aboard, the team members immediately diving into the task of chaining the small convoy to the overloaded cargo floor.

Sandra sat in the engineer's seat and turned to Will, who had already slid into the pilot's seat.

"Okay sir, here's the deal. *If* we could keep pumping for another five or ten minutes, we could get the pressure high enough in each accumulator to use one for APU start and keep the other in reserve in case the first starting attempt doesn't work."

Will nodded, tracking her words carefully.

"*Or,* with the lower pressure we've got now, we'd have to use both accumulators at once, but that probably *is* good enough to get the APU running. If I'm wrong and we use both and fail, we have to start pumping all over again."

Sandra watched her commander's face and waited for a decision. *At least, thank you, God, no one seems to be shooting at us!* she thought.

Will's eyes locked on the flight engineer. "What do *you* recommend, Sandra?"

Major Moyer had already scrambled up to the flight deck, adrenaline pumping through his system, wondering why the engines weren't already starting. They still had the main cargo doors to close, and for that they needed the APU and hydraulic pressure. He looked back anxiously in the direction of the cargo compartment, then glanced at Sandra and Colonel Westerman, barely restraining himself from asking what the hell they thought they were doing just sitting there.

Sergeant Johnson's voice echoed suddenly up through the cockpit door. He had come through the crew entrance door at a dead run. "Hey, we've got lights out there at two o'clock!"

Doug, in the copilot's seat, looked to the right, catching instantly the unmistakable sight of headlights shining in the distance over the desert floor.

"There's someone out there, all right," Doug confirmed. "He's quite a few miles away, but he's moving."

"Sandra?" Will asked again, this time with urgency.

She surprised herself. There was no hesitation, even though she'd lost the gamble the last time she'd attempted a low-pressure double-accumulator start. Her voice sounded like it came from someone else, but her fingers were already selecting "both" on the hydraulic accumulator switch as she spoke the words, "Let's try it, sir."

"Go ahead, then." Will held up a set of crossed fingers.

"Battery switch on. APU clear, APU start."

The sound of battery-operated relays was followed by the slow, laborious windup of a turbine wheel halfway back in the aircraft.

"Come on, *come on,* COME ON!" Sandra watched the APU panel, scarcely breathing, waiting for the sound of ignition. The igniters were firing sparks now into the small combustion chamber.

"Whoever that is," Doug continued, "he's headed for the same road we're sitting on."

"How far away, do you think?" The question came from Moyer as he leaned over the jump seat and tried to follow Doug's finger.

"Maybe three miles, maybe a bit closer."

The sound of the APU catching and winding up on its own filled the airplane, the noisy, diminutive jet engine stabilizing at normal power. Sandra exhaled an unheard sigh of relief as she flipped the electrical power on line, snapping the number-three hydraulic pumps on as Doug began reading the Before Starting Engines Checklist and the loadmaster began closing the ramp and the clamshell doors 160 feet behind them.

"What about the INSs?" Sandra asked. The inertial navigation systems took nearly ten minutes to spin up and stabilize, and they had been running only two minutes so far.

"We'd better not wait for them, engineer," Will said. Doug looked at the distant lights again, gauged the danger of going with minimal navigation equipment, and nodded.

The lights of the vehicle ahead were now at one o'clock, still headed at right angles to their "runway" as Will punched the starter buttons and toggled the four fuel and ignition switches on one at a time. The Before Taxi Checklist complete and the doors confirmed closed at last, Will snapped the two INS controls to the "Nav" position. They might just align in time, he thought, but if not, they could dead-reckon.

Feeling the pressure to move immediately, yet trying to stay calm and deliberate, Will pulled on his night-vision goggles and released the parking brake, holding the 141 to the center of the road as best he could see it in the black-and-white display. Doug, they had decided, would keep his goggles off, monitoring things with an unaided set of eyes.

"Are we ready?" Will's voice was steady but strained, fatigue apparent in his breathing.

"Lineup check complete." Sandra's voice again, this time in the headsets as Will advanced power on engines two and three—the inboard engines—and keyed the interphone. "As planned, I'm going to use the inboards until we reach sixty knots, copilot, to minimize sucking sand into the outboards."

"Roger."

The outboard engines were each hanging over open desert. They all knew that bringing them to full takeoff power at low speed was like thrusting the nozzle of a shop vacuum into a pile of shavings—guaranteed to suck a torrent of abrasive material through the whirling blades. Too much sand and grit could cause an engine to fail, sometimes explosively.

Sandra glanced to her left at the backs of the two pilots, sensing the visceral tension, and feeling it herself.

As they accelerated down the highway, what had been a gentle tailwind suddenly became an insistent crosswind from the left, and by forty knots, Will had to use heavy left rudder to keep the twenty-foot-wide landing gear on the narrow forty-foot-wide roadway, working to track the cockpit and nosewheel to the left of centerline in order to keep the eight massive main wheels in the middle some eighty feet behind him.

The distant vehicle had stopped. Whoever it was seemed to be waiting a few miles ahead by the road, as if he could see the darkened C-141 rushing his way. Certainly whoever was out there could hear the engines by now. The possibility that a shoulder-mounted SA-7 missile could be loaded and cocked, waiting for their passage, was a shared, unspoken thought.

At sixty knots airspeed, Will brought the power levers for engines one and four up to takeoff power, and Doug made the final adjustment, the Starlifter finally gaining speed at the rate they were all used to. It was getting more difficult to see the edge of the road with the 141's body canted slightly to counter the crosswind. The images were too indistinct in the night-vision goggles, and Will wished he had kept them off and just flipped on the landing lights. Interpreting the fuzzy white images was like driving through a downpour at eighty miles per hour; staying on the road was possible, but not guaranteed.

No matter. They would be at rotate speed in a few seconds, and then be safely airborne.

Computed rotate speed was 128 knots, but at 104 knots the C-141 drifted to the right a bit too much, the movement escaping Will's notice at first until the tires of the right main landing gear suddenly left the edge of the road and rolled into a section of soft sand, dragging the nose of the Starlifter to the right as the right main wheels began to sink down, plowing twin trenches in the sand and throwing up a monstrous roostertail of debris as Will's adrenaline level shot to emergency levels. He came left rapidly with the yoke and the rudder while pulling on the control column, trying to lift the right wing, which was now descending with engines three and four and the right wingtip toward the desert floor.

Too late! The impact of something on the right side hitting the sand was marked by a horrendous scraping as Will, praying he had enough airspeed to sustain flight, yanked the aircraft off the ground and rolled it back to the left to wings level, letting it climb a few yards, then leveling, letting it accelerate to full flying speed, thankful that he still had flight controls.

"Pilot, number four's vibrating . . ." The remainder of Sandra's sentence was lost in the noise of a soul-shaking thunderclap as an explosion rocked the entire aircraft, the sight of a fireball on the right side lighting up the cockpit. The Starlifter yawed immediately back to the right as Will hung on, pulling off his goggles with his right hand so he could look at the engine instruments clearly. In a microsecond he considered putting her back down on the roadway, then rejected the idea. They were still deep in enemy territory, although the vehicle that had spooked them had obviously been no threat.

The number-four engine readings were zero, and number three looked unstable. One and two were running normally, and the airplane was flyable, but they had dragged number four in the dirt with disastrous consequences.

One hundred twenty-five knots and accelerating. Enough speed to climb. Will pulled on the yoke and brought up the nose.

"Gear up!" At Will's command, Doug's hand lashed out and snapped the gear lever up, the sound of landing gear retraction lost in the overpowering noise of the engine fire warning bell.

The red light was on in the number-four-engine fire handle!

"Engine fire, number four!" Doug announced, his head jerking right almost instantly. "Scanner—pilot. Check engines three and four! Jump seat, turn on the leading-edge lights, please!"

Almost instantly Doug keyed the interphone. "We've got a fire, pilot!"

Bill Backus flipped the lights on as he lunged for the right cockpit window behind Doug, pressing his interphone button on arrival. Sandra glanced left in time to catch the garish orange light playing on Backus's face through the glass.

"It's on fire, all right, sir!" Backus confirmed, his voice nearly half an octave higher than normal. "Dammit! Number four's still there, pilot, but it's on fire and it looks like the cowling's off. We hit something, sir! I think it exploded!"

Will pulled the interphone switch, trying to keep himself calm and handle it by the numbers.

"Okay . . . okay, we're through a thousand feet, let's come right here to a southerly heading and keep climbing. We have an engine fire on number four, crew. I'm pulling the fire handle and firing the bottle. Copilot, confirm number four."

Doug turned toward the fire handles located on the glare shield above the center console and monitored Will's hand as he grabbed the correct fire handle. Doug nodded and Will pulled it all the way out, shutting off all fuel, electrical, and other lines to the ravaged power plant. Will pressed the fire-extinguisher button then for number four as Doug fished for the fire warning bell cutout button and turned off the loud ringing.

The red fire light, however, was still on. The fire-extinguishing agent in the single bottle hadn't been enough to kill the flames.

"Fire's still going, pilot." The scanner's voice was strained. "It's roaring out there! We gotta be trailing flames for miles!"

"Okay . . ." Will began, then stopped, his mind racing through the options as he checked their climb through two thousand feet and toggled the rudder trim to the left. He was aware of his left leg hurting. He had been pressing hard against the asymmetric power on the left wing, trying to keep her flying straight.

"Doug, better shoot the other bottle into that engine."

"Roger." Doug snapped the right-side fire-extinguisher bottle switch to the alternate position and pressed the button, the amber light indicating its contents were gone.

"It's *still* burning, pilot!" cried Backus, still monitoring in the right-side window, the significance of what was happening— and what might happen if they couldn't get the fire out—beginning to dawn on him. "We better do something, sir! It's getting bigger!"

Will toggled the interphone. "Okay, crew, this is the pilot. Think hard and fast. What do we need to do to isolate that engine and that wing from all fuel sources? What can we do that we haven't already done?"

Will glanced at the altimeter. They were through four thousand now, and climbing nicely. *If we can just get the fire out before we explode!*

There were no more fire-extinguisher bottles on the right side. The options were fly fast or land.

"Pilot . . ." It was Backus again, a bit calmer, his years of knowledge of C-141 systems serving him well. "The right wing and that engine are already isolated from the fuel, sir. Sandra's already done that. The problem is, number-four fuel tank's breached. I can see all sorts of holes under the wing from the engine where it disintegrated. The right wing itself is starting to burn!"

"The right wing is *burning*?" Will asked.

Doug was nodding, his head craned back to the right. "He's right, Will. It's a goddamn wing fire. We've got to put it out or get this bird on the ground!"

The sight of a huge fireball exploding from the desert in the distance off their right wing as the bunker disintegrated went unseen by the crew of Scorpion-1. They had their own fireball to contend with.

"I'm going to try to blow it out with speed," Will said. He shoved the throttles on the remaining engines up to takeoff power and leveled the aircraft, watching the speed build slowly toward three hundred knots.

"I'm going to take her to red line," Will added.

"Do it, man. Quickly," Doug responded. "I know that isn't av-gas in the wing, but . . ." Burning kerosene might not be as explosive, but it was quite capable of ending their flight prematurely.

"Copilot, you coordinate checklists and get AWACS up when you're ready, and I'll try to keep us in the air. Okay?"

"Sounds like a plan, pilot," Doug replied. *Good procedure, Will.*

The speed passed 320 knots as Will kept the nose down and let the aircraft accelerate while Doug ran the checklists with Sandra and tried to find options. With most of the fuel in number-four tank consumed, the flames began to diminish, and within seconds, what had been a fifty-foot trail of fire towed across the Iraqi night sky gradually became a small fire, then an occasional flicker.

Doug looked back at Will at last, almost breathing. "Pilot, the flames are dying down, but they're not out. I'm going to call Crown, let them know what's going on . . . just in case. Take the point for a minute." Doug checked the frequency on a classified list and clicked the digits into the control head at the same moment the engineer reported excessive vibration on number-three engine. Will jumped back on interphone immediately.

"Could number four have damaged number three, scanner?"

Backus was nodding vigorously in the right-hand window. "Damn right, sir. That looks like exactly what's happened. Number-three cowling looks like it's drooping."

"Pilot, engineer." Sandra's voice cut into Will's thinking.

"Go, engineer."

"We're losing it, sir. Exhaust-gas temperature on number three's climbing, fuel flow's climbing, my vibration meter is climbing, and N2 RPM is going down. We'd better pull the fire handle before it explodes too."

Will nodded, his right hand reaching out for the number-three fire handle as a part of his mind screamed at him to slow down and involve the copilot. His fingers closed around the red T-handle as Doug caught the movement out of the corner of his eye, his mind focused on giving the AWACS the vital statistics on what was becoming an increasingly desperate situation. Will yanked the fire handle back, and number three wound down to zero, the aircraft yawing even more precipitously to the right, one half of the flight-control hydraulics now gone with system number one, which was powered by engines three and four.

Doug looked up and let go of the transmit button, hitting the interphone instead. "Jesus, Will! I'm not completely out of the loop. You wanna wait for the rest of us, for God's sake?"

Will had his hands full of airplane now, with the two engines on the left wing trying to push the aircraft to the right and roll it over. He countered it with left rudder and left aileron and trim. The aircraft could fly just fine on two engines, provided it wasn't on fire.

Doug was shaking his head and Will caught the movement in his peripheral vision. He had known the second he snapped off the engine that doing it that fast was dangerous. But it was done. "Sorry. It was coming apart."

Doug nodded and went back to the transmit button, knowing there was a wide-eyed controller on the AWACS somewhere over northern Saudi Arabia, holding in mid-heartbeat, wondering whether Doug's truncated transmission meant the end of Scorpion-1.

Will and Sandra coordinated the emergency checklists for number-three engine and number-one hydraulic system loss as Doug finished with the AWACS and returned to the interphone. Rescue choppers would be headed north to intercept them shortly, and Crown—the AWACS call sign—was sending the two F-15s that had been standing by on fighter combat air patrol duty nearby. Doug dialed in the UHF frequency to talk to the Eagle jocks as he finished the report. Will saw him reach for the radar transponder. "Hey! What're you doing?"

"They want it on, Will. Sorry, I should have explained before I reached. Same mistake."

Will ignored the error and the *mea culpa*. "They forgetting where we are?"

"They're not *sure* where we are. That's why they need us on radar."

"Along with half of Saddam's remaining forces." Will looked disgusted and on the horns of a dilemma. "Oh, hell, do it."

Doug turned the wafer switch to the "on" position and toggled in the code the AWACS had requested. The little green light went on, indicating radar beams were being received and sent back with specific identification codes. Will could imagine the number of Iraqi radar operators who were also leaning forward in their seats at the sudden activity on their scopes.

"How're we doing on the right wing, scanner?"

"Diminished, sir. The speed's keeping it down, but we're still burning out there."

"Pilot, engineer. You realize we're down to one electrical generator?"

Will had forgotten. For that matter, so had Doug and Bill Backus.

"Are we going to be okay on one?" Doug asked.

"Should be," Sandra replied. "But if we lose number-two generator, we're down to batteries."

The sudden roll of the aircraft to the right punctuated her words, Will and Doug both grabbing the control yoke and rolling it left as the sickening orange glow through the right window increased in intensity.

"What . . . now?" The voice was Will's.

Bill Backus had been kneeling in the right window for what seemed like forever. His knees and feet hurt, and he was losing feeling in his toes, but none of that mattered. He had been watching the fire's progress on the right wing and *willing* it to go out as the pilots flew as fast as possible to the south. Now, suddenly, something new had happened, and in the glow of the right wingtip area, he thought he knew what.

"Pilot, we've lost the right aileron. I mean, the mother is literally off the airplane."

Doug looked at the hydraulic flight-control switches on the overhead panel. "We'd better get the right side on tab op . . . hell, if it's gone, that's worthless."

"Turn the system-two aileron off," Will ordered. Doug repositioned the switch immediately, feeling nothing in the response of the yoke. That meant the scanner was right: they had only the left aileron to control the roll of the airplane, and only one hydraulic system powering that.

"Where are we, Doug? Anyone know?" Will asked.

Doug looked at the FSAS screen again, scanning the error messages the protesting INS systems had thrown at them for trying to move too soon. It wasn't trustworthy.

"Just a second," he said, toggling the transmitter to Crown, then turning back to Will as the controller on the special four-engine Boeing AWACS measured their position on her scope and reported it back in the clear.

"We've come about fifty miles south, Will. We're about sixty north of the border. She says there's another highway strip off to the left about thirty miles, but it's still Iraqi. There're a couple of Saudi fields ahead. If we can keep her coming south, she says to steer two-zero-zero degrees magnetic."

"*Pilot, scanner!* We're losing chunks of the right wingtip!"

Will had felt it too; the heavy weight of the left wing, which had substantially more fuel than the right wing, had been somewhat balanced by the excessive force from the two engines on the left wing. But lift was another matter. The right wing was beginning to shorten, and the 141 was rolling even more to the right. Will looked down at the yoke and realized they were about

out of time. He was almost full to the left with the control wheel. Any more loss of lift on the right, and they'd be uncontrollable.

Will took a deep breath and looked in Doug's direction. "Okay, crew, this is the pilot. I want everyone's ideas right now. If we try to make it across the border, we may lose lateral control and be unable to land without dragging a wing and breaking up. If we go down now, we have to set it in the desert in Iraqi territory. I'm almost out of left aileron. Scanner, you first."

"Sir, we're coming apart. Let's get down."

"Engineer?"

"Concur, pilot."

"Loadmaster?"

"Yes sir. I concur. If we land intact, we can drive out. I'll open the doors before we touch."

"Roger. Copilot . . . Doug?"

Doug was already nodding his head. He pulled the interphone switch to sum it up. "No choice, old buddy. Let's do it."

Will lowered the nose as Doug radioed their intentions to Crown. Iraqi forces to the contrary, they would keep the transponder operating all the way down so that Crown and the choppers could locate them. The American F-15s were already on their tail, Crown said, confirming the trail of fire from the right wing. More U.S. fighters were launching, and two A-10 Warthog tank killers were being scrambled to deal with any ground interference. The challenge was to make an intact landing and get everyone out.

Doug coordinated with the loadmaster to get Moyer's and Johnson's people ready for the crash landing, and pre-positioned to get out once they came to a stop on the ground—hopefully intact. They would toggle open the pressure door and clamshell doors while still in flight, and land with the ramp down to a horizontal position, with the landing gear down and full flaps. When they came to a halt, then, the troops could get the vehicles out even if they had to smash through the upper tail structure to do it, and with any luck they could get safely clear and be waiting for the choppers within a few minutes.

They were down to a thousand feet now and slowing, the fire getting worse as the airflow diminished over the ragged remains of the right wingtip. With hydraulic system two, the landing gear came down without trouble, as did the flaps. Doug brought on all landing and taxi lights as Backus called off radar altimeter readings starting at five hundred feet above the desert.

"Wish us luck," Will said.

"Piece of cake, pilot," Doug responded, noting with pleasure that the pilot was wincing.

"You know I hate that expression, copilot."

"Yep. I know."

"Two hundred." Backus's voice again.

The plan was to stabilize at fifty feet and increase power, using only approach flaps until they saw a likely-looking stretch of desert. Such a spot seemed to loom just ahead now, flat and barren, with just a hint of a small rise to the left.

"Center the rudder trim," Will commanded, Doug's hand doing just that.

The throttles were back to idle now, the speed down to 130 knots, just above marker, as Will let the nose down a bit.

"Flaps landing."

"Roger, flaps landing." Doug's hand ran the flaps to the final setting, the barn-door appendages slowing the 141 even more.

"I'm going to try to touch at around stick-shaker speed," Will said.

Backus had already relocated to the increased safety of the navigator's chair, leaving the rickety jump seat empty.

"Twenty feet, ten feet . . ." Backus stopped the callouts. They were so close now, any more were unnecessary.

The wheels touched, unlike any landing Will had ever made, the sound of rocks and debris peppering the underside of the fuselage reaching his ears immediately as he called for the spoilers and slammed on the brakes, bringing engines one and two into idle reverse. At least they were on hard surface. The ship decelerated through 120 knots, bouncing and bucking as the uneven ground shot by beneath. Will transitioned to nosewheel steering at last as they came through 100 knots, hope alive that they might really pull it off without bending the aircraft.

The change from hard-packed desert floor to shifting sand was impossible to see in the landing lights until they plowed into it, the deceleration throwing them all forward into the shoulder harnesses, the 141 pitching forward as the nose landing gear broke away with a loud report, followed by the sound of sheet metal scraping over the ground. The right wing dipped down suddenly, and the ragged remains of its right outboard structure caught the ground for the second time in an hour, yawing the Starlifter to the right. The fuselage rolled left and dipped the left wingtip in the onrushing sand, causing an even more violent yaw back to the left as the battered Starlifter heeled into a modified ground loop and shed the left outboard engine. Once again the right wing dug in, the ravaged right outboard engine number four ripped away from its mounting. At fifty knots, engine number three dug into the sand like an anchor, violently slowing the aircraft until the fuselage came to a stop sideways in a towering cloud of dust and debris, the right wing all but disconnected from the wing root, and fuel spilling everywhere.

There was silence at first, then the sounds of powerful engines from behind them as Doug and Will realized the APC drivers were following orders and trying to get out at all costs. Somehow they had stopped with the fuselage rolled no more than fifteen degrees to the right. Will lifted the PA microphone and shouted, "EVACUATE NOW! EVACUATE NOW!" The echoes of his voice boomed back from the cargo compartment. He considered hitting the overhead bailout horn, but it was hardly necessary and probably too loud. Shouting and the sound of heavy boots pounding metal floors, hatches opening and closing, and sheet metal being shoved out of the way could be heard behind them as the vehicles roared away.

Will reached up and pulled the fire handles for engines one and two in coordination with Doug as Sandra switched off the battery. Doug thrust the night goggles up on the glare shield in the front window to get them out of the way as he pushed out of his seat. The roaring of the fire that was now openly consuming the right wing increased, accompanied by the sounds of tracked vehicles moving away to the right.

Bill Backus had slammed his head into the navigator's panel as the aircraft lurched across the sand. He was conscious, but moving slowly, as Will worked to get him out of the seatbelt, which was jammed.

The orange glow through the right windows became a transference of intense infrared heat, telling all of them there were mere seconds left. Doug and Sandra joined Will in trying to get Backus out. The belt finally came open, and the four of them turned at last toward the cockpit door. Doug leaned back toward the side window for one last second, trying to see whether the others had made it clear. Suddenly, a small but violent flash of hot orange light from the cargo compartment froze all of them in their tracks.

Major Moyer had made sure the cargo bay was empty before he leaped on the Bradley and motioned to his driver to floorboard the machine. They had reassembled some four hundred feet forward and to the right of the fuselage. Moyer was astounded at how fast the flames were growing.

"Is everyone out?"

"No sir. I can't find the cockpit crew. They may still be in there!" The speaker was at a dead run back toward the aircraft. Moyer recognized the loadmaster, Sergeant Casey, and took out after him, literally tackling him within fifty feet.

"Are you crazy, man?" Moyer said. "It's gonna blow up."

"My crew is still *in* there. Let go!" Casey struggled to break away, and Moyer considered letting him, but at that moment the major's eyes landed in the vicinity of the copilot's window. The image of someone—or was it several people?—became silhouettes for a moment as the interior flared bright orange. A small fireball incinerated the crew compartment a split second before the perfect fuel-air mixture in main tank number three detonated and brought the remaining fuel tanks on the right wing into the explosive conflagration, the 141's main wing box and center fuselage disintegrating into shrapnel, the upper portion of the left wing cartwheeling far above the wreckage, fire and flame and smoke billowing up in all directions.

"NO-O-O-O!"

"DOWN!" Moyer grabbed Casey and pulled him into the sand as the wave of heat and the whistle of fragments tore past them, something potentially lethal skimming lightly over his back. He looked up then, expecting to see the deadly rain of metal falling in their direction as well, but most of it seemed to be coming down on the left side of the wreckage near a small rise that was flickering a garish orange in the dying light of the now-dissipated fire. The half-musical sounds of large sections of sheet metal thonging, thunking, and clanging into the ground as they fell from where they'd been propelled overhead completed the surreal scene.

"Jesus . . . they were in there when it blew . . ." Casey was somewhere between tears and shock, staring in utter disbelief at the ruined aircraft.

"I'm . . . afraid you're right. I saw them in the cockpit."

Moyer was stunned too. Why were they still aboard? How could three large tracked vehicles, all those troops, and a Humvee have made it out and the cockpit crew hadn't?

Yet he knew what he had seen in the window, and there would have been no surviving that blast.

"Come on." Moyer pulled Casey to his feet, but the sergeant couldn't tear his eyes away. "We'll take the Bradley around and make sure."

Moyer had to pull Casey most of the way back. Sergeant

Johnson joined them then, and Moyer briefed him on what he had seen. They piled inside the Bradley as Moyer checked by radio with the other drivers, ordering them to stay put, and directing one of his men to make contact with the AWACS to coordinate the rescue.

Moyer took the controls himself and ran the Bradley back to the wreckage, circling slowly, as the radio crackled to life.

"Sir, the AWACS says to get all survivors and boogie south right now. Joint-Stars is picking up Iraqi vehicles, maybe even tanks, headed south toward our position. They want us out of here, *now*."

Moyer acknowledged and stopped the Bradley, thinking rapidly. The remaining fire was still intense, but it was obvious that the fuel tanks had all fragmented, and there was nothing left to explode.

He searched on all sides, especially where the crew entrance door had been, crunching over all sorts of debris, but seeing nothing resembling a body or a survivor. He jumped out one last time and ran to the remains of the cockpit, now little more than the front windscreen frames and the forward floor, one charred control yoke twisted but still attached. He even tried yelling into the night and listening for anything resembling a human voice. There were plenty of sounds, but no voices.

No one in there could have survived.

He looked back to the east at the small sand hill, now embedded with fragments large and small, and covered with tank-tread marks from several circuits back and forth.

"Sir!" The voice of the radio operator again. "They're really yelling at us to move. Range of the other force is two miles!"

It was decision time. Sergeant Johnson was standing beside him, but he was the leader, and this was a potential battlefield.

"Anywhere we haven't looked, Sarge?"

The Air Force combat support specialist looked at the field of debris with disbelief, the image of the four cockpit crew members fresh in his mind.

"Yes sir. Everywhere. There are large pieces of the wing over there, and back behind us. But if the crew was in the cockpit when it blew . . ."

"They were. I saw them."

"Then there's nothing left to save."

Moyer stared at him for a split second, then nodded. They scrambled back aboard the Bradley and accelerated toward the other vehicles as he relayed the word to bug out. He had living charges to get to safety.

The dead would have to wait.

Crown (E-3 AWACS—Airborne Warning and Control System) Thursday, March 7, 1991—5:12 A.M. (0212 GMT)

Captain Margaret Ellis acknowledged the radio check-in from Porky 22, a flight of two Air Force A-10s, and gave them a heading perpendicular to the oncoming column of Iraqi vehicles as reported by the airborne Joint-Stars radar aircraft some fifty miles away. The crash site of Scorpion-1 was tagged electronically by a small symbol in the upper quadrant of her radar display. Bambi 52, a flight of two Air Force F-15s, had been shadowing the C-141 since just before their crash landing. They were now setting up to shoot a warning barrage of rockets in front of the Iraqi force.

Margaret had worked the Bambi flight before. Their slogan always tickled her: "Where Bambi goes, nothing grows." She was glad to have their firepower on the scene, but if the vehicles moving toward the crash site were Iraqi Republican Guard, this would probably be a job for the A-10s, and Bambi flight would simply be there to keep Porky from getting jumped.

Not that Saddam had anything left of an aeronautical nature to jump them with.

Things had been quiet in the AOR for the past few days with the so-called end of hostilities. She still wondered whether someone had thought up the phrase "area of responsibility" in order to get the acronym AOR, or vice versa. "War zone" made more sense, though it wasn't supposed to be a war zone anymore.

The strange mission of Scorpion-1 had brought the crew of the modified Boeing 707 AWACS back to the same adrenaline levels as before. Whatever it was they were doing landing in the middle of Iraq in the middle of the night with a high level of CENTCOM and Pentagon interest, the mission had turned to shit, and lives had already been lost.

"Delta one, you still with me?" Margaret asked, envisioning someone in an armored vehicle sticking the antenna of his hand-held radio out a hatch to reply.

It was highly unusual for an AWACS to be controlling ground traffic, but the contingent of Coalition vehicles from the crashed C-141 was racing south, and it was up to the AWACS controller—her—to marshal the airborne force to give them time to reach safety. Without the amazing picture of ground forces and vehicles generated aboard Joint-Stars, however, her electronic eyes in the rotating, saucerlike AWACS antenna would be her only source of information—showing her only the airborne picture. There would have been no way an AWACS controller could direct air cover to precisely target moving ground forces without the C3 radio relay from the new system.

"Crown—Jolly twelve—confirm your instructions, please." The rescue helicopter leader interrupted her thoughts as she attempted to take a sip of cold coffee.

"Jolly twelve, roger, hold quad forty-eight, stay up this frequency. What's your bingo fuel time?"

"Bingo at zero-three-thirty Zulu."

Okay, she thought. He'll have to start returning to base no later than 0330 GMT. The two big rescue helicopters that had been assigned to stand by to protect this mission would just have to keep orbiting for now. CENTCOM was calling some of the shots on this one, and they wanted those vehicles back across the border if possible. She had suggested they abandon the vehicles and airlift the people out, but she had been over-ruled.

That was always the way it went when the damned Puzzle Palace got involved.

Margaret leaned over to the hastily assembled radar screen on her right and scanned the ground picture once again. The information was streaming at light speed in real-time format from the Joint-Stars radar, which was a boatlike antenna array mounted on the belly of a once-retired, now refurbished, commercial Boeing 707. Like nothing ever used before in warfare, Joint-Stars could paint a living, moving picture of what was happening on the ground hundreds of miles behind enemy lines using Doppler-shift principles and high-speed computers. It wasn't even supposed to have been ready for combat use. She shook her head and snickered quietly, remembering the amazed and excited expressions on the faces of the civilian technicians who had been quietly developing Joint-Stars as a multi-year project and who had suddenly found themselves in effect drafted into immediate service in the middle of a shooting war.

But they had been ready, and were doing a fantastic job!

Satisfied nothing had changed, Margaret let herself relax for a minute, sniffing the aroma of a fresh pot of coffee from the galley nearby, which would have to wait.

The message Delta 1 had asked her to relay to CENTCOM a short while ago was still playing in her mind, the stuff of a good mystery. What on earth did they mean, "We polished off only ninety-eight bottles of beer?"

Margaret keyed the mike again, one more nagging thought in her head.

"Delta one, Crown."

The voice over the weaker hand-held radio sounded very strained. She wondered what he looked like. Air Force people didn't get to talk to Army Special Forces commando types very often. They sounded normal on the radio, but who could tell? That was a trained killer down there.

"Delta one here. Go, Crown."

"Before I wave off the choppers entirely, you are confirming that there is no possibility of survivors at the crash site, affirmative?"

He seemed to hesitate, then the transmitter clicked on.

"We could find no one, Crown. We did look. We're sure the flight crew was in the cockpit when it blew. If the bad guys weren't approaching, it might be worth sending in someone to take a final look, but with bandits on the way, it's not worth the risk. No one could have gotten out."

She picked up the tie-line and briefed her counterpart at CENT-COM, who was back in her ear in half a minute with the decision. There would be no risking the helicopters at the crash site. When it was cool, they could go in with a special team and take a look. Not now.

But she *was* to dispatch one of the choppers to pick up two particular members of the Delta team. The rest would proceed on across the border on the ground.

"Crown, Bambi lead, we got their attention just north of the crash site, but they've barreled onto the site anyway and seem to be stopping there. We haven't tried to take them out yet. It's still dark out here, but we saw what looked like two tanks and several smaller vehicles."

Porky 22 was only twenty miles out. Margaret turned her attention to laying out an initial target angle for a fiery little line in the sand south of the crash site. The Iraqi goons could poke around at the crash site all they wanted, as long as they didn't come after the Delta team now eight miles south and hightailing it for the border.

Now to vector a chopper in and alert Delta 1. Some major named Moyer and one other individual CENTCOM had referred to as "the courier" were going for a ride.

In the central "war room" command post at CENTCOM in Riyadh, Army Brigadier General Herman Bullock disconnected from a secure radio link with his boss and, as per his instructions, picked up the satellite telephone link to the Pentagon. He was aware the information he was about to pass would make its way from the Pentagon to the White House situation room within minutes. Two containers of the biological agent were still at large, as was the scientist who had created them. Worse, the containers were reportedly headed for Baghdad. The response back home would not be pleasant.

31°57′ N, 41°55′ E, south central Iraq
Thursday, March 7, 1991—5:30 A.M. (0230 GMT)

The sounds of a high-speed pass in the darkness by a powerful jet, the rattle of an airborne machine gun, and the impact of several rockets made an already surreal dream seem even more bizarre. But it wasn't a dream. Will Westerman regained consciousness slowly, his face full of sand, something very heavy pressing on his back. He struggled to turn his head, and succeeded at last. He tried to spit out the sand and grit in his mouth, realizing as he attempted to bring his hand to his face that his arms were pinned, his left one only lightly by his own body, his right arm by someone, or something, in the dark. Slowly he worked his left hand free and up to his face to clear the grit and debris from his eyes and nose.

Another sound forced its way into his consciousness, a raspy, insistent whisper somewhere to his left in the darkness, pleading for help. He remembered now almost tumbling down the crew entry ladder with the others, and he remembered running and a terrible explosion. But after that, things were fuzzy.

Who was that? And where the hell were they anyway?

The whisper sounded like Sandra Murray, the engineer, he decided. He listened some more. It *was* the engineer, a few feet off to his left. The whispering had started as he moved his hand to his face. The words made little sense at first, but he thought he caught something about being pinned.

He drifted back into a semi–dream state for a moment, the sharp edge of the pain in his head snapping him back once more. *I should answer Sandra, but what in hell is pushing me down?*

He began to probe then with his left hand and arm, unable to fathom what was on top of his body. There was some free space vertically around him to the left, but not much. He could see nothing in the pitch darkness at first, and it scared him profoundly, wondering if he'd been blinded. But no, there was some faint hint of light in the distance to the left.

Sandra was whispering again. He wanted to answer, but his mind was completely focused on figuring out what was happening, and why he couldn't move freely.

His left hand probed down his left leg, finding the flight suit intact, the nerves in his leg confirming the touch of his hand. He wiggled his toes and moved his feet. It was difficult—whatever was on him had wedged his flight boots toes-down into the sand and was resting on the heels—but he at least wasn't paralyzed. Thank God for that!

He probed upward with the palm of his left hand, puzzled at the slickness of the solid object pinning him. It was some sort of metal plate, very heavy, obviously, but not heavy enough to crush him. He had enough room to breathe in and out. Will tried to roll to his right to raise the slab, but nothing moved. It was going to be a major struggle to get out.

Slowly he became aware that there was another body beside him to the left. He moved his arm out laterally and felt the flight suit, and recognized a sticky dampness that had to be blood.

He should answer the whispering.

"Sandra? Is that you?" His voice came out as a hoarse croak.

The voice came back with renewed vigor, if still just a whisper.

"I'm over here! Thank . . . God you're alive! I thought . . . I was alone." She was trying to yell, but it was as if she couldn't catch her breath.

"Is that you I'm touching?" he asked.

"No."

"Then who's next to me?"

"Bill. Bill Backus. I can't . . . get him to respond. I think he's dead . . . but I can't see anything . . . and I can't get my feet out."

"Something very heavy is on top of me, holding me down. Same over there?"

"Yes. A big piece . . . a piece . . . of the airplane. I heard it coming . . . after the explosion. It . . . it hit . . . behind . . . fell over us. I thought . . . you were all *dead!*"

Doug Harris's face loomed in his memory. Doug had been with them, of course. How could he forget? But where was *he?*

If Sandra and Bill were to his left, was that Doug on his right?

He struggled to turn his head back to the right. There was no easy way to do it, so he simply dragged his face back through the sand, trying to keep his eyes and mouth closed.

He could see nothing on the right, either. This couldn't continue. Whatever this immense weight was, he had to get out from under it. He had to breathe!

He tried to lift it by arching his back, struggling to budge it, praying he would feel some give. Finally, with great effort, it shifted ever so slightly. Or was that only his imagination?

He had to know.

He struggled to bring his left forearm up and get his palm into the sand to provide enough leverage to lift, as if doing push-ups. Finally, painfully, he succeeded, throwing all his strength into it.

At first nothing happened, and then there was an unmistakable shift.

So whatever this is, it isn't immovable!

"I felt that! Keep pushing!" Sandra cried out, her voice still hoarse.

Will didn't answer. He could hear her, but his mouth was now facing the other way.

Will took as deep a breath as he could and fairly yelled at the body to his right, *"Doug?"*

Nothing. A wave of claustrophobia passed over him then, the temptation to scream and flail almost overwhelming. He willed himself sternly to calm down and analyze the situation, just as he had done in one of the survival schools when they tested how well aircrew members could put up with cramped spaces. His head hurt terribly, though, and with his feet pinned and the immense weight on his back, being logical and calm was an agonizing effort.

At last he sensed movement to his right. Doug—if it *was* Doug—was beginning to respond, so at least he was alive. But they had to get out from under whatever this was.

Another round of gunfire and explosions suddenly echoed through the metal that was lying on top of them. The sounds of a low-flying jet followed.

He raked his face back through the soft sand to the left side again, blowing and spitting sand, remembering all the cautions about germs in the desert. Not a hell of a lot he could do about that now.

"Sandra?"

"Yes."

"What's going on out there?"

"I don't know. I think . . . our people left. I tried . . . to yell, but I couldn't get any louder . . . than this, and . . . I guess . . . I guess they couldn't find us."

Will realized she was having to stop to breathe every few words.

"The firing started . . . a few minutes ago. I . . . don't know who's . . . firing at whom."

"Sandra, we've got to lift this thing off us. Can you lift?"

"No . . . I've been trying . . . this thing's crushing the . . . breath out of me."

"Are you okay otherwise?"

"Yes. I can wiggle . . . my toes and fingers. I just . . . can't . . . move around, or breathe."

The overpowering scent in his nostrils began to register in his consciousness. It was the smell of jet fuel, along with a burned odor. Will dragged his face through the sand once more to try to rouse Doug, calling out to him, wondering how badly hurt he might be. The passing seconds of silence seemed endless, but eventually there was a moan and a small flicker of movement as Doug began to come around, very slowly at first, then snapping to consciousness with the same disorientation and whispered questions Will had asked.

Doug was, as far as they both could tell, unhurt, with all parts intact and functioning.

They began to work together then to lift the metal slab that covered them. It was huge and heavy, but by alternating, they both managed to get into the same push-up position, forcing the roof of their metal prison up a few inches while Sandra pulled her feet free and gained some breathing room. She began crawling forward on her stomach through the sand toward what seemed to be a strip of light, dragging an unconscious Bill Backus along with her a few inches at a time.

"Sir? Will?"

"Yeah?"

"How big do you think this thing is? The light seems to be another five feet away!"

"I don't know. I don't see anything behind us, but to my left, a long way off, I see light."

"We may be under one of the wings."

Bit by bit, alternating lifting and crawling and dragging Backus, they inched forward. First Will and Doug would lift and Sandra would pull herself forward a few feet, then she and Will would do the same for Doug, and so on. Inch by inch. Struggle by struggle, the goal exhaustingly distant and always receding.

It seemed a major accomplishment, then, when at long last Doug pushed one more time and suddenly felt something on his face, finding himself close enough to the edge of their prison to get a glimpse of the outside world. He could make out the first hint of dawn painting the horizon, and could feel the luxury of a small breeze leaking under the metallic edge, a feeling so grand he hated to report it to Will and Sandra until they could feel it too. It was the light at the end of the proverbial tunnel, water at the end of a drought, and food at the end of a fast, all in one. But as he struggled for the self-discipline not to make a sudden, all-out attempt to push free at the expense of the others, something else reached his ears that was deliverance itself.

Voices! He had heard them, he was sure, along with the sound of vehicles somewhere to one side or behind them, noises of tank treads.

The APCs!

So they're still looking for us! Thank God!

"Will! Our people are still out there. You hear them?"

The sounds seemed far away. Will strained to hear as Sandra wiggled closer to another sliver of light to their left.

"Should we start yell—"

"Wait! Wait a minute. Quiet!" Sandra cocked her ear and closed her eyes, trying to make out the words. She thought hard. There was no one on the attack team but Dr. Abbas who spoke Arabic, as far as she knew, and he had escaped. That wasn't English!

Sandra turned her head back to the interior gloom, her whisper edged with alarm.

"Oh God, those aren't our people! They're not speaking English. What do we do?"

Doug's heart sank as Will answered. "Shhh! Keep still and quiet."

There were footsteps then, and more clanking noises getting

louder fast as a tank approached from the left, roaring into prominence, stopping with a deafening squeal of metal on metal, its big engine idling, the fumes curling under the edge of the slab with sickening efficiency. Will toyed with the idea of calling for help and surrendering rather than run the risk of being crushed by a tank rolling over an apparently worthless slab of Yankee scrap metal. Backus probably needed medical help, but then Coalition forces weren't far away, either. He tried to remember how far they'd made it to the south before the forced landing.

There were voices on the right as well, and the sound of various chunks of metal being thrown aside as the Iraqis combed through the wreckage. The voices were closer now, and he could feel Doug tense next to him in the gloom as a pair of combat boots came into view standing just inches from Doug's face. If whoever that was looked in with a flashlight . . .

Gloved hands suddenly grabbed the edge of the metallic slab that was at once imprisoning and hiding them. They could feel the metal begin to shift and rise as the soldier grunted and strained, changed his footing, and pulled at it again. A cascade of additional light spilled under the slab, and for a moment Doug's eyes met Sandra's, exchanging a wordless prayer. Doug looked away, his eyes falling on the unconscious face of the other flight engineer, Bill Backus, whose eyes were closed. Blood caked the man's forehead.

The owner of the hands, having received no help from his fellows, gave up all at once, letting the huge metal panel fall back with laughter and what probably passed for curses in Arabic while the three conscious crew members below felt the breath shoved out of their lungs, and Will's back registered a stabbing pain of protest.

They waited an anxious half hour or more, until the last sounds of engines and voices had long since faded into the distance.

"What do you think, Will? Coast clear?" Will's mind had

drifted elsewhere, and Doug's whisper made him jump. He had been reliving the mission, trying to find the fatal flaw in planning. The road they had used for a runway was narrow, but there were so-called highway airstrips all over Iraq. It was supposed to have had only hard-packed shoulders.

"Will."

"What?"

"You ready to get out of here?"

"Hell, yes!"

Their efforts took on a shared, fierce determination then, and within ten minutes, with Sandra and Will making one final, Herculean effort to raise it and hold, Doug was finally able to squeeze out, ripping his flight suit in the process. Instantly he grabbed the first piece of angular metal he could find and shoved it under the edge to maintain the height they had achieved. He found more, they lifted further, and bit by bit they shored up a gap of eighteen inches between the sand and the huge metal slab. Sandra emerged then, Doug helping her pull Bill Backus free as Will pushed from within.

At last Will, too, rolled into the clear, utterly exhausted. He lay there a few seconds before struggling to his feet, then turned back to the west, expecting to see the burned-out hulk of their C-141.

Instead, only scrap metal and the remains of the T-tail were visible in the cold predawn light.

"Jesus Christ. There's nothing left!"

Doug looked up, preoccupied with the structure that had imprisoned them, a structure that had formed the upper part of the left wing. It was at least fifty feet wide at one end, and at the point where they had been pushed to the ground beneath it, about thirty feet in width.

"Will, you know what this is?"

"What?"

"We were under the top of number-two fuel tank. See the boost pump inspection plate here? The damn thing came down on us, but we were in the middle. It probably weighs two thousand pounds.''

Sandra got to her feet after checking Bill Backus over and finding him still unconscious, but breathing.

The three of them stood then for a minute, brushing off the coating of sand, a light breeze blowing in their faces. The overcast of a few hours back was now giving way to partly cloudy skies, and the multitude of tread and tire marks heading south from the final resting place of their aircraft were now all too visible.

Will broke the silence. ''The Iraqis couldn't have made all those tracks. That has to be our force moving south.''

Doug nodded, all their eyes following the same escape path to the horizon, which was empty.

And the reality sank in at last that they had been left for dead.

For the longest time, it seemed to Sandra, no one spoke.

They looked at each other in shock, each with the same thought. Will voiced it aloud.

''We've got to get out of here.''

Doug looked over at him with growing alarm, recognizing the set-jaw look Will had always worn when he was completely determined about something. And he was determined to leave! But it would be getting hot soon, and they were in the middle of a desert with no water or food. Leaving the accident site was exactly what they shouldn't do.

''I think we need to hunker down and stay put, Will. Our side will be back, perhaps in helicopters. We can make a lean-to out of some of this scrap and—''

''Doug . . .''

''What?''

''Look at those tracks, man. Tell me the Iraqis didn't go south.''

''I don't know whether they did or not.''

''Exactly. Neither do I. But if they did, and they come back, which they will, they'll find us. We need to scrounge whatever we can for survival use and get out of here. I'm not going to end up in an interrogation cell in Baghdad!"

Doug looked at him with disbelief. *Is he really going to insist on walking across this goddamned desert?* Will read his expression, and fairly exploded.

"Okay, *what?*"

Doug raised both hands, palms up. "Hey, you're in charge of this circus, okay? But I'm still gonna be the good copilot, Will. What the hell are we gonna do for water? You thought about that?"

"We'll search the wreckage."

"Fine. Right. And if there isn't any, what then?"

Will looked back at the wreckage rather than answering. He had come close, so damn close, to ending up captured and in the Hanoi Hilton once. It had scared him for years. Given him nightmares. He knew he was overreacting and scared and probably panicked, but the thought of chancing capture left his heart racing, which was something he simply couldn't tell Doug. Especially not with Sergeant Murray along.

"Okay." He turned to Doug. "We'll look around. If we can find enough stuff to sustain us, water included, we'll go. If not, we'll stay, okay?"

"Okay."

"Okay, Sandra?"

Will turned toward her suddenly, finding her eyes on the horizon. She pulled at a cascade of hair blowing in her face and focused on him vacantly.

"What?"

"We'll go only if we can find fluids to drink. Okay?"

She nodded, and he noticed her shoulders were shaking slightly.

"You cold?"

That was a good excuse, and she took it gratefully. "Yes. It's chilly. You suppose my bag's down there? My jacket was in it."

They fanned out with a coordinated purpose, searching rapidly and efficiently, tracking the path of disintegration of their airplane like a team of accident investigators, trying to figure out where various things had been hurled by the explosion.

The items that had not been blown away from the wreckage by the force of the explosion were burned or melted. The water jug at the head of the cargo compartment was crushed flat, partly melted, and empty. But two cases of Saudi Cokes had been blown out to the side, most of them surviving intact as they dug individual holes in the sand. The ends of each can showed up as small silver disks, but, one by one, the three crew members collected enough to last at least a few days.

Food was another story. Six of the heavy-plastic-packaged MREs—meals ready to eat—were found. The rest had vanished.

Their crew's bags had been with the water jug, and were mostly shredded and burned. But somehow a few leather flight jackets had survived, and both Sandra and Doug outfitted themselves against what they knew would be chilly nights. Bit by bit the rest of the necessary items were stacked to one side as all three of them kept a cautious eye on the horizon.

There were small but important victories. The first-aid kit near the ramp had survived, as had one of the life rafts in the tail section, and for a second Doug was ecstatic over the possibility of finding a survival radio in one of the rafts and simply calling in the rescue choppers. The accessory pack to the raft had been split open, however, and the radio was gone. He took the light-weight canopy for a tent and the remainder of the survival kit, and left the rest.

Will was in the middle of the wreckage, fashioning a sled from a piece of plastic sidewall, when Bill Backus regained consciousness.

''Will!'' Doug's summons from a hundred yards away was too sharp to ignore. Will came at a trot, fearing the worst, then flooded with relief, finding the injured man who had been under his command for four years sitting up at last, held gently by Doug and Sandra.

"Bill! Thank God. How do you feel?" Will knelt and put his hand on Bill's shoulder. "We thought we'd lost you, old boy."

Bill smiled a shallow, painful shadow of a smile, and winced at the effort. His voice was almost inaudible. "I'm . . . um . . . not feeling so good, Colonel."

"I filled him in on what's happened, what we're planning, and why," Doug reported. "His chest hurts, and it sounds like broken ribs."

"You rest, Bill. We're gonna fix up a sled and let you ride out of here in style."

They stood up, and Sandra stood where Bill couldn't see her and motioned Will over.

"I'm not a nurse, but I've had a lot of first aid, sir. I remember pulling him off a rock when we were struggling to get out. I think he fell on it, full force."

"You think there's more than broken ribs?"

She nodded gravely. "Collapsed lung, internal injuries, possibly internal bleeding. I'm not sure."

"Well . . ." Will began.

"What I *am* sure about is this. If we don't get him to a hospital soon, we could lose him."

Will looked off into the distance at the sunrise, estimates and probabilities all telling him discouraging things. A sigh told Sandra he understood the urgency.

"Let's get moving." There was nothing else he could say.

By 8:00 A.M. they were ready, Bill strapped to the makeshift sled amid the stack of supplies gleaned from the wreckage, the whole affair attached to a crude harness for the three of them.

"There's nothing but desert to the south," Will said. "We'll head southeast. Ten miles or so, then we hole up until night. Okay?"

"Ten miles?" Sandra looked shocked.

"We can probably pull this thing at three miles per hour, and I figure we can walk for three hours before it gets too hot, and that's nine miles."

"How far to friendly forces, sir?" Sandra asked.

Doug and Will exchanged glances. Sandra hadn't heard their previous discussion, but there was no reason to deceive her.

"One hundred fifty miles or more to the Coalition lines, *but...*" As he feared, she looked crestfallen, defeated, and he hurried to continue. "But the border's only fifty or sixty miles south, and we're likely to find a road."

Sandra's face betrayed despair as she worked to keep her voice steady. "That's ... fifteen to twenty-five hours of walking, provided we can keep up a good pace and nothing's in the way. Bill's ..." Her voice trailed off. "There are minefields out here, too, you know."

"What do you suggest, Sandra?" Will felt suddenly very tired and very unsure of himself. He wasn't angry with her, but he wished they could just start walking and to hell with the consequences. His back hurt, his head was still pounding, and there was nothing to be gained by arguing.

"I ... " Sandra began, reading Will's eyes as she tried to hold the enormity of what they'd been through, and where they were, at bay.

"You're right," she said at last. "Let's go."

As Sandra made some final adjustments, Doug put his hand on Will's shoulder and studied his face.

"If our choppers come, this will have been a big mistake. You know that, right? You've considered that?"

Will nodded.

"All right," Doug said. There was neither rancor nor resignation in his voice, and for that Will was glad.

The three of them adjusted their shoulders to the jury-rigged harness with Sandra in the middle, and stepped off together in a loose cadence, the makeshift sled with Backus and the supplies offering surprisingly little resistance through the sand.

10

Central Iraq, Ar Rutbah–to-Baghdad highway
Thursday, March 7, 1991—8:30 A.M. (0530 GMT)

Shakir Abbas jerked the steering wheel back to the left to regain the highway, cursing himself for falling asleep again, his heart pounding suddenly and his system awash in adrenaline. He had drifted off the ravaged road twice before, fatigue transforming the endless image of featureless concrete on featureless desert from mesmerizing monotony into the undulating, dreamlike shapes that had whispered to his subconscious from somewhere to the right. They were specters singing siren songs, evaporating each time the wheels of the speeding van rolled off the edge of the washboard highway surface and onto the far more serious washboard of the hard-packed shoulder, the sudden, seismic vibrations all but loosening his teeth and bringing him back to consciousness.

Wake up! Wake up! This is ridiculous!

He was appreciative of the clouds. If the sun had been out, it would have been worse. He knew that well from experience. All his life, whenever he was tired, sunshine had been as irresistible to him as a warm, fuzzy blanket to an exhausted baby—an instant narcotic.

But the gray, endless overcast had held the sun at bay as he raced eastward, pressing the gas pedal as hard as he dared while hoping that somehow he could catch up with Mahmed Ansallah.

Hopeless. Why even try? If I can't find him, then I collect Saliah and the children and try to get back to Saudi.

It wasn't much of a plan, but it filled the apprehension with some form and substance, directing the intensity of purpose that had propelled him through the dawn.

Ansallah was a fool. A sullen, distant young idealist with an aptitude for biochemistry, but the most miserable of researchers because he was not patient. Shakir did not dislike him. He simply didn't trust his lack of discipline. Time after time his assigned experiments had had to be rerun because Ansallah had let frustration lead him to try a shortcut, compromising his results. He couldn't really know what he was carrying in that van somewhere ahead. In clinical terms he did, of course. But there was something human missing in anyone who could confront the horrible threat to life contained in that canister and still contemplate handing it over to the military—*any* military.

Thank God the Americans did not ask me to preserve a sample for them.

He would have refused, of course. At least he was sure of that. The horrible culture he had created must be completely, utterly destroyed. Every last viral molecule of it.

Shakir's thoughts drifted back to the frantic dash away from the commando team. He had heard the departing C-141 transport as he raced away from the lab, but had made no effort to watch the takeoff. They should be safe now, both the big colonel who disliked him and the more friendly one who had seemed genuinely interested in, as well as frightened by, what Shakir had to say.

Now, of course, they would be cursing him, those Americans. They would assume that he had been some sort of double agent all along, though what such a "mission" would have accomplished for Saddam would be a puzzlement. Yet the fact that he had escaped would damn him in their estimation, and it hurt inside to wonder if there was anyone left who respected him—including he himself.

But his self-respect was not at stake. Shakir brought himself up short, sitting up a little straighter in the dusty seat of the van and setting his jaw.

Maybe I have acted late, but at least I have acted.

Bombed-out and burned-out hulks of vehicles and tank trucks had been flashing by at intervals since he had joined the main highway, which ran from Jordan to Baghdad. The Coalition had made a mess of it, but the traffic was still moving, and he'd had to pass several slow-moving, Baghdad-bound trucks coming in from the Jordanian border, filled, he was sure, with the very things the Jordanians were not supposed to be sending because of the embargo.

He had also passed a line of mobile Scud missile launchers headed west, and wondered what other acts of desperation Saddam was planning in his fog of criminal madness.

Shakir glanced at the speedometer, which now registered 110 kilometers per hour. The road was finally clear ahead again, and he saw nothing but flat desert on both sides with occasional lost hulks of various broken-down and abandoned vehicles alongside.

What was that?

Hitting the brakes at 110 kph was not the best of plans, but as the van lurched and protested, Shakir's right foot held the pedal hard, his hands steering the weaving vehicle as it slowed rapidly, the image that his eyes had seen but his mind had been slow to process having suddenly coalesced.

A half-mile behind, off to the right of the road and missing a wheel, had been a white Toyota van, with two men sitting to one side!

There could not be this much luck in the world, he thought as he wheeled around and sped back. It could turn out to be someone else. There were, after all, at least hundreds of white vans in his country.

He crossed the road once again and pulled up behind the van. It was obvious it had hit one of the ubiquitous potholes in the highway and shattered the right wheel assembly, and from the deep gouge marks in the desert, whoever had been driving had been faced with a genuine struggle to keep from turning over.

The two men did not get up as he approached, but the elation Shakir had felt began to turn to a knot of apprehension as he shifted to park and studied the face of the figure nearest to him.

It was indeed Mahmed Ansallah, the man who had probably already concluded that Shakir Abbas was a traitor.

Ansallah watched with emotionless curiosity as the stranger parked the familiar green van. Somehow it made sense that someone from the lab would come to rescue them. The fact that no one back there could have known about the broken wheel was immaterial and lost immediately in the shock of recognition as the face of his superior suddenly approached.

"Shakir? Is that you?" Ansallah scrambled to his feet, his eyes wide, the military guardsman doing the same beside him out of caution. "We thought you were dead!"

Shakir greeted Ansallah in a traditional embrace, then nodded to the guardsman, a Neanderthal he knew well from the lab. The man had the mind of a doorknob, which made him all the more lethal. Shakir was well aware of the pistol the soldier had pulled out, and was relieved when he saw the man stuff it back into his holster as they sat down cross-legged in the sand next to the crippled van. The traffic on the highway was sparse, the occasional passage of a truck or car making the setting even more desolate.

"We have no tea to offer, nor much of anything else," Ansallah began. "We were going to rest awhile, then try to flag down a military vehicle, but now that you're here . . ." He let his voice trail off, waiting for confirmation from Shakir that they were rescued. Shakir merely nodded, acutely aware of Ansallah's cold, suspicious stare.

"Mahmed, I have been on a very important, very secret mission for the government."

Ansallah looked at him without changing expression.

Shakir averted his eyes and continued.

"I know you and the others thought I had been killed. That was a purposeful deception."

"Where were you?" Ansallah asked with his typical, non-Arabic impatience.

"The nature of my mission and the locations involved are still state secrets I am not allowed to discuss. I would naturally like to, but . . ."

"Shakir, forgive my directness, but I am very familiar with how you felt about our last order to deliver the virus. You say we must never do this, then you disappear, and a burned body is found that is supposed to be you."

"And," Shakir broke in, throwing caution to the winds, "you assumed I had defected to the enemy."

Ansallah began to protest, but Shakir held up a hand. "Sandar told me this. He told me you were not convinced I was dead. Well, you were right, I was not dead. But you were wrong in thinking I was a traitor to Saddam. This is still my country."

"Why the trickery, then? Whom were you trying to fool? Our government thought you were dead, and Baghdad was frantic. Only you knew the formula. We searched your notes night and day and could find no clue, and you had refused to tell us."

"I have been your director for how long, Mahmed?"

Too long, old man, Ansallah thought, keeping his face impassive. Shakir was only twenty years older, but that seemed an eternity. He took a deep breath and answered Shakir at last.

"Two years."

"Two years. That's right. As director, have I told you about everything that goes on in our lab?"

"No."

"That's right, because while you have family political friends, I report to people even higher up. It was those people who determined that there was a spy in our midst. We even suspected you at one time."

As Shakir expected, Ansallah's eyes grew wide with shock. The consequences of being identified as a spy in Iraq were beyond the unspeakable.

Shakir raised a hand hurriedly to calm him down. "I quickly put a stop to that. My disappearance, though, was to see who did what when the lion was away. You acted properly. Others didn't."

The balance had shifted in a heartbeat, and a startled, frightened Ansallah was suddenly eager to please. Shakir ached to ask where the canisters were stashed, and to grab them and run. Fully half of his mental capacity was devoted to forcing himself to stay still and calm—to play out the scene—as he slowly coaxed Ansallah to talk about his colleagues in the lab and listened as a panoply of imagined intrigue and suspicions tumbled out of the young scientist's brain, enough to constitute a verbal dossier on just about everyone. Ansallah had indeed imagined himself as Saddam's personal representative in the facility. No wonder he had been such a poor scientist. He seemed to have spent all his time making notes on what everyone else was doing or saying.

Shakir had noticed the guard yawning earlier. Now he had slithered over beside the crippled white van and propped his back against it, and had gone to sleep, his snoring becoming increasingly audible.

"Ansallah," Shakir said at last, "who gave you the orders to deliver the two canisters you have before the main shipment?"

A look of sudden pride crossed the man's features, a look that just as suddenly faded to one of apprehension, a hunted look creeping into Ansallah's eyes as he tried to fathom which answer would satisfy Shakir. Danger signals were everywhere, and he must not speak the wrong words.

"I . . ." he began, " . . . *we* were ordered to bring the shipment to Baghdad."

"I know," Shakir answered hurriedly, "but you have only two of the containers. Why not wait for the main shipment tomorrow?"

"I don't have two, I have one," Ansallah responded. The words were not what Shakir had expected. He had two canisters, didn't he? Not one. Shakir concluded that he had somehow misunderstood, as Ansallah continued, "I . . . wanted to deliver at least one of them myself."

"To whom?" Shakir asked.

"The general who will use it to strike fear into the enemies of Iraq. If you had been alive, of course, I would have . . ."

"No, no! Go on. I wasn't there, so you *were* entitled to act. What else?" Shakir wondered if the feigned solicitous words were convincing enough, but Ansallah smiled and pushed his chest out another inch. "I knew General Sumed Hashamadi would be the first commander to have the honor of unleashing our weapon, and I wanted to put it in his hands myself. What they have done to our country must be avenged. Have you seen Baghdad? Have you seen what the Yankee bombs have done to us? I can't wait until they start dying by the thousands in agony, just like those dogs from Kuwait we tested it on. Remember how they screamed and cried? I want to see the Americans and the British and the Egyptians and Iranians, all the enemies of God, die the same way, in screaming agony!"

Shakir held his expression tightly in check as he watched rage and hatred consume Ansallah's mind. He let it subside before speaking again.

"Do you have any idea, Mahmed, how dangerous this virus is to Iraqis, too?"

Ansallah snorted. "Of course. But no more dangerous than the Americans who murdered my brothers."

There it was. Shakir had forgotten the two Ansallah brothers fighting in Kuwait.

"You lost both of them?"

He nodded, flame in his eyes.

"I am sorry, Mahmed."

"You understand, then?"

"Yes, but I must disappoint you." Shakir watched Ansallah's expression change again to puzzlement. "General Hashamadi is not to receive any canisters. These must go to headquarters in Baghdad, and I am ordered to deliver them."

Ansallah considered that for a few seconds. This was his leader, his commander. Since Shakir was alive and still in the country and driving an official vehicle, he was undoubtedly acting on official orders, and defying him could be fatal, especially now that the army was retreating and a civil war was beginning.

But he had referred to "them."

"Shakir, I have only one canister. General Hashamadi was sent the other one three days ago."

A courier had shown up at the lab, he said, in uniform, flown in by helicopter. The written orders were from the high command and signed. Ansallah had delivered the canister himself.

It was Shakir's turn to be off balance and confused, but he struggled to hide it as he stood up. The guard came awake at the same instant and leaped to his feet, and Ansallah stood as well.

"I'll send a car back for you in a few hours," Shakir lied.

The guard shook his head. "No. You take us in your van, Doctor."

"Look, I have no time to waste, and you two should go back to the lab."

Ansallah seemed passive, but the guard, for some reason, was not about to be left at the side of the road. As Shakir watched in amazement, the soldier unholstered his gun and aimed it somewhere in the vicinity of Shakir's feet. "We'll go in your van, Doctor. Now."

Shakir stood a second in thought, then nodded, watching for the guard to relax, which he did just a bit. Shakir motioned behind him and addressed Ansallah. "First there's something I need to show you. Wait here."

Praying that neither would follow, he walked the few steps back to his green van and opened the passenger door, reaching in and pulling the Uzi from the floorboard, feeling for the safety. He had cocked it hours ago, just in case.

The sound of footsteps shuffling through the sand announced the approach of the guard, and Shakir pulled himself back from the van in one calculated motion, pivoting to his left to hide the gun until he had swung completely around and brought its muzzle almost point-blank to the stomach of the soldier, who had made the mistake of reholstering his pistol.

Shakir had never killed a human being before. He had never thought of doing such a thing. The horrible testing of the virus on two hapless Kuwaitis had been an army atrocity carried out in spite of his protests. He had fired guns because the military insisted that the scientists at the underground lab know how to defend themselves and their project. But the sudden staccato burp of lead from the deceptively small Uzi caught Shakir off guard as he pulled the trigger. He was unprepared for the rush of noise, and the look of horrified surprise in the eyes of the guard whose lower chest and stomach had just been blasted away, his heart beating a few final, futile strokes as the ruined left ventricle deprived the brain of consciousness and the muscles relaxed, the body, blown backward a few feet by the force of the bullets, falling in a heap in a growing pool of crimson.

Ansallah's shock was visceral as well, but his response was catlike. As Shakir stared for a second at the body by his feet, Ansallah sprang behind the white van and drew his own pistol, cocking it loudly and peering around the corner to draw a bead on Shakir as he yelled in a shaky voice, "What are you *doing*, Shakir? Why did you kill him?"

"I . . . I have my orders, Mahmed. He would not listen. Put down the gun. I have no desire to hurt you. I didn't want to hurt *him*."

Ansallah's voice was rising to somewhere between a shaky, panicked cry and a scream of fright.

"Why did you do this? Why, Shakir?"

"Put the gun down and step out in the open, Mahmed. I won't hurt you."

Ansallah wasn't listening. "He was Republican Guard, Shakir! You have killed a Republican Guardsman!"

"Ansallah! Drop that gun and come out."

Ansallah was shaking his head, slowly at first, then with rapid determination, fully visible through the windshield of the white van.

"No. I don't trust you. I think you're trying to stop Saddam." Ansallah darted suddenly to the driver's side of the white van, putting the bulk of the van's body between himself and Shakir. Ansallah pulled the door open then, as if getting ready to start the engine and drive away.

What is he doing? That van's lost a wheel!

Shakir's puzzlement lasted only a second. As Ansallah moved to lean into the van, the image of the canister somewhere in the vehicle appeared in his mind, and in an instant Shakir had jumped over the body of the guard and raced to the right rear window of the van. Ansallah was struggling to lean past the driver's seat and reach a small Styrofoam box on the floor behind the passenger's seat.

"Stop! Don't move!" He knew the commands would be in vain, and his blood ran cold, but Ansallah could not be allowed to touch the container. Shakir yelled again, smashing the glass with the barrel of the Uzi in one lightning-quick motion, making sure Ansallah heard his warning as the younger man's right hand snaked toward the box, the pistol forgotten on the seat. Nothing else mattered to Ansallah but getting control of that canister, saving it from Shakir, and saving it for Saddam and his generals. His eyes were completely round with fear and determination, his mind focused on nothing else, and Shakir saw him launch his

body across the seat, his hand poised to snatch away the lid and grab the canister.

The Uzi was aimed this time, held in Shakir's shaking hands through the broken glass of the window, the barrel pointed at Ansallah's head and upper body. Shakir's finger held the trigger, waiting for the echo of his final scream to Ansallah to register and cause him to back off.

He knew, however, that it was hopeless.

Ansallah's hand touched the box, and Shakir's finger responded.

The now-familiar staccato report of the exploding cartridges as they hurled a lethal train of lead through the disintegrating head and torso of Mahmed Ansallah had a tragic inevitability as the entire sequence of horror seemed to stretch into slow motion. He saw the body flung back toward the steering wheel, the right hand shattered by the bullet stream, and was aware that with cold precision he had kept the aim above the box containing the deadly canister. But suddenly he realized the bullets were no longer firing. They hadn't been for some moments, though the ringing in his ears belied that truth. The clip had been exhausted, and he finally relaxed the pressure on the trigger and stepped back, shaken and dazed, then propelled into action by the sure knowledge that someone on the nearby highway must have witnessed the murders.

Shakir knelt by the right rear wheel of the white van and let the adrenaline shake him, for how long, he wasn't sure. The sound of a truck or car passing filled his ringing ears every few minutes, but the vans were parked in such a way as to hide the bloody scene from the view of anyone passing.

At last he forced himself to stand and slide open the white van's door, suddenly desperate to verify that the box he had killed for did, in fact, contain the canister.

It did.

Shakir's actions became deliberate and directed then, as his mind seemed to detach. He pulled the shattered body of Ansallah all the way into the van and closed the driver's door, then dragged the guard's body to the van as well and loaded it inside. He took one of the two jerry cans of gasoline for extra fuel, and used the other to douse the interior of the white van, soaking the two bodies thoroughly.

The canister was another matter. There was no kind of fire he could build rapidly that could reach a thousand degrees for five minutes, yet he had to be sure the virus was completely dead.

There were two choices. Take it or bury it. If he took it, it could still be used. If he buried it, the chances of anyone actually finding it were remote. The canister itself was glass-lined stainless steel. It could lie in the desert for a hundred years without risk of leaking. He could always come back later and neutralize it. Right or wrong, that seemed the best course of action.

There was a small wadi off to the south of the roadway, and Shakir walked to it, digging the deepest hole he could in the north wall and burying the canister without a trace, carefully spreading the sand back into place before leaving. He triangulated on a nearby rise in the terrain to the northwest, and another to the northeast, making careful notes on the location before returning to the vans.

There had been some military traffic on the highway all morning, but now there seemed to be less traffic of any sort, and Shakir waited until there was nothing in sight before lighting a small trail of twisted rags found in the van, the end of which lay in a puddle of gasoline that would ignite the van. He was three kilometers to the east when the sight of flames engulfing a speck of white metal bloomed in his rearview mirror.

Shakir drove for an hour before his self-anesthetized mind returned to the reality around him. General Hashamadi had last been the commander of the forces arrayed against the rebel Kurds in Kirkuk, which lay nearly 250 kilometers away, through countless military convoys and checkpoints. Somehow, he not only had to reach the general, he had to get possession of the most powerful weapon the man had ever commanded.

Baghdad lay dead ahead less than 150 kilometers, and to the south of Baghdad a few miles, his wife and children waited. He prayed they were all right. He could be there in just a few hours, load them in the van, and drive to safety. It would be foolhardy, if not suicidal, to go after the remaining canister. He had no orders, and he was already a dead man officially. Going to Kirkuk would be an act of desperation as stupid as Ansallah's suicidal attempt to reach that Styrofoam box in the face of an automatic weapon.

But, try as he might, the logic could not overwhelm the determination to right the wrongs, and recapture the genie.

And if those two men he had just murdered were not to have died in vain, he could do no less.

Shakir gripped the steering wheel a bit harder and began mentally plotting the course north.

Mildenhall Air Base, England
Thursday, March 7, 1991—12:00 noon (1200 GMT)

The sight of a uniformed major striding resolutely into the tranquil beauty of the Mildenhall woods on the west end of the base told Colonel Richard Kerr volumes. He recognized the major. He had spent most of the night in the man's airlift command post, monitoring the progress of the Balair DC-10 and Operation Scorpion Strike.

After catching a flight to Mildenhall from Keflavik the previous day, and spending most of the night in the command post, he had been exhausted. The minute the message had arrived that the C-141 had lifted off again from the Iraqi desert, he had headed for bed, still shaking his head over the call from Will Westerman that had set the whole thing in motion a few days before. They hadn't seen each other for a year, and suddenly his old pilot-training roomie had called from somewhere over the Atlantic in a presidential jet, trying to piece together a sneaky-pete mission by secure satellite phone. He had needed help with the logistics and clearances, and Kerr had responded immediately.

Kerr looked at the last of the ice cream cone in his hand, an indulgence from the nearby BX. He finished it in one bite and decided to let the major find *him* as he stayed put on the bench, enjoying the warmth of the sun.

The sun was straight overhead now, the temperature in the mid-sixties, with small, puffy cumulus clouds shooting by above in the teeth of a strong breeze that whispered at the surface through the pine needles like a gentle zephyr. He loved the UK in the springtime.

"Colonel Kerr!" Major Ben Campbell waved his hand and called out as he spotted Kerr and moved in his direction, then sat on the adjacent bench.

"Sir, apparently everything went to hell with the mission after you and I left last night." He filled Kerr in, holding back the one piece of information that had caused him to search out the colonel in person.

As the two of them had waited through the night, Kerr had regaled him with war stories of Colonel Will Westerman and the friendship that had begun in undergraduate pilot training. They were the type of stories senior officers love to tell to junior officers, and that junior officers have to pretend they enjoy. After that, the name Westerman was easy to spot.

"Sir, the names we had for the pilots were wrong. There was a crew change before the mission departed and two other pilots got on. One of them was a full colonel from McChord, a reservist named Harris, Douglas Harris, and—"

Campbell saw Kerr's face go sallow. He hadn't expected that reaction from the name of the first pilot.

"You know—uh, knew—him, sir?"

Kerr just nodded, Doug Harris's face swimming into his mind's eye.

Major Campbell continued, watching Kerr's face carefully.

"Sir, your friend, Colonel Westerman?"

"Yes?" The answer was impatient.

"He was the other pilot. He was killed, too. I'm sorry, sir."

Al Hajarah desert, south central Iraq
Thursday, March 7, 1991—7:00 P.M. (1600 GMT)

The purple twilight slowly engulfed them as Doug Harris sat with his back against the wall of a dry streambed and watched the stars emerge. Riptides of emotions were breaking back and forth on the shore of his resolve, one moment leaving him in silent, paralytic fear, the next propelling him to a false high of overconfidence. He knew fatigue was the driving force, but he couldn't stop the process, and he dearly wanted to hide it. The last thing they needed now was for one of them to start unraveling. *After all,* he reminded himself for the fiftieth time, *we're only a short distance from the border, the weather is reasonable, the enemy is all but defeated, and we've got food and liquids.*

But Bill Backus was dying before their eyes. It didn't take a surgeon to see that the big, affable sergeant was getting progressively weaker.

Will was still asleep, snoring soundly a few feet away, but Sandra had awakened after only an hour of rest to watch over Bill, who was drifting in and out of painful consciousness, his breath coming hard.

Bill Backus moaned softly again, and Doug could hear Sandra move to comfort him in the darkness off to the right. With clearing skies, the moon would rise in a few hours, and they could walk on in perfectly visible conditions.

The sled had proven harder to pull than they had imagined. When the sand was soft and easy for the sled to traverse, they had no footholds in the shifting dunes. When the surface was hard and easy to walk, it held on to the makeshift sled with a malevolent vengeance.

Will figured they had come no more than six miles before deciding to hide in the streambed.

Doug figured five.

What ate at them were the sounds they had heard before noon, the sounds of helicopters and jets coming from the direction of the crash site they had left.

It meant they had successfully evaded their own rescue force.

Will awoke on his own suddenly at 10:30 P.M. Within a half hour they were on their way again, their footfalls coming with a numbing cadence, the task of pulling together now achingly familiar, the navigation accomplished by reference to the star field overhead. There were no artificial lights on the ground, but occasional lights in the sky marked passing planes. They were Coalition planes, of course. If only that survival radio had been in the kit! Doug had concluded the Iraqis had taken it, probably to try tricking U.S. rescue forces the way the enemy used to do in Vietnam.

Midnight came and went, as did three more small wadis. They drank another Coke, nibbled on a shared MRE, and moved on, none of them speaking for a long time, until Will called for a rest.

"How is he, Sandra?" Will watched as she carefully checked Bill's pulse and temperature, trying not to rouse the unconscious engineer.

"As stable as possible, I guess."

Sandra looked up at the tall colonel, starkly visible in the soft moonlight. His voice was gentle, she thought, and tinged with deep concern for the sergeant.

"Do you remember Operation Babylift in Vietnam? The C-5 that crashed just after takeoff while bringing the orphans back stateside?"

Sandra searched her memory. She had joined the MAC reserves in the late seventies, and Vietnam was ancient history to her.

"I think I heard about it."

"Bill was a loadmaster in charge of the rear passenger section, upstairs. He was injured, but he personally saved a bunch of people, including some of the children. Very selfless and heroic. They had to force him to get to the hospital.''

"You were there, too?''

"Oh, no. No, I was flying F-4s in Thailand. Bill was in my squadron at Charleston when I took over. You do know he insisted on coming last night, don't you? After he survived the crash at Sandy?''

"He told me," she said softly.

Doug had walked a few dozen yards away to relieve himself discreetly. Now he was back suddenly, excited about something in the distance.

"Both of you, come here a second!''

Doug was moving faster than he'd moved in hours. Being in the middle of a desert was as barren an experience as being adrift in an endless sea, and he had just spotted another vessel on the horizon—another vestige of human existence—hostile or otherwise. He hustled them to the top of a small rise, pointing urgently to the east.

"What *is* it, man? Doug . . . chrissake . . . hold up! What did you see?''

"Watch. Just watch for a second. See if you see the same thing!''

At first there was nothing. Their eyes had long since adjusted to the darkness, and the stars and moon made a soft carpet of whiteness out of the desert surface.

But there *was* something, something artificial, in the distance.

"What the hell . . .'' Will began.

"It's a searchlight, or a headlight, or maybe an airport beacon, just over that hill. Can't see it directly, but it's there!''

Will peered into the darkness as hard as he could, slowly losing control of the tight rein he'd kept on his hopes. If there were rescue forces on the ground looking for them, would their headlights look any different as they bounced and lurched over the undulating surface? Of course, Iraqi headlights would look the same as American.

The light pulsed again just over the horizon, indistinct, enticing, and gaining in strength each time.

They watched, barely breathing, until what had been the hint of a glow emerged as a fuzzy spot of light, coalescing then into a single point of illumination that twinkled and undulated—the way celestial fires often do when they first swim into view over a distant horizon.

Will was the first to sort it out, disappointment dashing diplomacy.

"Jesus, Doug, that's a goddamned *star*!"

Doug realized it, too, at last, as did Sandra, her buoyed hopes collapsing in an instant.

Will shook his head in disgust, his expression plainly visible in the moonlight, the litany of the day's disappointments running like a roster of shame through his mind.

The sound of a nervous giggle emerged from the left, an uncharacteristic sound that caused Sandra to jump, until she realized it was coming from Doug Harris. The giggle became a nervous guffaw and grew to a hearty laugh as Doug dropped to his knees on the sand, laughing uproariously.

There was no sound from Will, and when Sandra looked in his direction, expecting to see a smile, the moonbeams caught an inexplicable expression of pure anger that stopped her cold. Will stood in the night air and stared at his friend with profound fury.

It's so damned easy for you to laugh, Harris! It was always so easy! The words rang in Will's mind now as if spoken over a bullhorn, the irritation dislodging the lid on some long-shut wellspring of anger, the intensity of his reaction surprising him as it rose out of control.

Can't you see how much trouble we're in? This is no damned laughing matter!

Will struggled to hold the anger inside, but he was losing the battle. His fists were clenched as he watched Doug now sitting in the sand, wiping away tears, oblivious of the fact that he was the only one enjoying the joke.

"I'm . . . ah . . . sorry . . ." Doug said between waves of laughter. "I don't know why this is so funny! Ca . . . cathartic relief, I guess."

"Harris, for God's sake, pull yourself together and act like a grownup." Will's voice was tinged with disgust.

Doug's eyes came open then, Will's stern demeanor registering at last a level of disapproval that brought back many memories for Doug. He got up slowly, brushing off sand, looking up at Will as the taller colonel stood, hands on hips, a few feet distant.

"Geez, Will, lighten up! If I can laugh at our miraculously successful escape and evasion of a U.S. Air Force rescue team today, you can laugh at *my* mistake, okay?"

The answer was instantaneous, and almost a hiss.

"You just couldn't wait to say that, could you?" Will said, his words dripping resentment.

Doug stared back for a second before answering, his mind narrating familiar laments.

Goddammit, Will, you always did take yourself too seriously.

"I only brought it up," Doug said, "to point out, in case you hadn't noticed, that we're both human." He could see the twin coals of anger burning in Will's eyes, the compressed lips, the clenched fists. *This is nuts! He's really* angry *at me! Jesus!*

"Will, look . . ."

"Don't forget I didn't want you on this trip. You begged me to go, and like an idiot I let you."

Doug's eyes flared suddenly, his voice taking on an equally angry tone. "Now just a damn minute, Will, I seem to recall a few times back there I helped out just a bit . . ."

Will had no response for that. He *had* blown the air-to-air refueling, and Doug had saved the day, as he'd done with the near-midair. Like Gladstone Gander, the cartoon character, Doug Harris couldn't get it wrong, and he was going to rub it in!

Mate and checkmate, Will thought, *and you take the game again.*

Will stared at Doug, who was staring back, both of them shocked at the vitriol that had spilled without warning. Even in the subdued moonlight, the familiarity of Doug's face erased the years, and for a split second Will was back in Tacoma, watching Doug marry the only woman he had ever truly wanted. After years of taking girls away from Doug Harris—a shared joke that spanned their teen years and extended into adulthood—the one time Harris had turned the tables, it had been devastating.

And Doug had never known.

Sandra had watched the confrontation from a few feet away in growing distress. She materialized beside them now, rank and caution overruled by the apparent need for a peacemaker. Her voice shook slightly.

"If we're going to get out of this, we've got to work together. You two have to work together."

Will nodded quietly, and Doug did the same, the fire suddenly gone, and both of them feeling off balance.

Sandra, however, had worked herself up to a frenzy of intervention.

"You're both acting like little boys! We've got to stay cool and coordinated and stay friends. We've..."

Will reached out and put his left hand on her shoulder. She was shaking slightly.

"Sandra...it's all right." Will's voice was different suddenly, soft and friendly again.

"It's okay, Sandra," Doug added, his tone also completely different, "we've just...I mean..." Doug's voice trailed off as Sandra tried to continue.

"I just can't stand by and let you two..."

"Sandra! It's okay. Really," Will assured her.

She looked at Will, then at Doug, her eyes still wide. "You're . . . sure?"

At last Will laughed. Not much more than a chuckle, but a milestone. "We've known each other for over forty years now, Sandra," Will said, gesturing to Doug, "and I'm afraid there's a lot of baggage."

She nodded silently, fighting embarrassment, and broke away gently from Will's hand, turning to head back to where they had left Bill.

Will took a deep breath and extended his hand to Doug, who took it firmly. "I'm sorry, Doug. I guess I'm exhausted."

Doug nodded, but something was held in reserve. Maybe he didn't really know Will anymore. Maybe he had never known him.

"Forgotten," Doug said.

Will fumbled for the right phrase. "Maybe . . . maybe we should talk later."

Doug nodded.

They resumed the trek then, hours of endless footsteps toward the endless horizon leaving them physically and emotionally numb.

At five in the morning they topped a towering sand dune and found themselves staring at a building.

Not much of a building, but the three of them dropped to the ground and studied it from a prone position, looking for lights, listening for noises on the wind, and hoping it was exactly what it seemed: abandoned.

Doug appointed himself the scout, dashing out in zigzag fashion, crouched over and cautious, returning a few minutes later standing upright and encouraged.

It was a squat masonry building with broken windows and a missing door, not that old, but almost reclaimed by the desert.

Will and Doug looked around the outside briefly, searching for the reason a building had been placed where this one was. The desert seemed unbroken in all directions, the moonlight showing them adrift in a sea of desolation. Who, why, and when would have to wait for daylight, which was an hour away.

The interior seemed free of vermin or insects, and there was a long wooden table, onto which they lifted Bill for protection against things that could bite or sting, shoving it against one wall, out of sight of anyone outside. Bill seemed unchanged, still in and out of consciousness, hurting when awake. Slowly, as light came in an eastern glow, they settled in, melding into the corner farthest from the broken windows, sleep overtaking them—until the distant rumble of engines spilled into the musty interior.

Doug heard it first, cocking an eyebrow, measuring the range and direction, waking Will as soon as it was apparent the noise wasn't passing or receding. There were engines, and tires, and what might have been the clank of tank treads, and the noise was getting louder with each second.

Sandra was awake then, wide-eyed and questioning, as Will crawled to the window closest to the oncoming sounds, well aware that it was too light outside now for them to run. Maybe, he hoped, the long-abandoned condition of the interior meant that whoever was coming would ignore the building as completely as the locals obviously had.

"Will! What do you see?" Doug's voice was a stage whisper as Will peered carefully above the broken masonry windowsill.

"It's military. A small convoy of some sort."

"Out here? *Why* the hell? What *is* this place?"

Doug began to move toward the window, but Will waved him back. "Stay down. Unless they're looking for us specifically, there's no reason to think they'll stop here."

"What are they doing wandering around with no roads, unless they're doing exactly that?" Doug asked. "Looking for us, I mean."

Will shook his head in shared puzzlement as his eyes saw the shape of the landscape change, a new perspective bringing a new reality. What had looked like a moonbeam in the predawn darkness now emerged from the natural camouflage of windborne sand as an Iraqi highway, a mere eighty feet away.

Will dove back toward the corner as the engines bore down closer to the abandoned building. Doug caught his arm, whispering, "Could they be ours?"

Sandra's heart sank at the expression on Will's face as he shook his head negatively.

"Iraqi. Stay down, and pray they aren't interested in a rest stop."

CENTCOM, Riyadh, Saudi Arabia
Thursday, March 7, 1991—11:00 P.M. (2000 GMT)

Air Force Brigadier General Herm Bullock sat across the ornate mahogany conference table from *his* boss, Army Major General Bill Martin, as the two-star mulled over his request for another rescue mission into Iraq. The first mission had officially found nothing, though one of the helicopter crew members—a sergeant—was convinced by footprints that some of the C-141 crew had survived, and that was good enough for Herm Bullock.

Martin, however, was skeptical. As the commander who had put Bullock in charge of Operation Scorpion Strike in the first place, he was already upset at accidents and suspicious of the so-called lethal virus.

A U.S. helicopter had rushed the tiny sample back to Riyadh nearly sixteen hours before, but the tests were still in progress in a well-equipped private Saudi biochemical lab that the Saudi government had commandeered for a team of U.S. Army scientists. If the results showed the virus was dangerous, okay. But if the results were negative, Martin and everyone involved were going to look very stupid.

And now Herm Bullock wanted to risk yet *another* penetration of Iraq. General Martin sighed loudly. "Herm, we've already blown plausible deniability out of the tub with this crash, *and* with the rescue mission we already flew. Your people died in the crash, man. I'm sorry. Accept it. At the very least we're asking for propaganda troubles with any more horsing around up there."

Bullock started to protest, but Martin raised his palm.

"We've already lost two airplanes and six crew members, though General Rice's boy and his aircraft commander look as though they're going to survive their injuries."

Herm nodded. "Jeff Rice is stabilized, and so is Collinwood. Both should make full recoveries."

"Good. But why risk more?"

"What if one of our people is alive and hurt up there, Bill?"

Martin drummed his fingers and stared at Bullock for a second before responding. "Find some evidence, Herm, and I'll launch in a second. Find me something, *anything,* to justify the risk."

Martin was on his feet now, signaling the end of the conference, and General Bullock got to his feet as well. "Political risk, you mean?"

The two-star shot the one-star a withering glance of disgust. *Of course* it was political.

"Herm, you're out of line on this! It's not a Pentagon show anymore, the civilians are involved again and we've got to be realistic about it. We've been walking on eggs with this operation of yours from the beginning."

And he was out the door, leaving an embarrassed and angered one-star general in his wake.

Operation of mine? *The damned thing was assigned to me by* you, *Bill!* Bullock thought to himself. Already Martin was shifting the blame.

Bullock returned to his office and turned to his aide, the look on his face confirming that the battle was far from conceded.

"That colonel who called here a while ago? The one we had setting up the DC-10 in Geneva?"

"Colonel Richard Kerr, sir," the aide replied. "He was at Mildenhall."

"Get him on the phone," Bullock told him. "I may be sandbagged here, but Westerman's a good friend of his, and Kerr has access to some heavy hitters at the Pentagon and elsewhere. Then we're gonna take a little stroll down to the targeteer's shop. If our crew is really out there and running, one of our satellites has to have taken their picture by now, and we're gonna find the right snapshot if it takes all night. I'll be goddamned if I'm going to take the chance of leaving one of our people in the desert!"

Al Hajarah desert, south central Iraq
Friday, March 8, 1991—7:30 A.M. (0430 GMT)

The first Iraqi column had passed without slowing—several heavy trucks, an armored personnel carrier, and a jeeplike vehicle from the USSR headed for the Iraq-Saudi border some fifty miles distant. If anyone in the column had even noticed the squat masonry building, he'd paid no official attention, but it had taken Sandra, Will, and Doug a half hour to get their heart rates back to normal.

The sun was climbing the eastern horizon now with classic intensity, a merciless spotlight poised to reveal any attempt they might make to move from the broken-down building. They were trapped by the proximity of the Iraqi road, and knew it.

By the time another rumble of engines and wheels reached their ears, the three of them had rearranged the sparse collection of supplies and the few sticks of furniture to hide them from any casual observer who happened to glance in the door. The table was turned on edge, a broken chair and a discarded piece of plywood placed to either side, and Bill was moved to the floor against the far wall behind the visual barrier where they all now huddled.

Bill Backus had been conscious for nearly thirty minutes, enough time to drink a can of Coke from the six they had left. His pain seemed to have subsided somewhat, but the flight engineer was still weakening.

As his eyes had begun to close again, Sandra had grasped Bill's hand in hers, her eyes locking on his with fierce determination. "You've got to fight, Bill. Fight to hang on! We'll get you out, but it will take a while. You've got to *want* to hang on!"

He had nodded dreamily, smiled, and gone back to sleep—or slipped into unconsciousness. The difference was esoteric at this stage, Doug thought.

Will was at the window again. Except for the presence of a single tank, the oncoming column looked like the last. This convoy, too, was headed south for the vicinity of the Saudi border, which seemed strange. Will knew Saddam wasn't totally defeated, and that stuck in all their craws, but why were viable military forces being used to guard the borders when the Butcher of Baghdad was busy exterminating Kurds to the north and Shiites to the southeast and needed all the murderous help he could get?

"Republican Guard, you think?" Doug asked.

"Probably," Will replied. "Their logo is a red triangle, though, and I don't see anything like that."

Will dove back into the shelter as the column passed, the noise of the tank and trucks just beginning to recede, when suddenly the squealing of brakes and the shouting of Iraqi soldiers sent shivers down their backs.

The column was stopped dead in the road only a hundred yards or so past the building. The shouting continued, obviously inflamed Arabic rhetoric, the words indecipherable, but the tempers clear. Someone was madder than hell about something.

The sound of sheet metal being hit by something else metallic reached their ears. A panel opened, then banged shut. More shouting, and the sound of footsteps.

But none of it was getting any closer.

"What on earth is going on out there?" Sandra's head was cocked in the direction of the window.

"Let's find out." Doug slithered out from the corner before Will could protest, and, keeping below the visual line of the windowsill, raised his head slowly and peered over.

For a few seconds he watched in silence, then turned back toward Will and Sandra with a stage whisper that sounded to Will like a shout. "One of their trucks has broken down."

Alarmed, Will tapped his lips with his index finger for quiet, and Doug nodded, turning back to watch, staying silent until one particular voice outside reached a new pitch of anger, loud enough to drown out any noise they could make from inside.

Doug turned his head toward them again, his voice a forceful whisper.

"I don't believe this."

"What's going on?" Will's whispered reply seemed just as loud.

"One of them is getting ready to shoot someone! I can't tell who. Maybe the driver." Doug looked back outside, gesturing with his right hand, narrating from one side of his mouth. "He's motioning everyone out of the back of the truck now, and he just cocked his gun . . . He's walking over by the hood, but I can't see anybody there. Now he's raising the barrel toward the side of the truck . . . What the . . . !"

Doug turned in disbelief to look at Will. "The sonofabitch is going to shoot his own truck!"

An automatic rifle rattled cacophonously, echoing off the masonry walls, accompanied by laughter from the troops outside, then applause, followed by a stern voice.

"Their sergeant is ordering them into the other trucks."

The tank started moving again, the distinctive tread noises

clanking away as other engines were gunned and the column moved off, leaving the unnoticed building and its relieved occupants in its wake.

"Where's the dead truck?" Will asked at last.

Doug turned with a growing smile, pointing outside. "Still sitting in the road. He only shot the *side* of it! You thinking what I'm thinking?"

Will was nodding. "Sure am. In fact, you have any idea what I've been doing with my spare time at Charleston the last ten years?"

"Something utterly responsible and boring as hell, I imagine." Doug smiled, hoping Will wouldn't take offense, but willing to test him regardless.

"No, wholly irresponsible and self-indulgent. I rebuild cars at the auto hobby shop on weekends when I should be taking Janice to the beach."

"Really?" Doug found the image incongruous. Since when had the cerebral Will Westerman started working with his hands?

Will was looking right through Doug, visualizing the truck just outside.

If there were no more Iraqi units nearby, and if they could get it running . . .

CENTCOM, Riyadh, Saudi Arabia
Friday, March 8, 1991—7:30 A.M. (0430 GMT)

General Herm Bullock had approached the intelligence analysis section to ask for urgent help. He knew there was a sizable flock of manned and orbital electronic eyes actively looking down on Iraq. That meant that the odds were good that somewhere in the resulting flood of surveillance shots, the crash site would appear.

Now the senior NCO he had tasked was back, with a triumphant smile.

"General, I may have something."

He led the way through a crowded warren of offices to a cluttered light table containing several transparencies, and motioned him to the eyepiece of a magnification device.

"This was taken at nine-nineteen local yesterday morning, several hours after the crash. It's an infrared shot. The sun's just come up, so we still have a relatively cool desert. Something measuring about a hundred degrees Fahrenheit will show up. See the small dark spot I've got circled?"

"Yes." Herm had to strain, but the spot was clearly marked.

"That's the crash site, full of hot metal. Now look to the southeast a little, where I've got a small arrow. Look to the end of that arrow. See the tiny dot?"

"Yes, I do."

"Something warm's out there. It could be a camel, or it could be one or more human beings. Probably the latter. Two hours later it's gone."

Another transparency slid into position, and Herm found the crash site marked as before, but the dot to the southeast had moved farther southeast.

"Now *this* one," the sergeant continued, "may be our smoking gun. The dot's the same size and type as before, and when you project a line back through the previous position, you've got a direct line to the crash site."

"They aren't Bedouin tribesmen?"

"Unlikely, sir, for many reasons. All in all, General, I'd say some of our people survived that crash and are headed southeast on foot, *and* . . ." he pulled another photo across the table and pointed to a highway, ". . . if they kept going in a straight line last night at a steady pace, they should have reached this highway before dawn, and there are some possibly abandoned buildings up and down here."

"Great!"

"Not necessarily, sir. If one of our people holed up in one of those, he'd have no way of knowing that right down here . . ."

The sergeant's finger dropped a quarter of an inch to the south. "... is a very active Iraqi military post. It's a very dangerous place to be, sir."

Herm Bullock straightened up and pointed to the table. "Can you bring all this with you right now?"

"Yes sir. Where're we going?"

"To launch a reconnaissance bird down that highway, and then get another rescue mission on the way."

Herm Bullock picked up the phone and punched in General Martin's intercom number.

Al Hajarah desert, south central Iraq
Friday, March 8, 1991—8:30 A.M. (0530 GMT)

Will's head was out of sight beneath the hood of the Russian-built army truck. The coup de grace administered by the angry driver had hit nothing vital. The battery was charged, there was plenty of fuel, and the starter worked, but the cylinders refused to fire. Nevertheless, the odds were good, Will had assured Doug and Sandra, that he could find and fix the problem.

"Either no gas or no spark," Will concluded.

The electrical system was working, and Will had drawn a healthy spark from the distributor on the first try, using a small tool kit from the cab of the truck. He began disassembling the fuel system then, while Sandra and Doug kept a tense lookout atop a small rise on the other side of the road, sitting side by side facing in opposite directions—she watching the north, he the south.

Sandra had been pensive and quiet for so long that when she spoke, her voice startled Doug.

"Sir, can I ask you something?"

"Sure." Doug's eyes locked on hers.

"I've known you through the squadron for years, but I don't

know Colonel Westerman. Is he going to be okay? I mean, last night . . . he was pretty mad at you.''

Doug nodded, letting his gaze return to the horizon.

"There are some things you ought to know about Will, Sandra. He's a very driven, intense guy, but he's also capable and determined. We've fought like cats and dogs at times over the years—we don't share the same sense of humor—but Will's a good man, and an excellent officer.''

Sandra considered that for a few seconds before replying.

"You said you and he grew up together?''

"Back in Dallas, that's right. Our families weren't close, but in the same social circles, and we started hanging out together at an early age.''

Doug paused and glanced at Sandra, gauging her interest.

"Will is like he is because of his dad, Sandra. For many years his dad was a raging alcoholic, severe, morose . . . one of the soldiers who returned from a prison camp at the end of World War II but in some ways could never leave it behind.''

"He was a German POW?''

"No, Japanese, in the Marianas. Much worse than the stalags the Germans kept our flyers in. Anyway, Will grew up being hard on himself and irritatingly responsible. *My* dad set a different example. He's fun-loving and about half-irresponsible, and I guess I take after him somewhat.''

"You and Colonel Westerman *are* quite a contrast,'' Sandra said.

"We complement each other. We always looked out for each other, you know? As kids, I was always getting in fights after school—fights that I couldn't win—and Will would always walk over calmly and flatten my opponent to save me. We went through school together, chased ladies together, only they'd''— Doug held his right hand out flat, like an airplane, sliding it forward—"shoot right past me after a date or two and end up in love with him. Really discouraging. I used to kid him that I was his procurer of females. Girls found him more attractive. Maybe because he seemed more solid and secure. I don't know.''

He fell silent for nearly a minute before speaking again, this time in a slightly lower voice, his throat tight and his thoughts far away.

"It sure was a shock to run into him the other night . . . not to mention all the other shocks. I don't have the slightest idea what we're doing here.''

"I know!'' she said. "I'm trying hard not to be, but I'm scared.'' She was looking north along the road again, and Doug looked away as well.

"We *are* going to get out of this, Sandra. But I've got to tell you I'd much rather be at home in Seattle right now with Kathy and my two boys. Or even back on the flight deck of a United 747, bitching about everything.''

Sandra looked at Doug's face and noticed he was not smiling. She looked at his hands and saw them shaking ever so slightly.

The sound of an automotive engine roaring to life suddenly filled their ears, startling both of them. Across the road, Will stood back from the hood of the truck and raised both arms in a victory salute.

"Jesus!'' Doug said. "He *did* it!''

Within ten minutes they had backed the truck to the door of the ramshackle building, loaded Bill inside, and drawn the rear flap of the heavy canvas cover closed. They threw the small amount of survival gear inside then, leaving the makeshift sled, and huddled briefly in the doorway.

"I'd say we go north as far as we dare, find a place to hide until nightfall, and then take the first turn eastbound,'' Doug said. "If we can make it to our lines to the west of Kuwait, we're home free.''

Sandra was nodding. "I'll stay in the back with Bill. The last thing you need is a female visible in an Iraqi army truck.''

"I agree. Let's get moving," Will added.

The sound of the RF-4 Phantom flashing down the road at barely five hundred feet caught them totally by surprise, the adrenaline level in all three jumping to alarm proportions, the smoke trail of the recon jet disappearing to the north before they could react. They knew it was an F-4, the distinctive sound and shape unmistakable to U.S. Air Force people. But without seeing the unique nose with the photographic port, there was no way to know for certain that the building, the idling truck, and a tantalizing glimpse of one of them had just been recorded on high-speed film of incredible clarity, and would be on its way back to Riyadh within minutes.

"Dammit!" Doug's eyes were locked on the remains of the Phantom's smoke trail to the north. "If that was one of our recon birds, he didn't see us. We were too far into the doorway. Damn!"

"Will he come back over?" Sandra asked, following Doug's thoughts. "Should we stay?"

Both Will and Doug were shaking their heads, but Will spoke first. "Probably not. Anyway, we can't stay here. Eventually Abdul's going to come looking for his dead truck."

They scrambled aboard then, Will jamming the truck into gear and accelerating noisily off to the north, their four identities now hidden within an image that, when viewed from the air or from space, could be identified only as one of the thousands of army trucks roaming Iraq.

Crown (E-3 AWACS)
Friday, March 8, 1991—10:42 A.M. (0742 GMT)

This one was personal. Captain Margaret Ellis felt anger and guilt at the news that yesterday's C-141 crash rescue had been botched, and fellow flyers had been left in the desert.

The briefing, which had come halfway through an otherwise uneventful airborne shift, had shaken her. An RF-4 had just returned pictures of two surviving crew members standing in a doorway by an Iraqi truck with a distinctive white smudge on top, and one of them was female. Intelligence had also concluded that the crew members had been captured and were being trucked north to Baghdad. Within an hour of that conclusion, a huge rescue effort had been thrown together to find and intercept that truck.

Margaret tried to concentrate on her display as a northbound flight of four F-15s came into her sector with a brief radio check.

"Magic one-two, Crown, loud and clear."

She searched her screen even more aggressively now for anything overlooked. Eight F-15s were flying CAP—combat air patrol—as an entire squadron of U.S. Air Force A-10 Warthog tank killers streamed north across the Iraqi border, each pair assigned to buzz down every road within the search sector, looking for a single Iraqi truck with a unique mark on top.

"Jolly thirteen, Crown, loud and clear."

Two MH-53J Pave Low Special Operations helicopters—Jolly 5 flight of two—had already penetrated the border and were closing on Point Alpha, a small building the American crew had been held in.

Four more MH-53s—including Jolly 13—were to land and sit on the ground just south of the border, waiting to be called in while a flight of eight Army Apache gunship helicopters followed the A-10s down each highway in the triangular search box. It would be the A-10s that would spot army trucks fitting the description she'd been handed, and the Apaches that would move in and verify that they had the right one.

The mission commander, a major using the unimaginative call sign "Airboss," was using Jolly 5 as his command ship. Margaret was responsible for keeping everyone safe from marauding airborne Iraqis—if such a thing still existed—and keeping the friendly traffic separated.

Jolly 5
0749 GMT

Major Walt Perkins had brought his MH-53J helicopter in from the east, perpendicular to the highway, with a second MH-53J alongside. The little stucco building was right ahead now, the highway secured by the Warthogs from unwanted traffic for miles in each direction. He added back-pressure to the cyclic stick held gently in his right hand as he rolled in more power and nudged the collective lever in his left hand up a hair, the big helicopter staying just ahead of translational lift as its airspeed dropped through thirty knots and the surface of the desert rose through fifty feet to meet them. With years of experience guiding his movements, he brought the big machine to a hover a few feet off the ground for a moment as they kicked up a hurricane of sand and dust, *thinking* the controls in the appropriate directions, before settling the final few feet to the surface.

Perkins stayed in position while Major Kent Kost accompanied several armed PJs as they jumped to the ground and scrambled to the side of the building, assuring themselves that no one was waiting inside.

In five minutes he was back on the secure channel to Lighthouse.

"There's a makeshift sled that appears to be a scrap of metal from the crashed 141, and judging from some of the trash— MRE packaging and so on—there's no question that at least one of our people was here."

The sled, however, indicated someone was hurt and being pulled.

But there were no signs of bullet impacts or blood in the building.

"How about the tire tracks from the door?" he was asked.

"North. They go north before entering the road, as we figured."

Kost noticed Walt Perkins looking over his shoulder from the right seat. He jerked his thumb in the direction of the ceiling, and Perkins nodded, rolling in power and collective as he pulled the helicopter back into a hover, gained altitude, and accelerated to the north.

Sandy 8
0756 GMT

The radar and computers on the Joint-Stars 707 had spotted it first, a lone target moving north from the abandoned building.

Captain Dennis Rounds had been vectored to the area minutes

before in his A-10, and now, with less than a mile to go, the target truck was just ahead, exactly as advertised.

"Airboss, Sandy eight lead, sector Echo Charlie. I've got the target by himself northeast-bound . . . Seems to be the right model truck."

Rounds brought the A-10 in from behind and slightly to the right while his wingman pulled up and established an orbit at two thousand feet to watch over his partner. Rounds throttled back his two turbofan engines and extended his speed brakes, slowing through two hundred knots as he maneuvered and closed on the lone truck from behind.

Easy, man, that machine could be full of guns and gomers, he cautioned himself. The A-10's cockpit was heavily sheathed in a type of lightweight armor, but even that couldn't protect him from a sudden hail of bullets through the canopy.

Yet he had to get a solid glimpse of the canvas top.

The A-10's huge gatling gun was fully loaded and armed, and he ran his finger lightly over the trigger as he stabilized the approach for the flyby. Not that it would do much good. The last thing he wanted to do was shoot at a truck that might be carrying captured Americans.

The voice of the commander of the rescue package—as the entire force was called—rang in his ears again, impatience eating at the man.

"Sandy eight lead, Airboss, you looking at his roof yet?"

"Stand by, Airboss, I'm closing."

The truck was less than a thousand yards away now, and he was slowing nicely. He would flash overhead at a closure rate of over 120 miles per hour, some fifty feet above them, if he did it exactly the way he was planning, and he'd have to take a mental photograph of the canvas top. That was going to be the hardest part. He considered extending flaps and slowing more, but he was already exposed enough.

One hundred yards left.

Hold it . . . hold it . . . steady . . . NOW!

Rounds snapped the A-10 into a left roll in a preplanned sequence, stopping the bank angle at fifty degrees just as the truck flashed by on his left, its roof fully visible. He brought in full military power then and pulled hard, holding the bank angle at the same fifty degrees to the left, the back-pressure causing the Warthog to climb smartly back to the left, reversing course, as he watched the truck for signs of hostility and keyed his radio.

"Airboss, Sandy eight. I *think* the mark is there, but I'm not sure."

It had amazed Rounds how rapidly they had sent the recon photo of the truck's roof mark to his squadron on a battlefield fax machine.

"Wait! The truck's stopping. I'm gonna circle here a second."

Aboard the AWACS, Margaret Ellis noted the position of Sandy 8 some thirty miles from the primary target, and did some quick math in her head. It was well within range of an army truck since the recon photo had been taken. Which meant it could be them!

She felt her heart rate increase slightly with hope and excitement, her mind's eye picturing what was going on down there a hundred fifty miles to the north, and wondering whether the captured flyers would be able to overpower their captors when the time came, or if the captors would try to resist. It could be a dangerous standoff.

At the same moment, another A-10 flight checked in with a visual on their assigned targets also being tracked by Joint-Stars.

"Airboss, Sandy twelve. I've got three trucks fitting the description eastbound in sector November Delta. Going down for a look."

The first A-10 driver's voice—Sandy 8—cut through again.

"Airboss, Sandy eight lead. We've got two figures emerging from the vehicle. They're waving, and they don't seem to be carrying guns."

"What're they doing, Sandy eight?" Airboss asked.

"Waving frantically at me. Bring on the Apaches and the Pave Lows. I'll bet these are our people!"

Airboss relayed the orders, the Army pilots acknowledging first as they shoved their cyclic sticks forward and accelerated their lethal gunships toward Sandy's position a few miles distant. With preplanned precision they raced in from the rear at less than a hundred feet, stopping one on each side at a range of a half-mile, then turned to bring their gatling guns and missiles to bear on the truck as they moved in. The two gunships slowed to a hover then, their huge rotor blades letting them hang ominously in the sky as they approached from either side at forty-five-degree angles.

"Airboss, Ops five. We confirm two figures out of the truck, hands in the air and waving. They appear to be male, both wearing uniforms of some sort—could be flight suits—and one of them is going around to the rear."

The pilot flying the lead Apache nodded to his wingman, who began swinging around to watch one of the men approach the rear of the truck.

Whoever these people are, Ops 5's pilot thought, *there's no fight in them. Thank God for that.* The weakest part of the rescue plan had been figuring how to deal with armed Iraqis who didn't want to let their hostages go once the Apaches had them cut off and surrounded.

They probably know what we could do with one burst of these guns.

His wingman was watching the rear now, his rotors kicking up a hurricane of wind and sand below, as the man at the front of the truck held his hands as far in the air as he could get them and began edging and motioning to the rear as well, toward his partner. Ops 5 lead followed, trying to see the faces clearly, watching with amazement as the rear flap was pulled back and another figure emerged, very obviously female.

"Airboss, there's a woman coming out of the rear of the truck . . ."

Major Kost slapped his knee and turned to one of the PJs. "That's one of our people! That's the flight engineer."

Aboard the E-3 AWACS, Captain Ellis looked up at two of her fellow crew members and flashed a smile and a thumbs-up.

In Riyadh, monitoring the radios, General Bullock quietly crossed his fingers and shot a quiet little prayer skyward.

And the pilots of Jolly 13, who were now streaking north of the border, nodded at each other as they increased their airspeed.

But the transmission from Ops 5 wasn't over.

". . . and now several others are getting out . . . looks like three children . . . and one, no, two men, one of them elderly, all in civilian clothes."

There was silence for a few seconds as the Apache pilot let up on his microphone button, then pressed it again.

"Airboss, these aren't our folks. What we've got here is an Iraqi family riding around in an army truck."

"*Shit!*" Kent Kost banged his fist on the small portable command desk so hard it hurt, reflecting the disappointment which, from the AWACS down to each member of the rescue group, was palpable.

But there was still hope.

Kost pressed his mike button. "Okay, people, back to work. Sandy eight and Ops five, wave 'em good-bye and get on with it."

Sandy 8 and his wingman resumed their search of the road as the two Apaches pulled away from the puzzled Iraqis, leaving them unharmed.

More Joint-Stars targets were tracked and passed, and one by one checked out by the A-10s. None of them matched the description.

Jolly 5, carrying Major Kost, continued to orbit about thirty miles north of the building the missing flight crew had occupied as each participant in the search checked in, the feeling growing in all of their minds that they had been too late. If the captors of the missing airmen had headed north at top speed, they could have been over a hundred miles away before the rescue attempt had even begun. That was probably it. As the minutes wore on, the gloomy assumption seemed all but conclusive.

At least some of the crew were alive. But they were headed to Baghdad now, for certain.

At the very moment when Sandy 8 was corralling the Iraqi truck, Will, Doug, and Sandra were scrambling to the top of a small embankment ten miles away and some four miles west of the main road, their "borrowed" Iraqi truck safely parked in the shadows of the twenty-foot-high south wall of a wadi they had crossed on foot in the moonlight less than twelve hours before.

"It was over there. An A-10, I'm almost certain." Sandra was shielding her eyes with her hand as she stood at the top and peered to the northeast, Will and Doug brushing off the sand and joining her as fast as they could.

"Which way was he . . . *There!*" Doug pointed farther to the north as the distinctive shape of a Warthog flashed into view perhaps ten miles distant, heading east.

The sound of a helicopter reached their ears within a minute, a sound coming not from the northeast, but from the direction of the road to the east. There was a small rise blocking their view at first, but the chopper suddenly emerged, moving north-bound and following the road at a very low altitude—*coming from the direction of the building they had just left.*

"Oh Jesus, *no!*" Will's voice was anguished.

"What? What is it?" Doug asked in alarm, noting the look of distress on Will's face as his eyes followed the helicopter north, watching it recede to little more than a small dot hanging against the northeastern sky.

"That," Will began quietly, "was a Pave Low. An MH-53J Special Operations chopper. The type you'd send into Iraq if you wanted to mount a rescue operation for downed flyers''—he hesitated, gritting his teeth, sighing loudly—''seen in a goddamn reconnaissance photograph.''

Sandra was studying both of them. ''Are you saying they *did* see us? That F-4 spotted us? And this is a rescue operation to pick us up?''

Will nodded with resignation as Doug pointed north suddenly.

''He's orbiting! The chopper's orbiting! Let's get that truck going and get the hell up there.''

The three of them broke at once, half-sliding, half-running down the embankment to the truck, Will firing off the engine, which didn't hesitate. He put it in gear and let out the clutch gently, mindful of the sandy areas beneath their wheels and ahead. Slowly, gingerly, they accelerated, bouncing down the length of the wadi until they regained the road, their view of the orbiting helicopter blocked by the north embankment, each of them praying that it would still be there when they reached the highway.

It was!

Will turned northbound again, accelerating as fast as he could.

''How far ahead do you think he is?'' Doug asked.

''Hard to say,'' Will replied. ''Ten, twelve miles when he's on this end of his holding pattern.''

''Turn on your lights. If we can get close enough, Sandra . . .''

She was sitting between them, leaving Bill in the back for the moment. She understood Doug's idea in an instant.

''Not many Iraqis have long blond hair, right?''

''Right,'' Doug agreed, as she scrambled past him, sitting by the window, ready to lean out and wave.

They were closing with agonizing slowness. There was no question now that it was an MH-53 U.S. Air Force helicopter, but there was also no question that something had changed ahead. Instead of continuing his left orbit, the chopper suddenly started moving north, matching the speed of their truck, becoming a stationary dot in the windscreen. They were close enough to see it, yet without a radio, they might as well have been a world away.

With fingers crossed and hopes high, they plowed ahead for interminable minutes, gratified that the MH-53's speed was no greater than theirs, but praying he would turn back on his course. They blinked their lights and Sandra leaned far out the window and waved frantically. Doug looked for the right angle to use the rearview mirror he'd already ripped from its mountings to reflect the sun in the pilot's eyes, a tried-and-true survival technique. *Anything* to attract their attention!

Ten minutes passed, but the ratios of the chase remained the same.

Then, without warning, the MH-53 stopped in a hover and began to grow *larger* in the windscreen. Will's foot was already to the floor, the army truck now bouncing along at nearly seventy miles per hour.

"Which way is he facing? Jeez!" Will's eyes were glued on the helicopter. If he was facing south, the pilots would surely see the oncoming truck, especially if a truck was what they were searching for.

But if he was facing north . . .

"Blink the lights! Quick!" Doug barked, as Sandra took it as a cue and leaned out the window, waving frantically, even though she knew deep down they were still too far away.

"He's turning! *Come on, baby! Turn that mother around!*" Doug yelled. But the turn stopped with the MH-53 facing east, not south. And as they watched with sinking hearts, it began to move in that direction.

"An A-10, to the right!" Sandra's voice rang out suddenly as a Warthog flashed across the horizon to their right and perhaps ten miles away, then banking back to the northeast. As they watched in disbelief, the MH-53 altered course to the northeast, in the same direction, and began moving away even faster.

The MH-53 had become nothing but an indistinguishable speck on the eastern horizon before Will realized he still had the accelerator to the floor, as if there were a purpose for the speed any longer.

They slowed then and stopped, letting the engine idle as they sat in stunned silence, willing their rescuers to come back.

But the horizon was now empty.

"That's it, people. Keep your eyes open coming back in." Airboss—Major Kost—spoke the orders with resignation as eyes turned away from the Joint-Stars scope at the moment its radar and computers noticed that the northbound movement of a new target in the south end of the search area had ceased. As it was programmed to do, it dropped the newly stationary target from the display. It did so at the same moment Margaret Ellis leaned over for a final check.

Five minutes elapsed with nothing but the sound of the truck engine in their ears before anyone spoke. And then it was Sandra:

"We'd better get this truck back under cover. That dry gulch worked before. I'd recommend we turn around. Or find another one."

No response. Will looked thunderstruck, and Doug seemed on the verge of tears. *So close,* they were all thinking, *so* damn *close!*

Again, Doug thought, *we've snatched defeat from the jaws of victory.*

Will drew a ragged breath at last and nodded, biting his lower lip before glancing at Doug and Sandra and gesturing behind them.

Doug merely nodded in reply as Will let out the clutch his foot had been jamming down since the chopper disappeared. His leg muscles were protesting, his foot bouncing on the pedal, but he didn't notice. They would have to revert to Plan A now, and wait until nightfall.

Samarra, Iraq, eighty miles north of Baghdad
Friday, March 8, 1991—12:05 P.M. (0905 GMT)

Shakir Abbas awoke with the sudden rumble of a car engine shattering an unplanned nap, the incongruity of bright sunlight disorienting him. The sunlight was streaming through the curtained window of an ornate parlor.

Where am I? Oh, yes.

The memory returned, and he came out of the rocking chair with a fluid motion to kneel at the window, relieved to see the owner of the house heading up the walkway toward a small stone gate, a package in his hands.

Muayad Damerji's name had entered Shakir's mind the moment he had decided to go after the missing canister. Longtime friend, roommate at Oxford, Muayad was more of a brother than a friend, and one of the few people on the planet he could trust with his life.

Which is exactly what I'm doing, Shakir reminded himself. *As well as endangering Muayad and his family.*

The door closed behind Dr. Muayad Damerji as he spotted Shakir standing by the window. He pointed to the package and

smiled, a toothy smile framed by a scraggly mustache and Van-
dyke beard.

"I startled you, Shakir?" Muayad asked.

"I had fallen asleep," he said, rubbing his eyes like a small
child. "Ghadah was gracious to let me do so."

Muayad smiled at the mention of his wife. She did not know
the reason for her husband's sudden midnight mission to Baghdad, and had been trying to wheedle it out of Shakir all morning,
giving up only when she noticed him snoring softly.

"I think I have everything." He shook the package for emphasis. "And no, I did not have trouble."

"I should not have let you—"

Muayad raised his index finger to his lips and shook his head.

"You came where you should have come, Shakir. You need
some money, some gas, some food, but you can do nothing
without information. That I have for you now."

Shakir looked around the warm, richly paneled room, making
certain Ghadah was out of earshot before speaking. He had told
Muayad too much—everything, in fact—but neither of them
wanted the circle to widen.

They sat in Muayad's plush wing chairs centered on a magnificent Tabriz rug from northern Iran, facing each other across
a small teak coffee table as Muayad patted the package in his
lap.

"When you told me all this last night, Shakir, I did not tell
you something. I did not say how much I admire you for what
you have tried to do."

Shakir shook his head in amazement. "Admire *me*? I'm a
traitor, a murderer."

"And Saddam is not? You have done nothing compared with
his crimes. He has raped our country, and you and I, all the
people I worked with in the nuclear program, all the people *you*
worked with, none of us wanted to admit it. Look what he has
done!" Muayad's right arm swept backwards toward the front
of his house, his eyebrows flaring. "He built a new Iraq. We

grew to like it. Now he has destroyed it! I had not"—his voice broke for a second, then recovered—"I had not seen all the rubble."

He leaned forward suddenly. "Oh, Shakir! Baghdad is in ruins! It will take ten years to replace just the utilities we have lost, but how can we replace an entire generation of young men? I heard the BBC say last week that the number of our soldiers he left to be slaughtered in Kuwait may exceed three hundred thousand!"

"I know. I know."

"Shakir, we both have sons. Allah be praised, they were too young to be taken, but nearly everyone here knows a family who has at least one son missing. And most will never know what happened to them. The graves, Shakir! Mass graves in the desert . . ."

Muayad looked down, working to contain his agitation for a few seconds before his head snapped up and his eyes locked onto Shakir's once again.

"We both lived so well, you and I, serving this animal and his criminals. I'm not brave enough to do anything but say 'yes, master, no, master.' I once was a research physicist, remember? For the last three years all I do with all that training is conduct scavenger hunts for forbidden materials and play stupid cat-and-mouse games with the CIA and Mossad."

He paused a moment, almost staring at Shakir, trying to decide how much to say. "Until you came to me last night, I did not know I could trust you, Shakir. I did not know that you, too, were sick of this dictator. I should . . . I should have been brave enough, like you, to walk out and tell the West what Saddam's *really* doing with the nuclear program.

"Perhaps you still can."

By 1:00 P.M. Shakir was on the road northbound, a carefully marked map by his side with a package of safe-passage letters written by several military directorates in Baghdad to Dr. Muayad Damerji. There was only one with a picture attached, and it was Shakir's picture—an old snapshot Muayad had kept in a desk drawer. Shakir had protested mightily against using Muayad's name. The dangers were obvious if his mission to Kirkuk ended in capture or discovery.

But Muayad would hear no dissent.

Shakir reached for a plastic bottle from the ample supply of bottled water in the backseat, munching on some pastries as he dodged potholes and military trucks, feeling much too relaxed.

Or am I just numb? he wondered.

The miles seemed to melt away, despite the deplorable condition of the highway. The desert on either side was the most depressing stretch he knew of in all Iraq. After leaving the fertile, irrigated greenery of the shores of the Tigris River, there was nothing but featureless, barren flatness and heat on either side. No sand, no hills, no rocks broke the flat expanse; it was only a geological purgatory of nothingness, with not even a hint that there were mountains somewhere to the east. Like a sickly yellow curtain, the heat haze and dust hung over the monotonous horizon.

Forty miles remained to Kirkuk, where the general had his field headquarters. Shakir checked the map and found the turn for a final shortcut, one that avoided the main highway—and, he hoped, the roadblocks.

He had been cleared easily through four checkpoints so far, but now, after traveling only three miles, another roadblock loomed in front of him. This one was different from the others: a battle-scarred tank parked partway across the road, leaving only one lane for passage in either direction, and three soldiers were standing on each side. The other checkpoints had been more organized, more professional. This one must have been thrown into place for some reason at the last minute. Kirkuk was just ahead, and the fighting with the Kurdish rebels had been raging all around for the last three days, according to Muayad.

Of course, he reminded himself, I'm *now Muayad Damerji.*

Shakir braked to a halt on the signal of an upturned palm from a raggedly dressed soldier who approached the driver's side now, his Kalashnikov rifle aimed right at Shakir's head.

"I'm no threat to you. Please lower your gun," Shakir said.

There was no response. The soldier's right hand came forward, palm up, silently waiting for Shakir's papers, and he fumbled for the ID card and the proper military pass, handing them through the window of the van—then realizing with a profound chill that the soldier was holding them upside down as he pretended to read.

Shakir looked at the face and saw a boy of fifteen, devoid of maturity, yet forced into a man's role. He was playing a part— only a part—and whatever lines he was about to recite were unpredictable.

And impervious to reason.

A full minute ticked by, Shakir memorizing the details of the muzzle of the gun as it hovered inches from his eyes, the young boy in a soldier's clothes still working to pretend he was absorbing the papers.

Finally he raised his eyes, his face a mask of impassivity.

"Out of the van!" he said at last, stuffing the papers and ID card in his pocket as he brought his right hand back up to the gun stock, his finger caressing the trigger as he stepped back.

Shakir complied quickly as he looked around for the boy's commander.

"Where is your officer?" he asked. "I am Dr. Muayad Damerji, on an important mission for the Revolutionary Command Council. You cannot detain—"

The boy seemed to come alive suddenly with anger.

"You will not speak!" the boy commanded. *"Down on your knees!"*

A cold ball of panic began rolling around in Shakir's consciousness, eluding his control and rattling the calm appearance he was trying to maintain. He had his hands in the air now as he looked at the boy quizzically. "You want me to do what?"

"*On your knees!*" the boy yelled at him, shoving the muzzle of the gun into his stomach so hard he nearly fell backwards.

Shakir complied, facing the boy.

"*I said turn around!*" he yelled again, pulling the barrel to one side far enough to strike his prisoner on the side of the head. Shakir beat him to it, turning instantly, his knees protesting as they ground painfully against the pavement by the front of the van.

"Where is your officer? You are making a terrible mistake!" Shakir was yelling now too, trying to treat a child like a child, although this one had a lethal weapon aimed at the back of his head.

The boy's response was swift and ominous: the sound of a bolt and a firing pin locking into position reached Shakir's ears.

"*Do not move! Do not speak!*" the young conscript said again.

Where is your commander?

Shakir prayed the thought would penetrate the thick skull of the boy behind him. His heart was now racing, his senses telling him to comply, yet his instincts telling him he had only seconds to prevent the trigger from ending his life—and the lives of many others if he could not neutralize that last canister.

"What do you have here, Private?" a voice asked behind him.

Allah be praised! That must be his officer. This nonsense will end now.

There was a hesitation as footsteps approached the soldier's position and stopped. The boy replied then, his words striking Shakir with the suddenness of a scorpion in a dark corner.

"This is one of Saddam's pigs, sir. May I kill him now?"

Shakir's mistake flashed through his consciousness in a split second.

These are rebel soldiers! And I just identified myself as—

The sound of another vehicle—a truck of some sort—came to his ears.

"Let me see his papers," the leader said.

The decision made to chance it, Shakir cried out, "Please, let me explain who I am!"

"Oh? And just who *are* you, *Doctor* Damerji?" the man Shakir assumed was an officer asked, a cold snarl in his tone. "This says you are working for the Revolutionary Command Council, which means you are working for Saddam. Why should I not let my man execute you right now? Saddam's jackals would execute *me* in an instant."

"May I turn around?" Shakir asked, his voice now clearly shaking.

A strong hand gripped his right shoulder suddenly and almost effortlessly yanked him to his feet, spun him around, and slammed his back against the door of the van. The boy-soldier was still aiming at his head, visceral fury on his face, but when Shakir looked left and into the eyes of the boy's leader, he saw weariness instead.

"You have one minute to tell me why you should live."

The sound of a heavy vehicle door opening met his ears now. Someone was starting to get out of the truck that had come up behind his van. The officer, a surprisingly tall man with weathered skin and a huge, sad mouth that seemed to cross his entire face, kept his eyes locked on Shakir's, but yelled out of the corner of his mouth suddenly: "Stay by your vehicle!" He snapped several orders in the other direction then, and Shakir could hear two of the other soldiers scurry to guard the newcomer.

Several seconds elapsed as Shakir's mind raced to find the right words to say. Suppose this was a trap? Suppose these were really loyalists trying to scare a confession out of him?

"Well, *Doctor*? What are you a doctor of? Death?"

The echo of Colonel Westerman's acid reference to him several days ago catapulted his decision past logic. He was *not* Doctor Death!

"I am trying to recover a deadly weapon before it can be used on your rebel forces, or on any other innocent people."

"What kind of weapon?"

"One that makes you sick. One that . . ."

"I'm not an idiot, Doctor. Are you talking about a nuclear weapon?"

"My papers indicate nuclear, but this is a germ weapon."

"And I'm supposed to believe you are trying to save *me*? You, who come down this road with papers proving you work for Saddam?"

"Yes. I . . ."

The officer let him go suddenly and stepped back, never taking his eyes off Shakir, but speaking as precisely to his young soldier as if he had been facing the boy. "I sentence him to the same treatment that was so graciously given to our comrade, Haamed Nashrani, two days ago. You understand?"

"Yes sir," the boy said, his eyes gleaming. "I know how to shoot him. He will die very slowly by the side of the road."

"Precisely," the officer said as he began to turn away. "Goodbye, *Doctor*."

The barrel of the gun dropped now from eye level as the boy stepped to one side and Shakir tensed himself to spring in a last-ditch effort to escape, the presence of another rifle now aimed at his head by one of the two soldiers standing across the road assuring that he wouldn't make it.

But he would go down fighting, at least!

Suddenly there was the sound of automatic rifle fire, and the young boy's head exploded in front of him, the Kalashnikov clattering harmlessly to the ground, rooting him to the spot. The other soldiers were turning now toward the newly arrived truck as the seconds stretched and fingers pulled on triggers too slowly. Shakir saw the two soldiers standing as if frozen, their bodies beginning to shake and jerk grotesquely as their torsos absorbed the impact of each bullet from the automatic weapons fire. The officer, who had been caught off guard when he turned to walk back toward the tank, tried to turn too late, catching the same lethal bullet stream full in the face, his magnificent mouth blasted away as his body flipped backward and crumpled.

There was gunfire to his right now, return fire, and Shakir slid to the ground and pressed his back against the right front tire of the van as he tried to get a glimpse of the source of the fusillade.

To the left of the door of the truck stood a solitary individual in a sports shirt and blue slacks, holding an automatic weapon. He pulled the trigger again to finish the slaughter, cutting down the last rebel soldier as he stood by the tank trying to cock his rifle, then he ran past Shakir to the tank, tossing a grenade in the open hatch. A horrible metallic sound assaulted Shakir's ears, as if a giant sledgehammer had struck the side of a massive piece of steel as he stood beside it. If anyone had remained inside, he was now dead.

Only then did the man walk toward Shakir.

"That was very close," the man said, offering his hand and helping Shakir get up, though his legs had turned to rubber.

"How . . . uh . . ."

The man smiled. "This is a government van. I know the look. I knew they were rebels, and I could see they were about to finish you. What more do I need to know?"

"You are . . . military?" Shakir asked.

"No." He smiled, a snaggletoothed, crooked smile set off by a set of cold snake eyes. "I am official security—secret police. And you?"

Shakir had little adrenaline left to add to his bloodstream, but a tiny spark of renewed apprehension returned.

Did he overhear what I said?

"I was saying . . . making up anything I could to save myself. You may have heard . . ." he stammered, after identifying himself as Dr. Damerji.

There was no acknowledgment. The man turned and walked over to the body of the officer. He knelt down and unfolded the dead man's fingers, retrieving the identification papers, which he studied before walking back and handing them to Shakir.

"Where are you going, Doctor?"

"I . . . must report to General Hashamadi in Kirkuk. I thank you . . ."

"You drive ahead, and I'll accompany you. If there are any more roadblocks ahead, stop and let me go around you first, and do *not* identify yourself. Let me do that."

"Certainly," Shakir said, fighting to contain the fact that he was thoroughly off balance. Conflicting loyalties and shifting alliances were flipping in and out of his mind. The danger he was now in was incalculable. One of Saddam's sadistic killers was going to lead him on a mission to destroy Saddam's most lethal weapon. If he weren't so filled with terror, the irony would have been hilarious.

But at least he was alive.

Shakir looked down at the carnage around the van, the grisly remains of the young boy in the soldier's suit just a few feet away. The boy had been almost the same age as his oldest son, his head now reduced to . . .

Shakir motioned to the secret policeman to wait a minute as he stumbled to the side of the road and vomited.

Riyadh, Saudi Arabia
Friday, March 8, 1991—7:30 P.M. (1730 GMT)

Another call to prayer was echoing from the loudspeakers of every minaret in Riyadh. General Herm Bullock rolled down the backseat window of the staff car as the driver rolled through the entrance to the air base. The mournful, musical incantations from the Koran were an exotic sound track to the glow of sunset in the west, the spectacular hues changing slowly to star-studded skies.

Colonel Kerr was sitting where he had said he'd be: on a dusty picnic table under a camouflage net just outside the collapsible

MAC ALCE command post. The driver scooped up Kerr's standard B-4 bag and a briefcase as Herm greeted him with a handshake. The chance to hop on a direct flight to Riyadh from Mildenhall had proven irresistible, especially after Herm Bullock's call.

"Good to meet you in person, General. My boss thought I could be of some help to you a little closer to the action, and since Westerman and Harris are pilot-training classmates of mine, I took him up on it."

"*Both?*"

"Yes sir. Class seventy-oh-eight at Willie." The reference to Williams Air Force Base, near Phoenix, brought back his own set of memories, but Bullock suppressed them, and merely nodded.

"I know you're with the Defense Intelligence Agency, but I didn't know you were a pilot."

"Former SR-71 jockey, sir, and U-2 before that. I got involved in surveillance mapping and other intelligence activities several years ago and got out of the cockpit."

"So now you're a spy?"

Kerr laughed at that. "Hardly, sir. I have a mixed bag of responsibilities related to satellite and other high-tech intelligence gathering and troubleshooting. What pulled me into this operation was a call from Will Westerman."

Bullock filled him in on the second failed rescue attempt, which had just gotten under way when Kerr's flight left Mildenhall.

"Let's go get something to eat," Herm said, "and I'll add the details. I'm glad you're here, by the way. I have a vague feeling I may need your help, especially if the Iraqis do what I expect they're going to do."

"What's that?"

"Pretend they don't have them."

"You *expect* that?"

The general was nodding. "That's why I insisted we formally notify the Iraqis that we know they are holding our people. General Martin's going to deliver that message tonight."

The news chilled Kerr.

My God, he thought, *what if they're not captured? We might as well paint a target on them.*

Al Hajarah desert, south central Iraq
Saturday, March 9, 1991—5:25 A.M. (0225 GMT)

"Slow down, Doug! You're leaving yourself no room for recovery."

They were going over sixty now, with nothing but moonlight illuminating the narrow desert road ahead. Will had been watching with alarm as Doug's foot got heavier on the accelerator, and he'd reached the breaking point.

"Doug, *please!*"

"Okay, okay." He let up on the power, feeling the truck slow.

It was a tightrope act without a net, balancing the remaining hours of covering darkness and moonlight against the need to use the headlights in order to maintain enough speed to get the most out of the remaining fuel. The equation was complicated even more by the fact that Bill Backus had developed a fever, and they were out of liquids.

"How far do you suppose we've come?" Doug's voice sounded dry, cracked, and unused. It had been over an hour since either of them had spoken, and over an hour since the last time they'd had to slow to a crawl to creep around a major desert intersection and its small settlement, bouncing over a rubble-strewn section of hard-packed desert to cut the corner by a mile. They couldn't chance using the headlights, but somehow they had pulled it off, navigating the roads by reference to the stars and zig-zagging first to the northeast, then the southeast, always trending in the right direction toward Kuwait and the Coalition lines.

"Since that last intersection"—Will pushed a tiny button on his digital watch and read the time, running some simple time and distance figures through his head—"about sixty miles. Since we came out of hiding, about a hundred and fifty."

They had returned to the wadi and slept in the back of the truck through the afternoon, Bill remaining mostly unconscious. Sandra had lain awake for hours imagining she heard more hel-icopter sounds in the distance before closing her eyes, cuddling against Will's back at one point as he slept—an unconscious act that had embarrassed Will when he awoke and felt her arm around his waist. Quietly he had disengaged, tenderly placing her arm back beside her and smoothing her hair as Doug watched, ad-miring the gentleness of his old friend. It had always been that gentle nature toward women that had drawn so many of them to him, Doug realized.

Fuel was a growing worry. There was no gas gauge, and Will's last attempt to dip the tanks had shown less than a quarter re-maining. When they ran out, the great escape—at least the easy part—would be over.

"Hey, what's *that?*"

Will's voice startled both of them. Something disturbingly familiar painted on the surface of the road had just flashed beneath them, too softly illuminated to be fully visible.

Doug raised up in the driver's seat. "I don't know, but I saw it too."

"There's another one. Slow down!"

Doug nodded, braking smartly.

The white stripes were large rectangles, side by side in the roadway, and placed at intervals, with bordering white lines on each side.

"The road's wider suddenly. You notice that?" Will asked.

There were no artificial lights on the horizon, and Doug's hand reached for the headlight switch as he looked over at Will. "Should I?"

"Go ahead. Just for a second."

The splash of glaring white light after hours of nothing but moonlight was a massive assault to their eyes. Doug had done little more than flick the switch on and off, but in the brief glare the meaning of the markings became crystal clear.

"Jesus, Will, this is a highway airstrip!"

They were used all over the desert nations of the Arabian Peninsula, highways which doubled as runways.

Doug braked to a stop now, aggressively, the headlights off once more. "If this is a highway strip, it's probably military, and it's probably full of holes from our attacks."

"There's a huge building over there." Will was looking off in the distance to the right as Doug pulled off to the side and stopped, letting the engine idle as the two of them climbed out, straining to see, both wishing again—as they had all night—that they had night-vision goggles.

Sandra jumped out the back and came up beside them as Will stared hard at the building, moving his focus to one side, letting his black-and-white night vision pick up more detail. It *was* a building, but more like a large hangar, and it looked like it might be bomb-damaged.

Will looked at his watch again. It was approaching five-thirty. The first light of dawn would be only a half hour away, with sunrise about 6:45 A.M. They couldn't afford to approach the border in daylight with no guns, no disguises, and no ability to speak Arabic.

"Will! Look here!" Doug had walked ahead of the truck a distance. His voice, tinged with amazement, carried back to Will and Sandra, and they followed, finding him standing on the edge of a jagged break in the road that ran fully ten meters from side to side and five meters across.

"This sucker would have eaten our lunch if we'd hit it at fifty! Jesus!"

"Did you see it ahead?" Sandra asked.

"No," Doug replied with a chuckle, motioning to Will. "Old eagle-eyes here saw the markings of a highway airstrip just in time."

They stood in silence for a minute, each running through a variety of thoughts as the night wind picked up and ruffled Sandra's hair. She pawed at it as Doug held his arms out, his hands palms up, and addressed Will.

"Okay, Kemo Sabe, what now? We can go around, of course, but daylight's coming." Will was still studying the ominous darkness of the large hangar to the right of the road, trying to let his eyes take the necessary time to sort out the image.

There were no signs of life. The hangar was only a few hundred yards off the roadway, but while a portion of it had collapsed from the impact of a bomb, one of the large doors seemed still in place. Maybe they could hide the truck and themselves inside and wait out the daylight again.

They drove off the road toward the hangar, the lights still off, Sandra sitting with them in the cab for the short distance, reminding both of them that Bill was burning with fever.

"If we don't get some liquids down him . . ."

"Infection, you think?"

She nodded, and somehow in the darkness they both understood. They needed to get him across the border to safety now, not the next night. Capture wouldn't help him either.

"Stay here. I'll take a look," Doug said, putting on the brake and leaving the truck idling as he scrambled out of the cab and walked toward the broken maw of the building.

It was huge, the entrance at least three hundred feet wide by ninety feet high, the body of it an imperfectly curved concrete arch, the doors heavy steel. The bomb—or bombs—had entered the right side of the roof, taking out the back corner and two of the five huge sliding metal doors, and obviously destroying whatever and whomever was inside. Doug imagined they would see some unpleasant remains when filtered daylight filled the interior in a few hours.

But somehow the structure hadn't collapsed, and as Doug looked up at the moon through the jagged bomb hole, he could see why the concrete was reinforced by tons of steel rebar reinforcing rods and girders. It had been an impressive installation.

But it had tangled with the wrong air force.

Something in the far, mostly undamaged left corner caught his eye. He saw the tracks of wheels through the desert dust and bomb-damage rubble leading in the direction of a vague shape. The tracks were obvious even in the reflected moonlight, and he followed them to the pitch-dark corner, almost bumping into a small airplane. A quick check showed it was operable, and at a dead run he quickly made it back to the truck, his breath coming hard.

"There's enough shelter to hide us, but you're not going to believe what's in there."

"Okay, what?" Will's impatience was obvious.

"An observation airplane. Single-engine. About the size of a Piper Cub. It looks flyable, it's undamaged, and it's fueled! Someone boogied in here with that bird, and it may be our ticket to getting Bill out of here."

"What do you mean, getting *Bill* out of here? Let's *all* get in the bird and get the flock out of here, buddy!"

Will's excitement was rising, and Doug felt guilty about raising his hopes. Will recognized the look on Doug's face.

"Okay, what's the matter?"

"Will, it's only a two-seat aircraft."

The information flow had gone on for the past twenty minutes
and was becoming repetitious. President George Bush raised his
right hand at the wrist, signaling enough. He had been director
of Central Intelligence. He understood only too well what the
proposed "finding" would say—and portend.

The grim-faced men and one woman sat around the plush
airborne conference room of the new Boeing 747 presidential jet
and kept quiet, letting the President think, his fingers drumming
the table for a moment.

The word had come from Riyadh an hour before that the virus
created by the Iraqis appeared on preliminary testing to be one of
the most virulent ever discovered. They had exposed several test
animals, the team reported, and death had been amazingly rapid.

The President leaned forward, rubbing his forehead, his eyes
wandering the cabin before coming to rest on the number-two
man at the CIA, William Gates.

"Okay, Bill. You know the limits and you know the risks,
but if this stuff is half as monstrous as it sounds, I can't sit around
and hope it'll go away. You prepare the finding, then use everything we can, *including* the few human assets you say we've got
on the ground in Iraq, to find the rest of it. I'm impressed with
the fact that you can't safely manufacture more of it without an
appropriate lab, so if we can find any other infant-formula fac-
tories Saddam has redecorated in pink"—the group chuckled at
the reference to the bombed biological weapons factory in Baghdad—"we gotta shut them down somehow."

"Maybe Peter Arnett could locate it for us," one of the group
said.

More laughter.

"Now," the President responded without a smile, index finger in the air, "that brings up something. This is, and will remain, top secret. There had better be no leaks on this one, folks. Everyone got that? There will be no mention of, or confirmation of, anything to do with Iraqi biological weapons, or our desert raid on that lab, or the sample we got, or the tests, the missing crew—anything."

"Unless, of course," one of the analysts replied, "they actually use it on someone."

At the same moment, in the Situation Room at the White House, Dr. Alan Benedict, a biochemical advisor to the National Security Council, was taking a call from a civilian member of the Army biological warfare team at the commandeered and heavily guarded lab in Riyadh.

Dr. Walter Hajek had driven across Riyadh to use a secure phone at CENTCOM and stay out of earshot of his boss, whose plans had upset him.

"Alan, they want to ship about half of the viral serum we've got back to *Washington*, for God's sake! We've been able to get a look at it here with an electron microscope, and there's nothing you can do there that we can't do here."

The reply had been hesitant. "What's your point, Walter?"

"My point is that I don't want something this dangerous to human life back in our country. What if an accident occurred? What if . . . what if the plane crashed at Andrews? Remember that movie, *The Andromeda Strain*? This stuff is worse than the fictional virus they created in the movie because it's so resilient it can live in ordinary water."

"Walter, I don't control—"

"Can't you call someone? Can't you call Scowcroft, or the President?"

"I got your message earlier, Walter. They don't agree with your worries. The sample is to be shipped as scheduled, and I suggest you not make a big deal about this."

"Alan, for God's sake, man, think about it. We destroy all there is over here, right? What, then, if some of our bright pragmatic thinkers decide that having the worst biological weapon in the world is a good deterrent? Suppose *we* decide to grow more of it?"

"That's a different reason, now, isn't it? Walter, you're getting paranoid." Benedict fairly snapped the words at him. "You know damn well we don't do such things."

"I'm glad *you're* sure of that," Hajek replied, "because I'm not."

Al Hajarah desert, south central Iraq
Saturday, March 9, 1991—6:30 A.M. (0330 GMT)

Sandra had protested, but she was qualified in tail-draggers—light airplanes with tail wheels instead of nosewheels—so Sandra would go. That one fact had let Will and Doug both off the hook. As much as they wanted out, neither could tolerate either the thought of leaving the other behind just to save himself, or the idea of leaving behind an enlisted crew member under his command. Will was the aircraft commander, but Doug was Sandra's squadron commander.

And there was the fact that Sandra was a female, and decent males don't leave females in the desert. That factor was chauvinistic and unspoken, but a factor nonetheless.

"Sandra, listen to me. I fly airplanes with cockpits forty-five feet in the air! Will flies cockpits twenty feet in the air. And neither of us has ever flown a tail-dragger. This is no time to learn."

"That's B.S. and you know it, Colonel, *sir*." She was upset, and the words were impassioned. "Either of you could fly this thing in your sleep."

"Don't you want out?" Will had said at last, almost exasperated with the "No, please, after *you*" debate.

"Yes," she said quietly. "But this is a Hobson's choice. I want both of you out, too."

Will had looked at her for several seconds before he realized why the reflected light of early morning was glistening in the corners of her eyes. He nodded at Doug as Sandra looked down, his right hand finding her left shoulder. "I've got to make a command decision, Sandra. That decision is, you go. You fly Bill out and to the nearest base, get him to a hospital, then debrief rescue and send them back in for us. We'll pull the desert in around our ears and sit tight this time. We'll be back with you in no time."

She nodded and said nothing. It was done.

Doug rechecked the control cables and quadrants in the airplane for the third time as Will helped Sandra load Bill into the rear seat. The move hurt him, and he regained consciousness long enough to hear what was happening. But he was in pain and beginning to hallucinate with the fever. They were thankful when he slipped back into a deep sleep.

The three of them pulled the little airplane over to the entrance, keeping it hidden as Sandra hugged each of them, fought back tears, and strapped in.

"Taxi straight out to the highway, the way we came in, take off that way, then turn back immediately and keep it at treetop level. I figure we're no more than fifty miles north. Go due south, but avoid anything and everything human. Highways, towns, troops—"

The sound of her soft voice interrupting had stopped him. "I know. I got it all the first three times."

There were yellow and orange light rays painting the eastern horizon as Sandra touched the starter button, giving a silent prayer of thanks when the prop whirled and the engine caught almost immediately. The familiar sound of a fixed-pitch prop slapping the air was music to her ears. She nudged the throttle and began rolling toward the highway, Doug walking beside her right wing, the noise of the engine obscuring sudden shouts from behind them as two figures in fatigues raced toward the front of the hangar and the departing airplane, waving automatic weapons.

Standing partly behind the hangar door, Will was out of their line of vision. He started to yell a warning, but realized he'd never be heard over the noise of the engine.

Doug was still beside the airplane, seventy-five or so feet from the hangar, as Sandra accelerated slightly. Will calculated the intended path of the two soldiers who were now sprinting toward the airplane in a path that would take them past Will by some fifty feet. They had not seen him, Will realized. They were focused on Doug and the airplane, and as they closed on the boundary line marking the hangar entrance, Will found himself running to intercept them as if he were playing forward tackle on some bizarre football team where the quarterbacks carried assault rifles.

The two men were forty or so feet from the entrance and gaining speed, their eyes glued to the departing single-engine planc. Will accelerated as well on a ninety-degree intercept course. The man closest to him raised his weapon, aiming in the air over the departing airplane. Will wondered if it was by chance or by choice. The bullets were long departed before the sound waves hit Doug's ears as he paced the accelerating airplane, which was now halfway to the road. Will could see Doug turn in puzzlement, and could see the look of shock as he turned back toward Sandra and gave her a frantic, wide-eyed gesture that said, *Go! Go now!*

The two Iraqis—for that's what they had to be—spotted Will now. The second man fired his gun, also aiming harmlessly in the air, and somewhere in his head Will realized they didn't want the airplane full of holes.

They would have no such attachment to Doug or Will.

Doug was fully exposed now, standing clear of the accelerating aircraft as both soldiers stopped in their tracks, the muzzles of their guns both dropping from a high angle to a flat angle. Will knew they had seen him approach. They were less than twenty feet away now. Will had to alter course to the left to reach the two as they took aim, presumably at Doug. Will could see in his peripheral vision that Doug's hands were in the air. He could see directly ahead of him that the nearest Iraqi was turning, bringing the barrel of his gun around. Their fingers were both inside their respective trigger guards. There was simply no time left.

"NO! STOP IT! HOLD ON! DON'T SHOOT!" Will screamed the words at the top of his lungs, waving his arms in the air as if trying to block a basketball shot, his body coming to a halt in their line of fire, between them and Doug. He braced mentally for the impact of bullets. It was a clinical, detached thought, but he wondered if it would hurt.

The two soldiers had not moved. They stood stock-still, their guns both leveled at Will, who was now standing less than five feet away. Doug was behind him somewhere, and the sound of the departing aircraft engine told him that Sandra was off the ground. Mission accomplished.

Still the two men stood there. If they were going to shoot, why didn't they get it over with?

"You . . . *come!*" one of them ordered, motioning to Doug. Will prayed that Doug would run. Instead, Doug's footsteps approached from behind, and then he was standing beside Will, both of them holding their hands in the air.

The two Iraqis looked at each other and said something in Arabic, their voices chattering in staccato bursts as they kept their guns aimed at Doug and Will, their fingers holding firm on the triggers.

"You . . . *Americans?*" one of them finally asked, pushing his gun forward for emphasis.

Doug and Will nodded slowly. Their flight suits were hardly civilian camouflage.

"Surren . . . surrender!" The Iraqi turned the word over tentatively, his agitation growing.

Doug and Will, their hands still in the air, glanced at each other. Doug shrugged. "I thought we already had."

The order came again, even more insistent.

"Surrender!"

Will nodded slowly, painfully, every movement of his head a confirmation of his worst nightmares. His voice was almost inaudible.

"Yes," he said, "surrender."

"I . . . ah . . . do, too," Doug echoed, equally subdued. "I surrender."

The two soldiers stepped back, talking rapidly to each other, keeping their weapons pointed directly at the two colonels. They stepped back suddenly, almost in unison.

This is it, Will thought.

"Surrender, *yes?*" the one said again.

"*Yes,* dammit! Surrender!" Will repeated.

Simultaneously the two Iraqis raised their guns to a port arms position, sank to their knees, and placed the guns on the concrete floor of the hangar, raising *their* hands in the air.

"We surrender now! You will take us please . . . Saud Arabia. Yes?"

16

Sandra Murray put a couple of hundred feet between the small aircraft and the desert floor and tried to concentrate on the horizon ahead, seeing nothing but flatness and desolation in all directions.

She felt empty inside, as if she'd turned her back on her family in a time of crisis. The sounds of gunfire behind her as she taxied out of the hangar and seeing Doug Harris standing there, frantically motioning for her to gun the engine and escape, had triggered an instinctive reaction.

She had responded by jamming the throttle to the stops, raising the nose, and yanking them into the air before even reaching the highway—and feeling instantly guilty for doing so. There was nothing else she could have done, of course. Logic absolved her. But somewhere deep inside, loyalty condemned her.

Once airborne, she was supposed to turn and fly south, but she couldn't do it. She had to know. Carefully staying at a half-mile range, she circled behind the hangar and flew past the open doors once more with the engine back to idle, expecting a hail of bullets for her trouble.

Instead, she saw just for a split second an image that hung in front of her like a nightmarish hallucination: Doug and Will, their hands in the air, facing the two gunmen point-blank.

There was nothing I could do!

Sandra closed her eyes momentarily to exorcise the memory, praying they were merely captured, and not dead. She turned her thoughts to her unconscious passenger instead.

If I can save Bill, then maybe leaving them will make sense.

The highway had long since disappeared to the left, angling to the southeast as Sandra flew due south instead, popping up a few hundred feet every few minutes to check for military installations ahead. If the hangar where they'd found the airplane was fifty miles north of the border as Doug had surmised, Saudi Arabia would be just ahead.

The fatigue of running all night, coupled with the trauma of the last hour and the incredible noise and vibration of the engine through the poorly insulated firewall of the Soviet-built aircraft, fuzzed up her thinking, amplifying her fears and muddling her judgment. She recognized the signs of fatigue, much like the cumulative fatigue of MAC aircrews flying nonstop Desert Shield–Desert Storm missions over the previous half-year.

A roughness seized the engine suddenly, drawing her attention, the sound suggesting carburetor ice—a near impossibility with the warm temperatures and low humidity of the desert climate. Sandra fumbled with what looked like the carburetor heat knob nevertheless, getting no response. There was another lever next to it that looked very much like a fuel-mixture control, and she pulled it now gently, feeling instantly better as the engine smoothed out.

Fifteen more minutes on this heading, she promised herself, *then I turn southeast and look for a Coalition base.*

The morning sun had just begun to heat the sands. By noon, any small airplane flying in the same place, she knew, would be bounced all over the sky by thermals—rising columns of heated air.

But this time of the morning it was smooth, which was a blessing for Bill. The last thing he needed was more jostling around.

She checked the gas gauge again. It was marked in liters, but if Doug had been right, she'd had about three hours of gasoline to start with. That should be enough—unless, of course, she flew right past Saudi civilization and right on into the Arabian desert.

An overwhelming thirst gripped her again. She knew she was becoming dehydrated. She was already hungry and filthy and scared, and very aware there was no time for errors. She had to find help as fast as possible.

Sandra looked at her watch and decided the border was just a few miles ahead. There was supposed to be a road of some sort running on the Saudi side parallel to the border, but she had yet to see it. If she could spot it, she could follow it to what she knew would be Coalition forces. Most of the supplies for the incredibly successful ''Hail Mary'' maneuver Schwarzkopf had pulled off had been trucked along that road.

The flash of silver to the extreme left margins of her peripheral vision didn't register at first. Sandra's eyes had been drawn to a needle advancing toward a red arc. She assumed it was an oil temperature gauge, but with everything labeled in Arabic, she could only guess. Whatever it was, the temperature it was measuring was going up.

She looked forward, sensing something new, something amiss, though the desert was bare before her. She looked to the right, letting her eyes run carefully over the horizon, finding nothing there.

She looked then to the left, and caught a small metallic glint to one side of the rising sun. The glint increased in size.

Something coming this way! Let it be one of ours!

The smoke trail angrily billowing from the back of the on-rushing fighter was a dark shadow against the intense brightness of the horizon. He was turning now, back to the north, probably trying to maneuver in on her, she concluded. She strained to see the outline of it, noting the fact that it seemed to be alone. U.S. fighters would be flying in two- or four-ship formations.

It had twin tails like an F-15, but . . .

The outline of something on the belly and the shape of the upper body in silhouette took shape just for a moment in a chilling form.

That's a MiG-25!

She knew the Coalition controlled the skies. But she also knew that many Iraqi fighters had escaped destruction in hard shelters and by running to Iran.

Almost instinctively she pushed forward on the control stick, diving the tiny aircraft toward the desert floor, wondering if she'd been seen.

She had.

Sandra glanced at the altimeter, trying to interpret it. The rocks were getting larger as she kept the nose down, listening to the rising sounds of the wind in the face of the stubby little craft as it accelerated in the shallow dive. Her training as a flight engineer in C-141s came back now, all the things she'd heard the pilots say about how they'd been trained to make a last-ditch effort to evade a fighter if their lumbering transport was ever jumped on a low-altitude mission.

Fighters hate low and slow, and they hate tight, sudden turns!

The sound of the engine changed suddenly, the noise level rising. She wanted to look at the oil pressure, but there wasn't time.

He was back at her eight-o'clock position now, streaking north. Sandra felt a hope rise in her middle that he didn't consider her a worthwhile target. After all, she was just a little fluff of an airplane in the huge desert sky. Hardly worth the bullets.

Where are our guys when I need them? They should have seen this bandit! AWACS should have seen him!

Perhaps whoever was at those controls was more interested in running to safety than in shooting down a single-engine airplane.

Or perhaps he was one of the few remaining Iraqi fighter pilots who hadn't gotten the word it was all over.

Jesus! He's turning!

There was no doubt now. The fighter had gone into a tight left turn behind her and was rolling in on the tiny single-engine. One burst of his guns and she and Bill would simply disintegrate in midair.

She was down to fifty feet above the desert now, but pushed the nose even lower as she searched quickly for the oil gauge. She remembered an F-15 pilot telling her once he could "lock up" trucks on a German autobahn with his fire-control radar. Even sitting on the ground she wasn't safe, but she wasn't going to make it easy for the bastard.

Turn! Got to out-turn him!

She looked over her left shoulder again, following the smoke and realizing he was almost directly behind her now, perhaps five miles in trail, and undoubtedly locking up a "firing solution."

It was anger now that guided the sudden violent right bank as she kicked the right rudder for good measure and almost pirouetted the single-engine aircraft around to the right, coming about almost 180 degrees before rolling out to face the oncoming jet.

Okay, Abdul, I'm gonna screw up your shot!

But it hadn't fazed him. As his target, Sandra realized, she had simply moved a click to the right, and he could easily correct for that! She would have to wait until he was almost on her to turn again.

The position of the needles on the gauges she had looked at a minute before finally registered, and she looked back, startled to find the needle for what she assumed was oil temperature pegged in the red, and the one she assumed was oil pressure reading very low. If those were right, they were going to be coming out of the sky soon, one way or another.

The ground was within thirty feet now, and so low she dared not bank very steeply without climbing. The engine was getting louder, and she assumed it would continue to rise in volume until it seized. She was losing oil somewhere, and would have to make a forced landing.

The fighter was less than two miles away now, his speed seeming to slow, his form growing larger in her windscreen, and with the full expectation that she would see his guns spitting fire and bullets at any second, she watched him approach, amazed to see that he was aiming to her right as if not interested in blowing her apart, and even more amazed as he came nearly abreast. What had been a Russian-built MiG-25 Foxbat to her mind a few seconds before coalesced into a similar-looking American-built F-15!

He flashed by safely to the right then, trying to slow as much as he dared, the passage incredibly fast even though the pilot was barely hanging in the sky at the slowest possible airspeed of around 180 knots.

Sandra was breathing hard, her heart pounding. *I was so damn sure he was hostile, I never even stopped to think he might be one of ours!*

She banked right again, the engine still turning, but the oil pressure gauge moved even lower as she turned back to the south. The Eagle driver kicked up his power and pulled several G's around to the left, setting up for another low-speed pass, this time with Sandra going in the same direction.

She pushed the throttle in now and brought the little airplane to the highest speed it could manage, close to 120 knots, surprised when the engine complied, expecting a smile and a wave from the F-15 pilot as he came by again with flaps down at an airspeed only sixty knots faster than hers.

But the chatter of the Eagle's powerful guns reached her ears instead, at the exact moment her mind registered the fact that live tracer rounds were snaking south over the desert.

He's FIRING at me! He's WARNING me! He thinks I'M hostile!

Again the Eagle accelerated and began a left turn as his wingman, who'd stayed high and out of sight until now, slowed in trail for a low-speed pass.

There was no radio in the little airplane. She hadn't considered the fact that she was flying an Iraqi military aircraft into Saudi and Coalition airspace without a clearance and at low altitude. She had to signal the guy she was a GI.

How?

He's closing again back there. No, that one's still maneuvering out to the left. This must be his wingman.

She assumed he wanted her to land. She was going to have to do so momentarily, anyway. The other pilot had made some sort of gesture on his last pass, but he was too far over for Sandra to make it out. This time the F-15 seemed only inches away as he approached, pulling abeam with a sixty-knot closing rate again as Sandra reached up and clawed at one of her Velcro patches, the American flag on her left shoulder. She opened the window on her left, then, and held the patch out as far as she could, waving it vigorously up and down as she leaned her head in the same direction, letting her blond hair trail outside the window as obviously as possible.

Sandra had no way of hearing the radioed comment of the Eagle pilot to his flight lead somewhere above. As he accelerated and pulled in his flaps, Rover 21 punched his mike button and said, "You're not gonna believe this. There's a blond broad in a flight suit at the controls of that Iraqi crate, and she's shaking a U.S. flag at me!"

The reaction from his controller aboard Crown was almost instantaneous.

"Watch the sexist remarks, Rover two-one. That's a female of the GI persuasion to you."

The AWACS controller reached for the tie-line phone to

scramble a rescue helicopter for the intercept at the same moment the engine in front of Sandra Murray gave a last sound of screeching protest and stopped.

Pick a suitable field, set up a glide . . .

She reran the single-engine-aircraft forced-landing procedure through her head at the same time she realized that half of Saudi Arabia constituted a suitable emergency landing field, and from a hundred feet she had little time to glide.

She sideslipped just a bit to avoid a small depression and held the little aircraft off until it stalled, then touched down. Braking sharply to a safe stop, she got out immediately to wave at the two F-15s as they made one last flyby.

She looked in at Bill then, relieved his chest was still rising and falling.

There was still a chance.

CENTCOM, Riyadh, Saudi Arabia
Saturday, March 9, 1991—8:30 A.M. (0530 GMT)

"Sergeant Phillips, come here and look at this."

Colonel Richard Kerr looked haggard and alarmed after poring over aerial surveillance shots since an hour before dawn. Officers usually didn't do the grunt work of photo analysis, but Kerr was an acknowledged expert, and he was determined to find Will and Doug, if they were findable.

"Sir?"

Phillips took the photo, spotting the telltale mark on the roof of what was clearly a truck of some sort as it sat tucked away in a ravine north of the abandoned masonry building the missing 141 crew had used.

"Okay," Kerr began, "check my logic. I've got four shots of the same spot in a ravine not too far from that highway they were searching. One was taken just before the RF-4 took the picture of the building and caught two of our crew members, one as the rescue mission was beginning, one ninety minutes later, after the mission ended unsuccessfully, and the last in midafternoon. The truck's not in the first shot, it *is* in the second shot, gone again in the third shot, and back in the last one. *And we've found no infrared returns on the satellite orbit after midnight, meaning the truck was gone again after dark.* At last I've got a blowup of the same spot that shows the truck in the ravine is the same one that was at the building with Westerman. What do you make of all that?''

Phillips studied the colonel's face, recognizing a rhetorical question.

"What do *you* make of it, sir?''

Kerr nodded, the key to the puzzle in his hands.

"They're *not* captured! I don't know how they got an Iraqi truck, but if they'd been captured, their captors wouldn't be hiding in the desert, they'd be heading for Baghdad or somewhere else. If you were Westerman and Harris, though, and you'd captured a truck, would you want to drive in daylight with pale faces and a female engineer?''

"Hardly. I'd wait for darkness.''

Kerr thumped the picture again. "Exactly what they did!''

Will hadn't disappointed him. He knew his old friend would find a way to wiggle out of the net.

But now the Iraqis knew as well.

Kerr collected the photos and supporting materials and charged upstairs, finding General Bullock in the central command post.

"Sir,'' he explained carefully, "this means our people were *not* captive as of yesterday morning.''

"They are now.''

Kerr was confused. "I don't understand. What's happened?''

Bullock filled him in on the flash message from Search and Rescue. Sergeant Sandra Murray and a seriously injured Sergeant Bill Backus had just flown out of Iraq and were en route to a U.S. field hospital at Dhahran.

Bullock pushed his right hand under his glasses and rubbed

his eyes briefly before continuing. "Colonels Westerman and Harris were taken at gunpoint by Iraqi soldiers as she and Backus got away. She's not even sure they weren't shot."

Kerr threw the satellite transparencies down on the console. "Shit!"

"Tell me about it," Bullock said, looking up. "You remember I was insisting we tell Iraq we knew they had our people? That was done at ten P.M." Bullock heaved himself out of the chair and instinctively straightened his uniform. "So at dawn this morning, guess what? Thanks to the fact that we told them all about the American crew they were supposed to have captured but hadn't, the Iraqis went right out and captured them."

"General"—Kerr was shaking his head—"that's probably just a coincidence. There wouldn't have been enough time to mount a search, especially with the civil war and the lack of command communications."

Bullock nodded slowly. "I hope you're right."

"Well, sir, it's a moot point now, apparently."

Bullock sighed again. "We'll know more in an hour. We're sending a new rescue package in to find that hangar and look it over, just in case."

Provisional Regional Military Command Headquarters, Kirkuk, Iraq
Saturday, March 9, 1991—8:30 A.M. (0530 GMT)

"Doctor Damerji, can you hear me? Doctor?"

The words were Arabic, but for some reason Shakir's mind transposed them into English. He was sitting naked in the middle of a huge bed in what had to be a whorehouse in the middle of Arizona, or maybe Montana. It was the Old West, and beside him, asleep in the bed, was an extremely sexy woman, and someone was calling his name. Only it wasn't his name, it was the name of his classmate, who didn't have his doctorate yet. That was what puzzled him, why the owner of the voice would ask for *Doctor* Damerji before Damerji was a doctor. Most unusual!

"Doctor, are you okay?"

His eyes finally focused as the dream—and the girl—evaporated. He felt himself mentally grasping for the memory as it slipped like sand through his fingers, and was gone.

He was back in Iraq, sitting on the floor in the corner of the commandeered room of a Kirkuk house taken over by General Hashamadi and his staff, one of whom was leaning over him with a worried expression.

"I'm . . . I'm fine," Shakir croaked, his mouth as dry as powder, his voice protesting the call to duty.

"Would you like some tea, Doctor? Or some water?"

Don't forget who you are! You are Muayad Damerji! Remember that!

Shakir looked up and smiled as much as he could, sitting up and readjusting his back, which was hurting. "Thank you, yes, I'd like some water."

The aide nodded and turned. He looked more like an Iranian, Shakir thought. Drooping mustache, jet black hair and eyes. But it was the stocking hat and the oversized army fatigue jacket that made him look Iranian. That and the fact that he couldn't be much more than twenty years old.

Shakir rubbed his eyes and looked at his watch, trying to ignore the wave of body odor the aide had left in his wake.

Eight-thirty. I've been asleep about five hours.

General Hashamadi was still away, but expected back by midmorning. The fighting to the north was serious, the Kurdish rebels having gained the upper hand in ways that were unclear. Shakir overheard a few sketchy conversations while waiting, but nothing reliable.

The aide returned with a ceramic cup of water of questionable origin, but he drank it down rather than examine it.

The secret police officer who had rescued him was nowhere to be seen, but Shakir couldn't help but imagine him around the corner, listening carefully for Shakir's slightest slip or mistake. The man had escorted him right to the military post and inside, then frightened Shakir even more by insisting on waiting with him. Around midnight he had tired of the wait and taken his leave, or so he had said.

Shakir had never hidden behind an alias before, and it unnerved him profoundly.

Muayad—the *real* Muayad—had agreed to lie low at home for several days to prevent being seen at two places at the same time. The greatest danger, both of them knew, was Shakir running into someone who knew Muayad—or him. Or someone who had seen pictures—someone like the secret police officer, perhaps.

Shakir looked around at his surroundings—a half-destroyed living room—and caught an unpleasant whiff of raw sewage from somewhere outside the open door. Some poor family had been kicked out of their house so the army could use it. Like animals, the soldiers had simply tossed most of the personal items outside in a heap, breaking whatever would break. Keepsakes and heirlooms now mixed indiscriminately with garbage and dirt in the courtyard, as if those material items had never had meaning for any living person.

Then again, perhaps the family had been declared an enemy of the state, like me, Shakir thought. Perhaps their lives had been deemed as disposable as their property.

There was an animated conversation going on to his left between an officer and someone he could not see. Shakir had paid no attention, but a word—or phrase—had suddenly snagged his ear. They seemed anxious to communicate back to Baghdad that Saddam's loyal forces in Kirkuk were not holding whomever Saddam's Baghdad staff was looking for. At least that's what it sounded like, and the words froze Shakir's blood. He zeroed in on the conversation as best he could, trying to mentally filter out the noises of trucks passing outside, the clopping of heavy boots on the tile floors, and the background hum of other voices. He strained to listen for the names "Shakir," "Abbas," "Damerji," or the name of the former colleague whose body he'd left to burn in the desert.

They were looking for someone. No, they had *captured* someone, but Baghdad didn't know where they were. He must have misunderstood that part, Shakir concluded.

He closed his eyes and concentrated, trying to unravel the garbled portions of each sentence, and realized suddenly that several of the last words he had just heard were neither words nor Arabic.

They were names. Two familiar names, which sounded like "Westaremon" and "Hair-*ees.*"

Shakir's eyes came open instantly. He got to his feet somewhat painfully, but ignored the discomfort, moving rapidly into a better position from which to overhear.

Al Hajarah desert, south central Iraq
Saturday, March 9, 1991—8:45 A.M. (0545 GMT)

Leaving the bombed-out Iraqi hangar had been one of the most difficult things Will Westerman had ever had to do. He knew American rescue forces would be on the scene within hours—at least he *hoped* they would—and moving away from rescue once again seemed stupid.

But the two defecting Iraqi soldiers were spotter pilots. They had already radioed their officers that the hangar complex was a good place for their retreating armored column to hide while waiting for orders. Then they had gone to sleep in the hallway of an underground bunker beneath the hangar, only to be awakened by the sounds of the four Americans stealing their airplane.

The motorized infantry brigade was due by midmorning. There was no time to lose. What persuaded Will to go, however, was the chilling news that Sandra had flown off in an airplane hemorrhaging oil. The two Iraqis had planned to fly right past the hangar and on to Saudi Arabia to defect, but were forced down by the oil leak. They had radioed their main force, hoping to get the leak fixed when the column arrived. All they would have needed were the rudimentary tools the brigade mechanics carried to tighten the lines. Then, they had figured, they could try again.

Sandra, in other words, might not have made it all the way to a friendly air base. Rescue could be days away, not hours—while capture could be imminent if they dawdled.

With great reluctance Will and Doug loaded themselves in the truck and headed out again, this time bouncing east straight across the desert with the two Iraqis—brothers named Amal and Harun—sandwiched between them on the front seat.

Doug braked again, another stretch of loose sand looming ahead.

"Are you sure about this, Amal?"

"Yes, yes! I am sure. This . . . is right . . . is right point for to get . . . for going to American base."

Amal could speak broken English, Harun could not, which made for a hilarious routine of not-so-simultaneous translation. Harun would speak in rapid Arabic and Amal would get wide-eyed trying to keep up, occasionally hitting his brother in the arm to slow down and let him catch up. When Will or Doug spoke, Harun could not wait for the translation and pressed Amal unmercifully to hurry up and explain—which he did now.

"What'd he say?" Doug asked, trying to suppress a smile.

"Harun agrees this is right, sir." Amal nodded, his head continuing to bob in affirmation until Doug raised his hand to indicate enough.

Will sat by the right door of the crowded cab of the truck in deep worry, the desert wind blowing hot in his face now as the temperature rose into the upper eighties on its way higher. They had water, thanks to Amal and Harun, and they had some sense of direction. But they had no more gasoline, and the tanks were getting dry. Will estimated they had no more than an hour's worth left. Once again they would be on foot.

He had tried to convince the Iraqis of this. Amal understood, but insisted there was a road, always "a road there . . . up there!"

It seemed as if they had been on the run forever, though only two and a half days had gone by since the marathon disaster of a mission had begun.

Will rested his right arm on the windowsill and looked absently at the horizon as Doug spoke and laughed with the two brothers.

Doug could make friends with Attila the Hun, Will groused to himself. It was a talent. An irritating talent, but a talent nonetheless.

Sandra's face swam before him suddenly. He supposed he was just worried about her, but there was something more.

He missed her.

No, he corrected himself, *I* miss *Janice back home. I'm just worried about Sandra.*

Bullshit! something in his brain shot back. *You miss her, bub, because you like her. Quit kidding yourself!*

The truck bounced painfully hard suddenly, the engine and transmission protesting as the wheels began to slide on more sand and Doug fought successfully to recover, pushing ahead toward the spot Amal kept shaking his index finger at through the windshield.

"There . . . please go in there direction . . . *that* direction. We have the day before now come from there. American military is there."

Once again Harun demanded an immediate translation, and he and Amal fell to speaking rapidly in Arabic.

In spite of himself—in spite of his anger at all things Iraqi—Will was beginning to like these two comedians. Somehow the fact that they could fly made it all right—as if he needed an excuse.

And the idea of these two killing anyone—or anyone killing

them—didn't make much sense either, whether they were military or not.

They had gotten stuck in deep sand and worked themselves free twice when the gasoline ran out. They climbed from the truck then to see for the first time a wall of brown approaching from the east, a sudden dust storm that engulfed them in minutes. They began trudging toward the southeast, the two Iraqis leading the way with surprising strength.

"You not worry," Amal had told them while showing Will and Doug how to fashion face masks of simple cloth and bundle up against the choking grit. "The road is there, and after, American military. I know this."

For hours they walked, Will and Doug staying in line behind the two brothers, guided as much by the sharp sound of their footsteps as by any visual reference, until the intensity of the wind at their backs and the impossible concentration of grit in the air made stopping a matter of survival. Virtually nothing was visible beyond ten feet ahead.

As Will and Doug sat, Amal pulled yards of parachute cloth and several collapsible aluminum poles from a small pack he had brought, and within minutes the four of them were huddled under a lean-to tent buttressed by sand piled behind them in a quickly made berm.

"Do they teach you to do this in military training?" Doug asked Amal.

"Teach? This . . . tent?" he asked, a puzzled expression coloring his swarthy features.

A smile broke out then, toothy and broad. "Oh, no no no. I am Arab. We are Arab. Arabs know to do this. This desert is home, no?"

They were conscripts from a merchant family in Baghdad, young men in their early twenties who had girlfriends and parents and brothers and sisters and cousins they hadn't seen in a year.

"We have no choice," Amal said of their induction. "We do not go, the army take us anyway and shoot us for not going. Either way we lose."

"How long have you been out here in the desert?" Will asked.

Amal looked out at the swirling dust, his chin trembling slightly, ignoring Harun's request for instant translation.

"We come here when Saddam invades Kuwait. We have no letters from home for many months."

They fell silent as each in turn nursed the remaining water in two canteens and the brothers shared the food they had—which was little more than dried dates and hard bread—waiting for the storm to blow past, which it began to do in late afternoon.

As suddenly as switching on a bright light, the skies cleared, the sun began beating down on the makeshift shelter, and they started digging out. The four of them had begun walking southeast again, Amal leading the way over a low, shallow sand dune, when Doug suddenly saw him drop to his belly in the sand, motioning the others to do the same.

"Ahead! Republican Guard!" he whispered over his shoulder. "Not our . . . unit . . ." Amal gestured to his brother. " . . . but I know this one."

A group of personnel carriers and tanks were parked in a ragged circle a quarter-mile distant, a few soldiers sitting or standing near their machines, but no one apparently looking in their direction.

Harun was obviously upset. He spoke rapidly and urgently to his brother before Amal translated.

"Harun say these are the . . . the . . . soldiers who came to shoot any Iraqi who try to run away, they come from units like this. They must not see us!"

Will turned his head toward Amal, kicking up sand with his chin.

Amal turned to Will and spoke at last. "It is better . . . if we are here until sun is gone."

Amal's sudden tugging on Will's sleeve caught all of them off guard. He had been studying the far horizon.

"Sir, look there! You see helicopter? American military are there."

Will followed Amal's finger toward a small dot on the horizon that coalesced into a helicopter. The chopper was disappearing to the north, but in its wake they could almost make out something on the ground from where he had taken to the air. Eight to ten miles away, the suggestion of dark shapes that could be tents, tanks, or vehicles hovered in the slight mirage of residual heat in the waning sunlight.

"If those are our people . . ." Will began.

The helicopter was returning, closer to their position now, yet still at least five miles distant. Nevertheless, its shape was distinctive.

"Those *are* our people, Will!" Doug's voice was tinged with excitement. "That's an American Blackhawk!"

Will sighed a close-to-the-end-of-the-race sigh as the Blackhawk sank out of sight over the horizon. "Okay, we'll do our usual trick of waiting until nightfall, then get around that Iraqi unit and make the dash as fast as we can. If that's ten miles, it'll take us, what, two hours?"

Doug was nodding, a broad smile on his face.

Amal was excited too. Excited and vindicated.

"I told you American military was there. You trust me, I say. They are there, I say, and now, there they are!"

Will smiled, reached over, and patted the Iraqi on the shoulder, a gesture that at first surprised the young soldier.

"Well done, my friend."

As Doug watched, Amal's face softened to an expression of gratitude, and he nodded solemnly to Will before turning to Harun to deliver the inevitable translation to Arabic.

Doug looked at his watch. It was 5:00 P.M., and two hours to darkness. It was too far away to see, of course, but he could almost feel Old Glory waving over the encampment out there in the desert only a few miles away.

Doug let himself think of Kathy and the kids. They would have been notified by now that he was missing, and she would be in agony.

There would be at least a field telephone over there on the American side. He'd call home the moment they made it over the line.

Two more hours!

Iraq Military Command Headquarters, Baghdad
Saturday, March 9, 1991—4:00 P.M. (1300 GMT)

General Hassoun of the Iraqi army tossed the teletype message on the scarred wooden surface of the makeshift desk and scowled at his aide. His tooth was hurting again, but there was no time to attend to it. He rubbed his right cheek and motioned for the man to sit down as he pulled a cigarette from a small silver case and lit it. He had too few left to offer one to the aide.

"When did this come in?" he asked the younger officer.

"About ten minutes ago, sir. It was brought here by courier, from the other communications center."

The general nodded. To call this a command anymore was a ridiculous joke. For the last five days what remained of Saddam's command staff had been scrambling out of hardened shelters and into ordinary civilian neighborhoods to hide from the new laser-guided American bomb that had punched through thirty feet of concrete and taken out a vital command post—along with several lifelong friends and a senior army commander—in the last day of the ground war. Bunkers were no longer safe, regardless of the concrete. Yet residential areas had no communications. It was like fighting a war with postcards.

And there was still a war to fight, though it was now a civil war.

Hassoun had made his own plans. If the worst came and Bush decided to invade all the way to Baghdad, he would escape to Jordan. His family was already there, though Saddam did not know that.

"Where were these American colonels supposed to be again?" the general asked.

The aide spread a tattered map on the desk and indicated a point in south central Iraq. "Their transport crashed here, General. They were supposed to have been captured"—his finger moved the equivalent of a hundred and fifty miles—"here."

"We have checked with all the outposts in that area?"

"The ones we can reach, sir. They are all, as you know, scattered badly."

Hassoun nodded, and sighed deeply.

"If the Americans are convinced these two colonels are our prisoners, they will push and scream at us until we send them home, and we cannot send them home until we have first captured them. We do not want to hand Bush another reason to start bombing again. So we must find these two colonels by whatever means necessary."

"Sir, that's what we've been trying to do. The message—"

"The message simply says, Captain, that none of our people who have reported in are holding them. The message does not say they cannot be found. They are obviously still out there somewhere, and obviously, if they aren't stupid, they're heading for the nearest border or for their own forces. It shouldn't be too hard to figure out where to look. Start notifying all the units we can reach that these two are to be found and brought immediately, and in good condition, to me. Whoever makes the capture will be rewarded with either money or a discharge, whichever they want."

"Yes sir."

Hassoun watched the man leave before getting to his feet and walking to the window. There were several helicopters in a small village on the outskirts of the city under his control alone, fueled and ready to fly him out if the time came. He didn't trust helicopters, but those were the only Iraqi craft the Americans would allow in the air unchallenged.

With the latest dispatches from Kirkuk, and the noise the Americans were making about protecting the Kurds and the Shiites, his escape plan was looking more attractive by the hour.

Al Hajarah desert, south central Iraq
Saturday, March 9, 1991—6:05 P.M. (1505 GMT)

The sun was hanging low in the western sky, the temperatures starting down from the upper eighties, as the lengthening shadows began to creep toward the crest of the small sand dune hiding Doug Harris, Will Westerman, and their two Iraqi deserters.

They were all lying on their stomachs, partially burrowed into the sand and hiding, Will to Doug's left, the two Iraqi defectors on Will's left. As the day wore to a close, the angled sunbeams began highlighting features in the sand they hadn't noticed before.

Like the others, Doug was lying with his chin resting on his crossed hands. For several minutes he'd been studying two small bumps in the sand an inch or so apart and lying directly in front of his face.

"Will?" Doug's voice was low and questioning.

"Yeah."

"Ask Amal if they have horned toads in Iraq."

Will didn't answer at first. The question sounded like a typical buildup to a joke, Harris-style, and Will wasn't in a joking mood.

Nor was Doug.

"Ask him *what*?" Will said at last.

"Horned toads, like in Fort Worth. Ask him if they have them here."

Will turned his head to look at Doug, a scowl on his face.

"Why the hell would—"

"Just . . . just *ask* him, will you?"

Will sighed and turned to Amal, relaying the question, then describing what a horned toad was. He turned back to Doug.

"No, they don't. But he wants to know why."

"Because I see something in front of me that looks like a horned toad."

"Right in front of you?"

"Yeah."

"Where?"

"Look about a foot in front of my nose. See those bumps?"

Will turned toward Amal, and the conversation took on an urgent tone before Will turned back to Doug, speaking slowly, his voice now tense and little more than a whisper.

"Okay, Doug, listen very carefully. Do exactly what I tell you . . . okay?"

"Okay."

"Okay." Will cleared his throat as quietly as he could.

"Doug, that's *not* a horned toad."

"What is—"

Will cut him off. "*Just* . . . just, when I give the word . . . I want you to flip your entire body . . . to your left . . . over the top of me."

"To the left?"

"To the left. Got that?"

"Yeah. But what *is* it?"

"Just . . . do it. Don't ask." Will's words were quiet and urgent.

"*Now!*"

Doug rolled with a sudden, fluid motion across Will's back, landing between him and Amal, and simultaneously Amal, Harun, and Will leaped to their feet, pulling Doug along with them as they all ran a dozen yards away, bending over to stay out of view, before once again dropping to their stomachs in the sand.

"Now what the hell was *that* all about?" Doug asked, irritated.

"That, old friend," Will answered as he caught his breath, "was a sand viper. They do that. They bury themselves in the sand, and all you see are those little horns. He was close enough to strike you on the nose."

"They're poisonous?"

Doug heard Will snort. "You ever hear the expression 'two-stepper'? He bites you, you take two steps and drop. Horribly venomous snake."

The sound of Doug scrambling to his feet accompanied the last of Will's explanation.

"Get down!" Will said, craning his neck to the right to look at Doug, who was edging farther from the crest of the dune.

"Like *hell* I'm going to get back into that sand pile if there're snakes in it. I hate snakes! You know that."

"You like Iraqi bullets any better? Get *down*, man!" Will was gesturing with his palm down, and Doug gingerly sank to his knees as he pointed in the direction of the Iraqi unit now out of sight across the dune.

"They can't see us," Doug said.

"They will if you keep moving around with the sun at your back."

Amal had been moving carefully back toward the crest of the dune, taking care to stay clear of the viper's location. He was back now at Will's side, excited.

"Sir, the guard unit is moving away!"

"Away from us?" Will looked alarmed.

Amal nodded and pointed north as the faint sounds of engines firing up filtered over the sand dune. They watched as the Iraqi unit moved on toward the north.

Will brushed back his sand-caked hair and looked at his watch. Thirty minutes to darkness, he figured. A forelock of hair fell right back in his eyes and Will pawed at it once again, shaking his head disgustedly as Doug started laughing at the futility of the effort.

"My kingdom for a shower and some deodorant," Will said.

"Amen to that. We smell worse than we did after that two-night hell week at survival training."

"Spokane in the winter. God, don't remind me of that," Will snorted. "I'll never forgive the Air Force for that."

Doug glanced around to the west at exactly the moment the sun began undulating into the horizon, its passage a conflagration of oranges and reds against deepening purple overhead. They all fell silent then, following Doug's gaze, Harun catching Amal's sleeve and pointing at the solar beauty as the disk sank out of sight at last in the barren majesty of a living painting framed by an endless horizon.

"Okay," Will said at last, "let's get ready to move. As soon as they're out of sight, we go toward the Coalition base as fast as we can walk."

CENTCOM, Riyadh, Saudi Arabia
Saturday, March 9, 1991—6:30 P.M. (1530 GMT)

The radioed reports of the short-lived battle inside Iraq had already been relayed to the Pentagon as General Martin joined General Bullock and several other senior officers in the war room.

"In brief?" Martin asked.

Bullock nodded and grimaced. "We had to hold off until the dust storm blew over, as you know. That was around sixteen hundred local, but as soon as the first Warthog did a flyby on that partially destroyed hangar, he was fired on. We brought in the Apaches and flushed out two tanks, but just as the hogs were rolling in on them again, white flags came out all over the place. They all wanted to come back as POWs. Our people inspected the hangar and found no trace of the truck, or of Westerman and Harris. They also found no evidence that anyone had been shot. Instead, they found truck tracks leading off to the southeast.''

"Meaning what?'' Martin asked.

"It's anybody's guess. The Iraqis claimed they hadn't seen any Americans. But they did confirm that two of their spotter pilots and an airplane were missing.''

"That would be the one . . .''

"We think so, yes. The one Sergeant Murray used to fly out. The two soldiers she saw in the hangar were probably the two spotter pilots. But where *are* they? That's the question we haven't yet answered, though we're running some additional RF-4 recon missions now, and one of the choppers has been trying to follow the tire tracks. And that's the other question. Why did they head southeast with American prisoners?''

"We left those Iraqi troops at the hangar, didn't we?'' Martin asked.

"Yes sir. They were pretty disappointed, I'm told, but we disabled the remaining tanks and left them. They were not Republican Guard.''

At the same moment, two floors below, a nervous Dr. Sandar Almeany, former research assistant to Shakir Abbas, was nudged around a final corner of the linoleum-tiled hallway and into a small conference room, a poker-faced Army MP on each elbow. Since suffering through a plane crash and a mad dash through the night in a wildly bucking armored vehicle, he had been kept locked up and isolated, even though he had asked for asylum.

Colonel Richard Kerr and three other officers were waiting and motioned him to a seat. They gave Almeany a carefully rehearsed briefing on what they already knew about the virus he and Shakir Abbas had developed, and about the events leading to Abbas's escape—which they called a "disappearance.'' The Iraqi listened impassively, then waited an uncomfortably long time to reply. He knew the key question they wanted answered: how much of the virus was out there, and *where* was it? Sandar was defecting. He had no intention of being elusive.

"Dr. Abbas is my colleague for many years," he began, "and he asked me similar questions the night of the attack. At first I thought he had been captured, then I understood he had come to you for help. This . . . this *thing* we developed is too deadly to be left in the hands of our leader."

The word *leader* was spoken with a snort. In Baghdad, that slight nuance could get him shot. In Riyadh, he figured, it would not be ingraciously received.

Sandar looked at the men in the room and continued, telling them what he knew about the two missing canisters, who had taken them, and where they might be headed.

"Why did Dr. Abbas break away from the force we sent in?"

"I *suspect*," Sandar answered. "I don't *know*. From the questions he asked me, he would have gone after Ansallah and the canister, or canisters, Ansallah took. Shakir is a determined man when he decides to do something."

They talked about routes and highways, the Abbas family, the location of General Hashamadi, and what Shakir Abbas could be expected to do when on such a vital mission. Richard Kerr had needed an edge —a lead—to have any reasonable hope of using satellite surveillance shots and other intelligence reports to reconstruct Abbas's whereabouts, and try to find the canisters. The pressure was building rapidly on Kerr. With two other senior intelligence officials on their way from Washington to join him in Riyadh, the needle-in-the-haystack search was becoming frantic. Where were Abbas and the missing viral canisters? No less a personage than the President of the United States had decreed that every effort would be made to recapture the man and his lethal creation, regardless of cost.

Richard Kerr made a few final notes, thanked Almeany, and charged out of the room then, heading back to the basement and a growing stack of satellite surveillance pictures of the area around the destroyed desert lab. Principally, he was looking for the tiny image of a green Toyota van. "All I have to do," he had said sarcastically, "is follow that van and its occupant across Iraq and, days after the fact, figure out where that driver is now." And regardless of the increasing number of personnel he had at his disposal to help, he couldn't ditch the fatalistic feeling that they had already exceeded the limits of electronic surveillance.

Behind him now in a far corner of the conference room, Dr. Walter Hajek of the biomedical research team had been listening quietly and waiting his turn. Now Hajek started in like a gentle professor, quietly building a bond of scientific kinship with the researcher as he probed the details of how the virus had been created.

His mind, however, was elsewhere, and he found himself checking his watch with embarrassing frequency. In approximately two more hours a small vial shipped against his wishes from Riyadh would arrive at Andrews Air Force Base and be rushed to a top-secret biological research facility somewhere nearby.

Hajek knew neither the code name nor the location of the secret facility, and that was fine. What he *did* know, however, was that all hell was going to break loose when they tried to test that sample.

U.S. Forces Field Hospital, Dhahran, Saudi Arabia
Saturday, March 9, 1991—6:50 P.M. (1550 GMT)

Sergeant Sandra Murray replaced the handset at the nurses' station and stood there for a moment, her eyes on the door of the operating room where Bill Backus was still in surgery. Her thoughts, however, were still in the desert, searching for Will and Doug.

"You all right, honey?" The concerned voice of the nurse

behind the desk barely registered at first. Sandra turned, a puzzled look on her face, as the words came together in some recess of her brain.

"Oh yes. I'm . . . I'm fine. Just waiting for word, you know." Sandra smiled as she felt her right hand twirling the telephone cord—a symmetrical, back-and-forth motion she couldn't seem to stop. It was soothing somehow. Like a physical chant.

"Was that call about the other crew members?" the nurse tried again. "Your two colonels?"

My two colonels?

Sandra looked at the major, who was at least ten years older and an activated reservist like herself. What was her name? Oh yes. Sara. That was the third time she'd forgotten, and it was embarrassing.

Sandra nodded and took a deep breath. "Yeah. Rescue has found the truck we were in, about eighty miles from where I left them. It was out of gas. It's strange, but hopeful at the same time. I thought they were captured, but they seem to be heading for the nearest Coalition base."

"Well, that's great news, then, right?"

"Yes." Sandra knew her face contradicted her words, but something seemed very wrong—or was she just exhausted? The doctor who had refused to let her out of the hospital an hour ago had said she was suffering from exhaustion, and she had looked in his eyes and said, "Bullshit, sir."

Sandra gestured toward nowhere in particular, ignoring the antiseptic smell that seemed to waft over her suddenly as an orderly bustled by with open bottles of unknown content on a cart.

"I should be out there on one of those rescue choppers right now, helping to find them. There's nothing wrong with me. Why won't they let me out of here?"

The question was swallowed by the sudden movement of the doors to the operating room as a surgeon came out, pulling off his latex gloves, his mask askew, and a tired smile on his face. He winked at Sara and nodded at Sandra before raising his hand to silence her impending questions.

"There is a rather massive infection, but it's already responding, and we've repaired the internal damage and reinflated his lung."

"Why'd it take so long? You've been in there for hours, sir."

"I know it," he said, tugging at his surgical cap. "One of his ribs not only broke, it serrated, and even though I know you folks tried to be gentle, it ripped him up rather badly inside as he was moved around. We had to restructure a few things."

"Do you think he'll be okay?"

The doctor nodded. "He's tough. I think he's going to be just fine."

Sandra thanked him and headed for the phone. Bill's wife was waiting on tenterhooks back in South Carolina for what was going to be good news.

She punched in the numbers as Sara's words echoed in her mind again.

Your two colonels, she had said.

Al Hajarah desert, south central Iraq
Saturday, March 9, 1991—8:00 P.M. (1700 GMT)

The glow on the horizon was close now, Will figured. Perhaps three miles, and nothing but open desert between them and freedom. They had left miles behind the road where the Republican Guard patrol had stopped.

The base ahead was American. The sight of a Blackhawk helicopter lifting off from a bright circle of floodlights had put their fears to rest.

All that remained was to get there.

Will stood in the night wind and scanned the eastern horizon, noting the distant orange of the oil fires punctuating a background of stars, the enticing glow from the base pulling at him to hurry.

Will glanced back at the dark shape they had passed ten minutes ago. It was the hulk of a burned-out tank that had loomed in front of them suddenly in the darkness. Several hundred yards farther on, the remains of a small truck appeared bathed in ghostly light from the distant mercury-vapor lamps. Moonrise was several hours away, and without flashlights, there was no way to tell what else might be strewn on the desert before them.

What happened here? Will wondered. *Aerial attack? Ground attack?* The tank had lost its treads as well as having been burned, and the truck seemed to have been blown on its side.

Very strange. There was an explanation for the abandoned hardware, but it was eluding him, while fatigue numbed his need to know.

Harun was thirty yards ahead now and moving impatiently forward, periodically silhouetted by the lights of the base. For many steps he would be only a dark shadow to one side, then suddenly his form would move across the field of light, only to disappear in the darkness to the other side once again. Will had watched the routine oscillations with amusement, waiting each time for Harun to reappear, which he did now, stopping in full silhouette and turning around suddenly.

What's he up to? Will wondered.

Will could see Harun bend over abruptly, as if examining something on the ground a hundred feet ahead, and at the same moment the image of the burned-out vehicles merged with the fact that they were approaching a battlefield boundary, tipping the last mental tumbler in place, and unlocking a chilling conclusion.

Oh my God!

The unspoken thought that flashed through Will's mind was punctuated instantly by a blinding explosion of light from Harun's direction, followed by a soul-shaking THARRUMPP!

A scream of anguish met his ears, then. Not from Harun, but from Amal, who had just seen his brother's legs vaporized by a land mine.

"Minefield!" Doug yelled. "Oh Jesus, Will! We're in a live minefield!" Doug's voice was up half an octave as he held Amal back. Harun could be seen writhing on the ground in the distance, trying to sit up, waving at them weakly and moaning.

Amal was fighting Doug now, and Will moved to him, holding his arms, talking to him firmly.

"*Listen* to me! We can't help him if we hit a mine too. You can't run out there!"

The cries from Harun were in Arabic, and Doug turned to Amal. "What is he saying? Quickly!"

"He tell me not to come, but I must help!" Amal cried.

"What do we do, Will?" Doug asked. "Do you have any training in this? Are we in the middle of more of them?"

Will's eyes were glued to the mortally wounded brother, trying to calculate whether he could be reached by exactly the same steps. There was too little light. A step in any direction could be fatal.

Harun's voice cut the air again, in agony, but insistent.

Amal yelled back and, giving a sudden heave of his body, broke away from Doug, sprinting ten feet toward his brother before Harun's voice met them again. Even without a translator, it was clear Harun had ordered Amal to come no farther. Amal protested, but Harun yelled the same demand again, his hand weakly motioning his brother back.

Amal stepped forward anyway, slowly, gingerly, trying to see his brother's footsteps in the darkened sand. Will and Doug were frozen in their tracks, grappling with the futility of following him and realizing that they couldn't run back out either.

Harun saw what was happening. He knew his brother would have no choice but to come to his rescue, whatever the consequences. He knew there was nothing he could say to stop Amal from making the same error.

But there was something he could *do*.

Harun accepted the fact he was dying, the pain from his ruined body almost unbearable. As he watched Amal take another perilous step forward, he reached his decision, and felt a great calm come over him.

Will saw Harun raise his gun into the glare of the background lights—the shape of it melding with the silhouetted image of the Iraqi's head.

There was a brief burst of automatic fire then, and Harun's body lurched back and disappeared from view, leaving only the lights of the base, now less than two miles away.

Amal fell to his knees in agony, understanding his brother's last act. Will walked the ten feet to him and put his arm around the young Iraqi's shoulder, drawing him back to where Doug was standing in shock.

"I'm sorry, Amal. I'm so sorry!" Will repeated, holding one shoulder, as Doug held the other.

Several American soldiers had already gathered next to the perimeter guard post by the time the company commander appeared.

"In the minefield out there, sir. I thought I could see a couple of figures after the explosion. One of them may have taken a mine, but they're too far away to make out clearly."

The major took the nightscope binoculars and examined the scene, agreeing with the assessment. He handed the scope back and stood in thought for a second.

"Keep watching. I'll see if we can find an Apache to go take a look."

The Iraqi Republican Guard unit that had moved north also heard the report from the exploding mine. Having received orders earlier by radio to find two American pilots trying to get to Coalition lines in the desert, they had been searching the perimeter of the minefield they had laid several days before. The Iraqi lieutenant, frustrated in their search, had stopped the column of four armored personnel carriers and ordered the engines killed so he could feel the desert night. Together they had stood on their machines and scanned ahead, intent on being the patrol that brought back the missing American colonels, and well aware that the glow four miles to the southeast was that of the conquering enemy.

The thump of the mine was too distinctive to ignore, especially since it was his unit that had laid the minefield.

Now, like a spider moving to its struggling prey, they were rolling again, their headlights off until the landmark hulk of the burned-out tank loomed just ahead, giving the driver the precise guidance he needed to avoid their own death traps.

Doug saw the headlights snap on in the distance and was grateful—for the few seconds it took to realize whom the lights probably belonged to.

There was nowhere to run that wouldn't be a game of Russian roulette. Somehow they had blundered many yards inside the minefield, and whether in darkness or daylight, a single step could kill them.

They had talked quickly, urgently, looking for a way out, but there was only one: wait until daylight and walk back in their own footprints.

Now even that option had been canceled.

"Maybe somebody on our side heard the explosion," Will said hopefully, but without confidence.

The Iraqi patrol, if that was what it was, had them bracketed in headlights now, the APCs coming to a halt less than a hundred yards away.

Doug turned to Amal and shoved the remaining gun into his hand. Amal's face, ghostly in the distant headlights, was streaked with tears.

"Amal, listen carefully." Doug's voice was little more than a whisper, and Will moved between them and the lights, understanding what Doug was planning. "Hold the gun on us. We are your prisoners."

Amal jammed the gun back in Doug's stomach and shook his head. "No! I cannot! You were kind to . . . Amal . . . and . . ." He gestured limply behind him as the gun once again was shoved into his hands and Doug's voice became an insistent growl.

"They will kill you on the spot, Amal, if they think you were escaping. We need you alive to help us. We need you to get out of this minefield, get around it, and make it to the base over there. We need you to tell them where we were captured. If you're dead, there's no trace. This is for us, Amal, understand?"

Amal nodded, slowly, reluctantly, as voices began shouting at them from the direction of the headlights.

"One more thing, Amal. Tell them . . ." Doug fumbled in a flight suit pocket for a scrap of paper, hoping his pen would still work.

It did. He wrote out the names of Sandra Murray and Bill Backus. "Give this to an American officer."

Doug wrote as clearly as he could a brief message, folded the paper, and stuck it in Amal's pocket.

"Now. Hold that gun on us and call to them. Tell them you have taken the gun away from us."

Amal complied, his voice rising, submerging his anguish in the act of convincing the oncoming soldiers who were picking their way through the last few yards with flashlights and a map.

Doug and Will were led out at gunpoint, Amal following behind, his story accepted with scorn. This conscript wasn't going to claim their reward. They would leave him behind to shift for himself.

One of the soldiers shoved Doug in the back, knocking him into the rear of one of the armored personnel carriers as his lieutenant yelled at him to be careful. The Americans were to be delivered in good condition. He had told his men the reward would be for all of them.

It was Will's turn then to climb in the rear hatch, and with his hands now bound behind him, it was difficult. The final soldier joined him inside, leaving the door open as the column lurched away, the noise of the engine covering the sound of an American helicopter approaching from the southeast.

Amal was visible through the hatch, his face caught in a rear searchlight from the APC, standing at the edge of the minefield with glistening eyes, his gun held limply by his side, his shoulders slumped, helpless to rescue the Americans who had tried to rescue him.

To Will, he looked like the saddest man on earth.

Airborne, north of Kirkuk, Iraq
Sunday, March 10, 1991—7:00 A.M. (0400 GMT)

Shakir Abbas watched the ground drop away, carrying his stomach with it.

His left hand hurt from gripping the life out of the side rail on the seat, but with the main door of the helicopter wide open, the intimidating mixture of engine and rotor noise with the shocking blast of cold morning air made it impossible to relax his near-death grip.

The helicopter pitched over sharply then, as if the floor were dropping out from under him. It felt as strange and frightening as the roller-coaster ride he had taken in an American amusement park once, that catastrophic feeling of uncontrollable emptiness in your middle when you rocket over the top and head down again—not quite a pain, but very alarming. Shakir closed his eyes momentarily, opening them again when he realized the helicopter was simply picking up speed as they headed north to pick up General Hashamadi.

"Are you all right, Doctor?" One of the crew members was yelling at him in Arabic, and Shakir smiled and nodded. Not a very convincing show of confidence, but at least he was hanging on.

In the guise of Dr. Damerji he had fumed, paced, sat, and slept for an entire day waiting for the general to return. Sometime before dawn, the same secret police officer who had escorted Shakir into town had reappeared, seemingly delighted with what he had arranged for the good doctor. Damerji, he announced, would be allowed to fly on the general's helicopter when it left to fetch him from somewhere closer to the fighting. Shakir had tried to act appreciative, but deep inside was the latent fear that his true identity was known to the man, and that he was being toyed with. A fatalistic image of being kicked out the door of the helicopter from a thousand feet up had played repeatedly in his mind. Saliah might have to get along without him after all.

With the guards used to his presence in the makeshift head-quarters, Shakir had begun wandering the halls the previous afternoon, letting each excursion take him farther and farther into the various rooms until he found himself in the general's office. He had come back twice, as casually as possible, both times with his hands shoved deep in his pockets in case he was discovered there, and both times letting his eyes touch every object in the room.

But there was no sign of the distinctive little canister, and he dared not open any of the desk drawers.

The hunger pains that had nauseated him earlier came back for a moment. None of the soldiers was eating well, and Shakir had asked for nothing and received little more. He needed food, he needed fluids, he needed sleep, and he needed clean clothes and a chance to bathe. But more than anything else, he needed to speak with the general absolutely alone.

His plan required that.

The helicopter was descending now under a canopy of dank gray, the orange and yellow sunrise off to the right suppressed by a thick layer of clouds, the chill of the morning air causing him to hunch over in an instinctive attempt to preserve body heat. Why they flew with the door open he couldn't fathom, but the other three crewmen didn't seem interested in closing it.

They were in the mountains now, or at least in the foothills. The hint of greenery and trees below through the mist and clouds gave way to a verdant scene of highland meadows. A poor substitute to anyone who had seen Scotland, as he had while at Oxford, but to the desert-parched eye of an Iraqi it was an Eden indeed.

The pilot circled and banked sharply, another helicopter—a gunship of Russian design—pacing them off to the right. Shakir could see a small group of vehicles ahead on the ground, and a group of military men standing nearby.

Their American-built helicopter was dropping sharply now and slowing, the sound of the engine and slapping of the blades increasing as the ground came up and gently kissed the skids in a perfect landing.

Almost instantly there were men at the open entrance, helping two others through the door and into the seat along the rear wall. Shakir instinctively moved over, looking for his seatbelt as the chopper leaped from the surface again and turned back to the south.

"General?" One of the crew members was standing in front of the man next to Shakir, whose rank he had not seen.

"Yes."

The crewman gestured to Shakir then. "This is Dr. Damerji, of the Nuclear Research Division. He needs to talk with you, sir, and we were given permission to bring him." The man was searching the general's face in subdued panic, obviously unsure he had done the right thing.

General Hashamadi nodded then and turned to Shakir, extending his hand.

"Doctor? How may I be of service?"

Shakir had feared this very moment the same way a guilty student faces an angry principal, submerging fear in constant rehearsal of what to say to this stern, unyielding military butcher.

Hashamadi must be a butcher if he worked for Saddam, who surrounded himself with the vicious and the brutal. Weak generals seldom lasted in the Iraqi army. They were often shot. Sometimes by Saddam himself.

Hashamadi's eyes, however, were warm and kind, which was as much a shock as the huge, beefy hand that carefully squeezed his in greeting. The general's face had seen bitter storms and better days, the lines detailing the history he had witnessed, the permanent puffiness beneath the eyes the baggage of time and dedication. His hair was showing silver at the edges and thinning, his almost English-style mustache more befitting a swarthy-complected earl in Cornwall than an Iraqi general.

Shakir realized he was staring, and looked away.

"Ah, I need desperately to talk with you in complete privacy, General."

Hashamadi gestured around the helicopter. "We have privacy here. Speak close to my ear, and your voice will carry to no one."

Shakir hesitated only a heartbeat, but the general caught the indecision and smiled again. "This must be quite serious, then."

"Yes sir, it is," Shakir said, drawing a deep breath and trying to remember all the carefully constructed phrases that now seemed to evaporate in his mind. He drew a deep breath and leaned closer.

"One of your staff, sir, came to one of our labs in the western desert last week—the one called Saad-18—to pick up a small canister containing a new weapon. We made a terrible error, and I am supposed to retrieve that canister, and later bring you the replacement."

"I see." Hashamadi's reply was matter-of-fact. "And thus it is ineffective in battle?"

"That . . . would be one way of characterizing it, sir."

"Saddam has ordered this weapon used tomorrow morning. Did you know this?"

Shakir forced himself to nod, and the general continued, "It will make the enemy sick within one day, I am told. Low fever, stomach trouble, and generally a bad feeling that lasts a few days. While they are feeling ill, they cannot fight well, and we can finish their rebellion quickly, which is important.''

Shakir's stomach was doing strange things again, though the helicopter was flying straight and level.

"So, this agent is not effective, but you will bring some that is? When?'' the general demanded.

His first words finally coalesced in Shakir's mind. "Make people ill,'' he was saying, not "kill people.''

Could it be he doesn't know?

Shakir could feel the general's eyes on him.

For the longest time Hashamadi studied the scientist without moving a muscle, as Shakir prepared for the worst.

"Doctor,'' the general said at last, his voice low and steady, "I think there is something more here you are not telling me.''

Shakir nodded. "Who told you, General, that this agent would only make people ill for a few days?''

Hashamadi ignored the question and grasped the meaning. "It does not sicken, then? It kills?''

Shakir explained in great detail the scope of the plague that lurked in the single canister he had been given to use, encouraged that Hashamadi seemed suddenly off balance and shaken, especially when told that he and his men would certainly die as well. And horribly at that.

"It will stay in the water, you say?''

Shakir nodded.

"For how long?''

"Long enough, sir, to kill anything human or animal that drinks it for many months, and perhaps years.''

Hashamadi fell silent then, and spent the rest of the return flight looking forward, his face hardened now and expressionless except for a small muscle in his lower left jaw, which seemed to be twitching every time Shakir glanced to the right.

They landed a hundred yards from the commandeered house,

Hashamadi motioning Shakir to follow, then striding at an uncomfortably rapid pace into the building and into his office.

Shakir trailed him through the office door and closed it behind them. The general opened the door of an armoire and poured some sort of liquor, turning then to Shakir.

"I am not a very devout Muslim. If you are, Doctor, I apologize for drinking in your presence. If not, would you like something?"

"Some mineral water, if possible."

Hashamadi pulled a bottle of water from the interior and handed it to him with a clean glass, before walking to his desk and sitting down heavily, his eyes focusing on the courtyard visible through shades on the window.

There was a tense silence before he spoke again, still looking outside.

"You are not Dr. Damerji, of course."

Shakir's heart flip-flopped and he felt dizzy—and dead. The charade had been discovered. He began to speak, but words would not come before the general's hand went up to silence the attempt.

"How did I know this, you were about to ask?"

Shakir nodded.

The general turned around toward Shakir, resting his elbows on the desk, and smiled.

"Until your reaction just now, I didn't. I merely suspected. You were introduced as a nuclear scientist. Nuclear scientists know little of biological work, because Saddam wanted it that way."

Still Shakir's voice wouldn't quite come.

"So who are you, Doctor?"

"My . . ." He coughed and tried to clear his throat. "My name is Shakir Abbas. I am a biochemist in the Saad-18 facility."

"That's interesting. It was destroyed in an American raid a few days ago. You know this?"

Shakir nodded. "I had just left when it happened. Otherwise . . ."

"Otherwise you would be in Saudi Arabia as the guest of Bush and Fahd."

Shakir nodded. "I suppose so."

"So!" Hashamadi got up and walked around the desk, leaning on the front of it and balancing his glass on partially crossed arms as he looked down at Shakir. "I am told to release an agent that makes people sick, and instead it will destroy tens of thousands of lives and make Kurdistan uninhabitable for generations, correct?"

Shakir looked up at the mention of the forbidden name of the Kurdish homeland, a place that existed only in their dreams. Saddam had forbidden the use of that name. This was one of his generals.

"Is what you told me correct, Dr. Abbas?"

"Yes, General, it is."

He nodded, giving no hint of what was coming as he pivoted suddenly and, with a great heave of his arm, propelled the half-filled tumbler of brandy into the masonry wall, where it exploded in a shower of glass fragments and alcoholic mist, the roar of his voice as startling as a gunshot.

"That bastard!"

Hashamadi stood now, shaking with anger, his face reddening and his breathing like the exhalations of a stream engine at redline pressure. With a fluid motion he turned back to the cabinet and threw open a lower door to reveal a small safe. He spun the combination on it and pulled at the lever, the door swinging open then to reveal a small metallic canister, which he pulled from the safe and held out to Shakir.

"This is it?"

Shakir nodded, his eyes wide.

"In this container are human-killing germs?"

"Virus, actually."

"How do I kill them?"

"You . . . I need the appropriate equipment, sir. I have to heat it . . ."

Hashamadi handed it to Shakir and walked back to his desk, staring out the window.

"You can do that? You can find the equipment?"

"Yes, General, I—"

He turned toward Shakir suddenly. "I'll give you letters of safe passage. And I will give you what is essentially a blank order, signed by me. You can use them to get into any place except headquarters in Baghdad. But you'll have to hurry. When tomorrow comes and this horrible weapon is not used, Saddam will go crazy."

"What will you do?" Shakir asked.

Hashamadi looked up, surprised, and smiled. "Concerned about an old warhorse you've never met before? You're too softhearted, Doctor, to be making weapons of mass destruction, as Bush calls them." He sat down at the desk and began writing as he talked. "Do you remember the air force commander Saddam executed in January? He was vice-commander in Baghdad, and tried to save our best fighters rather than lose them to the American force."

"I . . . think so."

"Saddam shot him. Just pulled out his gun and shot him in the headquarters bunker." Hashamadi looked up. "Saddam did not know then, and does not know now, that the man he shot was like a brother to me. I shall not forgive his murder, but I have tried to stay loyal to the regime—until now."

Hashamadi looked right through Shakir, his mouth drawn tightly, his eyes flaring hate. "This is the day it all ends! I cannot shoot him, but I can block his evil. I should have done so long ago."

The general looked back down and finished writing, folding the three separate sheets of paper before getting up and handing them to Shakir.

"These will get you what you need. But as soon as you have killed the virus in that bottle, I suggest you get across the border rapidly and seek asylum. You have a vehicle?"

"Yes. But I have family . . ."

"Take them, but go. In twenty-four hours you will be a wanted man." He came around the desk and shook Shakir's hand. "Tell anyone of this, Doctor, and we are both dead. You understand this?"

"Yes, General. Thank you, I—"

"I am in *your* debt, Doctor. In another day, I would have become a mass murderer, remembered for being another Eichmann or Himmler. Now take that infernal canister and go, and Allah be with you!"

Shakir turned to leave the office, but something on the general's desk which he had been staring at unconsciously had snagged in the back of his mind. Suddenly it coalesced into a piece of yellow teletype paper, a message in Arabic directing all units to search for the American colonels Westerman and Harris.

Shakir had been horrified at hearing their names many hours ago in the hallway. He had assumed the strike force had flown safely back to Saudi territory. Something catastrophic had obviously happened, though the aide he dared to ask had called them spies and knew nothing of a plane crash. Sandar and other subordinates he knew well had been aboard that airplane, and he had no idea of their fate.

There was, however, another realization that tugged at his conscience: if he hadn't come south asking for help, those two colonels wouldn't be in trouble.

The teletype had mentioned only the two pilots. They were to be found and captured as fast as possible and brought to Baghdad, which was an ominous order. After all, Doug Harris and Will Westerman had destroyed Iraq's most promising biological lab, an act that would trigger Saddam's instincts for homicidal revenge. If nothing was done, Westerman and Harris could easily end up tortured and killed, and Shakir could not stand by and let that happen.

I got them into this, I've got to get them out!

Shakir's decision took less than a second to make. He had to take the gamble, though he might be pushing much too far.

"General . . ." Shakir turned to face Hashamadi. "May I ask you, have those two American colonels been found?"

Hashamadi froze, searching Shakir's face once again with those penetrating eyes. He sat hard against his desk then, a slow smile creeping across his face. He knew all about the two Americans who had flown the attack team into the western desert. Being one of the key commanders, he saw most important messages, and the story of the desert raid and the subsequent crash had been very curious. How could such a precision raid have been done without outside help? The question had surfaced in his mind the day before.

"So you know the colonels who destroyed your lab? I should have suspected as much. It makes sense." Hashamadi cocked his head, his eyes still locked on Shakir. "You are a very brave man, Doctor, to come to me under such pretenses. If you had asked about these two when I first got in my helicopter—if I had figured this out before you told me what this canister really holds—I would have dropped you out the door with a bullet in your head."

Hashamadi stood away from the desk and paced heavily toward the window. "And then, my friend, we would both have died, along with many others."

He stared through the shutters for a few seconds before turning back to Shakir. "These Americans, you care about them? They are friends?"

"General, if they had not been brave enough to fly that mission, there would be many more of these containers for Saddam to use. They worked very hard and against grave difficulties to bring me . . ." There was no sense in holding anything back, now. They had given each other enough damaging information to condemn both of them. "They brought me back to Saad-18 so that I could kill all the virus we had created. There were two canisters missing. I found one of them. This"—he held up the one Hashamadi had given him—"is the other. There are no more."

Hashamadi sighed. "Your two colonels were captured late last night far to the south. They will be detained pending a prisoner exchange."

Shakir simply stood there, in a quandary. How far could the man be pushed, he wondered. Was there any chance . .

General Hashamadi leaned forward as if examining Shakir's eyes. "Are you serious, Doctor? Do you really want to dare to help them?"

Shakir nodded.

"I respect your loyalty, Doctor. It is that of a true believer, even though it is a couple of infidels you want to help."

He returned to his desk and scribbled two more notes, folding both of them before drawing a crude map of western Baghdad on another page and looking back at Shakir.

"You will be in danger every inch of the way. I can only give you the basic tools. I cannot guarantee that you—or they—won't be shot trying to get out. And Saddam may have to let them go soon anyway. This risk may be unnecessary for them. Think on these things, Doctor."

"I'll take the risk," Shakir said quietly.

"Very well. This . . . is where they are being taken. It's not a prison, but a temporary outpost. Go there after midnight. Stop somewhere and commandeer a couple of basic soldiers with this letter to go with you and look official"—he held up another sheet of official stationery—"then present this other one to the guard. Be demanding, be firm, and be insistent, and don't give him time to check with anyone. He will have no telephone. Only radios. Since he can't check with me, he will have to obey this order. Collect these two then and get out of there immediately, across the border."

"This will work?" Shakir asked, holding up the paper.

"Headquarters will call me later on the radio, screaming, and I'll say I moved them on Saddam's orders. It will take most of the morning for anyone to get up enough courage to ask Saddam. Be gone by then."

Shakir started to thank him again, and the general waved him out.

"Go! Someday we will talk about this, Dr. Abbas. Perhaps in exile, perhaps in hell."

CENTCOM, Riyadh, Saudi Arabia
Sunday, March 10, 1991—8:30 A.M. (0530 GMT)

Walter Hajek looked at his shaking hands and tried to calm down.

You knew there would be an angry reaction! he told himself.

But he had failed to think it through.

The three military policemen had come for him in his Riyadh hotel room, and suddenly his GM-15 civil service rating—which normally entitled him to respect and careful treatment—was worthless. They had gently but coldly forced him into the back-seat of a black sedan and whisked him to the basement of CENT-COM, and then to a small office within the cipher-lock-secured intelligence analysis section. He had asked if he was under arrest, but the MPs had refused to answer, which was even more chilling.

The door to the office opened now, admitting a contingent of grim-faced men, most of them military—several of them CIA.

"Dr. Hajek, I am Jon McCarthy of the National Security Agency." McCarthy did not offer his hand.

"Am . . . am I under arrest?"

"If that time arrives, Doctor, you will be read your rights and given access to counsel. This is an emergency inquiry convened under the authority of the United States government and the office of the President as well as the National Security Council."

Hajek sighed deeply and tried to look puzzled. "What's this all about?"

McCarthy cleared his throat and spoke at last. "Doctor, the sample of the Iraqi biological agent that you were assigned to test and safeguard was shipped on orders from your superiors to Washington, correct?"

"Yes."

"What did you place in that container before you sealed it and gave it to the courier?"

Hajek described the hazardous biological agent sample containment vessel, and the safeguards for sealing and resealing it as the small central core was placed inside a glass-lined container, which in turn was inserted in other containers.

"I'm not interested in the packing, Doctor. I'm interested in hearing about the contents of the central container. What was in it?"

"Nothing," he said at last. "I forgot the final step—placing the active viral sample in the core container. It was empty, I, ah, discovered that later."

"In fact it was empty on arrival, after the expenditure of approximately sixty thousand dollars of flight expense to rush it to Washington. Why was it empty, Doctor?"

"I made a mistake."

McCarthy pulled out a sheaf of papers and consulted them, letting seconds tick by as Hajek sweated and tried to think ahead. His insides were shaking, and his voice sounded wobbly.

At last McCarthy looked up.

"Dr. Hajek, this is a statement from Dr. Alan Benedict, a government consultant to the National Security Council. Did you call Dr. Benedict yesterday at 5:30 A.M. local time on a secured telephone and ask him to intervene with the President to stop the shipment of the sample you had been tasked to provide?"

Hajek nodded.

"And then you *accidentally* forgot to fill the sample vial? A bit coincidental, don't you think?"

Walter Hajek took another deep breath and opened his palms to the air.

"All right. There's no use pretending, Mr. McCarthy. I *elected* not to send that sample, because I don't believe anybody involved in the order to bring it back understood what we were dealing with, and how deadly this stuff is. I was trying to buy some time to convince the people in Washington they don't want this on our shores."

McCarthy was listening dispassionately, his eyes boring into Hajek as he waited for the silence to become too uncomfortable. It was a learned technique of interrogation that failed only with the pathologically self-assured.

Hajek could stand it no longer. "I . . . I don't understand, though, what this is all about. Why not just fire me and send the sample yourself? I knew, of course, this would be discovered."

"Yet you started to lie about it. You told us a minute ago it was a mistake."

Hajek's palms were offered to the ceiling again. He placed his hands back in his lap then, and looked at McCarthy.

"So I guess I'm fired, and somebody else can package the sample and send it."

The impassive, silent stare remained for fully thirty seconds, no one else in the room moving, before McCarthy spoke. "You most likely will be fired, sir. You are already suspended and your security clearance has been canceled. But no one else will be sending that sample."

Hajek brightened at that. "Really? They changed their minds? Thank God! Was it the President who changed his mind?"

"No sir. The remaining samples of the biological agent retrieved from Iraq—which was the only key the United States and the Coalition had to formulate an antidote or any personnel defense strategies—are still here in the lab, but all of them have been neutralized. Someone purposefully put both vials in that kiln and killed the virus."

"*What?* You don't think . . ."

McCarthy stood up and addressed an Army colonel. "Read him his rights, Colonel, and let's put the rest of this on the record. When he's had access to criminal defense counsel, we'll proceed."

Walter Hajek was on his feet then, his eyes wide with shock and fright.

"Mr. McCarthy! I didn't . . . I mean . . . I didn't do that! *It wasn't me!*"

McCarthy barely turned his head as he pulled open the door. "That's a question for a prosecutor and the courts, isn't it?"

The slam of the door punctuated McCarthy's words, leaving Hajek standing in a panic, looking from face to face and finding no solace. He looked at the Army colonel in desperation.

"What are you charging me with?"

The door opened again as several of the men began filing out, one of them stopping momentarily to answer.

"Don't worry, Doctor, we'll think of something."

Two floors above, General Herm Bullock was stuffing his brief-case with a legal pad and a sandwich for a meeting across town as Colonel Richard Kerr walked in, responding to his summons for a quick meeting.

"You've heard about the Iraqi pilot, Richard?"

"Yes sir. Your aide filled me in about the note he was carrying from Doug and everything. I can't believe we—*they*—came so close to getting out!"

Bullock snapped the unassuming Samsonite case closed and straightened up, wincing as his back protested the action. "Well, there's no doubt at all now. They're in Iraqi hands and headed north. I'm afraid we've lost the gambit, Richard."

Kerr walked the general to his staff car before turning to go back inside. He should resume the search for Shakir Abbas, but the morning was pleasantly mild and clear, and he hesitated. The attempt to find Abbas was essentially hopeless anyway, without agents behind the lines. Abbas had simply disappeared into the Iraqi gulag, and no amount of technical wizardry from space was going to find him *or* the virus, let alone kill the last of the deadly strain. Only Abbas could do it now, and in that the doctor was on his own.

Kerr knew he should return to the basement and get to work on organizing a new photographic search for the APCs that had hauled away Will and Doug, but that too would be fruitless. Westerman and Harris were as submerged now as Abbas.

The silent acknowledgment of defeat triggered the first relaxation he'd felt in two days. Suddenly he was taking a deep breath and looking around as his mind leaped at the chance to consider something simple, such as the dusty beauty of this desert capital city of strange customs and stranger attitudes, as it awoke under a morning canopy of fresh air.

There was an outdoor restaurant less than a mile away, and he needed the exercise.

Iraq Military Command Headquarters, Baghdad
Sunday, March 10, 1991—3:00 P.M. (1200 GMT)

"This is insane, Ihsan, surely you know that."

General Hassoun stood with his back to the Interior Ministry official and studied the tactical map of the deteriorating civil war, an almost illegible copy hastily pinned to the wall of the makeshift war room.

Ihsan Fethi, a small, thin man whose leathery skin seemed painfully stretched over excessively angular bones, had been an archeology professor of considerable intellect, but that was long ago, before his submersion into the Ba'ath party. Now he was little more than a "gofer" carrying messages back and forth to the exposed military command headquarters while the Iraqi president stayed in hiding. Saddam's terror of the new American bomb and the possibility of assassination was earning the growing contempt of his senior military officers.

There were, of course, far too many loyalists hidden in various posts to safely give voice to such thoughts. Especially in front of Fethi.

Hassoun turned and looked at the man. The little toady was

obviously tired of relaying ill-advised commands to military commanders and having to carry back the muted, upset replies. General Hassoun suspected few of those dissents ever reached Saddam's ears.

"Well, Ihsan?" the general prompted.

"Saddam is furious about the destruction of the new biological weapon. You know that, General. We informed him of the capture of these two American officers and that they came from the transport that crashed two days ago, the one that brought in the attackers who destroyed Saad-18, and he went crazy. He wants them questioned until we know everything that happened. He wants to know if any of our people were involved, or even failed to resist. He wants names, times, places—everything. And then he wants them killed—slowly—as criminals of the state."

The general let out a disgusted sigh and shook his head. "Hasn't anyone bothered to tell him the war is over and we *lost*?"

"He knows—"

"Does he not understand that if we damage these two prisoners, we can't send them home, and if we don't send them home, we'll hand Bush another excuse to bomb us to rubble? Doesn't he understand we can't survive another month of bombing? Doesn't he understand that this is exactly the excuse they need to invade Baghdad? Is there no one with enough backbone to explain these things to him? Where the hell is Tariq Aziz?" Hassoun already knew the answer. Aziz was little more than a poor actor playing the part of foreign minister, and scared to death of Saddam. There was no one in the inner circle who dared expose the dictator to international realities.

Fethi studied his shoes at length before replying. "He has issued the orders, General. The Americans are to be told that these two were never captured. They must have died in the desert. We have searched, we will say, but we are not holding them. That way they cannot use it as an excuse."

Hassoun shook his head sadly as Fethi continued.

"General, all the work we've done to prepare the long-range cannon will be lost if we don't have the biological agent it was supposed to deliver. They can stop our missiles from hitting Tel Aviv and Riyadh, but they can't stop a cannon shell filled with disease and death. We could have wiped out half of Israel, as Saddam promised, in a matter of weeks if Saad-18 had not been destroyed. But now there is only one batch of the agent left, and it goes to the Kurds. Only one! Can't you see why Saddam is so angry? And these two Americans are to be held responsible."

"I suppose," the general began, turning back to the map, permitting himself a little sarcasm, "that he wants to shoot them himself?"

"Perhaps after we are finished with them."

"You want them moved to the security facilities under your control, correct?"

Fethi nodded. "We are better equipped."

General Hassoun looked back over his shoulder at the little man and gave him a scowl. "I've met some of these twisted ghouls your security force employs."

Fethi pointedly ignored the remark. The army had used such interrogators with equal readiness when it suited their purposes.

"When may I tell Saddam the transfer will take place?" he asked the general.

Hassoun swept his hand toward the ceiling. "With their satellites always looking at us? Not until tonight. Provide the location to my aide. We'll transfer them sometime late tonight. And Fethi, one more thing."

Ihsan Fethi kept an even expression as he waited for the inevitable postscript he was supposed to deliver, but never would. It would be suicide to say such things to Saddam.

"Tell our esteemed leader that this is against my recommendation, and he cannot hold me or my staff responsible for the consequences."

"Of course I'll tell him, General."

Western suburbs, Baghdad
Sunday, March 10, 1991—5:30 P.M. (1430 GMT)

Doug sat bolt upright in the pitch darkness of the cell, his heart racing wildly, the sound of heavy footsteps in an outside corridor rising in volume, and headed his way.

Unseen prisoners on both sides of his cell had been pulled screaming into that corridor in the past few hours and taken some distance away to be beaten, the muffled sounds of heavy blows and cries of pain unmistakable. One had been thrown back in later, moaning and crying. The other had never returned.

None of the voices belonged to Will. So far. He was sure of that and thankful for it. But whoever the Iraqis were beating, they spoke English. He had heard their cries for help and their screams as doors had opened and closed.

The guards were getting closer, the reverberation of their heavy boots striding resolutely right toward his door.

Doug had been in pitch blackness for many hours, and no one had even touched the door, as if he had been walled off and forgotten. He was exhausted, but unable to sleep with footsteps marching back and forth constantly.

At least three guards had gathered outside his door now. Doug could hear their guttural voices speaking in Arabic, and he could hear something hard slapping against the wall with rhythmic malevolence.

An unseen hand gripped whatever doorknob there was and rattled it, the sounds of jingling keys giving way then to the scraping of a key in a lock—*his* lock—*his* door!

Instinctively he found himself edging toward the back wall, trying to remember all the things the Air Force survival school had taught him about interrogations, and how to survive. He had no information they really needed—except for one particular name.

A blaze of white light flooded the room at the same instant the door was banged open, and Doug shut his eyes and folded his hands over them to block the painful glare.

The owner of the heavy boots pushed roughly into the room but stopped suddenly, responding to a distant voice down the corridor, which was yelling something in Arabic.

The guard backed out of the door then, his voice low and menacing as he mouthed a few words in English.

"First your friend. Then you."

The door slammed with unbelievable force and the lights went out again, the footsteps clumping down the corridor a short distance where another door was yanked open. Doug could hear an order given in English to get up, and a surprised, belligerent reply. Whoever they were yelling at was protesting, but the voice was covered by the angry shouting of the guards, and then silenced by the sound of a body being slammed into the wall and dragged off in the distance.

There was silence for a few minutes before a new vibration crept into the room, moving without warning like an assassin, very distant at first, and then more plaintive—the high-pitched wail of someone screaming in terrible pain.

Doug's heart began to race again. He had heard nothing like that earlier. There had been people beaten, true, but no more.

The wailing ceased then, and tense silence surrounded him. Minutes passed, then a half hour, before the sound of a door somewhere being thrown open shocked him upright again.

This time someone was moaning incoherently in the distance, the sound clearly audible through an open door.

The sound of a small gasoline engine began sputtering nearby as well, growing into a warbling noise that could only be the sound of a chain saw. The sputtering accelerated, and a long, sustained, unearthly shriek echoed through the building and lingered.

Exactly how much time passed after the sounds stopped he didn't know, but suddenly the light in his cell snapped on with full intensity and the door crashed open. He had not heard a key.

"On your feet, pig!" Someone snarled the words in perfect English, and Doug tried to open his eyes and get to his feet shakily, gathering his courage as best he could and squaring his shoulders as he tried to make his voice work. "I . . . demand to know what you have done with Colonel Westerman."

The Iraqi was smiling. That was exactly the question he had expected, and he shrugged in response. "He wouldn't answer our questions."

"What have you *done* with him? You're bound by the Geneva Convention! You cannot physically mistreat us!"

The man turned toward the door and motioned to someone outside, who came in lugging a large plastic tub. The guard carried it across the room then and held it high in front of him, lowering it slowly until he couldn't avoid looking at the contents.

"You asked about your friend?"

Doug's knees turned to rubber as he staggered back against the wall.

"You . . . you goddamned animals . . . you . . ."

The man's smile broadened. "We have some questions, Colonel. In about an hour you will have one single chance to answer them."

The commander known as Akhmed closed the door to the American's makeshift cell and locked it noisily. He and his team of guards moved down the corridor then and reentered their small office, locking the door carefully behind them as Akhmed checked the time.

Central Baghdad
Sunday, March 10, 1991—6:30 P.M. (1530 GMT)

The physician Shakir had asked to see was before him now, deep lines creasing his tired face, his hair askew, his hands shaking slightly as he stuffed them in the pockets of a dirty white smock, almost knocking his stethoscope on the cracked linoleum floor.

The hospital was filthy. There had been no direct bomb damage, but power and water had been intermittent for weeks and the staff was traumatized by lack of supplies but no lack of patients. Now they were seeing dysentery, and feared cholera. The entire population of Baghdad, it seemed, was using the filthy waters of the Tigris River.

"What is your name?" he asked in Arabic.

"Damerji. Dr. Muayad Damerji."

"And you need to use *what*?"

"A kiln or oven. I need to sterilize some military equipment."

The physician just stared at him until Shakir wondered if he'd fallen asleep with his eyes open.

Finally he spoke. "That is not possible. All we have is an autoclave, and it is in constant use, and then only when we have power."

"I have authorization from—"

"I don't care if the Prophet himself sent you!" he yelled. "You damned military people think you can hijack everything! It is impossible!" The physician turned away abruptly and disappeared around a corner, ignoring Shakir's final attempt to communicate.

An overweight nurse with a surly disposition smirked knowingly and nodded an I-told-you-so at Shakir as she, too, turned back to more pressing matters. The military no longer impressed them.

Shakir left the building then, and returned to the dirty green van. The drive back from Kirkuk had beaten the machine into a filthy rattletrap. Three times he had been forced to drive off into the desert to navigate around roadblocks.

He had stopped in Samarra to thank the real Muayad and warn him that he was to know nothing of Shakir's actions, or the use of his name. Shakir begged him to gather his family and flee for the nearest border.

"I cannot do that, my friend. We'll be all right here, but Allah be with you and Saliah, wherever you go."

So he had driven on to Baghdad alone.

Shakir stood on the concrete curb by the van and looked around him. The day was pleasantly warm, with a slight breeze bringing the fragrance of flowers and trees, which unfortunately mixed with the noxious aromas of uncollected garbage and raw sewage from a city whose infrastructure no longer worked.

Baghdad had taken one hell of a beating. Muayad had been right.

Shakir opened the back doors of the van and checked the spare-tire compartment to assure himself the canister was where he had left it. The hospital had been his last chance. He had no idea what to do now, other than keep carrying the tiny biological bomb until he could find something capable of destroying its contents by heat. Muayad had suggested an open fire, but it might not reach a high enough temperature. No, better to keep carrying it until he could be sure.

He checked his watch again, which read a quarter to seven. The general had told him to wait until after midnight.

Shakir climbed back in the driver's seat and fired the engine, rumbling back into the streets in search of a gas station—only to find he needed an authorization slip he didn't possess. The harassed attendant pointed him in the direction of a police sub-station where he found a long line of irritable citizens waiting for the same thing. The temptation to yell Hashamadi's name and bypass them all was great, but the last thing he needed was undue attention.

When his turn came at last, one glance at the official orders he carried was enough for the policeman behind the desk. Then it took another hour of waiting in line to fill the tank.

By then it was dark and he felt safer and more anonymous.

At nine he parked the van near a small restaurant a half-mile from the Al Rashid Hotel, carefully taking the distributor cap off the engine to prevent theft. He went in quietly to eat, sitting in a far corner. Since there was no electricity, he wondered how the restaurant was managing to stay open, but he knew good Arab merchants were born knowing how to stay in business, and restaurateurs would always find a way to serve something—even by candlelight.

He had run the plan in his mind a hundred times as the day progressed. He would gather the two soldiers he needed, then drive to the western edge of the city, to the nondescript building that had been pressed into service as a military holding tank for POWs, and try to remember the lines he had memorized to say to the guards when he walked into their lair.

During the fruitless search for a kiln, he had driven by the building several times, memorizing the approaches and escape routes.

Thoughts of home and Saliah slipped in, and Shakir found himself fighting an overpowering longing for his family. He ached to drive the thirty miles southeast to be with them, but until this obligation was played out one way or another, he could not.

Shakir finished his coffee and paid the bill quietly, reentering the quiet streets to find the van untouched. He had spent too much time thinking, and the enormity of what he was about to attempt had begun to scare him profoundly. These were not amateurs he was about to fool around with, and if they were already waiting for him . . .

But there was no way they could know! General Hashamadi would not have led him into an elaborate trap. If the general had been insincere, he could simply have killed him then and there in Kirkuk.

Or were there more complex plots of which Shakir was dangerously unaware?

He took a deep breath and closed his eyes for a moment, trying to shake the jitters and wondering how he could be anything but numb after all he'd experienced.

The next step, after all, would require nerves of steel.

The sound of a jet engine at treetop level suddenly assaulted his ears as someone flew over at near supersonic speed. The Americans, probably. They continued to harass the city with flyovers, just to demonstrate they owned the sky. It was a startling sound, triggering even more adrenaline in Shakir's bloodstream as the unseen intruder roared on to the west and out of sight.

There were no tracers in the sky now. The antiaircraft batteries had probably grown numb too, as well as disinterested, especially since they had proven all but worthless during the six weeks of aerial bombardment.

The drive to the army staging outpost on the northwest edge of town was filled with conflicting thoughts and fears, but when Shakir walked in the door and approached the outer guards, he was calm and steady.

One by one they looked at his authorization from Hashamadi and ushered him farther and farther into the barracks. The three clips for his gun were provided without question, as were the two soldiers, both of them buck privates carrying guns and a noncommittal attitude. The three of them had left the building headed for the van, and Shakir had almost relaxed when the sound of footsteps running after them and a voice calling— yelling, actually—sent little shivers of impending doom up and down his spine.

Shakir turned as one of the younger officers came racing up, his expression invisible in the single light of the parking area.

"What's the matter?" Shakir managed, trying to keep an even demeanor.

"You are Dr. Damerji?" he asked.

Shakir tried to fathom what was behind those dark eyes, but couldn't.

"Yes," he replied, feigning as much disinterest as possible.

The officer—a lieutenant—took Shakir's hand and began pumping it.

"I did not recognize you, Doctor. You look different." He was smiling, and Shakir tried to do the same.

"Where have we met? You must forgive me, I don't have my glasses and probably wouldn't recognize my own son."

"You don't remember? I'm devastated!" the young man said.

"No games, now. I can't really see your face clearly out here, but your voice sounds like . . ."

"Ali Mahmadi!"

"Of *course*!" Shakir replied.

"My father asked you to help with my appointment to the army, and I owe this rank to you! You do remember?"

"Yes, yes, I do!" Shakir's mind raced ahead, improvising as he went. "I'm delighted to . . . get to say hello . . . even though it's in an unexpected time and place and I'm in a rush on a special assignment I can't discuss."

"I understand, Doctor. I know this is for General Hashamadi." Shakir saw the young man wink conspiratorially, and nodded in return, at the same time catching sight of a flurry of activity to his left. Headlights from several vehicles were approaching rapidly, and the need to break away and *run* was rising like an uncontrollable reflex.

Shakir forced it back, however, and willed himself to be cordial.

"Were you in the fighting, Ali?"

The face of the young man grew serious now. He had struck a nerve, which was not surprising.

"I was there . . . but . . . we were ordered out before . . ."

"That's all right." Shakir put a hand on his shoulder. "We'll talk about it some other time. Perhaps, when all this military activity has calmed, we can get together." The urge to say "How's your father?" or "*Where* is your father?" slammed into a wall of caution. Suppose the boy's father was dead, or worse, and Shakir should know?

Or Muayad, he corrected himself, should know.

The headlights were turning into the parking area now and

illuminating Shakir, young Lieutenant Mahmadi, and the two privates who had been leaning against the van.

"I appreciate to the depths of my heart your condolences, Doctor, on the death of my father. I know you were with him, and I want to ask you questions, but I know we must wait."

Two small army vehicles roared past on their left now, followed by a nondescript gray sedan. Shakir noticed the two privates suddenly come to attention before he glanced to his left to see why. The lieutenant had also snapped to attention, his face a combination of surprise, fear, and excitement.

"Allah be praised!" the young man whispered.

The sedan stopped almost beside them, and a guard from the lead vehicle scurried back carrying an impressive automatic weapon and opened the rear door, saluting the occupant as he climbed out.

Shakir looked disbelievingly at his face as the man straightened his uniform and smiled.

This is not happening!

He would play along as if it were, of course.

Of all the people on the planet I did not want to meet in person ever again and especially tonight . . .

Saddam Hussein walked slowly the few feet separating Shakir and the lieutenant and returned the young officer's salute before shaking his hand.

Lieutenant Mahmadi couldn't restrain himself.

"Mr. President," he gushed, "may I have the honor of presenting one of your most loyal and accomplished scientists, Dr. Muayad Damerji, whom I'm sure you know very well."

He will recognize me! He will know this is a fraud! I am dead!

The thoughts were a jumble and his knees were turning to jelly, but somehow he managed to smile and extend his hand, the look of sheer terror passing for the sort of excitement Saddam was used to seeing in the eyes of his intimidated countrymen. It was the look and the attitude he had wanted to see.

— *312* —

"We are fortunate to have this opportunity, Doctor," Saddam said in his low, gravelly tones. "Do you wish to see me about the progress of our bomb?"

"Not . . ." Shakir's voice was a hoarse croak and he cleared his throat. "Excuse me . . . no sir, not tonight, if you don't mind. I will have a formal presentation for you in two days."

"You were to see me in four days. All of you in the program. Is something wrong?"

Shakir shook his head. "No sir. *That* meeting will go on as planned. I would like a few minutes of your time a bit earlier."

Saddam nodded, his interest waning, and began to turn away. But something stopped him, and he turned back to Shakir, his eyes almost looking through him.

Shakir had met the dictator on many occasions and was always nervous in his presence. The knowledge that he could just as easily pull his gun and blow your head off as talk to you was unnerving.

Saddam was staring at Shakir now, studying his face very carefully, the implications in Shakir's mind approaching the apocalyptic as the dictator cocked his head slightly and stared.

Finally he shrugged and placed a beefy hand on Shakir's shoulder.

"You look very tired, Doctor. We are all tired. But tomorrow morning we will gain the upper hand. Wait and see."

And then he was gone, sweeping into the building with his guards.

"What great good fortune, Doctor!" Lieutenant Mahmadi said, elated. "I was so fortunate to catch you."

Wrong word, Ali. Wrong word, Shakir thought.

"I am very glad as well, Ali," Shakir lied, "but I must go. We'll talk soon."

The lieutenant waved good-bye and hurried inside as Shakir motioned to the two soldiers to relax and get in the van. He started the engine and forced himself to motor out of the drive at a reasonable speed, though the inclination was to floorboard it. The two privates were still wide-eyed. Whatever reservations they might have had about this odd civilian with a secret mission were gone.

Obviously he worked for Saddam.

Western suburbs, Baghdad
Sunday, March 10, 1991—11:00 P.M. (2000 GMT)

Akhmed looked around the small office of his makeshift jail and sighed. It was a municipal building, of course, but their hard work had made it an effective interrogation and holding facility. Especially all the work that went into installing the tape recorders and speaker system, all of which had been ordered from the United States before the war. The irony always made him chuckle.

A messenger from army headquarters had been left waiting in the outer chamber of the building, and Akhmed motioned to him now as one of his men placed the plastic tub back in a large freezer after yet another highly effective session of scaring the enemy half to death. It had been a stroke of genius, he thought, to stay on good relations with one of the army morticians. Whatever body parts were needed to terrify prisoners, the proper size and color could usually be provided in short order, then frozen and thawed when needed. It was macabre, but no more so than the horrid deeds they pretended to be doing.

Both Americans would be basket cases of terror in a few more hours, Akhmed knew, even if they didn't continue the carefully prepared program of gruesome tape-recorded screams and chain-saw sounds accompanied by his men howling and screaming and thrashing about on schedule.

Akhmed acknowledged the messenger and signed for the classified dispatch from military command headquarters somewhere across town. He tore open the envelope and read the cold Arabic words with resignation and disgust.

"So, Assid," he said to the nearest guard, "we are directed to deliver these two Americans to a representative from the Interior Ministry around midnight tonight. And so we are out of business again."

He refolded the dispatch and handed it to one of his men. They were taking his last two prisoners. It was a disappointment. All he would have needed was two days. Just forty-eight hours, and he could have squeezed out all the information they had before having to send them home in the impending prisoner exchange. It would have impressed his superiors, or so he had hoped. But now he was ordered to deny the Americans had ever existed and turn them over to the real sadists.

Which meant they were as good as dead.

"Saddam must be even angrier than we thought, eh?" Assid answered, as Akhmed nodded.

Akhmed shuddered inwardly to think of what lay ahead for those two. He and his guards were trained to *pretend* to be bloodthirsty homicidal maniacs.

But the ones the two colonels would face by midnight would not be pretending.

Shakir Abbas pulled up to the temporary jail at eleven-forty and turned out the lights, having already given careful instructions to the two soldiers with him. They were to keep their guns on safety at all times. Under no circumstances were they to harm the prisoners or injure them or treat them roughly. They were to answer no questions asked by the keepers of this facility, and they were to obey only Shakir's orders.

Thanks to the encounter an hour before, there was no way either man was going to question a word he said.

The door to the squat, undistinguished cinderblock building was opened without hesitation, and much to his surprise, Shakir was ushered inside with nothing more than a cursory look at the papers Hashamadi had prepared.

"I am here to collect the two Americans, in accordance with the orders of—"

A heavily built man in civilian clothes motioned for his guard to close the door. "The Interior Ministry, yes I know," he said, shaking Shakir's hand briefly. "I am Akhmed Anbarra, commander of this facility." He turned to lead the way to an inside office then, glancing back over his shoulder as they walked. "I must tell you this transfer is unnecessary. We could extract all the information needed from these two by ourselves, but I know you people don't believe that." He shrugged, and gestured toward the door. "You want handcuffs and blindfolds?"

"I'm sorry?" Shakir's face had already registered surprise before he realized Akhmed meant the prisoners. "Oh, of course. Real handcuffs only if you have a spare key. Otherwise, use the plastic ones. I don't want to go through *that* debacle again."

Good, Shakir thought, *at least one rehearsed line I can use.* "Blindfolds are unnecessary. Where they're going, you see . . ." He let his voice trail off with the implication Akhmed had expected.

"I understand. Wait here, if you don't mind." He disappeared into the hallway then, leaving Shakir in a quandary.

How could they be expecting me? And what of the mention of the Interior Ministry? Interior controlled Saddam's hard-core goons—his secret police. Could General Hashamadi have sent them word? That wasn't possible! It would have tipped his hand. It would have—

The banging of doors and the sound of feet in the corridor

prompted Shakir to step out of the office at the moment Will Westerman was shoved around a distant corner, his hands cuffed behind him as he fell against the far wall and one of the guards yelled at him.

He looks awful! But I mustn't notice.

Westerman had a four-day growth of beard, his hair was scraggly, and his flight suit was ragged—and he was barefoot.

"Do they have shoes?" Shakir asked in Arabic.

Akhmed nodded, shooting him a slightly puzzled expression that seemed to require an explanation.

"*Our* rules," he said simply.

Akhmed shrugged and disappeared back around the same corner as Westerman was brought within ten feet of Shakir. The colonel had not looked up yet, and as more commotion around the corner of the hallway announced the arrival of Doug Harris, Westerman looked back over his shoulder instead, his jaw dropping open in surprise at the same moment Harris's eyes grew wide with equal shock.

"Doug—"

"*Shut up!*" Akhmed snarled at Will, and then glowered at Doug.

Will had turned back to the front of the corridor, his eyes landing on Shakir and his eyebrows flaring slightly in recognition.

Shakir quickly filled the silence by ordering his two soldiers into position, their guns pointed at Will and Doug just as he had instructed them. There was a danger, however slight, that one of the colonels might say something if the seconds weren't filled with sound and motion. Shakir could tell they were both taking it all in and trying to fathom the Iraqi scientist's role.

And he couldn't give them a chance to get it wrong.

Shakir switched to accented English then. He had to assume someone in the facility also spoke the language. "You two American swine will keep your mouths shut and follow my orders exactly, or I will have you shot here and now, you understand?"

He kept his voice low and tense and angry, noticing the slight nod of Akhmed's head as he brought Westerman's and Harris's boots around the corner and threw them at the two men.

"Take the boots and move. *Now!*" Shakir yelled at them, issuing a final order in Arabic to the privates as they marched the two colonels past him.

"Lock them in and keep them under guard."

Don't, please don't try to say anything to me as you pass, Shakir pleaded silently, pushing past them as rapidly as possible, averting his eyes from theirs, and turning instead to Akhmed, who handed him the key to the handcuffs, which were the traditional type.

"I'm on a tight schedule," he said simply. "Thank you for the smooth transfer."

Akhmed looked shocked. No one from the secret police or the Interior Ministry had ever *thanked* him for anything before. They were always contemptuous of the military being involved in questioning. Who was this Dr. Damerji, anyway?

Shakir saw the look and knew he had overplayed the part. He should have acted more in charge and haughty. The secret police wouldn't be friendly, especially not a "doctor."

But there was no way to repair it without making it worse.

Shakir turned toward the door then, and followed the men into the drive, feeling Akhmed's eyes on him every inch of the way. He nodded in approval as the two guards climbed in the rear and shut the doors. His hands began to shake suddenly as he opened the driver's door, climbed in, and started the engine.

Akhmed was standing in the doorway now, his image reflected in Shakir's rearview mirror. Two of Akhmed's guards also appeared with him at the door, and as Shakir put the van in gear, he could see them conversing.

Did I get the orders back? What if I left them?

Shakir fumbled for the paper with General Hashamadi's signature on it, relieved to find it was still in his shirt pocket. But the guard would remember the name of the man who had signed it, and that name was all wrong if they were expecting the Interior

Ministry. Why would an army general be signing orders for the Interior Ministry?

The van was clearing the gate now, but Shakir could see Akhmed take a few steps into the drive, still staring at the van, his head jerking back and forth between one of his men and the disappearing prisoners. There were no other vehicles near the door, and Shakir prayed there were none parked nearby.

You're being paranoid. He has no reason to suspect . . .

The van's license plate suddenly loomed large in Shakir's memory. He had meant to remove it, but hadn't. A secret police van might not have a license plate at all. Could Akhmed have noticed that?

One block between us now!

Will and Doug were quiet in the darkness behind him, for which he was thankful. There was no time to explain yet what was going on.

Shakir had turned right out of the driveway of the building, the taillights of the van disappearing from Akhmed's view off to the west as the road curved slightly. Now Shakir turned left and left again, doubling back to the east on a different street that crossed the main road leading directly to the detention building.

There were lights to the right now, headed for the same intersection he was approaching and moving in a direct line toward the detention building. They would reach the intersection first, so Shakir slowed to let the dark, unmarked panel truck and the black sedan pass.

He accelerated then, crossing the intersection, glancing left to see their taillights enter the driveway the van had just left.

Bringing another hapless prisoner, I suppose, Shakir said to himself, the realization taking a few seconds to hit.

No! That's not it. They said they were expecting a transfer when I arrived. So I must have arrived first! When they discover what's happened . . .

Cold fear pressed his foot to the floor as Shakir rocketed the van around corners and threaded his way to the south through back streets on a route he had carefully preplanned at a slower speed.

There was an empty military warehouse several miles away where he would leave the two soldiers, and he couldn't show panic or explain things to Westerman and Harris until that was done.

Shakir kept watching the rearview mirror, fully expecting to see headlights chasing him. It would have taken Akhmed no more than a split second to figure out he'd been duped, once the real secret police showed up.

The sudden appearance of a vehicle behind them in the distance pushed up his heart rate, but the car turned off in another direction.

Perhaps he should pull into an alcove somewhere, kill the lights, and just sit.

No, he had to stay calm and stick with the plan. Baghdad was a large city, and there were several miles between them now.

At last the gates of the warehouse were just ahead. Shakir braked and killed the lights, letting the engine idle as he briefed the two privates, having first pulled his Kalashnikov into his lap to show he was adequately armed.

"You are to get out here," Shakir began in Arabic, "hide yourselves, and guard this entrance until dawn. Then you will walk back to your barracks. You are not expected back until the day after tomorrow, so you may take your time and relax. But under no circumstances are you to report to anyone what you have seen tonight. None of this happened. If you care for your lives, you will obey me. I can handle these two."

Having completed the short speech, he got out and came around the van, opening the rear door to let them out and making a show of handcuffing first Westerman and then Harris to one of the arms of the bench seat. He slammed the doors again and locked them from the outside as the soldiers took up their positions inside the gate and waved good-bye, happy to be given the next two days off for an easy night's work.

Shakir had found the rear exit to the warehouse earlier in the day. He drove into the middle of the facility now and rolled to the far end, out of sight of the guards, killing the lights and letting the engine idle as they rolled quietly out the far end and through a large break in the fence.

Shakir put a mile and a half between the warehouse and the van before stopping. He cut the lights and the engine and opened the rear door with a sheepish grin that Doug and Will could see in the reflected glow of the city lights.

"Can we talk now?" Doug asked.

"Yes, but quietly. There are homes around here," Shakir said.

Doug shook off the second handcuff and helped unlock Will before jumping to the ground and grabbing Shakir's shoulders.

"I knew the moment I saw you back there that you weren't the enemy! Thank you, Doctor! I can't tell you . . . I . . ." There was a large lump in his throat suddenly, the memory of what had transpired six hours earlier washing over him in an uncontrollable wave.

Will jumped out as well, his hands scooping up Shakir's right hand and squeezing it until it hurt.

"Where on earth did you come from, Doctor? How did you know?"

Will could feel tears in his eyes. A familiar face had never looked so good, though Will thought with a deep pang of remorse that he had treated Shakir as anything but a friend during the mission.

Shakir had placed his left hand on Doug's forearm and had tried to jar Will into letting go of his right, but it wasn't working. They were delirious with appreciation, and the chase had just begun.

"*Listen* to me!" Shakir said in a harsh whisper. "We are all in great danger. I can explain more as we go, but we must get moving! They will already be looking for you, and for me."

The two colonels fell silent and glanced at each other for a second before nodding and hurrying back to the front seat.

Shakir rolled clear of the neighborhood with the lights off, barely touching the accelerator, before using more gas as he continued to weave through residential and rural areas, trending always toward the south.

The next few miles were a blur of exchanged information on Shakir's search for the canisters and the cooperative turncoat general and Doug and Will's crash in the desert followed by their struggle to get back across the border, but within ten minutes all three of them realized that something vital was missing.

"What's our plan, here?" Will asked at last. "Do we have a plan?"

Shakir shook his head. "To be honest with you, I'm not sure. I guess I'll drive you out."

"You'll go with us, then. Good."

"No," Shakir said, surprising Will and Doug. Shakir had been suppressing the realities of what might happen—what *would* happen—afterwards. General Hashamadi had been right. Get your family and leave, he had said. But getting these two Americans across the border with the last canister was the most important duty. They could be trusted to destroy it. Then he would head back for Saliah and the children and pray to Allah he could get them all out in time. It would probably be a day or two before they connected the name Shakir Abbas with all that had transpired.

Maybe.

"I will go back for my wife and children after you are safely across," he said.

"Where do you live, Doctor? Where is your family?"

"Please, just call me Shakir." He pointed to the right of the van at a splotch of lights on the near horizon. "A small village over there about five miles."

"Well, then," Will said, "if we're that close, what's wrong with right now?"

Shakir seemed confused. "I . . . beg your pardon?"

Will glanced at Doug who was nodding vigorously.

"Turn right. Let's go get your family, and then we'll all get the hell out of here!"

Shakir hadn't considered the possibility. He looked back at Will, then at Doug, surprised at their resolve. That part of his plan had been the shakiest. It *would* be best to get his family now, but that would put these two Americans in more danger.

"I thank you, but it will take an extra hour, and it is dangerous enough for you now."

"We'll take the risk," Will said.

Strange, Shakir thought. *That is exactly what I said to General Hashamadi.*

Will's right hand squeezed Shakir's right arm then as Doug's voice rang in his ears.

"We're all in this together, my friend."

Southwest of Baghdad
Monday, March 11, 1991—12:45 A.M. (2145 GMT)

They had seen the roadblock in time, but just barely. Shakir had planned to cross the main highway from east to west to get to his village, but sirens and blinking red lights in the darkness had made them all uneasy. So he kept to the back roads, unobtrusively paralleling the highway until he spotted a formidable collection of military vehicles blocking the route to Kuwait.

He cut the lights then and turned before they were seen.

But the back roads were being cut off progressively as well, and as Shakir tried to stay ahead of the closing net, a military car of some sort moved into position a half-mile ahead of them on the last available escape route south.

They drove north and northeast then, watching yet another roadblock go up behind them just after they'd shot through a rural intersection. It was painfully obvious that an angry regime was trying to seal off any possible escape route.

Blocked to the south and west by the military and hemmed in on the east by the Tigris River, Shakir continued north, worried that even if they got to his village, it too would be surrounded, and his family perhaps already arrested.

And within an hour they were back on the streets of Baghdad just south of the old city, feeling like a cornered fox run at the hounds' pleasure back to the hounds' lair.

Yet there were still options, and one of them appeared ahead suddenly in the form of a black van parked along a deserted street. Even though they had shed the license plates miles back, a green Toyota van dashing around after midnight would have no trouble attracting attention, especially if half of Saddam's security forces were looking for it.

As Shakir pulled to the curb, Will spotted a line of headlights at an intersection several blocks ahead, turning in their direction.

"Stop! Kill the lights and get down!" Will's voice was an impassioned whisper.

Shakir quickly killed the engine and all three of them dived for the floorboards.

"They're military, I think," Shakir said. "Their running lights looked like military."

The sound of automotive engines rose to a crescendo, marking the passage of a small convoy, the sound falling steadily behind them with no hint of applied brakes.

They remained still for nearly four minutes before Will cautiously peered over the dashboard.

"We're alone, and the black van's still there."

"I assume," Doug whispered, "that you're as good a van thief as you are a truck thief."

Will crept to the other van and opened the door, relieved that the ceiling light didn't work. Using matches for illumination, he found the wires he was looking for under the dash and made the necessary connections, and within minutes they were pulling quietly away from the curb, the deadly canister carefully stowed in the new van's spare-tire compartment.

Shakir cut back to the west then, finding at last a quiet side street that took them under the main freeway. They watched the rearview mirror constantly for signs of anyone chasing them, but saw nothing.

Shakir drove west and occasionally north to make sure they hadn't been followed, turning south at last to follow featureless desert roads toward his home, the subdued lights of Baghdad serving as a compass on his left.

Slowly they closed on the village, all three of them knowing now that daylight would overtake them long before they could reach the border—and knowing as well that with roadblocks everywhere, their chances of getting out of the country undetected were almost nil.

It was nearly 3:00 A.M. when the lights of Shakir's village grew bright in their windshield and Doug's eyes began to make out two distinctly familiar shapes to the left of the road ahead.

"Are those helicopters?" Doug sounded incredulous.

"Yes," Shakir answered matter-of-factly. "But I don't know why the army started keeping them here."

"Was this some sort of barracks?" Will asked.

Shakir nodded. "Many of the conscripted young men from our village were based here, but they were all sent to Kuwait."

Doug's eyes were glued to the two helicopters.

"Those are Soviet Mi-24 Hind gunships, Will! Two of them."

Will was on full alert now, worried that where there were sophisticated military aircraft, there would be military guards.

Shakir killed the headlights and rolled to the shoulder of the road while Doug and Will talked it over. He let the engine idle, trying to ignore a small curl of exhaust fumes that wafted around and through his open window.

"Nothing's moving up there," Will said at last. "You see anything?"

Doug was nodding. "I sure do."

"What?" Will's voice was low and cautious, his eyes searching for whatever Doug was seeing.

"What I see, old buddy, is our getaway car."

There was silence for a second as Will thought through any other possible meaning to Doug's words.

There were none.

"Our *getaway*...You're not seriously thinking of...of *flying* one of those out of here, are you?"

"If either of those birds has fuel and a good battery, it's the answer to our prayers," Doug said, his voice low and excited.

"Doug—"

"They're looking for us everywhere, right? We either dig a hole and pull it in over us for days, or we risk going back to a worse version of...of..." The images of what he had gone through earlier flooded back, and words failed him.

"Or we fly out."

"You've made your point," Will said quietly. "But can you fly something like that?"

"If it can be started, it can be flown."

"They're Russian, for God's sake, with placards probably written in Arabic."

Doug shook his head and raised the palm of his hand to quiet the torrent of objections.

"You get speed to the turbines, you initiate a fuel source and a spark, you vary the throttle setting until you get adequate RPM on the blades, and the rest is standard helicopter. No sweat."

Will just stared at him, the van's engine sounding like a roar in the silence between them. Shakir nervously watched both men, his eyes darting back and forth.

"You're crazy, Doug, but—" Will said in a mixture of fright and awe.

"Do we have a choice? A *good* choice? Come on, Will. We don't."

Will was nodding. "I know it."

"It's this or nothing, man."

Shakir could stand it no longer. "You are discussing flying one of those helicopters to Saudi Arabia?"

"I think so, Shakir," Will affirmed.

"Won't the fighters shoot it down?"

"No," Doug said. "Saddam can't fly any fighters. He's been warned that any fighter he puts in the air will be destroyed. But *helicopters* are okay. Our side won't shoot them down."

Doug paused, then continued, "Shakir, are those helicopters guarded?"

Shakir nodded.

"Would they take note of a van like this as it passed at three in the morning?"

"I doubt it," was the quiet reply. "There is routine traffic on this road all night."

They formulated a plan before moving. Shakir would drive slowly and steadily past the helicopters on the road into town. Several hundred feet on the other side—provided there was no activity around the choppers—Doug and Will would leap from the open sliding door of the van with Shakir's gun and make their way back to overpower whatever guards might be there.

Shakir would go to his home, wake his wife and children, and try to bundle them into the van without attracting the neighbors' attention.

"How long do you think, Shakir?" Will asked.

"It is hard to say. If my wife isn't slow . . . ."

"They took our watches," Doug said. "What time is it?"

Shakir consulted his digital watch. "Three-twenty. I have another watch at home. You take mine"—he struggled to get the clip open and handed it to Will—"and let us say that I will be back at exactly four-ten. You start the helicopter at four exactly. If anyone starts firing at you, or if I do not show up, you go on."

Will shook his head. "Even if you're late, keep coming. We'll wait as long as we possibly can, and then some."

Doug opened the sliding door then, positioning the two of them for the jump as Shakir turned on the headlights and began rolling south past the makeshift desert heliport. At the appointed spot he slowed to fifteen and looked over his shoulder.

"Now!"

Even at slow speed, Doug was too bruised and stiff to keep his balance. He rolled on the ground as soon as his feet touched, bruising himself even more on the small rocks along the road.

Will's long legs served him well, however, and he landed upright and running. Within seconds they were creeping together toward the nearest Hind, their night vision improving with each passing minute.

Both helicopters were facing the road, their large, sliding side doors on the north as Will and Doug approached from the south. Distant sounds of car engines miles away melded with the engine sounds of a high-flying jet in the night. The only light ahead was a single incandescent bulb hanging from a small building on the other side of the helicopters.

Slowly, carefully motioning to Will to kneel down and keep a watch beneath the huge Soviet gunships, Doug moved toward the side of the first one and pressed his face to the window.

The sliding door on the other side was open, the light filtering in and clearly illuminating the interior—which was empty.

They slipped quietly under the tail then, staying in the shadow cast by the muscular housing of the twin turbine engines on top of the second helicopter, and moved closer to peer in one of the windows.

A scorpion as big as a child's fist suddenly scurried out of the way as Will knelt down to look beneath the belly of the Hind. The movement startled him, the scuffling of his feet sounding horrendously loud to Doug as he looked back at Will in near panic, waving his index finger in front of his lips for quiet. Will sidestepped a few more inches to put some healthy distance between his feet and the fleeing scorpion and resumed his look-out, giving a thumbs-up to Doug, who raised his head slowly and looked through the window.

What greeted Doug through the window of the helicopter was

too good to be true. Two guards—little more than young boys, it appeared—lay snoring their heads off in the sidewall seats, their guns neatly placed on the floor out of arm's reach.

Doug pulled Will to the window to see for himself, whispering the strategy.

They crept around the stub wings and under the tail then, satisfied there were no other guards. Slowly they approached the open sliding troop door, Doug covering Will as he slipped into the helicopter and silently lifted one of the Iraqi rifles, handing it back to Doug, who laid it on the ground.

Now Doug eased himself inside as well, amused at the volume of the snoring, momentarily unsure what to do next.

Will produced the handcuffs Shakir had removed from their wrists earlier and placed one of the manacles around the recumbent wrist of the nearest soldier, slowly closing the other one around a metal tie-down loop on the floor.

Still neither of them stirred.

Slowly working his way to the aft end of the compartment, Will repeated the maneuver with the second young soldier, threading the other end of the cuffs into another tie-down loop and locking it with a sudden click.

The soldier came awake without warning, giving a cry of surprise that woke his companion at the same moment.

Will jumped back, scrambling to get his hands on the rifle while Doug leveled his at the head of the first soldier, who had just discovered his hand was attached to the floor and couldn't quite figure out why.

"Hold it! Don't move!" Doug barked. The words were indecipherable to the young Iraqis, but the meaning was clear—reinforced as it was by the barrel of a Kalashnikov, which both clearly recognized.

"I'll cover them. You take a look at the cockpit." Will's voice was still a loud whisper.

Doug climbed to the single pilot's seat and pulled a book of matches from his pocket. As Will had predicted, the placards were all in Russian and Arabic, and the arrangement of switches and indicators was foreign as well.

But somewhere there had to be a master switch that could route ground power and battery power to some basic electrical buses—and at least one cockpit light. There was a ground power cord leading from each Hind to a small shed. Doug had nearly tripped over it in the darkness.

Doug lit a match, the light flaring brightly and startling him, the flame dying before his eyes had focused on the panel. He lit the second one then, working to keep it burning before looking back to the panel.

There were switches everywhere, and a flight engineer's panel behind him in the cargo compartment with more switches, but several had metal guards around them to prevent accidental operation.

A master switch would look like that.

The second match died, but Doug reached into the darkness from memory, feeling for the switch he had just spotted that *might* just do it . . .

He flipped up the switch guard and moved the switch.

Electrical cooling fans and gyros began spinning up as a set of red overhead lights and the instrument lights came on.

"Got it!" he whispered to himself.

Now to figure out the starting system—and sequence.

To the left side of the panel was a lighted gauge which caught his eye. Two gauges, to be exact, both of them measuring fuel quantity.

On both, the needles indicated near empty.

Doug scanned the panel again, looking for some other explanation.

There was none. Those were the gas gauges, and there wasn't any gas to speak of.

Doug killed the master switch and scrambled out of the pilot's seat, briefing Will as he hopped out the door and headed with pounding heart to the adjacent Hind. Familiar now with the cockpit setup, he slid into the pilot's seat and flipped on the master switch, his eyes going to the gas gauges as the red lights came on and the same galaxy of gyros and fans came to life.

The needles hesitated at the far left side of each fuel gauge, then began moving to the right, every millimeter an indication of more fuel.

Doug was back at Will's side in half a minute.

"That one's full! Both tanks. I have no idea how many pounds, but I'll gamble it'll get us across the border."

Will laughed at that, a short, truncated snort. "We're beginning to sound like desperadoes. 'Get across the border,' indeed."

"We *are* desperadoes." Doug motioned to the two soldiers. "What about them? Leave 'em or take 'em?"

Two sets of wide eyes were fixed on them from the back of the helicopter.

Will thought a moment. "We'd better take them. If we leave them behind, they can provide descriptions, time, method, everything. Otherwise they'll have to guess who took the chopper."

"They'll figure it out, Will," Doug said.

"Yeah, but why make it easy?"

They transferred the soldiers one at a time to the other Hind, Will handcuffing them to the tie-down loops as before, while Doug climbed into the cockpit.

Switch by switch, gauge by gauge, Doug probed the instrument panel and control switches, finding what appeared to be the critical controls to start the two turboshaft engines. He killed the master switch then to conserve power as Will moved into the open space between the single pilot's seat and the large Plexiglas bubble that covered the cockpit area. Both of them fell silent.

Doug looked at the watch Shakir had loaned him. Slightly more than ten minutes left before the agreed engine-start time.

The sound of boot leather moving on the aluminum flooring below reached their ears as one of the soldiers shifted position slightly, and Doug double-checked to see that all the guns were in the cockpit with them.

Then all was quiet again.

The blanket of silence surrounded them totally, amplifying the call of a distant night bird and the whir of some flying insect through the open cockpit window as they sat in the midst of what in other circumstances would have been a peaceful scene.

Doug stared through the Plexiglas at the canopy of stars overhead and tried to hold on to the reality of where they were, but it was too frightening. The utter terror of what he had been through in the detention cell had to be suppressed.

Think about flying. Think about home. Think about anything but that!

Doug glanced over at Will, who was also deep in thought, his hands folded in his lap, his eyes focused many miles away. Doug followed Will's gaze off to the west before speaking, his voice catching Will by surprise and causing him to jump slightly.

"We can do this."

"What?" Will seemed distracted.

"We can do this, Will. We're going to get out of here."

Will nodded slowly. "We have to." Doug saw him look away to the left and out the side of the bubble canopy.

There was silence between them for a few seconds as the memories of a few hours before flooded back with frightening clarity.

Will's thumb gestured back over his shoulder. "Back there—in that prison—they had me believing they'd taken a chain saw to you." Will's right hand waved in frustration, a gesture of dismissal. "They said they were coming back in a few hours to do the same to me. It terrified me, Doug."

Doug was nodding. "Me too, old friend. They made me think exactly the same about you. The noises and screaming—all an act, I guess."

"A damned effective one."

Will's voice became stronger with anger and emotion as he told Doug of the plastic tub and its contents, and he was surprised to hear that the same scam had unnerved Doug as well.

Will turned suddenly, his face starkly visible in the subdued light. "When they made me think they had . . . killed you, I sat there . . . thinking about all those wasted years of no contact between us. I . . ."

Doug was nodding. "I know."

Will was looking away again, but his words reverberated clearly from the plastic canopy. "I've never been so terrified. They never even slugged me, and I feel like a rape victim must feel."

Doug was nodding silently, his fists clenched, but Will was looking outside as he continued, "I've always had a phobia about being captured, Doug. I guess I've been a bit of a coward about it, especially since 'Nam."

"Bullshit! You were never a coward about anything, Will Westerman. You survived back there, didn't you?"

"Inside I didn't, Doug. Inside I died a thousand deaths."

"Look, with what your dad went through in the war, of *course* you'd be fearful."

Will turned to face Doug. "No, it's more than that. You never wanted to see it, or you've been kind enough not to rub my nose in it, but I've always been a bit of a coward about a lot of things. I've always been afraid, deep down. Afraid of being captured, afraid of taking a chance with the airlines and leaving the service like you, afraid to have fun and be content with lousy grades like yours."

Doug laughed a shallow laugh. "I'll have you know I was a very good high-C student."

"Yeah, and you had fun with your life! That's the point. You were never afraid to take a chance and have fun. It didn't make you irresponsible, it let you live. *I* was always the anchor, stuck down in the mud, afraid to take a chance, always dragging you and everyone around me back to responsibility and caution."

There was silence again for a few seconds until Doug's voice, quiet and firm, filled it. "You were never a coward, Will."

"Then why did I run? Tell me that! Why am I still afraid to . . . discuss Wendy with you?"

How did Wendy get into this? Doug thought. "I don't understand."

The sound of a long, deep breath being drawn and let out was followed by the creaking of seat covers as Will sat forward and turned to Doug.

"I was in love with her, Doug."

The words fell like a load of bricks at Doug's feet, an instant weight off Will's back that just lay there.

"It was the first time I had ever fallen like that, and the last, I guess."

"With *Wendy*?" Doug was incredulous, and somewhere a final piece of a very old puzzle fell into place in Will's mind.

He never even suspected, Will realized.

"You two had an *affair*?" Doug asked.

Will shook his head. "We met at U-Tapao in Thailand while she was stationed there as a nurse. You remember? I told you that."

"I remember that part okay, but when—"

"In U-Tapao, on weekends, slowly at first. I was practically flying a daily parts shuttle run for the squadron. I'd use any excuse to fly down there to see her. By the time she rotated back stateside and settled at Madigan Army Hospital at Fort Lewis there by McChord, I knew there was no one else I wanted, but what I *didn't* know was how to tell her—or you."

"I always thought you transferred to McChord to get the old team back together."

"Partly, yes. But Wendy was the driving force."

"My God, Will, I had no idea. I . . ." Doug's right hand waved in confusion. "I used to joke that I had taken her away from you, and . . . and it was the first time that had ever happened, because usually you took 'em away from me, remember?"

Will nodded.

"So now you're telling me that the one girl I took from you, the one you introduced me to, the one I married, was the love of your *life*?"

The reply was very quiet. "That's why I left after the wedding. That's why I've kept from calling all these years. I'm sorry, Doug."

"*You're* sorry? *I'm* sorry! Oh Jeez, Will."

"I know."

"All these years."

"I know."

They fell silent again as Doug checked his watch, reading 4:00 A.M. Engine start could wait a few seconds, he decided. There was one more piece to the puzzle that Will didn't even know was missing.

"Will, it wouldn't have worked for you two."

"Probably not."

"No, I mean there's something you don't know. Wendy was very sick, and it took me years to find it out, and I was too slow."

"What do you mean, sick?"

"Manic-depressive with schizoid tendencies, I believe was the diagnosis. She even dragged me down half a dozen times a year."

"Yeah, but you can't say—"

"Will . . ." Doug's hand came up in a "stop" gesture. "Will, she killed herself. Three years after we were married."

That stunned him as Doug knew it would.

"How?" Will finally managed.

"She'd tried twice before. The first was an overdose, but I found her in time. The second attempt was in the garage, with the car engine running. The third time she didn't want to take any chances. She used a twelve-gauge shotgun."

"I'm sorry, Doug."

"I found her . . . well . . . that's another gruesome story."

Will's head was spinning slightly. There were too many emotions tugging at him even to categorize, so he began pushing them all aside.

"What time is it?"

Doug leaned forward and flipped on the master switch before replying.

"Three minutes after four. Let's get going."

The gyros and gauge stabilized as Doug brought on two additional switches that he assumed were fuel-boost pumps. The satisfying sound of pumps of some sort reached his ears. He checked for a locked rotor brake then, and, finding nothing similar, toggled what he assumed was the start switch.

Sure enough, the right engine began to spin, the needles on the Arabic-labeled RPM gauge moving to the right. Doug estimated twenty-five percent before moving what he hoped were the fuel-start and ignition switches to the "on" position.

Nothing happened. The engine continued to turn on ground power, but there was no sign of ignition.

Doug looked down again, trying to fathom what was wrong, panic welling up in his stomach.

"Wrong engine, Doug. You spun the right one, but you're on the controls for the left one."

"Jesus!" He moved his hand over and threw the proper switches, hearing almost instantly the satisfying *thump* of a flame front inside the combustion chamber of the right engine as the hot gases began forcing the turbine blades behind it to spin the engine faster and faster up to idle RPM.

"Lawd awmighty, Willard, m'boy, we've got an engine started on this Russky craft!"

"You do good work, Doug. Now do it again."

Doug repeated the sequence, toggling the fuel and start switches for the left one, hearing the same sound as the second engine came on line and the huge rotor blades began to turn over their heads, slowly at first, and then becoming a blur as Doug worked the motorcycle-style throttle on the collective lever to the left of his seat, bringing the RPM above idle.

"There's a car coming from the town," Will reported, raising his voice over the din of the engines and the steady *whump-whump-whump* of the rotor blades.

Will looked back to the right then, his eyes widening. "And we've got lights from the north. Several vehicles. You haven't turned on any position lights, have you?"

"Nope. How far are they?"

"Almost twice as far away as Shakir—if that's Shakir—but they're coming fast."

Doug nudged the RPM up a bit more, calculating his takeoff run and moving the cyclic stick between his legs in all directions, feeling the big helicopter follow his movements by leaning in whatever direction the stick was shoved. He tapped the tail-rotor control pedals as well, feeling an instant response.

The lights to their left were racing toward them, a single vehicle, but too far away still to make out. To the right, the approaching lights coalesced into a string of three vehicles, one a truck. Will could barely see them around the corner of the building. The helicopter would still be out of their view and shielded for a while longer, but if those vehicles spelled trouble, it was going to be close.

Doug turned to Will and gestured to the nose of the helicopter.

"You suppose that minigun in the nose of this beast is loaded and armed?"

"In other words, will I go check it out and get ready to use it?"

"Something like that."

Will leaned down and moved forward into the weapon operator's seat, situated under a smaller bubble canopy. Doug could see his head appear in the canopy as he bobbed around, apparently looking for the controls.

The single set of headlights racing toward them from the village coalesced at last into a black van.

That's Shakir! Thank God—or, in his case, thank Allah.

Will reappeared alongside his seat at the same moment.

"I think it's loaded, but I don't have a clue how to work the damn thing, and we're out of time. I'm going to get Shakir and his family in here first."

Doug nodded and edged the throttles up a bit more as the black van reached their position, braked hard, and turned along the right side of the helicopter.

Will was waiting for them. He yanked open the van's side door and grabbed the first child he saw, swinging him around and into the helicopter as Shakir came out of the door holding two others, one under each arm, both wide-eyed with apprehension as their father carried them into the helicopter.

Will helped Shakir's wife inside before jumping in himself and pulling on the door to close it.

"Not yet!" Shakir yelled over the noise as he scrambled back out of the helicopter and moved to the rear door of the van, fishing for something inside as Doug yelled back over his shoulder into the cargo compartment.

"They're getting closer. We'd better get out of here!"

"He's coming right back," Will yelled, but Shakir was still standing at the back of the van and pulling at something.

Will leaped out the door then and hurried around the aft end of the van.

"We've got to go!" Will told him.

Shakir did not look up. His eyes were glued to something inside a floor compartment.

"It's stuck," he said. "This canister is wedged down here on the side."

"Let's use this tire iron," Will suggested.

"*No!* That . . . that's one of the containers of the virus."

Will looked in shock at the silver canister. He had assumed it had all been destroyed in the desert. Suddenly to confront the cause of this entire debacle was something he had not expected.

Doug slid open the small hatch in the cockpit canopy and put his mouth close to the opening.

"*Will! For chrissake, you two get in here!*" Doug's voice was barely audible above the roar of the helicopter. Will looked around, the reflection of headlights approaching from the north unmistakable now.

"It's now or never, Shakir. We're out of time."

Working together, they got their hands around the edges of the canister and pulled hard, but it wouldn't budge, and even in the subdued light, Will finally saw why. Part of the metal flange that formed the floor of the tire compartment was bent down, and the canister had slid past it. It was holding on now with the tenacity of a Chinese finger trap, which gave Will an idea.

"GODDAMMIT, GET IN HERE!" Doug's voice again, but there was no time to acknowledge him. The sound of the engines and rotor blades seemed deafening.

Will grabbed the tire iron and positioned it to bend the metal flange down. Shakir understood at last and held the canister steady as Will worked the end of the bar in place. They could hear the sounds of powerful truck engines now within several hundred yards, and Will could hear the RPM of the rotor blades increase even more, Doug throttling the engines up to takeoff power.

"WILL! GODDAMMIT!"

Will ignored him and kept working. He only had one chance. If the end of the iron slipped, it would take too long to reposition it.

"Got it!" The flange gave suddenly and Shakir yanked the canister free.

Will dropped the bar where it was and raced after Shakir to the door of the Hind, both of them rolling inside, Will turning back then to slide the door closed as he yelled forward. *"Now, Doug! GO!"*

The sound of truck engines rumbled in front of them at the same moment, the startled drivers distracted by the sight and sound of the helicopter as it came up to takeoff power just to the left of the road.

There were two trucks and a jeeplike vehicle. The trucks rolled

clear, but the occupants of the small four-wheeler had spotted
the black van and slammed on their brakes, trying to figure out
why such a vehicle would be sitting next to General Hassoun's
personal helicopter.

They stopped squarely in front of Doug twenty feet away,
blocking his takeoff path.

To make a standing, hovering takeoff would be suicide, even
if they decided not to shoot. The other Hind was too close. One
mistake and they'd smash into it.

The only way, Doug figured, was to jam the cyclic stick
forward to get the helicopter rolling in that direction, then yank
the collective up to get airborne. Whether or not they took that
jeep with them would be an open question.

Doug's hands pulled at the controls as an officer alighted from
the far side of the four-wheeler and came around to the driver's
side, waving at the unseen pilot to shut down as he brandished
his gun.

Instead, Doug let the Hind leap forward at the startled Iraqi,
who took a step back and found himself pinned against his driver's door. There was a split-second choice to be made. The
helicopter was on the ground and accelerating toward him now.
He could try to shoot it, or try to escape from it. He could not
do both.

The officer chose the latter, yelling at his driver and holding
on to the window post as the small four-wheel lurched to the left
just before the huge helicopter rolled over the very spot he'd
been occupying a second before.

They were across the road now and still on the ground, the
rear end of the chopper lifting up before the single nosewheel,
scaring Doug, who had the distinct feeling that he'd already lost
control.

Too much cyclic! Doug pulled back on the cyclic and the two
rear wheels fell back to the ground with a frightening thud, the
front wheel lifting off then as the machine lurched backwards,
the mains following the rest of the machine into the air as the

Hind became airborne in a unique fashion. The Iraqi officer who had let himself be dragged clear lifted his gun to aim at the big machine, but it was coming back at him now, lurching backwards and to the left.

That was enough. The officer yelled and ran past his car, motioning the driver to follow. Whoever was at the controls of the Hind, he decided, was dangerously insane.

Once again Doug pushed forward on the cyclic, but not as violently this time, feeling the Hind stop its backward motion and wobble to the left, then pitch forward a reasonable amount as it yawed violently to the right.

Doug realized he was fighting the machine. He pressed the left rudder pedal, feeling the nose swing back forward, and pulled up even more on the collective, raising the pitch of the rotor blades and lifting them faster into the air.

Once again they were sideslipping, this time to the right, the forward pitch excessive, the extra power being eaten up in additional forward speed rather than lift.

Doug nudged the cyclic back a bit this time instead of pulling it, correcting the pitch problem without overcontrolling, and pressing the left rudder pedal to correct for the yawing motion as the ground fell away—the instrument he assumed was an altimeter beginning to wind up to what appeared to be several hundred meters above the ground.

Airspeed! Where the hell's my airspeed indicator!

The labels were all indecipherable, but the airspeed needle was unmistakable, and Doug included it in his frantic instrument scan as the gyrating, slipping, yawing, and pitching Hind began to increase forward speed, stabilizing slowly as it went.

At last they were moving forward, at least fifty or sixty knots and accelerating—enough forward airspeed for the helicopter to take on the normal feel of an airplane. Gentle movements of the cyclic stick to the left, then, accompanied by a nudge of the left rudder pedal, would produce a smooth turn to the left, and vice versa.

Aerodynamically, Doug was back in familiar territory.

As long as he didn't slow down or try to hover.

Doug had located the compass and was in the process of verifying that they were headed south-southeast across the desert when Will appeared by his seat, his eyes wider than Doug had ever seen them.

"I thought," Will said slowly, "you said you knew how to fly a helicopter!"

Doug looked over and smiled. "Nope. I didn't say that. Never learned."

"But you *said* . . ."

Doug was laughing, but the noise was drowning out anything but his smile. "What I said was, if we could get it started, it would fly. I never said *I* knew how to fly . . . uh-oh . . ."

A sudden gust of wind shoved them into a left yaw momentarily and Doug had to fight the controls for a second to get it back under control.

"There." He glanced over at Will. "You were saying?"

Will's fingers were about to squeeze through the armrest of Doug's chair as he held on for dear life. After being tossed all over the cargo compartment, he had tried to convince himself that the alleged takeoff was by design. Doug was confirming it had been by default.

"I told you it would fly," Doug continued, "and see, it's flying!"

"No thanks to you! Now, if you can keep us in the air long enough to get over the border, how are we going to land this thing?"

Doug kept his eyes ahead. "The same way porcupines make love—very carefully."

"You *are* crazy, Harris!"

Iraq Military Command Headquarters, Baghdad
Monday, March 11, 1991—4:45 A.M. (0145 GMT)

Ihsan Fethi, his ears still ringing from the diatribe of his leader, scurried out of the car and past the guards into headquarters, looking for General Hassoun's aide.

The place resembled a kicked-over anthill, he thought. Not only were plans for a counteroffensive against Kurdish forces in the north and Shiite rebels in the south beginning to coalesce in a frenzy of activity, but now there was the matter of these escaped Americans to deal with.

The officer he was looking for had a field telephone glued to each ear and motioned him to wait. Communications to most field units were almost nonexistent, but a few hardened lines and radio circuits were working, and the sound of people yelling into archaic handsets was perhaps his most vivid memory of headquarters since the bombing had begun.

And now they would have to drop everything they were doing and use every communications line available to the south.

The aide and his general were going to be dumbfounded when they heard Saddam's latest order, but if the president wanted to defy the Americans and put a fighter in the air to shoot down a helicopter, that's exactly what would happen.

Airborne, 200 miles southeast of Baghdad
Monday, March 11, 1991—6:05 A.M. (0305 GMT)

Shakir Abbas sat on the left sidewall seat, holding his wife and three children, trying to keep them warm in the cold air streaming through the partially opened main door.

Will had tried to close and lock the large sliding door, but the Russian latch had defied the American's attempts, and now it had crept open again—a two-foot gap of nighttime blackness admitting a hurricane of wind.

The two guards were cold as well—one hunched over trying to retain body heat, the other rolled into a ball on the floor around the tie-down loop that restrained him. For two hours they had rumbled along through the night without challenge, and now the orange and pink glow streaking the eastern horizon was a welcome sight as Will came back once again to reassure them.

"We should be across in less than ten minutes now, and you want to make sure those seatbelts are fastened for landing."

"Do we really have a chance to make it?" Shakir asked. "I expected they would chase us and try to shoot us down."

Will shrugged. "Even if they know where we are, Shakir, all they can chase us with is another helicopter, and so far there's been nothing."

He returned to the cockpit then, glancing at the defiant door and deciding it wasn't worth another struggle.

Shakir had kept one of the rifles by his side on the floor. It was safe there—out of reach of both soldiers, who, in any event, were harmless, shackled as they were to the floor.

An abrupt blur of movement on Shakir's right caused his head to jerk suddenly in that direction. He saw the young soldier who had been lying in a ball on the floor leap forward like a tiger past Shakir, scoop up the rifle, and come to rest with his back against the forward left-hand corner of the cargo compartment, by the flight engineer's station.

Within a heartbeat, Shakir found himself staring down the barrel of an automatic weapon, the unmistakable sound of the firing mechanism being cocked reaching his ears with chilling clarity.

The young soldier's eyes were narrowed with determination, his right wrist still encircled by one side of the handcuffs, the carefully removed tie-down cleat dangling from the other end.

"Land this machine! NOW!" he yelled in Arabic at Shakir.

Saliah stifled a scream as she gathered the children closer around her. The youngest whimpered as he clutched his mother, too frightened to cry out.

Will heard the command and looked around from where he was standing to the left of the pilot's seat in the cockpit, seeing only Shakir as he motioned for Will to stay where he was, speaking in English.

"One of the guards has broken loose and taken my gun. He wants us to land."

That brought Doug to full attention. He and Will looked at each other, searching for split-second answers. Then Doug, reading Will's thoughts, nodded once, smiled slightly, and turned back to concentrate on flying.

"Good luck, old buddy," he said under his breath.

"LAND! NOW!" the soldier repeated, pushing the barrel of the gun at Shakir with each word. His eyes kept darting to the left toward the cockpit entrance, bracing for a challenge.

Will grabbed one of the other guns from alongside the pilot's seat and checked the safety as he analyzed the situation.

There was no way even to see the soldier from the cockpit without coming back, which would put Will in the line of fire before he had a chance to raise his gun.

There was only one solution apparent. The soldier would have to be moved.

Will was on his feet now beside the pilot's seat and facing backwards. He leaned over and spoke directly in Doug's ear.

"Can you bank suddenly to the right and then stand this thing on its tail? You know, a sudden nose-high deck angle?"

"We can try."

Will caught Shakir's eyes and described with his hands what was about to happen. To his relief, Shakir merely blinked twice with a neutral expression.

Doug yanked the cyclic stick to the right then and kicked the left rudder pedal. The helicopter rolled to the right and gravity went with it, propelling the soldier unceremoniously against the middle of the partially opened door as Doug pulled back just as suddenly on the stick, the Hind's blades protesting with mighty slapping noises as the nose of the chopper rose suddenly to a steep nose-up deck angle.

The soldier had tried to get to his feet after hitting the door but the floor wouldn't cooperate. With his sense of balance out of service, he flailed the air for something to hold on to as he tumbled backwards, his foot inadvertently kicking Shakir's hand as he rolled by—dislodging the canister Shakir had been holding.

Soldier and canister now ended up in confusion against the rear bulkhead of the cargo compartment as Will emerged from the cockpit, rifle raised and aimed, safety off. The helicopter was pitching forward again, picking up speed as Will braced himself on the slippery metal floor, acutely aware of the yawning hole to his left. The main sliding door was now almost two-thirds open and a clear danger, and Will fumbled for a solid handhold as Shakir's voice reached his ears.

"Don't shoot! He's got the canister! We can't take a chance that a bullet might hit it!"

The words didn't make sense, though the tone of voice did, and Shakir read the confusion on Will's face as he realized he had yelled in Arabic.

The soldier, however, understood instantly. Whatever was in that silver canister was important to these thieves. He scooped it up then and held it against the muzzle of the gun, realizing he now held all the aces.

"LAND NOW, OR I WILL SHOOT THIS!"

One hundred twenty miles north of Riyadh, Saudi Arabia, the radar displays aboard the AWACS covering the Kuwait theater of operations confirmed that the fast-moving target that had popped up moments earlier from a marginally operational Iraqi air base northwest of Basrah was not a "friendly." The transponder codes were all wrong, and it was going too fast to be a helicopter.

The sector controller calculated the time to intercept for the flight of four F-15s on combat air patrol and keyed his transmitter to turn them in that direction. Whoever was flying that Iraqi fighter had to know he was committing suicide—*unless* it was a defection.

The controller raised the possibility to his boss, who relayed it on up the line in a flash of telecommunication coordination as the F-15s turned to make a supersonic dash at the intruder, who was now within thirty miles of a Coalition forward base.

"There's something else here." The controller's finger traced the slow-moving helicopter he had been monitoring for the past hour. It, too, seemed headed for the Coalition line, and the projected path of the fighter was aimed right at the rotorcraft.

In the cockpit of the Iraqi MiG-21, the thirty-four-year-old squadron commander twisted his head around again to check his six-o'clock position before turning his attention to the target. The slow-moving helicopter was doing a little over one hundred knots and he was closing on the target at over four hundred. It would be so easy if he just had a single air-to-air missile, but it had been all he could do to get the aircraft out of the bunker and launched with the guns armed.

The MiG shouldn't even be flying, of course. It was one of the few that had too many maintenance problems to make the dash to Iran at the first of the air war. And there was the matter of the American Air Force fighters who would be sweeping down on him in minutes. He'd have to shoot the stolen helicopter out of the sky with his guns, then turn and run on afterburner to the nearest runway—or punch out before they blew him out of the sky.

His radar screen came alive suddenly with the indication he feared the most: someone's fire-control radar was tracking him, and lock-on was imminent.

The smoke plumes from the hundreds of Kuwaiti oil wells the departing Iraqis had set ablaze were now visible in the windscreen ahead as Doug looked over his shoulder again at the standoff in the cargo compartment. The soldier had been dislodged once, but he'd learned his lesson. He was propped against the rear bulkhead now, with his feet wedged against the sidewall seat stanchions, holding the rifle muzzle to the canister and yelling periodically in Arabic, which Shakir kept translating with increasing alarm.

"I think he means it! I think we'd better land!" Shakir yelled at Will, who was trying to keep the bead of his gun on the Iraqi's forehead and calculating whether shooting might cause his trigger finger to twitch.

It was too great a chance.

Will turned then to warn Doug at the same moment the image and sound of something large and loud flashed across their windscreen. Doug instinctively shoved the cyclic stick forward, pitching the Hind more than thirty degrees nose-down at the same moment they flew through the slipstream of whatever had passed them. The burble was like hitting a four-foot-diameter chuckhole at sixty miles per hour in a car, and everybody and everything in the helicopter catapulted up, then smashed back down.

Will felt himself hit the ceiling and lose control of the gun as the helicopter now lurched upward to meet him, combining with gravity to knock the wind out of him, the rifle clattering toward the open door where it hesitated for what seemed like a lazy few seconds before tumbling out toward the predawn desert below.

Shakir's family had been belted in, and fared better than Shakir, who hit the ceiling too, then came down hard on his wife's lap.

The soldier had worked his feet into an immovable position before the upset. Suddenly his body was being sent to places his feet could not follow, and he found himself slammed back into the deck with two broken ankles before being rolled forward past his comrade toward the open door, his grip on the rifle lost—his grip on the canister firm.

Shakir saw what was happening and lunged from the sidewall seat toward the outstretched hand of the soldier, grabbing for the canister as the helicopter rolled to the right, still canted nose-down, the soldier concentrating for a critical split second on the pain in his ankles, failing to realize he was sliding backward inexorably toward the maw of the open door.

Shakir's hand swept toward the canister, but missed. He gathered his knees under him and tried to propel himself forward as the soldier's legs slid over the edge of the door and the man clawed for a handhold with his free hand. Once again the canister was inches away but unreachable.

Shakir's mind shifted its personal time-base to high speed now as he analyzed the deteriorating situation. If he made a final lunge for the canister, he could propel himself right out the door with it, which would accomplish nothing. If he didn't lunge, it was gone. The soldier's hips were now sliding into the slipstream as he flailed for something to hold onto, finding only the slick metal floor and the rounded edge of the doorjamb itself.

There was no choice.

Shakir gathered his left foot under him and launched himself toward the right forward corner of the cargo compartment, his hand grabbing the soldier's arm as the man went fully over the edge with a scream of surprise, his arm and wrist and hand progressively slipping through Shakir's grasp until only the canister was left behind in Shakir's hands.

Now Shakir's body was rolling toward the door, and somewhere in the background he heard Saliah scream.

The Hind was still rolled to the right, though the steep deck angle was coming back up as Doug pulled on the cyclic and tried to catch a glimpse of the fighter that had caused the upset.

Shakir's feet were hanging on to the edge of the open sliding door. His right hand held the canister, his left the forward doorjamb, and his body straddled the gap—a thousand-foot plunge awaiting the slightest slip.

Will had recovered enough to get to his knees and grab a handle on the forward bulkhead with his left hand as he reached out with his right in an attempt to capture Shakir's arm and at least stabilize him, but Shakir slapped the canister into Will's right hand instead.

Shakir held on now with both hands to the forward doorjamb, his fingers curling around the lip of it, the sharp metal beginning to cut his flesh.

"Doug!" Will yelled forward without looking. There was one chance, and as Will hoped, Doug looked around.

"What?"

"I'm throwing the canister forward."

Will let his right arm and hand accelerate the canister gently into the cockpit, the silver container seeming to hang in the air as it passed through the opening and clattered onto the floor, rolling forward toward the weapon operator's compartment before coming to a stop.

Will grabbed a handle on the right side of the bulkhead, closer to the door, as he yelled again at Doug. "Roll left! Roll back to the left!"

In the time it took for Doug to respond, Shakir's feet slipped off the edge of the sliding door and the door slid fully open.

Will saw Shakir's body swing into the windstream then as his hands held on to the forward doorjamb, pivoting around its sharp edge as Will reached for Shakir's left forearm and caught it.

The weight was incredible. Will was in good condition, but Shakir was an immovable dead weight on his hand and arm. He could barely hang on, let alone haul him inside, and he could feel Shakir's grip on the doorjamb slipping. He saw crimson around Shakir's hands, the bleeding making the metal slippery and loosening his grip even more.

Shakir's left hand slid off first, and Will used every ounce of strength he had to haul in on his forearm, which slipped out of his grip until he was hanging on to a wrist—and that too was slipping.

Shakir was looking up, trying to pull himself in with his right hand but not succeeding. Will could see his fingers loosening on the doorjamb. It would be a matter of seconds until all his weight would hang from Will's right hand.

Pull, goddammit! Will yelled to himself, giving one last grand effort to yank Shakir in at the same moment Doug glanced behind, assessed the situation, and rolled the Hind to the left sharply.

Shakir catapulted back in the door and into Will, knocking them both into the left side of the cargo compartment.

"Strap in!" Will yelled at him, watching as Shakir dove for the seat next to Saliah and did exactly that as she enfolded him in her arms, her eyes wide with terror.

Will pulled himself up to the left seat and strapped in as Doug pivoted the machine around to the north, his eyes locking in on the smoke trail of the fighter, his mind working the problem of identification down to a chilling conclusion.

"Jesus Christ, Will, I think that's a MiG-21!"

The fighter was rolling out on a head-on course now and closing, the black smoke from its engine indicating it was accelerating.

"If he's got missiles, we're dead," Will said calmly.

"If he had and he's chasing us, he would have used them. He's coming in on a strafing run."

A tentative few flashes of light from the MiG's wing roots underscored Doug's fears as tracers from the small squeeze of bullets passed just beneath them. Doug could see the nose of the MiG adjusting the shot.

"Doug—"

"I know!" Doug's hand was already pulling on the collective and cyclic simultaneously, causing the helicopter to pop up suddenly in the fighter's perspective as it slowed. They could see the MiG pilot adjusting even more and waited for him to do so before Doug fairly yanked the cyclic to the right as he pressed hard on the rudder pedals and dumped the collective, causing the helicopter to spiral down to the right suddenly with a sickening sink rate.

Once again the MiG's target was out of the cross hairs, and this time he was within three miles and closing fast.

Another stream of tracers snaked by on the left as Doug dove to the right and then reversed direction, climbing and banking back to the left as the MiG pilot struggled to follow, his bullets still wide of the mark.

The fighter shot past on the left as Doug pirouetted and followed, accelerating as fast as he dared, knowing that even at one hundred fifty they were no match for the MiG's speed.

"Where the hell are *our* guys?" Doug yelled.

"We're an Iraqi helicopter being attacked by an Iraqi fighter. You think our guys are going to help? This looks like civil-war stuff. We're on our own!" Will yelled back.

"Then get up there and figure out that minigun. We've got to fight back."

I've got to hover. I've got to hover this baby and keep screwing up his shot, Doug decided.

Will was clambering beneath the cockpit now toward the nose gunner's position, and within seconds Doug could see his head appear in the Plexiglas in front of the cockpit bubble as he searched for the cocking and firing mechanisms.

The MiG was turning back toward them again as Doug pulled on the cyclic and increased the collective and the power, bringing in some compensating rudder as he slowed under fifty now and started flying in a speed range reserved mainly for helicopters.

I'm overcontrolling again!

Almost immediately the Hind became a beast, wanting to gyrate in every direction at once and defying Doug's attempts to hover.

He estimated his altitude now at a thousand feet, and as the MiG rolled out on course and wings level some five miles distant, Doug waited for the right moment to slam the collective to the floor and literally drop out of the MiG's sights.

The fighter was steady on course now and aiming straight for them. The pilot would be fingering the trigger and waiting for the right moment. Doug could see Will's head still bobbing around up ahead, meaning he still didn't have the gun figured out.

NOW!

Doug's left hand slammed the collective into negative pitch, feeling the bottom fall out from beneath his stomach as they suddenly accelerated toward the desert floor with almost no forward flying speed.

A crowd was gathering rapidly four miles to the south at the American encampment. The sight of a Soviet-built helicopter in an apparent duel with a Soviet-built fighter was amazing and entertaining at the same time. As the GIs watched, messages were being radioed for assistance in case it portended an attack on the base, and antiaircraft batteries were being brought to bear on the potential intruders.

Aboard Crown, the reports of the duel were coming from

ground observers and reaching incredulous ears. It did indeed look like a defection of some sort, but who was defecting?

"Probably the chopper. I've been watching him come steadily south for an hour. The other guy was probably launched to get him," the duty controller told his commander as they watched the F-15s streaking into the battle scene now only four minutes out.

The helicopter was a steady, sitting-duck target in the Iraqi pilot's gunsight, the shot almost too good to be true. His own fire-control radar was showing he had been locked up now by several incoming American fighters who had missile guidance heads tracking his tailpipe. There had been no missile launch yet, but there would be, and the Iraqi knew he had precious little time.

There was a wild card, though. As long as the helicopter he was stalking remained airborne, the U.S. fighters would probably do a flyby before starting an attack. Perhaps that would give him time for one final pass if he didn't get the Hind on this one.

The pilot steadied the MiG and began using his rudder to walk the cross hairs of his gunsight into position, his finger caressing the trigger as he waited to get slightly closer.

There was a powerful Gatling gun on that Hind, he knew, but obviously whoever was flying the helicopter didn't know how to use it.

Still another radar lock-on showed up on his screen.

He had decided on a plan. Since there would be no time to run, he would shoot down the helicopter as ordered and then immediately punch out.

His jet would never fly again anyway. There was no way the Americans were going to give him enough time to reach a runway anywhere.

The pilot turned his attention back to the helicopter in his cross hairs.

It wasn't there!

Doug brought in the collective once more to arrest the wild vertical descent. He had intended to stop in another hover, but the machine balked. Suddenly they were flying backwards, and then to the side, and then forward as he began fighting the gyrating machine, almost losing it. The fighter was still aiming at the spot five hundred feet overhead that the helicopter had occupied seconds before, but at a range of two miles he saw the MiG pilot figure it out as he nosed over and began walking his tracers across the Hind. The sound of a bullet ricocheting off one of the rotor blades was followed by four noises in the cargo compartment that sounded like BBs transiting a tin can.

The MiG pulled up suddenly, his firing solution too dangerous. He would have to dive toward the ground to keep shooting.

Doug fought to move in a straight line again as he swiveled to the left, catching sight of something on the ground.

"Will, there's a base over there!"

No answer, but Will's head was steady now and not moving. It looked like he was hunched over something.

Doug tried to peer to the left even as he started swinging the bucking chopper back to the right. Was he imagining things, or was that Old Glory on top of a tent?

Maybe, he thought. *Just maybe!*

He had the chopper in a right turn again, looking for the MiG, which, ominously, was nowhere in sight.

Doug pivoted more to the north and kept coming around, searching the sky for the smoke trail. The sun was almost on the horizon now, and if it came up before the fighter made his next pass, he would try to position himself between the sun and the fighter.

Doug glanced back in the cargo compartment. Shakir was holding on to his wife, who was holding on to their children. The remaining soldier was hanging on too, apparently uninterested in doing anything but surviving.

He checked the instrument panel as best he could, considering the Arabic labels. There were no red lights blinking and nothing to indicate they had taken any serious hits from the bullets he had heard.

Where the hell is he?

Doug had almost let himself hope that the MiG had been chased off when a slight smudge of smoke at ten o'clock high caught his sight.

Oh Jeez! The sumbitch is diving!

This was the last pass, the Iraqi pilot told himself. This time he wasn't about to let a damned helicopter weasel out of his gunsights. As long as he maintained a steep vertical intercept angle, the helicopter down there could gyrate all over the place and still not spoil the shot.

He heard the airspeed increasing as he centered the cross hairs and prepared to readjust to whatever the target tried to do. He would get the shot, pull up, head north, and eject—probably just as someone back there launched a missile down his tailpipe. It was all or nothing now, and all his concentration and training and survival instincts focused on making these last shots count.

The first tracers snaked by on the right as Doug pushed over and accelerated as fast as possible in the direction from which the MiG was diving. He yanked the cyclic back and forth, banking wildly and hoping the rotor blades could take it, while the deadly stream of bullets and tracers followed him, as if a determined little boy with a hose were trying to soak his target.

Will had still not moved and Doug was becoming alarmed. Those hits had been in the back, hadn't they? Had Will been hit?

Again he jerked the chopper to the right, hearing another sickening sound of penetrated metal behind him as several bullets found their mark through the body of the Hind, one of the hits sounding like shrapnel.

The MiG was still two miles or so distant. He stopped firing suddenly at the same moment Will's voice rang out from the bubble ahead. Doug was so glad to hear him, he almost ignored the words.

"Pitch up! I've got it! Pitch up now!"

The MiG was firing again, the deadly trail of tracers starting low in front of them and coming forward as the pilot corrected his aim.

And without warning a strange sound and vibration shuddered through the helicopter. Doug thought one of the engines or the tail rotor had been hit.

The cyclic stick was vibrating badly, the vibrations shaking his spine.

What the hell is causing that?

Suddenly Doug realized it was *they* who were firing and fighting back. The vibrations were coming from the minigun.

The first tracers that snaked past the cockpit of the MiG had been dismissed by the pilot as his own. Then he realized that he was also being fired on. Someone in the helicopter had discovered the minigun.

He had only seconds left in his attack dive, but the chopper was still in the air and unhurt. He could break off now and punch out, or give it five more seconds and one more burst.

The thought processes took less than two seconds to rocket around his brain, but the prospect of having to punch out without completing his mission was unacceptable.

One more shot.

The helicopter was firing wide as the MiG pilot popped his stick downward and dropped away from the oncoming stream of tracers, steadying out again as the cross hairs centered nicely on the Hind. His brain began the process of triggering the motor response to his index finger to pull the trigger—but the message never arrived.

The lethal stream of flying lead that Will had been firing wide of the mark suddenly found its target, obliterating the canopy, the cockpit, and its occupant before chewing up the engine and igniting the ammunition and fuel tanks in a single explosive event.

"You got him! You got him!" Doug yelled at Will.

What had been a MiG-21 one moment was now a fireball of falling debris to be avoided.

Doug threw the Hind into a left bank as Will realized he no longer had a target. He let up on the trigger, amazed at the result.

Will turned in the nose gunner's canopy and looked back at Doug with an unusually broad grin, his right thumb held against the top of the Plexiglas in a victory salute.

In the cockpit of the lead F-15, the locked-up target had suddenly flared and disappeared, leaving only the slow-mover that AWACS had ID'd as a helicopter.

"Good shooting, Ranger one-zero-one," the voice of the AWACS controller sounded in his headset, and he pressed his transmit button in reply.

"Ranger one-zero-one never took the shot. I don't know who got him."

Will made his way back to the cockpit and appeared at Doug's elbow, a grin still on his face—until he glanced to the north.

"Oh God, more fighters!"

Doug jerked his head around and spotted the smoke trails—and the twin tails.

"Those are our Eagles," Doug said, "and here we are in an enemy chopper. Got anything white to wave like maybe your life depended on it?"

To his surprise, Will nodded. "I already borrowed this from Mrs. Abbas. She pulled it out of her bag for me."

He held up a white nylon slip and raised his eyebrows.

Doug laughed, then began urging the helicopter toward the

camp he had spotted earlier, having just as much trouble staying steady at low speed as before.

"I'm going to keep us slow in case anyone down there is nervously fingering a trigger."

"You can't fly this thing slow," Will told him. "I saw you try to hover before, remember? It was a disaster."

"Hey, it's just a steep learning curve, okay?" Doug tried to look offended, then his expression became serious again. "You better start waving that thing."

Three miles distant, the lead F-15 pilot calculated the remaining distance between the helicopter and the U.S. base and decided his shot was too dangerous. He had been locked on the target for several minutes, his missile giving him a steady tone as the radar and the missile guidance package tracked the Hind and waited for the order to drop off the rail and fly.

But the wreckage might fall in the camp, and there was still the chance this was a defector who just hadn't heard all the radio energy directing him not to overfly the camp.

The F-15 driver broke right and began a circle, advising his wingman to slow up and fly by for a closer look.

Will slid open a small window and waved Saliah's white slip as the F-15 passed.

"We've got a defector here with a white flag," was the message radioed to Crown and his lead. There was no way to see more detail inside the helicopter, but with the fighter attack, it made sense.

Nearly two hundred U.S. servicemen and -women were gathered now along the north edge of the camp. The rumor that they were watching a defector trying to reach safety had rippled through the throng, and everyone had cheered when the Hind fired and the MiG-21 disintegrated in a fireball.

Now a pair of incoming F-15s had broken off without attacking, which seemed to confirm the rumor.

The Hind was approaching the camp as if the pilot were determined to put on a flying comedy show. As they watched, the Hind did a sudden pop-up climb, turned to face the camp, promptly sideslipped off to one side, turned to the west and backed up, then pitched forward and turned completely around to the right before starting for the camp again, the machine yawing back toward the east as it continued sideways toward the boundary line.

Up and down, rocking, gyrating, and yawing, the craft was more or less trending in their direction.

When the helicopter was within a tenth of a mile, it swung around to the west again and the entire camp saw for the first time the white slip fluttering along the left side.

Another cheer went up.

The wild gyrations had been almost comical, but now they were becoming alarming.

"Doug, can't you stabilize this tub?" Will asked, concern showing on his face.

"I'm working on it." Doug saw the camp off to his left. He wanted to put the camp directly on the nose, but the Hind was exerting a will of its own. It either wanted to slip left or right.

"I can't make this damn thing go forward!" Doug cried.

"Well, just put it down somewhere in the open," Will yelled back over his shoulder as he struggled to hold on to the white slip, which was threatening to tear loose from his grip.

They could see the crowd gathering below as the Hind gyrated back and forth.

Doug gestured with a slight tilt of his head. "There's a clear area way over in the middle of the camp. I'm gonna put her down there."

"That's too crowded," Will shot back, but he could tell Doug was determined. "We'll hit something!"

"No, we won't. Trust me!"

The cyclic was almost behaving now as Doug worked to get the right combination of power and pitch to keep moving. He kept telling himself to just "think" the controls in the appropriate direction, but his movements were still too abrupt.

"Doug, they're going to want you to take a Breathalyzer test when we get down there. We're all over the sky!"

They were over the edge of the crowd now and bobbling between fifty and eighty feet above the ground as Doug once again felt himself sideslipping. He brought in a bit more collective and nudged the cyclic back to the right, causing the inevitable overreaction, and remembered at last a long-ago snippet of advice from an instructor who had almost despaired of teaching Lieutenant Doug Harris to fly formation.

"Keep the stick moving," the instructor had advised. "Average your corrections."

Doug began stirring the cyclic, causing a seasick motion that nevertheless gave him more control.

Will held on to the pilot's seat and glanced back, noting the pallor of Shakir Abbas's face as he and Saliah held on to each other and their frightened children.

From the ground it looked like some sort of aerial victory dance, and within seconds someone in the crowd punched on a boom box, which began pumping a driving rhythm that almost matched the movements of the Hind as it came directly over their heads now, wobbling like a top.

"By George, I think I've got it!"

Doug could feel the machine obey him at last. He was still wobbling, but it was a controlled wobble, and he pushed it toward the small clearing in the tent city beside several larger tents a few hundred yards inside the compound from where the crowd had formed.

"I don't know, Doug."

Doug moved toward what had to be a shower tent before inching the collective down as he kept stirring the cyclic, urging the Hind toward the targeted landing zone.

Fifty, forty, thirty, and finally twenty feet, Doug let the ship settle as he turned his head for a final comment to Will.

"Hey! I think I'm finally getting the hang of this!"

Unconsciously, his hand moved the stick ever so slightly at the same moment, and the Hind sidestepped in response.

Suddenly they were ballooning more than twenty feet above the ground as the left main landing gear snagged the tie-down ropes of the men's shower tent, the Velcro seams holding the interior structure of rubberized canvas shower stalls and plastic hose plumbing intact as the helicopter neatly lifted the entire assembly clear of the dirt floor before tossing it to one side in the hurricane force of the wind from the rotor blades.

Doug urged the machine back to his right, and with a clear area beneath them again, unloaded the collective and let the Hind settle to the ground, fighting to throttle down the engines and stop the rotor blades—which had picked up a loose section of the tent fabric, the KA-WHUMP, KA-WHUMP, KA-WHUMP of the gyrating canvas making a horrendous noise until the blades finally flung it clear, sailing it off into the distance.

"Was anybody in there?" Doug asked, alarmed, as he strained to see the site of the missing tent. He toggled off the master switch.

Will nodded. "You might say that."

Three customers had been taking showers when the incongruous sounds of an approaching helicopter finally grew louder than the noise from the shower heads. There had been no time to react, and now the three officers—a brigadier general and two captains—were standing unhurt but completely in the open next to a large Russian helicopter with Iraqi markings, holding their bars of soap and wearing nothing more than startled expressions as a cheering crowd approached and the collapsed rubber-hose plumbing continued spraying hot water at their feet.

It was all very confusing.

The two captains retreated to the side of the denuded tent platform to find their clothes, but the general stood his ground, studying the cockpit windows, realizing from a face looking back at him that at least one American GI was involved in the strange arrival of the enemy craft.

He saw the flight suit then, and the flash of a set of colonel's eagles on the shoulder.

The crowd surged forward and surrounded the helicopter. The Hind had settled between the shower tent and the audience, but now they could see the general and they began applauding and hooting, blocking the military policemen who were rushing to the scene.

The one-star waved to the crowd *au naturel,* took a bow, and walked slowly over to retrieve his towel. He wrapped the towel around his waist, found his hat and an unlit cigar, put on the hat, stuffed the cigar in his mouth, and strode around the front of the helicopter.

Doug saw the general, who was obviously uninjured except for his dignity, and slid back the window, a grin of immense relief at having landed safely still covering his face.

"We're American GIs! Air Force!" Doug yelled.

The crowd surged even closer as the general took the cigar from his lips, cleared his throat, and looked up.

"First," he said, "I'd like to take a peek at your pilot's license."

Will was the first out of the Hind, followed closely by Doug, both of them smiling broadly, intent on identifying themselves as they shook hands all around. They had seen Shakir and his wife huddled together in the corner of the helicopter's interior as they left—the remaining Iraqi soldier still shackled to the floor—but they hadn't noticed the anguish in the eyes of Saliah Abbas.

The crowd pressed around them, diverting their attention, but a small voice from within the helicopter caused both Will and Doug to turn around.

"Please . . . help, please!" The accented plea came from Saliah Abbas, who was still sitting on the sidewall seat, holding her husband's shoulders and staring in horror at a growing patch of crimson on the front of his shirt, his head lolled against her shoulder.

Will was in the helicopter in an instant with Doug close behind as they opened his shirt and saw the entry wound.

"Help . . . please!" she was saying again in the only English she knew, and several GIs jumped in to comfort her and the children as Doug yelled for a medic and Will helped Shakir lie down on the bench seat.

Will looked up at the bullet holes in the interior, unaware until now that they had taken so many hits. Most were clean entry and exit trajectories that blessedly had bypassed the Abbas family and the soldier by many feet. But one had apparently come out as jagged shrapnel. One of those pieces of shrapnel had apparently entered Shakir's chest.

He roused from his half-conscious state and grabbed Will's arm, holding it with inordinate strength.

"Do you have the canister?" Shakir asked desperately.

"Yes, we . . . Doug, you better get that thing down from your seat."

Doug nodded and moved to the cockpit, returning with the silver container and holding it in Shakir's view as he nodded painfully.

"You promise me it will be incinerated? You give me your word as an officer?" His eyes were boring into Will's.

"You have my promise, Shakir. But just hang in there and you'll be able to verify that yourself."

"I . . . am dizzy. I did not realize . . . this was a bad wound."

"Easy, Doctor," Will said. "We'll get medical help on the way." Will turned and yelled through the open door at a half-dozen faces to get an ambulance and saw at least one officer nod and race away.

"Lie back and rest," Will told Shakir. "You'll be okay, we'll make sure of that."

But Shakir's grip increased on Will's arm as he pulled himself up again, struggling with pain and an increasing mental fog to focus on something he wanted to say.

Doug moved in and supported Shakir's back as Will looked him in the eye, saying, "We owe our lives to you, Doctor. You came through for everyone on this."

The sound of a siren outside heralded the approach of an ambulance.

Doug was nodding firmly. "He's saying it for me, too, I . . ."

"You must listen, Colonel." Shakir was focused on Will. "There is . . . another . . ."

Shakir's eyes rolled back and his body went limp as unconsciousness overtook him. Will checked for a pulse and felt a faint beat. A team of medics had arrived, and they clambered aboard and began work immediately, transferring Abbas to a stretcher, then into the ambulance, which roared off with its siren in full cry.

E P I L O  G U E

CENTCOM, Riyadh, Saudi Arabia
Tuesday, March 12, 1991—4:00 P.M. (1300 GMT)

Forty minutes at one thousand degrees was finally up. The lab technician switched the machine off and turned to a small group of assembled officers who had witnessed the procedure.

"It's done, and as you gentlemen saw, it was all in there. That eliminates the last of the deadliest human virus ever discovered, and I'm damned appreciative of that fact." He took out his pen and leaned over a desk to sign the certification paper that had been drawn up, then stood and shook Colonel Richard Kerr's hand.

"It was really that bad?" Kerr asked.

"You can't imagine the suffering and destruction it could have caused, Colonel. You can't *begin* to imagine. The tests we ran in just ten hours on lab animals were gruesome. We diluted it to one-five-hundred-thousandth of its original strength and it still killed a rhesus monkey within two hours."

Kerr and Jon McCarthy of the National Security Agency walked together toward the security door lost in thought before Kerr broke the silence.

"We need to tell Dr. Hajek he's off the hook before he shoots himself," Kerr said. "How are you going to handle that little task, Jon?"

"Me?" McCarthy feigned amusement, but he had effectively caused the arrest of Dr. Hajek on suspicion of destroying government property, and it fell to him to undo the deed. He knew Hajek was waiting in his Riyadh hotel room in mental agony for the next shoe to drop.

"Yes, you," Kerr echoed, grinning. "Poor guy. A lab assistant simply tries to follow the doctor's orders to sterilize 'everything' and gets hold of the live samples by mistake, and we jump to the conclusion that Hajek's guilty of sabotage."

"He is," McCarthy reminded Kerr. "At least guilty of sabotaging our attempts to send that sample home."

"Hajek was right in one way, though," Kerr added. "I don't ever want anything that dangerous back in the States."

"Well, it's a moot point now," McCarthy said.

"Is it? I mean, yes, *this* stuff is history, but what about the next time someone stumbles on a biological weapon and our side decides to take the Trojan Horse home? That's what it might turn out to be, you know."

"I don't understand what you're getting at," McCarthy said.

"I mean, Jon, I hate it that we have to keep this whole thing secret. I understand why, and I know we have no choice, but it's a damn dangerous shame. The people need to know what happened, and what could have happened."

"Are you talking about what Dr. Abbas did, Richard, or about the virus itself?"

"Both. Abbas didn't have to put everything on the line like

that, and he certainly didn't have to rescue our men. Even though he created that bug, he also made it possible to get rid of it. But he risked everything warning us, and what do we do? Keep it secret. I'm upset about the President sealing the record.''

McCarthy started chuckling again, as he had been doing off and on all day after getting the full report from Kuwait. ''I just can't believe that those two crazy colonels of ours flew a god-damned Hind right out from under Saddam's nose! And neither of them had ever flown a chopper before. *That's* what I'd like to publicize. Everybody in the Air Force would've gotten a kick out of that!''

Richard Kerr bade McCarthy good-bye and headed for the air base to catch a ride back to Dhahran, where Doug Harris and Will Westerman were about to be released from the hospital and debriefing. He would need to make arrangements for the Abbas family.

And as for Dr. Shakir Abbas himself, there was the matter of a funeral.

The tragedy of Dr. Abbas's death had been compounded by the mysteries he had left behind. The stories of how he had retrieved the remaining canisters, how and where he had disposed of the first one, had died with him.

But at least the threat was over.

Western Iraqi Desert
Tuesday, March 12, 1991—5:45 P.M. (1445 GMT)

The sun dipped large and fiery orange toward the western rim of the desert, casting long shadows from a single Bedouin as he led his camel across a small wadi. The man moved slowly and with timeless deliberation as he thought of making camp and looked forward to his tea. He would rest somewhere on the other side.

He had topped the rim of the wadi when his camel stumbled,

the beast's rear hooves churning the sand of the wadi's steep side as it struggled for footing. The man turned and hauled at the line, willing the camel up with prayers, oaths, and muscle.

When the camel had crested the wadi at last, the man set course for a point somewhere on the other side of the intrusive highway before him, ignoring a passing truck and the burned-out hulk of a smaller vehicle on his right.

Unseen behind him, a small rivulet of sand began falling steadily from the wall of the wadi, a tiny record of the camel's momentary struggle, which grew to a trickle and continued un-abated, even after the Bedouin and his camel had disappeared over the horizon. The sandfall persisted until at last it began to reveal something hard and shiny within the bank—something alien to the rhythms and substance of the desert.

A small metal canister rolled into the open then, and accel-erated down the side of the wadi, tumbling across its floor before coming to rest in the middle—its polished silver surface reflecting the last dying rays of the setting sun.